THE DEAF HOUSE

THE
DEAF HOUSE

ALEXANDRA HAMPTON

MACMILLAN

First published 1995 by Pan Books Ltd

an imprint of Macmillan General Books
Cavaye Place London SW10 9PG
and Basingstoke

Associated companies throughout the world

ISBN 0 330 33088 8

Copyright © Alexandra Hampton 1995

The right of Alexandra Hampton to be identified as the
author of this work has been asserted by her in accordance
with the Copyright, Designs and Patents Act 1988.

All rights reserved. No reproduction, copy or transmission
of this publication may be made without written permission.
No paragraph of this publication may be reproduced, copied or
transmitted save with written permission or in accordance with
the provisions of the Copyright Act 1956 (as amended). Any
person who does any unauthorized act in relation to
this publication may be liable to criminal prosecution
and civil claims for damages.

1 3 5 7 9 8 6 4 2

A CIP catalogue record for this book is available from
the British Library

Phototypeset by Intype, London
Printed and bound in Great Britain by Cox & Wyman Ltd,
Reading, Berkshire

The book is sold subject to the condition that it shall not,
by way of trade or otherwise, be lent, re-sold, hired out,
or otherwise circulated without the publisher's prior consent
in any form of binding or cover other than that in which
it is published and without a similar condition including this
condition being imposed on the subsequent purchaser

This book is dedicated to my grandfather, Jack Worthington, the most honourable of men.

> There are some who walk under silence;
> And some who walk always alone.
>
> *L. Grinling*

PROLOGUE

I am a deaf man in a deaf house.

Deafness has a colour to it. It is bone-coloured and soft like unworn wool. At night it intensifies; it warms itself in the brain; it makes little noises, brain mewls. And deafness has moods. Outside the world is soggy with sound, but inside, in a deaf head, the quiet is so absolute that any noise seems to have an electricity of its own, and a meaning which goes beyond understanding. This is the instinct of silence.

I was deafened after a fight. I had been a heavyweight boxer for years, earning good money in a rough world, using my head. Listening. Watching. Quick on my feet. It was obvious, the fight world; you moved faster than the other man and threw a heavier punch, and you won. Well, one night I was slow and that slowness deafened me.

At first the silence made me clumsy. You don't hear a car horn or music, or the roar of a crowd before a game. People's lips move without noise, and all the world's sounds come down merely to vibration. You live on another level; the shudder under your feet is all that is left of music; the quick judder of floorboards tells you a door has been slammed; and if you rest your head against a wall only the vibration tells you of traffic. It speaks in another language, as I do now.

Unable to hear my voice, I stopped talking. I learned that the world has no understanding of silence and fills up every pause with sound, so that a person thrown into unending, unceasing noiselessness is left without guidance, only instinct, only memory *of sound*, memory *of voice. To be deaf is to be diminished and exalted; to exist in one world whilst occupying another. To be deaf is to be aware of your life every second. My heartbeats are the metronome by which I live, and the rhythm by which I walk the world.*

When you close your eyes, what is there? I see only a series of hollows in vacuums and walls without doors. For many years civilization slid away from me. Until now. Now I see six people coming; six hearing people coming.

Coming to the deaf man, in the deaf house.

The Beginning

If you stand at the entrance, looking in, the vaulted ceiling rises almost fifty feet above you, white-painted and gridded with black girders, the vast unholy arch flanked with circular fluorescent lights the size of lorry wheels. The cold makes the meagre warmth from the lights steam meanly into the freezing air, the metallic sounds from below clanking upwards hideously into the vaulted roof. Gradually your eyes move slowly downwards and then, finally, they come to rest uneasily on the panorama which confronts you.

The perspective is terrifying; the vanishing point almost two hundred feet away – the exit like a contracted black pupil – and in that two hundred feet is a scene from hell. Stretching out on either side of you the rows of dead meat extend; yard after yard of carcasses – beef, lamb, game – the bodies stripped of their hides and hung, sometimes whole, sometimes dismembered, on iron hooks from iron rails. And because of the height of the chamber all movements echo, the scrape of the iron hook on the iron bar barking harshly into the biting cold.

All manner of men work here, porters, butchers, bummerees, loaders, all dressed in long white overalls, some ghostly in caps, the white cotton flaps at the back falling down on to their shoulders. The material is streaked with blood, as are their shoulders, but there is no smell, no sick hot stench of the abattoir. This is not a place of dying, but of death. In fact, there is no smell at all. Only noise; the men shouting, hoarse in the cold; the metal clanking; and the turning tumbrel sound of the cart wheels grinding on the flat cemented floor.

Hesitating at the entrance, Rachel Crossley glanced round, then winced as a cart passed her, brushing against her coat. Slowly she took out a notepad and began to write. It was two o'clock in the morning. At Smithfield market, in the dark, dead city of London.

The men were used to her now. At first they had teased her, wolf-whistled when she came in, made comic-book gestures when she told them she was training to be an architect.

'I'm doing research.'

'Why? So you can build more places like this?'

She shrugged, looked round; her actions slow with the cold. 'Smithfield's a historic place,' she explained. 'It's built like a church.'

'Some bloody church, luv,' the porter replied, banging his feet on the cement floor. 'Mind you, it's cold enough.'

They took her for a cup of tea later – before dawn, around five – and bought her a bacon sandwich. Bread half an inch thick, bacon cooked pink, limp, greasy. Hot on a February morning whilst the streets were still dark. Gratefully, Rachel ate with them as they sat huddled in a steamy café on the corner facing the entrance to the market – and then she saw him.

'Who's that?'

The nearest porter turned. Red-eyed, with a long white bone of a nose. 'Who?'

'That man . . . look, over there,' Rachel answered, wiping away the gathering steam on the window and pointing across the dark street to the solitary figure standing, unmoving, at the entrance to Smithfield market.

The porter laughed sharply and then winked at his companion across the table. 'You want to stay away from him, Miss. Stick with the likes of us instead.'

Her eyes were still fixed on the man outside.

'Why? Who is he?'

The porter shrugged: 'Him? Well now, he used to be a big man. He did. A real big man. Tough as they come. A boxer. Heavyweight...'

Rachel frowned, trying to make out the stranger's face in the darkness.

'... you want to ask Titus Brand the details. He knows all about it.' The porter jerked his thumb towards the figure outside. 'All I can tell you is that he used to work part-time here, lifting and humping the carcasses about. He could lift *any* bloody carcass. Jesus, he was strong. It was his way of weight training, you see. A cheap way to build up muscle; work out. He was so poor then he couldn't afford to pay for sparring partners.'

Rachel wiped the window again with her hand. The figure came into clearer focus immediately. Standing, stock still, a dark shape at the Dantesque market entrance. 'What's his name?'

The porter raised his eyebrows. 'I dunno. Never found that out—'

'But everyone has a name!' Rachel said incredulously. 'Didn't anyone think to ask him?'

'No, no one asked him, Miss – because he couldn't tell them even if they did,' the porter replied patiently. 'He doesn't talk, you see. He can't hear, and he can't speak.' He peered at the figure outside; just as Rachel did. 'He's no name, he's just known as *the deaf man* – and if you take my advice you'll stay away from him.'

She looked over her shoulder curiously. 'Why?'

Gently the porter turned her around so that she was staring out of the window again.

'Look at him... watch him,' he urged her. 'What do you see?'

Her voice was puzzled. 'I see a man on his own.'

'And what else?'

She frowned. 'Nothing.'

'Well, I see a man who's at home here,' the porter replied quietly, dropping his hands from her shoulders. 'I see a man who comes to a hell-hole like this and *likes* it. He doesn't *have* to come here; he doesn't have to work here. He comes because he's *comfortable* here... Now that worries me. It doesn't seem right.'

'Why not? I come here for my work,' Rachel answered. 'Maybe he has equally good reason.'

'Maybe so, maybe not,' the porter replied. 'But he worries me, unnerves me. You see, once I found him sitting on the back steps of one of the lorries – this is months ago – just sitting in the bleeding cold. Watching. He saw me looking at him, but never moved a muscle, and I kept staring for some reason – like I couldn't tear myself away.' The porter paused, the window was steaming up again, misting the deaf man. 'Well, he keeps staring at me and then finally he unfastens his coat. It was an overcoat like the one he's wearing now. He opened it wide. Very wide... I can't explain *what* I saw, I mean, it makes no sense... but as he opened the coat the lining was ribbed with bone and covered in blood. It was like he was opening his own chest...' The man hesitated, his voice dropping. 'Christ, I backed off those lorry steps just as fast as I could go, and when I finally looked back he was still sitting there – but there was no blood and no ribs showing. It was just like the inside of a normal coat...' The porter's gaze moved slowly away from the window. 'He was warning me off, you see. Telling me to keep my distance – and, if you've any sense, you'll do the same.'

Almost half an hour later Rachel left, walking out on to the chilled street, illuminated intermittently as she moved in and out of the lamplight. She was aware all the time of the deaf man watching her; she could sense his interest and listened for the footsteps following her. But there was none, and when she turned at the end of the street, the vast inverted V of the market entrance was empty.

The First Day

CHAPTER ONE

You have one week to live.

Harry Binky blinked at the words, stared at them as they appeared on the menu card. Six words, clearly defined on the white paper, coming somewhere between the first and second courses. Their appearance jolted him, and then he felt a creeping desire to laugh, glancing across the table to his companion. It was then that he realized that the room was suddenly quiet. Not simply a falling off of noise, a lull in conversation from the tables which surrounded him, but an *absolute* quiet.

The paper shook noiselessly in his hand. He reached towards his wine glass, watching as it struck against the side of his plate. Noiselessly. The impulse to laugh vanished, his eyes turning back to the menu card as he read the words again, his left hand moving up to his ear. Gingerly he felt it, then felt his other ear. Then he rubbed the skin of his cheeks, smiling nervously as his companion glanced over to him and spoke.

But he *heard* nothing. He saw the man's lips move, and heard nothing. The menu fluttered in his hand, the realization that he was deaf causing a rush of blood to his face. Yet he heard *that*; heard the noises *inside* his head, and thought he heard, for an instant, the sound of his own brain fighting panic. Relax, he told himself, relax, it'll pass, it's just a momentary blip. His companion kept talking, apparently unaware of his alarm, and then signalled to the wine waiter again. The man appeared silently; his lips moved silently; his feet made no sound. Nothing made a sound, only the words on the menu card hummed incandescently.

You have one week to live.

But *they* had sound. They rippled with sound; they poured into Harry Binky's deaf ears just as they tapped out a rhythm in front of his eyes. He began to sweat; feeling a sudden tightness around his chest; a quick speeding up of his breathing; he felt nauseated and became horribly aware that he was about to faint. Soundlessly his mouth opened, but his lips hung without words, his hand losing its grip and dropping the menu to the floor.

Where it fell *loudly*. So loudly that he jumped, automatically putting his hands over his ears to block out the noise.

'What's the matter, Harry?'

He blinked. The deafness had gone and his companion's voice echoed unbearably in his head as he forced himself to smile.

'Earache,' he said quickly.

'I'm not surprised,' the man replied. 'A morning in the House would give any sane man earache.'

Gingerly Harry Binky glanced back at his menu. The words were gone; in their place was only the promise of an unappetizing fish starter. Again, he fought an impulse to laugh, relief making him giddy. No one had *really* written the words there. It wasn't a genuine threat or even a crude joke. He had imagined it, that was all. He was working too hard, pushing himself too much, something like this was bound to happen in the end, his doctor had warned him about it only the other day, nagging him about his long hours.

'I'm an MP, what the hell am I supposed to do? I have hundreds of people calling on my time.'

'Pace yourself,' the medic replied. 'Don't risk your health for your career.'

'Believe me,' Harry had replied with confidence, 'I can look after myself.'

But now he could feel the uncomfortable stickiness under his arms and his ear drums seemed exposed, peeled, each sound unbearably loud.

I need a holiday.

'What?'

Harry raised his eyebrows. He was thinking aloud now. God, what a mess.

'I said I was thinking of taking a holiday.'

'It would be rather a bad time to pick at the moment, wouldn't it?'

'Well . . .' Harry said half-heartedly, ' . . . it was only a thought.'

'I need to talk to you about that new road in Shipley . . .'

Stuff the road, Harry thought, discreetly rubbing his left ear.

' . . . the locals are getting together a petition and I talked to Gordon this morning about it . . .'

You have one week to live.

What kind of a message was that? Harry wondered irritably. Maybe he *was* pushing himself too fast. After all, even if he had only imagined it, it might be a warning of sorts.

' . . . we could have some trouble with them . . .' the man went on.

Harry emptied his glass of wine, the liquid lifting his spirits and pulling him back into reality.

'Nothing we can't handle,' he said confidently, pleased to find that his hearing was fully restored and that his voice no longer sounded loud in his ears. 'You worry too much.'

'I'm not worried now,' his companion replied easily. 'Now that I know you're looking after it.'

They talked for another hour and a half, Harry Binky relapsing back into his usual easy good humour. Copious amounts of wine were drunk, a good lunch eaten, the time for the lighting up of cigars coming as the *maître d'hôtel* walked over to their table. The man leaned down, his face for an instant divinely wreathed in an aureole of Havana smoke as he spoke quietly to Harry Binky.

Discretion was important, he knew, especially in the breaking of bad news. And this was some of the worst news a father ever had to hear.

Harry sat rigidly in his seat, the cigar in his left hand, his face turned upwards.

'Did you say my son has been in an accident?'

The *maître d'hôtel* nodded, low-voiced with sympathy. 'He's at St Thomas's Hospital, sir. I'm very sorry, very sorry indeed—'

'Chris is at St Thomas's?' Harry repeated, struggling to his feet, the table pulled away to allow him to pass easily. 'Did you say he was in St Thomas's?'

'I did, sir. Shall I get you a taxi?'

Harry nodded, walking stiffly to the door.

'I'm so sorry, sir,' the *maître d'hôtel* continued. 'I'm sure everything will be all right . . .'

Harry moved towards the exit blindly, his legs carrying him without any sensation of walking, his hand still clasping the cigar as he moved out on to the street. The rain drummed against him, it snuffed out the expensive cigar, it stained the shoulders of his suit and it dampened his carefully cut hair. Harry Binky, forty-eight years old, divorced, with a burgeoning career, two houses – and one son on a life-support machine.

The deaf man had taken several hours to prepare the meal and had now laid it out on the table in the kitchen. It steamed invitingly; the meat blood-red at the centre, the butter-sheened vegetables luridly enticing. The house was in darkness apart from the kitchen. And silent; but then everything was silent to him ... Carefully he scrutinized the two place settings on the white linen cloth, and then slowly poured out two glasses of wine. Ssssh ... sssh ... he crooned to himself, tipping his head to one side and frowning slightly. You're hungry, I know that, but wait. Wait a little longer.

It was their anniversary. Twelve years since the deaf man had come to the house. Twelve slow-motion years. Twelve years in which he had turned from hopelessness to a position of strength. You nurtured me, you loved me, he thought, glancing around him. You took me in ... He looked at the food again for a long instant, a deep dark warmth flooding him and turning the juices in his stomach. No, he wouldn't eat yet, not yet. He had to feed her first. He had to reward her, to show her the love she had showed him.

It was dark. February. Matt black sky, too cold even for dogs to be out, as he made his way into the garden at the back of the house. He needed no light – he knew every morsel of ground intimately – and when he reached the spot he had selected earlier he knelt down. Somewhere there was a moon rising in another place; somewhere day waited; but in that instant he dug at the black unilluminated earth and then, when he had made a hole, he placed the meal in it.

Eat, he willed the earth, the garden, the house. Eat ... take ... live ... Eat.

His hands smoothed the earth, pressing the food down into the soil beneath.

Eat ... eat ...

His eyes were quick in the darkness, his hands stroking the ground, his thanks murmured unintelligibly, repeatedly, his mouth only an inch above the soil.

Jeanie Maas had had two Guinnesses and was pleasantly giddy. She hummed to herself as she walked round her bedroom in the basement of the house in Portland Place, the tune unrecognizable, a quick curse escaping her lips as she bumped into the bedside table. Painfully slowly she undressed, tossing her clothes on to a chair, her underwear tucked modestly under the little pile, her stockings draped over the chair arm. In the morning she would have to darn them again; she always pushed her feet through the ends, her toes red-ringed at the end of the day.

Her mother had taught her how to darn. *If you can darn socks you can keep a man happy. Men like women to be frugal.* Jeanie doubted it, she had a belief that men only pretended to like sensible women, in reality they liked silly, extravagant females who looked good. And looking good meant not wearing darned stockings. Looking good meant having silly underwear, those scooped-up bras which pushed up the breasts ... Giggling softly she pulled back the bedspread. What was the use of even thinking about it? She was seventy years old, she didn't need a bra to lift her breasts, more like a fork-lift truck.

She hummed again giddily, slipping off her glasses and polishing them. After *Coronation Street* she would go to bed – that was if she could stay awake long enough to watch it. Chances were that she would fall asleep in her chair like she usually did when she had a drink, and wake later with a crick in her neck. Still, she felt good; her employer was preoccupied; the house was quiet and she could afford to indulge herself.

The TV flickered in the dim lounge as Jeanie walked in, tapping her hearing aid impatiently and fiddling with the volume control. The Guinness had made her artificially happy, but clumsy, and her fingers struggled to turn up the sound as her eyes fixed on the TV images. The characters were engaged in some kind of brawl, she realized, her attention riveted to the set – and then the sound failed.

Damn the National Health! Jeanie thought irritably, her good humour evaporating. The bloody thing was useless! Her hand fiddled with the hearing aid in her ear, her fingers fumbling with the tiny switch. Damn and blast it! She had been looking forward to watching TV all day, and now this... There was a sudden loud crackling in her ear, and she winced, then realized that *she could hear nothing*.

Now she'd really gone and done it! Jeanie thought angrily. Now she'd broken the flaming thing. She sat down heavily holding the hearing aid. What was she supposed to do now? If she couldn't hear, she couldn't follow the programme. Her irritation accelerated, then she frowned, her hands going up to her ears in panic. What the hell was going on? She couldn't hear anything at all! Her head swam; her eyes on the screen. The mouths of the TV characters kept moving, but there was no sound of voices. *Nothing*.

She was used to having impaired hearing – but not *deafness*. Annoyed, Jeanie wrenched the hearing aid out of her ear. She banged it on the back of her hand. Nothing happened. She then wiggled her index finger in one ear and then the other. But she still heard nothing. Then she glanced at the screen.

You have one week to live.

Jeanie Maas saw the words and frowned. She then took off her glasses, polished them, and looked back at the screen, trying hard to concentrate.

You have one week to live.

She tittered softly, her mind mushy. She must have changed channels by accident, and this must be a trailer for a film. The words flickered in front of her. *Well, go on*, she willed it, *get on with the programme*. But nothing happened. Jeanie frowned again. Then shook her head, trying to dislodge the pressing silence. But it persisted.

Suddenly she was frightened. Struggling to organize her thoughts she staggered to her feet and stood unsteadily in front of the TV, staring at the words and then at the useless hearing aid in her hand. It was light pink, flesh-coloured plastic, the outer ring clear. Roughly she rubbed the back of her reddened ear, surprised to find that her eyes had filled and that she felt suddenly vulnerable. *If I look again at the TV the words will have gone*, she thought helplessly, half turning and then turning away again. *Come on, Jeanie, force yourself to look, and they'll be gone.*

And they were. As Jeanie Maas fought oncoming panic she turned to the screen and saw that the words had disappeared – and realized in the same instant that she could hear the low rumble of speech. Silly with relief, she tucked the hearing aid back into her ear and turned up the volume to maximum. The sound blasted into her head and made her laugh outright, her hand extending automatically to the bottle of Guinness beside her.

Titus Brand was smoking a hand-rolled cigarette at the back entrance of Smithfield market, his rheumy eyes narrowed against the wind blowing down the alleyway. He coughed once, narrow-chested, diabetic, thin, and then nodded as Rachel approached him. She came dressed in trousers, a scarf over her face, her dark hair hidden under a man's cap.

''Morning,' Titus said affably.

'God, I can hardly breathe in this cold.'

The porter laughed. He should have retired years ago; he was too old and too sick, but he had friends at the market and it was quiet at home now that his wife had died. Automatically he reached into his pocket for some chocolate. He shouldn't eat it – he was diabetic – but it never stopped him.

'Tom said you wanted a word with me,' he said, offering her some chocolate.

Rachel tucked the scarf under her chin. Her mouth was pale with cold. 'I was asking about the deaf man,' she said simply, stamping her feet on the pavement, her breath a white vapour.

'I thought you wanted to know about the market,' Titus replied, sucking on his cigarette before biting into the chocolate again. 'Someone said you were a builder.'

'I'm training to be an architect—'

'Same difference,' Titus said blithely.

Rachel let it pass. 'So, what *do* you know about him?'

'He's deaf.'

'What else?'

The old man narrowed his eyes. His false teeth clicked as he chewed, his buckled hands clenched around the pinched stub of his smoke.

'He was a boxer, a winner too. I saw him fight once. Even put a bet on him.' Titus paused. He seemed oblivious to the cold, although he couldn't have weighed more than seven and a half stone. 'He was beaten, deafened, and then . . .'

'Go on.'

'He couldn't hear, you see. He didn't hear the men come up behind him that night. They jumped him, beat the hell out of him – it was a grudge or something. They'd never have dared to take him on before, but when he was hurt, well, then they set on him. He went downhill after that. He'd always thought of himself as a hard man, an iron man, frightened of no one. A man who could always defend himself. But he hadn't heard them coming up behind him and they left him for dead . . . He never got over it. He felt he'd lost respect.' Titus glanced over to the young woman standing beside him. 'In fact, he felt he'd lost everything. I shouldn't tell you this, but he's got a scar across his throat almost four inches wide. I don't say he did it – I don't say the bastards who worked him over did it – but someone did.'

Rachel stared into the old man's face: 'D'you think he tried to kill himself?'

'No,' Titus replied, stubbing out his smoke. 'Not that he didn't think about it. He was crazy, mad with the world for months. You wouldn't have dared to go near him then; no one would. He was shit mad, and frightening.' Titus paused. 'He's *still* frightening . . . Listen, love, I'm a man, I can handle it, but you couldn't.'

Rachel hesitated. 'But how does he live now? I mean, what does he do?'

'Who knows?' Titus said, shrugging. 'I don't. I just know that he went crazy for a while, and wanted to die – and then he changed. Calmed down. Funny thing is, when he's calm he's more frightening than ever.'

Rachel frowned. 'He doesn't look frightening.'

Slowly Titus turned to look at her: 'How close have you got to him?'

'What?'

'I said – how close have you got to him?'

She hesitated. 'I've just seen him across a street, that's all.'

Titus nodded. 'Well, keep it that way, luv. Across a street is close enough.'

Father Michael was in a foul mood at breakfast. His irascible temper was due to an undercooked egg running rawly off his spoon and making a mess down the side of the egg cup. He had poked at it with his spoon, the liquid slipping around the plate as his disgust rose.

No matter how many times he told the housekeeper, his morning egg was seldom cooked enough. At first he had thought it was merely inexperience but the woman had been working for him for two years now and there were still many times when his egg was vilely underdone. He thought it was deliberate. In fact, he was sure of it. Especially as she always managed to irritate him when he had to face a particularly difficult day. Unchristian, he called it. And spiteful.

He poked at the underdone egg for several moments, smearing it over the plate, making a slime trail with his spoon.

Oh yes, she did it deliberately, he knew that. It was her way of getting her own back, of repaying him for his irritability or for one of the many slights she imagined. Suddenly, he struck the egg hard, hearing the satisfying crunch of the shell and watching as the glutinous mess oozed out.

Perhaps she asked forgiveness for her cooking at confession. Behind the ecclesiastical grille, perhaps she confided to some other priest her culinary acts of revenge. He wondered what her penance would be, two Hail Marys seemed inappropriate somehow—

'What's wrong with it?'

He turned his face upwards. A young face cheating its years, the dark hair suspiciously full. No one had hair like that naturally, the woman had confided to a friend, and no priest should be *allowed* to have hair like that. It wasn't Godly.

'The egg's raw,' he said flatly.

'I did it for two minutes.'

'Then perhaps you should turn the gas on next time,' Father Michael replied, getting to his feet and walking out.

He paused in the hallway, picking up the newspaper and glancing into the mirror over the table. His reflection pleased him, even though he tried half-heartedly to fight his vanity. The cool morning light paled him, his eyes, rested and welcoming, looking back from the mirror and appearing full of kindness. Fascinated, he touched his skin – and then frowned.

His hands were ugly, they let him down. Too large, the nails spatulated, the skin coarse. They were another man's hands, out of context with his face. Instinctively, he tucked them into his pockets and returned to the scrutiny of his face. Women had fallen in love with him, and he liked that. He liked adoration without commitment, even though he knew that parishioners were often attracted to the unavailability of the clergy, and not to the man himself.

It had been very nearly his downfall though. Ten years

previously his looks had enticed a woman and she had, in turn, fascinated him. He winced, pained by the memory, and disturbed, not by the thought of love gone, but by the realization that his sexuality had almost lost him his place in the world. His *status*. It was one thing to be the object of adoration, quite another to enter into its steaming grip . . . Caution was all, he knew; caution and control. Stay remote, he repeated to himself, take the admiration – but stay remote.

An hour later he was giving Mass to a paltry congregation, the words of the service intoned by rote as his eyes flicked from the Bible to the people ahead of him. He was aware of their interest, flattered by it, and yet irritated as he laid out the wine and wafers, the ringing of the bell encouraging the faithful to the altar rail. There were ten kneeling supplicants, mostly women, their hands cupped to receive the sacrament as Father Michael began to walk the length of the row. He noticed how the light played on the bent heads, making pockets of darkness under the cheek-bones and crescented shadows under the down-turned eyes. He noticed, too, how many of their hands shook, and how a faded label curled slyly out of a woman's collar.

The words came from his lips to the rhythm of ritual, the smell of incense, the ringing Mass bell and the intermittent coughing of an elderly man. Then he saw it. And blinked, halting for an instant as he stared at the communion wafer in his hand.

You have one week to live.

The words seemed burnt into the whiteness of the wafer and, as he drew his hand closer to read them again, the priest became aware that he could no longer hear the old man coughing, or the bell. *He was deaf.* An involuntary grunt escaped his lips – but it came without sound, and he knew, with mounting panic, there *should* have been a noise. The wafer lay unmoving in his hand. It seemed threatening, the words damning, and yet for a shimmering instant the priest had an unexpected sensation of excitement. Perhaps this was an omen; perhaps he would receive other messages; stigmata; the voice of God – perhaps he was to be one of the chosen. At that moment the priest could see in his mind – in his deaf head – little plaster figurines of himself which would be sold to the faithful, together with plastic-coated cards adorned with medals. They would be carried in a thousand pockets and prayed to, mumbled to, wept over in the lonely early hours, pleaded to . . .

His vanity inflated, it bloated in silence, it swelled as the wafer swelled in his palm, and then, in the instant of almost physical excitement, it suddenly *moved*. It undulated, took on short white legs; it wriggled, the words on its back growing smaller, then expanding again. It breathed, its hot belly pressing against the priest's hand – and then it seemed to lock into his flesh.

He screamed. He couldn't hear his own fear, but the kneeling supplicants were startled, watching with horror as the priest tried to brush the communion wafer from his right palm, the fingers of his left hand scratching at the white disc, pulling at the swollen back of the pulsing object. But it held on, its legs pushing agonizingly through the flesh of the priest's hand and creeping up and around his wrist as he screamed again, the words expanding in front of his eyes.

You have one week to live.

He began to pray then, the words making no sound as they came from his lips. Panicking, he stumbled away from the watching figures kneeling in front of him, and in desperation turned and slammed his hand with full force against the altar. The pain was so intense that he thought he'd broken his wrist, even though he didn't hear the sound of the bone cracking – and then he saw, with frantic relief, the wafer fall away.

It fell in slow motion, it turned in the air; the writing

fading, the legs disappearing, the long dream-time of its fall watched by the priest who stood with his back against the altar, his right hand hanging uselessly by his side.

It finally came to rest on the marble floor by his feet. Circular, white, pure as a crystal, without words. Benign. But as it landed it fell with a booming sound and jolted his ears back into full hearing, his head crammed suddenly with the noise of beating wings.

Intensive care units are always dark, the lighting subdued, the monitors easy to decipher in the warm gloom. Harry Binky stood by his son's bed in silence. He could have sat down – a seat had been brought for him – but he remained standing, half hoping that by refusing to accept the situation, it would cease to exist. If he continued standing – ready at any moment to go – Chris would wake up; they would remove the tubes; unhook him from the monitor; and prop him up against the pillows. He would talk about the crash, make a joke, using the sense of humour he had inherited from his father to make light of his injuries. Food would be brought for him, and he would grimace, asking for a steak, calling for the phone to talk to his friends. If Harry Binky just remained standing, it would all be all right...

But it wasn't that easy. Harry knew that he should leave, go to vote on a motion at the House – but he didn't. He didn't sit down either; even though his legs ached from standing after an hour; even though the rain dried on his suit and on his hair. Even *then* he stood, breathing in rhythm with his son's breaths, watching the green line of heartbeats and knowing that they wouldn't alter for a long time – even *then* a stubborn reluctance to admit the truth kept him upright.

Chris had been knocked off his motorbike on Hammersmith Broadway. That would have been bad enough, but a car had been unable to stop and had struck him as he lay on the road. Internal injuries, the doctor said, and possibly . . .

'What?' Harry had asked.

'Brain damage.'

Brain damage.

'Permanent?' Harry's voice was controlled. The MP taking on problems, taking it all in his stride.

'We won't know until he recovers consciousness.'

'He's my son,' Harry said helplessly. 'My *son*.'

'I know, Mr Binky.'

'It should have been me.'

Oh no, Dad, no . . .

Open your eyes, Chris. Open them. It can't be that difficult. Try. Your father's here.

Dad, listen, listen to me. You can hear me. Dad . . .

'What can be done for him?'

'Nothing, we just wait,' the doctor replied. 'The next few days will be vital.'

Dad, look at me, I'm OK! I'm here. I can hear you, why can't you hear me? I took a risk, overtook some bloody van. It was my fault. Jesus, Dad, listen to me. Get me out of here.

'Can I stay?'

The doctor nodded. 'You can stay as long as you like.'

'Fine,' Harry said quietly, lowering himself at long last into the chair. 'That's fine.'

Dad, don't give up, get me out of here. I'm not dying, I'm just stuck... That's kind, I don't remember you touching me for a long time. I can smell you as well as hear you. Bloody cigar smoke on your hands! You won't leave me, will you? Not here. They don't understand, but I can hear everything that's going on. I can't see though. Why is that, Dad? Why can't I see? Why can't I open my eyes? I can see inside my head though. It's almost like dreaming, if only I wasn't so afraid...

But I am scared, Dad. Dad! Oh God, are you still there? I can't hear you! Yes, yes, you're there, I can hear you breathing now. But it's too fast, Dad, slow down, or you'll have a heart attack and we don't want both of us ending up in here. Don't move your hand away, please... oh, you did. Why? Does it embarrass you? Make you feel stupid because you think I can't feel it? But I can, Dad, and I need you to touch me... Hold on to me. Hold on to me.

Harry kept staring at his unmoving, unresponsive son. 'Chris, you'll be OK.'

I know, just stay with me, that's all.

'We'll get you patched up,' Harry said vigorously, furiously. 'You'll be fine soon enough. Hang on.'

Only if you hang on to me too. Stay with me... Oh God, I'm drifting, but I'm not tired, so where am I drifting to? I have to stay here, I have to! I have to stay in the hospital. They've drugged me, Dad; they've sedated me even though I didn't want to be sedated. I can still hear the monitor, still make out dim lights through my eyelids. I should be awake, Dad. I should be

*awake, walking out of here, but I can't move. I can't move!
... Dad, someone's talking to me, but it's not you, or the doctor.
There's a man here with me ... No! It's not possible. This is
crazy, Dad, but you have to listen to me. Listen to me. I want
to tell you what I see. Listen carefully, I'm going somewhere and
I want you to know all about it.* You have to know. *Follow me,
Dad, follow me ...*

*I'm in a house. A house with three floors set away from other
houses. Dad, take my hand, take it! Dad! Yes, that's it, hold on
to me. You see, you know what to do, you don't think you do,
but you do ... This house is old, no curtains, just shutters. It
could have been a great house once. You'd have liked it, it would
have impressed all your pompous MP friends ... Dad, listen, it's
important. The rooms are all wood panelled, the floors wood too,
with fireplaces and grates with mounds of ashes under them.
There are logs burning ... Dad? Breathe, talk, let me know
you're there! Good, I heard you move, you're shifting in your
seat. You're still there. Stay, stay with me.*

*I'm in one room now, Dad. It's got a low ceiling, wood walls,
wood floor. It smells of earth. There's a fire here too and it lights
the room, but there are only two pieces of furniture here — a
chair and a clock. The clock has a pendulum, Dad, and as it
swings it's ticking loudly. Very loudly. Just a minute, that's
it! That's what's so strange, there's* no other sound here. *The
fire's silent — but how's that possible? There's no sound of logs
crackling. This is a deaf house ... God, that's crazy.* Isn't it
crazy, tell me it's crazy, Dad ... *Dad? Keep breathing, that's
it. I can't slip away if I can hear you.* Keep breathing, *keep
touching me ...*

*The chair's in front of me now, Dad, facing me. A high-
backed chair, dark leather, well used, smelling of earth. Soil, wet
earth. I'm afraid ... I want to come back, Dad, but I can't
open my eyes or move! God, I'm not paralysed, am I? Please,
God, don't say I'm paralysed ...*

Someone's here. There's a man in my head with me ... *Dad, listen to me. Listen! He wants something from me – but he doesn't say what; he's just looking at me. Looking. I'm afraid. The clock's getting louder and now you're breathing to the rhythm of the clock ... Dad? Slow down, please!* Slow down!

Good, that's better. We can't both panic, can we, Dad? We can't panic ... I'm still in the room and the man is still here. I don't know if he hears me. He doesn't talk, he just points to the clock ... The dial's changed, Dad. No numbers, letters instead. I can't read it yet. Yes, yes, I can now ... It says. What? It makes no sense at all, but I'll read it to you anyway. You have one week to live ... What's that supposed to mean, Dad? ... Dad? ... DAD! I can't hear you. I can't feel you. Don't leave me! This house has no sound, this man doesn't speak. Dad, I'm not dying, am I? I don't want to die here. Not here, not in a dead room that smells of earth. Don't let me die and be buried here. Get me out! Listen to me! Hear me! I'm begging you, Dad!!!

'I think you should go home and try to get some rest,' the doctor said, glancing at the monitor next to Chris Binky's bed.

'He is my son. He needs me,' Harry said quietly.

'But there's nothing you can do for him at the moment. He's not aware of your being here.'

Slowly Harry took his hand away from his son's.

'I'll come back in a little while then.'

The doctor nodded. 'That would be best.'

No, no it wouldn't! God, Dad, don't go. Don't leave me. You're getting up, you're going! Don't leave me here. I can't move, Dad. I can't follow you. I don't want to stay here. Don't leave me, you bastard! Don't ... *Dad, get me out, please ... If*

I promise to stay very still, you will come back, won't you? Won't you?

You've gone now. Gone. So has the house and the man. I can hear everything again clearly, just as I heard the door open and close when you left ... I'll stay here quietly. I'll be good and I'll wait for you to come back. I won't panic, I'll just wait for you to come back ... You will, won't you? You won't let anything happen to me, will you? You won't let me die, will you? ... Dad? Dad?

The deaf man knew he was being watched. He liked the feel of Rachel's attention, the soft stroke of interest which followed him towards the exit of the market. Before, when he had turned round, she had pretended to be making notes; scribbling busily on a little white pad – but he hadn't been fooled. She had been flushed slightly – her lips for an instant parting – when she knew he watched her.

Under the white light she was bleached, her flesh dead, the cold making her skin bloodless. *Look at me*, he whispered in his head, *look at me. I know who you are; I know all of you; and I know that you will bring the others to me. Rachel ...* He saw her stiffen. *Yes, you heard me call. I'm in your head, Rachel, creeping into your brain. What did he tell you, old Titus Brand? What stories? What excuses did he make? Did he tell you how I live, Rachel? Did he tell you what feeds and nourishes me? I doubt it, you have to find that out for yourself. And you will. You will ...*

At first she woke without knowing why she woke. The curtains blanked out the moonlight, the clock by her bed reading two-thirty. Languorously Ahlia moved her legs, waking slowly, drawing herself out of sleep. Her head moved on the pillow, the full length of blonde hair falling across her forehead, one arm stretching out for the light switch.

The lamp brought the room back to her as she drowsily turned over. He had gone, she realized without regret. Good, she liked to make love, but she preferred to sleep alone. Her bed snuggled around her, her toes exploring the cool corners of the sheets. Reluctantly she woke, longing to continue sleeping, her eyes opening only momentarily.

You have one week to live.

Her eyes widened as her hand extended to the words written on the pillow. What on earth was that! she thought, as she sprang up in bed and backed away from the pillow. If he thought this was some kind of a joke, he was crazy. Writing on her pillow – what the hell had possessed him?

But angry as she was, Ahlia couldn't touch the pillow and instead she slid out of bed and continued to back away, her breathing and heart rate accelerating rapidly as she fought to control herself. I'm only dreaming, she told herself, I just have to force myself to wake up—

'Wake up!'

She knew that she had spoken; knew she had formed the words, *but there was no sound*. At least, none she could hear. Again she spoke – and again there was silence. In blind panic, and tripping over the sheet wrapped round her, Ahlia ran in to the bathroom and snapped on the light, staring at her mouth as she repeated her name over and over again.

Jesus, Dear God, I'm deaf!

Her hands went to her mouth, her fingers moving against her lips as she talked. She could feel the vibration of her words, but heard nothing, and panicking stumbled back into the bedroom and snatched up the phone.

Hurriedly she dialled her lover's number, then realized that if he answered she *couldn't hear his voice*. She was deaf, *she couldn't hear anything!* Hysteria winded her, and when she saw the marked pillow she lunged at it, clawing at the silk with her nails, the pillowcase ripping, feathers frosting over her, her mouth working uselessly... Finally, after several minutes, she stopped. The silence fell over her and she curled up on the floor exhausted, her fabulous legs tucked against stomach, her fist pressed tightly against her mouth.

The only person to whom the silence was welcome was Rachel Crossley. She sat with her knees clasped together in the board room and felt her hearing slide away from her. There was no panic – she had had too much of that – the silence was simply comforting. If I cannot hear, I can remove myself from this place, I can leave the world. Her calm was vast, without fear. The board room was filled with men, all partners, the Managing Director making notes on a huge white board in front of them.

It was an important meeting; one to which she had been invited to watch, not participate. She was training to be an architect, not yet one of the hallowed breed of the qualified. *Was she really deaf?* she wondered drowsily as she stared at the board in front of her. Was she really *deaf*? The words appeared suddenly on the table in front of her:

YOU HAVE ONE WEEK TO LIVE.

What? she thought, blinking. What did it say? Her eyes fixed on the words. One week to live – why now? Why not years ago, when she had wanted to die, begged to die? Why now? After years of inescapable torment, why was she being offered peace now? And why was she *deaf*? Oh, once she would have longed to be deaf. Then she would no longer have heard the opening of the bedroom door and then heard, in the dark, the changing of her breathing – and of Leon, her widowed mother's step-son. The child her mother inherited from her second marriage. The only thing left of the man she had loved. Leon.

The abuse had started when Rachel was a child, and had continued. She wanted to tell; always wanted to tell; but how could she? Leon was mentally retarded. But very strong. Leon was everything to her mother; the only one who had remained with her.

Rachel had wanted to stay at home. But couldn't. So she left when she could, without ever telling her mother why. Letting her mother think she was a bitch. Letting her mother lavish attention on the one who remained – Leon. Rachel had believed that she would forget – and she was right. But after a while, she remembered, and lately she had begun to dream of Leon again.

Her hands pressed together, her head bent towards the words on the table in front of her.

You have one week to live.

What was it supposed to mean? Why was she being threatened now, now that she had escaped? She didn't want to die any longer; she wanted to live. She had reasons to live – Chris Binky, for one. They were talking about living together, and with him she could make love properly for the first time. She even believed that one day soon she might be able to tell him about Leon.

So why had the words come now? Wasn't it over – all the horror and the disgust? Was that why she was dreaming of Leon again? Had the few quiet, whole years she had spent been just a temporary safety? The room was silent around her and she sat, closed off, in her deaf world. I'm twenty-four years old, not fourteen, I got away. I got away... didn't I?

The words disappeared suddenly, her hearing returning with such force that she gasped loudly and clasped her hands over her ears. Startled, the men in the board room turned to look at her – and in every face she saw something of Leon.

And so ended the first day.

The Second Day

Chapter Two

Harry Binky stood in the small sitting room and waited for Father Michael to appear. He hadn't thought of his religion for over a decade, had rejected all the trappings of Catholicism as archaic. His world had been the world of the achiever; he had no time for, or belief in, the spiritual. His faith had been enforced by his mother and when he was old enough to move away from her, Harry moved from religion too. It embarrassed him. He resented the idea of a priest being able to absolve sins – what made a priest, a man, able to forgive another man?

Invoked or not invoked the God will be present. The words came back to him and he struggled to remember where he had heard them. It had been during a holiday and he had seen them carved over a doorway in Greece, the words of the Delphic oracle seeming trite under a hot and libidinous sun. But now they didn't seem banal; they didn't seem comfortable either, but they did offer some kind of promise of hope. While Harry Binky had followed his ambitions, cheated a little, done his fair share of petty-spirited things, God had been with him. He found the notion oddly affecting . . .

He coughed, uncomfortable with his thoughts. The room was heavy with furniture, a mixture of styles all crowding together like ill-matched guests at a party. An old-fashioned plant stand stood next to a modern gas fire, the curtains tasselled with worn fringe. Outside the window the day hovered disinterestedly over Peckham, the untended garden fierce with vegetation, a rose bush marshalled with suckers. The room smelt of indignity.

'Mr Binky?'

Harry turned, surprised by the man standing in the doorway.

'I'm Father Michael,' he said, introducing himself and walking in. The room stood back for him.

'It's good of you to see me,' Harry replied, scrutinizing the priest.

Around six feet in height, heavily built, the man was dressed in a priest's black robes, a circle of white around his throat. The collar seemed to sever his head from his body – to divorce the disturbingly erotic from the clerical garb.

The priest leaned down and turned up the gas fire, glancing over to his visitor.

'What can I do for you?'

'It's my son,' Harry said simply, sitting down. The chair sagged under him, old springs sucking him in. He wondered fleetingly why he had come.

The priest stood in front of the fire; cutting off the meagre warmth.

'My son is very ill . . . he's in St Thomas's Hospital.'

'I'm very sorry . . . are you a Catholic?'

'Pardon?'

The priest repeated the question.

'Yes . . . I don't go to Mass any more, though,' Harry admitted. It was one of his saving graces, being truthful at times. Truth was a useful weapon for an MP. 'Does that matter?'

Father Michael smiled and moved away from the fire. The room acted as a backdrop for him and Harry realized with grim humour that he was fully aware of the effect his actions had. At first the priest stood by the window, then moved away, then sat down, leaning towards his visitor. You can trust me, the action said.

Harry doubted it.

'He's critically ill.'

'How old is your son?'

'Twenty-five,' Harry said, shifting his position in the chair.

'Only twenty-five . . .'

The priest gazed at his visitor. 'Do you want me to see him?'

'Well . . . no. Not really.'

Father Michael hid his surprise well. 'You wanted to talk then?'

'Yes, to talk.'

The silence which followed denied it. A bus passed on the street outside, changing gears at the bend. Harry couldn't remember how long it was since he had travelled on public transport; one of the perks of being an MP. Working for the people, yet removed from the people. The irony made him smile.

'So talk, please.'

Harry glanced at his hands, aching to light up a cigar, the gas fire in the room made him drowsy.

'Do you hear confessions?'

His own words jolted him. Confession. After all he had said about priests over the years, here he was asking for this man to hear his confession and offer him forgiveness. His hypocrisy made him clumsy.

'I can come back another time . . .'

'Now is fine.'

'But if you're busy . . .'

Sitting next to Harry, Father Michael turned his body to face him. He saw a man who was well known, respected, an MP whose features had stared at him from many windows during the last election. A tailored face, suited to his profession and his tailored clothes; a face at peace with its owner. A face which was arranged to shock no one, entice no one, threaten no one. A face for all men.

'Do you want to confess in church? Or would you rather I listen to you here?'

The room hummed with the noise from the gas fire, a soporific hum. Harry's thoughts swung back to the previous day, and for an instant his hearing again slipped and the words juggled in front of his eyes. *You have one week to live.* Anxiety shook him and his body tensed, his hands flexed against the arms of the chair.

The priest saw and misread his action.

'Relax, Mr Binky. Just take your time. It will feel strange at first. Just talk when you're ready.'

Harry looked at him blankly and then exhaled. Perhaps the experience of the previous day had been a premonition of his son's accident. But reasoning did nothing to lessen the swamping sense of dread and he found his voice wavering.

'I've been a shoddy father . . .' he began, talking automatically, running in his mind from the fear which was threatening to immobilize him. 'I love Chris. My son. I love him, but I never talk to him. Not really. I talk to everyone else instead. Constituents, agents, other MPs. I talk for a living . . .' The gas fire hissed on. 'I don't want to believe that I'll never get the chance to say the things I wanted to say.'

'What did you want to say?'

'What would be the point in telling you?' Harry asked honestly. 'You're not my son. It's Chris I should be telling.'

Father Michael remained impassive. 'Tell me anyway.'

Harry felt into his pocket and drew out a cigar, fingering it without lighting it. 'I'm very jealous of my son. Of his life . . . I never wanted my child to have better than I had.' He refused to look at the priest, ashamed of his confession.

'Other parents want just that, don't they? They strive so that their children have more than they had . . . Well, I didn't want my son to have more advantages than me because if he did I knew he would achieve more than I could ever hope to. He's only twenty-five, but he's clever in the way that changes people. Intuitively clever. He can recognize reality and yet he understands how perception changes things too. People, situations. He sees how the soul moves in people . . .' Harry stopped, embarrassed by the extravagance of his speech. 'I saw him in the hospital – he's unconscious, on a ventilator – and I saw how they had taped his eyelids closed. And I was *glad*. You see, I didn't want him to see me, to see *into* me . . . My son is transfixing.'

'He sounds exceptional.'

Harry nodded. 'And I am jealous of him.' Suddenly chilled, he leaned towards the gas fire and warmed his left hand. 'Chris could do anything. His mother knew that, his teachers know that, I know that, and do you know something, Father, when I looked at him in that hospital bed, I was for an instant, *glad* that he was there, that his wonderful progress had been stopped . . .' Harry breathed in, sucked at the air, suddenly winded with the reality of what he had said.

'But you love him?'

Harry glanced at the priest, quick with contempt. 'Don't tell me that loving him makes it all right.'

'I wasn't going to,' Father Michael replied. 'I just wanted to know if you loved your son.'

'I love him by rote.'

'If you learn something by rote, you learn it by heart,' the priest replied.

'Clever,' Harry said wryly. 'But not convincing, Father. You see, it doesn't matter a damn how we behave, or how we are perceived by others. What matters is how we would behave if there was no one to judge us. If no one knew how we lived, if there was no punishment for our actions, no sense of guilt, *then* how would we behave? I'm not talking of how we appear in order to conform or be approved of, I'm talking of our emotional intentions. And my emotional intentions towards my son are not just.'

'But you treat him well—'

'Because I'm afraid to treat him badly. Conscience and circumstance affect my behaviour, not honour,' Harry said emphatically, looking at the priest. 'If you were assured that whatever you did would go unpunished, then how would *you* behave? Always honourably? I wonder . . .'

Father Michael leaned back in his seat, suddenly aware that the positions were reversed and he was now the weaker of the two. Harry Binky had unnerved him, his theories tapping away at his guilt. If there was no judgement on earth, how *would* he behave? How would he then react to those women who fascinated him? And to what lengths would he go to satisfy his vanity? He felt his confidence ebbing and a low resentment building up. Harry Binky had asked for his help, had come to him for religious aid; he had no right to question the one person who could offer him forgiveness.

'Well?' Harry said simply. 'What do we do now?'

'Have you told me everything?'

'How could I? I've only been here a little while.'

The priest sighed. 'Mr Binky, I don't think that you really want my forgiveness—'

'You're right, Father, I don't. Because I don't think that you can forgive me, just as I don't believe in the Catholic church's pecking order.' His voice dropped. 'But I would like to talk to you a little longer. You see, I don't have anyone to talk to; not anyone that would listen, and at the moment talking seems the only way to prevent myself from going mad . . . When I saw my son I thought that it should have been me in that hospital. It was not a thought born out of nobility, but cowardice. You see, I don't want to have to face his recovery or his death. Both would be so demanding, and so chock-full of guilt. If he lives handicapped, how can I come to terms with such a waste of promise? And if he dies, he will have the power of all dead martyrs. I wasn't supposed to be the father of a special child. *I* wanted to be the special one . . .' Harry stopped, the truth nauseated him. 'Something very terrible is coming, Father. Something very much beyond what I believe I can stand.'

His words jolted the priest and for a long instant he stared at Harry Binky and saw in him a premonition of his own fate.

The deaf man began the morning as he always did. He rose early while it was still dark and made his way down to the kitchen on the ground floor. There he cut four inch-thick slices of brown bread and then diced them, finally putting the cubes into two plastic bags. He then walked over to his coat hanging on the back of the door and unzipped the inner pockets, placing one bag in the left pocket and one in the right. He always had to have food about him so that, wherever he was, he could never be hungry; he had to feel the bread in his pockets to feel safe.

When he had finished he switched off the light and made his way back upstairs. There was no heating in the house, and every window was shuttered. The floors were bare-boarded, the bathroom walls covered with Victorian ceramic tiles, a few cracked behind the wash-basin. Slowly he drew some water and leaned down to rinse his face, glancing into the small mirror only to shave. His hair was short, close to his head, his face square, the bones wide under the weathered skin. His mouth was narrow-lipped, his eyes unblinking. His nose was broad across the bridge and hinted at an early break. Carefully Kaine Lukes shaved, then took a flannel and washed his ears, drying them thoroughly on the towel.

He heard nothing, although his left hand fingered the

implants behind both ears; cochlear implants which had been inserted surgically and which, when he fixed his deaf aids on to them, could afford him a little sound. Not that he used the aids often; he was adjusted to his deafness, and besides, he had grown used to another form of hearing. Closing his eyes Kaine Lukes ran his hands up and down his arms and soothed himself, stroking himself as he listened. How would the noises sound that day? The brain mewls, he called them.

At first the deaf man thought that the tinnitus would drive him insane; the unending noises inside his head rising and falling, fading and increasing. But always there. Now a siren, now a buzz, now a humming. Noises of a world beyond worlds. He was deaf – all Kaine Lukes would know from then onwards was the voice of the brain. And it cheated him; it failed him; it stopped him from hearing the men who came after him . . .

A while later, after he recovered, he came out of hospital and organized himself. Having been careful with his money he could afford to invest in a property. A man of substance, at last. He found the house – or it found him – he was never sure which; only that on seeing it he felt a childlike sensation of having finally come home. It had been unoccupied for over six years and before that an old woman and her brother had lived there for decades. The world had been closed off at the turn of the century; time had passed by the gates, but never visited the house.

No one else visited it either, even though it was massively large for a single man. On three floors, there were six bedrooms, three bathrooms, four receptions rooms and a cellar. The front door was shielded by a porch, a light always left burning overnight, the letter box fused shut over the years, so that the meagre amount of mail Kaine Lukes received was tucked under an old gridded mat. There was little furniture. Even in the one downstairs room he used frequently there were only two worn leather chairs and a mahogany clock, the dial painted with the four seasons, the night moon looming out of the ornamental arch. Otherwise there was only a large ebony mantelpiece and iron grate where he burnt the logs brought in from the stone outhouse, logs delivered punctually three times a year.

The cold clawed at him, the old walls sucking up any warmth so that the only real heat came from sitting directly in front of the fire. And here he read. And absorbed, and here for twelve changing years he educated himself to the ticking of the clock. For the clock was the only clear sound the deaf man *could* hear when he used his hearing aids. The slow, resonant rhythm clicked in time to his heartbeats and rocked him in the crib of the worn oak room. It ticked as its pendulum swung; it ticked as he breathed in and out; it ticked in time to the words on the page, and in the end it ticked to the rhythm of his speech.

Drawn back from human voices, the deaf man seldom talked, and when he did he talked to himself, repeating what he had learned, timing his knowledge to the pendulum's swing. Time fell by, and the world shrank down to the wooden confines of the clock. He absorbed facts, consumed knowledge; he turned pages and under his hands books surrendered themselves, his fingers running over the print, his skin sensing the words as his eyes read them. In the early hours the fire often burnt down, Kaine Lukes throwing a couple of logs on to restart the blaze. The smell of the wood burning nuzzled into his clothes and hung about his hair, along with another smell – the smell of earth.

He smelt of earth because he worked in the earth; and in the vast, untended garden Kaine Lukes pursued a ritual which he had undertaken from the first days he had moved there. On reading a book, and understanding it, he would go out into the garden and bury the volume, setting above it a slat of wood on which was written the title and the date it was interred. After a few years there were several rows of wooden labels, some weathered, some new, each spelling out the dead route of his education. And under the markers lay the books. Buried, deafened, and blinded, beneath the dark earth.

Only one book remained above ground. A volume which had expanded into several volumes; a book in which Kaine Lukes talked. As other men dined, joked and confided to their companions, the deaf man talked to the page, and as he wrote he left his history for someone some day to read and follow. His life was buried, isolated, but his thoughts were above ground, and they spoke for him.

3 October
Three months after retiring from boxing.

It is a coming in from nowhere. I did not hear, but felt myself losing my place in the world. Deafness capsized me, tipped me over, filled my lungs with despair; it took me into silence, under the weight of water noises, drowned me under a crush of stillness. Green dreams came to me, bearing my soul weightless and soundless on a night without voices. I could not hear; the mouth was no longer a place of communication; words no longer bore the impact of sensation or remorse. The lilt of language was gone, and in its going, I was lost also.

I walk around in my head, moving memories like furniture. What I was, shifted under what I was to become, so I kept what certainty I knew about me. I carry my world with me – a poster of the last fight, an old publicity photograph, a knot of money – all in the pockets of my coat, next to the body, moving with the swell of breath. Beyond God, there is no faith, only the certainty that when God has gone from you, the Devil leaves you also.

And the deaf house was glad of me. There was a silence about her which moved to the rhythm of my own stillness; the brain mewls in my head caught time with the old voices in the walls. I touched her and knew her to be mine. The windows vibrated, the floors shuddered, the fireplace echoed with the sound of flames burning. The noises were not to be heard in the ears, but under the hand and at the back of the throat. I sensed speech, and felt sound, I smelt the warm scent of communication. My fingers groped at the wooden walls, my nails scraped at the dead film of voices left there, and in my hands the world turned, and burned.

I have green dreams and walk where the saints walked; and I know where the smallest of deaths begins.

He wrote in the book until, exhausted, he went reluctantly to bed. The light burned over the porch, and fingered at the boarded bedroom window; the night crept up the dark stairs and over the hearing aids laid out on the table by the deaf man's bed. He undressed slowly, lying down on the mattress and smoothing the blankets over him. Then in the instant before sleep he spoke his name into the darkness – and heard nothing.

CHAPTER THREE

Harry Binky, Chris Binky, the priest, Ahlia Bell, Jeanie Maas and Rachel Crossley. Each had received the warning – *You have one week to live*. Each had experienced the terrifying deafness before recovering their hearing again. Only Chris Binky found no escape. The others convinced themselves that they had merely imagined what had happened, but Chris was locked into immobility, the deaf man sliding, unbidden, in and out of his head and taking him to the deaf house. Behind his taped eyelids, Chris could only watch the activity in his mind's world and wait, terrified, for the deaf man to come again.

His father couldn't understand what was going on, that much was obvious. Harry Binky understood only what the doctors told him – that his son was unconscious, unfeeling, possibly brain-damaged – nothing more. He hadn't the intuition, or the will, to perceive anything further... Chris tried to alter his position on the bed, his limbs unmoving. *Don't let me be paralysed*, he wished repeatedly, *I don't want to live paralysed*. His panic closed over him; it fixed around his chest, and when he tried to cry out there was no response. *Don't panic!* he willed himself again, *If you panic, you're lost. There must be a way out of this, there must*...

He could hear the monitors next to him, and the sound of feet on the floor. Hands touched him, the sensation of a needle breaking into the skin of his arm making him wince inwardly. All he had to do was to relax, to plan, to think . . . There *was* a way back, a way to escape . . . An image of the deaf man came into Chris's head unbidden – together with the smell of damp earth and wood smoke.

No! he thought hurriedly, *Think of the living, of something good . . . Another picture came to him immediately.* A young woman, dark haired, standing under an archway. Rachel Crossley. Chris sighed, deep into the thought. Desperately, he caught on to the image of her, as a man might run for a midnight train to take him home; he grabbed at her and in his head she turned to him, shrugging her shoulders as she laughed.

She had been nervous the last time he saw her. On edge, uneasy, and unwilling to talk.

'Have I said something?'

'What?' she answered, turning her eyes on his. It was obvious that she had had little sleep the previous night – the dark brown pupils were hazy, without their usual alertness.

'Are you OK?'

'Fine,' she said simply. 'Don't fuss.'

Her rebuttal, although gentle, left him helpless and clumsy; and for an instant, bewildered. She was cold, blowing on her white hands, her feet stamping at the flagstones. The temperature had dropped, winter afternoon night coming quick and ill-tempered.

'How's your father?'

He was surprised by the question. Rachel knew Harry well, liked him, but wasn't fooled by him. She had his measure, they all knew that.

'He's fine,' Chris said drily, 'How's your mother?'

She smiled and then linked arms with him.

His stomach tightened. Oh God, Rachel . . .

'Can't you tell me what's bothering you?'

She shook her head. 'Really, it's nothing.'

'Work?'

'No.'

'Money?'

'No.'

'Not love, surely?' A sudden thought overtook him. 'You're not going to tell me something, are you? This isn't going to turn out to be the worst night of my life, is it?'

Her eyes fixed on his in bewilderment and then she smiled and leaned towards him, brushing his hair from his forehead.

'No, Chris. I'm not worried about us – there's something else I have to sort out.'

'But I could help—'

'Not with this.'

'I could,' Chris insisted. 'I love you. You love me – why can't you confide in me?'

She flinched, her arm stiff against his. He had overstepped the mark, and he knew it.

'I'm sorry.'

'It's OK,' Rachel replied, her face ghostly under the street lamp.

'D'you want to get something to eat?'

Her dark hair was pushed into the collar of her jacket, her expression shuttered.

'No . . . I should get back to work. I still have some things to do at the office.'

He had been wretched with unease. 'But we'll meet later?'

She smiled again, distantly. A faraway smile.

'I thought you were working on that piece for the paper. I thought you had a deadline.'

'It'll wait.'

She stopped walking suddenly. The previous night had been a long one, mottled with dreams. With Leon. And then, even when she woke she was startled by shadows, the past coming back, full blown, to saddle the present . . . She should tell Chris what had happened. Should explain . . . but what if he was disgusted by what she told him? What if – oh God – what if she lost him?

'Rachel, tell me what's wrong. Please.'

But he knew it was useless. He might question her for ever, but the answer would never come. Some old terror had slid between them; some word, or memory, unbeknown to him, had tainted their relationship. It couldn't be seen, or felt, but it was there, huge and malignant.

'Do you love me?' she asked. 'Do you?'

He replied in the only way he knew how, kissing her softly on the forehead – and then she linked arms with him, her shadow matching his on the lamp-lighted road . . .

The monitor bleeped on beside him, Chris's thoughts turning back to the present. If he was paralysed he would never be able to make things right with Rachel; would never be able to touch her, make love to her, or look after her – and he didn't want her to look after him. Of that much he was certain. She *mustn't* see him like this. If this was to be his life, caught dying between daylights, he didn't want her to know. It would be more than she could bear, he said to himself behind taped eyelids. More than she could bear . . . And then unexpectedly, and unwelcomely, he saw the deaf man again.

His fear was potent, cloying, as he faced him: '*Talk to me!*' Chris demanded.

But the man said nothing, just dug into his inside pocket and brought out a plastic bag. Carefully, Kaine Lukes took out two pieces of the diced bread and then extended his hand, palm upwards, towards Chris.

'*What is it?*'

Silence . . . But not quite total silence. In the background Chris could hear the ticking of the old clock and a sudden vast intake of breath from the deaf man.

'TAKE IT.'

Chris blinked.

'TAKE IT.'

In his head, Chris watched himself move and saw himself take the bread from the deaf man's hand. Slowly he chewed it, swallowing with difficulty.

The deaf man breathed in deeply, then laboriously began to speak:

'I CAN
GET YOU
OUT OF
THIS PLACE.'

His voice was disembodied, without expression. A voice from memory, coming from under the throat. Behind the deaf man the clock continued to tick loudly. *Too loudly*, Chris thought, realizing at that very instant that it was in fact *ticking to the rhythm of the deaf man's speech*.

Get me out! he begged the man, *Now, please . . . I have to go home. I have to get out of here.*

'NOT YET,' the deaf man replied, turning suddenly and walking away.

And Chris ran after him; down the uncarpeted stairs of the deaf house; down into the deep room where the fire burned; down, down into the damp dark smell of the earth . . . Finally, Kaine Lukes paused and then lowered himself into one of the chairs which flanked the fire, his hands reaching out towards the warmth. He said nothing and did not turn when Chris sat in the chair next to his. For a long time they remained seated side by side – while the monitors bleeped in the intensive care unit and the nurses turned and bathed the still form of Chris Binky – for a long time they continued to sit together until another sound crept slowly into the still room.

The clock still ticked, the fire burned on, but some other noise took form as Chris slowly and reluctantly turned to look at his companion.

The deaf man was asleep, darkly, deeply asleep, and as he slept a noise came from him. A night noise; a noise from the back of a sleeping throat and a deaf head. In the earth-smelling room, within the wood walls, under the shuttered windows and deep in the dark leathered chair, Kaine Lukes purred.

Rachel knew that she didn't really need to go back to the market – not for a while, at least – but she couldn't sleep and the night was long and very lonely. Dressing quickly, she drove over to Smithfield and parked opposite the entrance. It was morning. One o'clock. Dark. The hour when the body is at its lowest, when the senses slow and the heart rate lessens. One o'clock – the dying hour.

She got out of the car and crossed the street, dodging an oncoming cart and acknowledging the good-tempered nod of a porter. Her body ached from lack of sleep; but she couldn't risk losing consiousness – because then she would dream. Of Leon. Then she would fall back into her teenage years and remember what he had done to her; and remember too the betrayal of her mother. *Why didn't you know? Why didn't you guess? Why did you love him more than you loved me?* Rachel's memories raced angrily. Leon was ugly, slack-mouthed, sly – how could her mother choose him?

Her thoughts preoccupied her so much that Rachel hardly realized where she was walking, and after turning a corner too hurriedly, collided with someone.

'God, sorry!'

His face was impassive, very still. *How close have you got to him?* Titus Brand had asked. *How close have you got?*

'. . . I wasn't looking where I was going,' Rachel blundered on. The deaf man didn't move, but his eyes watched her mouth; reading her lips as she talked. Around them the market clanked with sound, the heavy whoosh of a cleaver slamming into a meat block behind them. The noise made Rachel jump and she turned round. When she looked back, the deaf man was walking away.

'Hey, wait!' she shouted, then cursed herself under her breath and began to run after him.

He walked lightly, balanced, carrying his considerable height and weight well. Her feet sounded loud on the cement floor and when she caught up with him she was about to touch him on the shoulder when the deaf man turned suddenly.

He caught her arm and quickly moved her along the aisle between the meat rows, so unexpectedly that she didn't cry out or even try to resist. The metal sounds echoed around them, the dark, fat-gridded meat swinging from iron hooks to left and right. Then he stopped. They were standing by a far wall, the stall in front of them empty. Only yards away men moved and worked on, but Rachel had the sudden and unpleasant sensation that they were unreachable, and that she was somehow unseen.

'What do you want?'

What do you want? Her words came back into her head as she thought them. Rachel stared at the deaf man blindly, her mouth drying. *Get out, get out now!* she told herself. *Get out!*

Talk to me.

His face was heavy under the light; his eyes fixed; his coat collar drawn up around his chin, hiding the scar.

Someone did it. I don't say he did – but someone did . . . Do you want to know a secret, Rachel?

Terrified, she backed away, then paused as more words began filling her head.

I know you. Come on. You can trust me. You can tell me what happened. I can make the dreams stop, Rachel. I can make the dreams stop.

'I have . . . I have to go.'

He read her lips, his gaze moving from her mouth to her

eyes, and then back to her mouth again. His eyes concentrated on her lips, focused on them, stared at them – and slowly, deeply, a flickering began under her flesh. It was soft, gentle at first, then became harder, more emphatic, her lips beginning to move as words were *forced* out of her.

What is it, Rachel? Tell me ... Look how we talk, how we communicate. We can talk to each other in our heads ... Talk to me ... he coaxed her, leading her out of the market exit and into the dark street beyond. *Talk to me. Let me have the secrets, Rachel, I can take the misery away. Tell me ...*

And she told him; the words compelled from her, torn from her mouth, each syllable dragged into the winter night. At first she tried to resist, to hold back, fighting to keep her humiliation secret; but she couldn't stop talking, confiding, pouring her sour history into the dead night. And as the story of Leon unfolded, Rachel felt her resistance dwindle and then collapse entirely ... The words bled from her uncontrollably, they streamed from her, sweated from her, wept from every pore until she was finished – and when she stopped talking the deaf man turned his gaze on to his own hands.

Slowly, he extended his outstretched palms, and on them were hundreds, thousands of pulsating, wriggling black maggots. And each maggot had a letter on its back.

Watch.

Rachel heard the command in her head and obeyed, watching the maggots as the deaf man reached into his pocket and took out some cubes of bread. She wanted to run, but couldn't move, could only watch as he took the letter maggots and then pushed them into the cubes of bread, cramming them, pressing them into the soft dough. Then he paused ...

No, she thought, no, don't eat it, please don't eat it ...

The movement was sudden, quick, violent, the deaf man throwing the cubes of bread up into the black air ... And the night took them. Mesmerized, Rachel waited for the bread to fall again, but it didn't. Every syllable she had spoken, every word, every foul remembrance was gone.

I can take away the misery, Rachel. I can take it all away.

'I had a nightmare,' Ahlia said dismissively, throwing her tights over the back of the bedroom chair and signalling for Jeanie Maas to pass her a towelling robe. 'I dreamt I was deaf. God, it was so real!'

Jeanie paused, a memory stirring inside her. Hadn't she dreamt something like that only last night? Ahlia peered at her reflection in the mirror, one hand trailing over the line of her neck. She looked tired, the night had been a long one and the fear hadn't left her at dawn. Slowly she glanced at the older woman behind her; poor Jeanie, drinking alone in the basement whilst she was upstairs making love. A quick whelp of pity rose up in her, but was dismissed as quickly as it came. She rose to her feet and walked over to the wardrobe.

She wanted to look good tonight. Wanted to impress her lover; wanted to hear the words she needed. Love words, couched in admiration; longing words, the words she lived for. Harry had been good at words. Darling Harry Binky, MP, clever with words in bed and out of it. But Harry had gone, moved on – just as she had. Ahlia's hands trailed over the line of clothes, her fingers finally pulling out a black silk dress.

'What d'you think?'

Jeanie glanced at it: 'Fine.'

'Is that it?' Ahlia asked sharply. 'Don't overdo the enthusiasm.'

'You look good in anything.'

Ahlia was immediately mollified and stepped into the dress, zipping it up and turning back to the full length mirror to admire her reflection. Behind her, Jeanie picked up the discarded day clothes, her hearing aid turned up to its full volume, her glasses firm on her nose. If she managed to get her employer out early she could retire downstairs in plenty of time to watch the film on BBC 2.

'It *was* a dream, wasn't it?'

Jeanie glanced up: 'What?'

'Last night – it was a dream, wasn't it?' Ahlia repeated, her voice quiet.

The older woman recognized the familiar plea for reassurance. 'It must have been,' Jeanie said firmly. 'After all, you're not deaf now, are you?'

Ahlia touched her ears.

'No . . . but it just seemed so real.' Her thoughts wandered. To be really deaf; never to hear a man whispering to her in the dark; to miss the compliments. Worse, to be seen as handicapped! God, what chance had she then? A handicapped woman, someone others would pity, not envy—

'You don't think it was a premonition, do you?'

Jeanie regarded her employer thoughtfully. She knew that Ahlia pitied her, but also realized that the feeling was mutual. But how that would hurt her if she knew! Jeanie thought. A rich, handsome woman pitied by her ageing Northern housekeeper; a woman with many men pitied by a frigid woman; a woman with all the world's advantages needing a woman with none.

And Ahlia *did* need her, Jeanie realized. She might be dismissive, peevish at times, but when she was afraid – and she often was – it was to her she turned. *Help me, Jeanie . . .* The neurotic turning to the pragmatic. *Help me, sit with me, talk to me, tell me everything will be all right . . .* She had worked for Ahlia for nearly ten years, soon after her employer had come to live in London. After her second marriage Ahlia had gone into therapy, visiting Harley Street daily, her childhood, relationships and anxieties picked over and massaged; the ectoplasm of past griefs materializing daily. The therapy hadn't helped, in fact it had hindered any progress; Ahlia didn't need to remember the past, she needed to believe she had a future.

Which was where Jeanie Maas came in. She had no family and needed a home; Ahlia had no family and needed a confidante. The two women, totally dissimilar, came to rely on each other; each supplying the other's needs. Ahlia gave Jeanie security and money; Jeanie gave her employer sense. So she stayed, and nine years on she was still working for Ahlia and still listening to her premonitions, although at times Jeanie turned off the volume on her hearing aid when her employer's strident whining got on her nerves. All she had to do was to keep nodding and looking sympathetic and Ahlia kept talking, her mouth moving like a fish's underwater, her words blessedly unheard.

But at this precise moment Jeanie *was* listening, her own experience of the previous night oddly similiar.

'. . . there was something written on my pillow last night,' Ahlia went on, about to tell Jeanie what the words said, then hesitating, for once unwilling to confess everything, 'and when I saw it I couldn't hear, Jeanie. I was suddenly *deaf*.'

Jeanie thought back; hadn't *she* seen something odd on the television screen last night? And hadn't she also lost her hearing? She had thought it was just her hearing aid packing up, but now, after what Ahlia had said, she wasn't so sure.

'To be deaf would be awful. Oh sorry . . .' Ahlia paused, glancing at Jeanie. 'I didn't mean—'

'I'm not offended,' the older woman replied. 'Besides I'm hard of hearing, not deaf.'

'But *if* you went deaf, stone deaf,' Ahlia persisted, 'as I was last night—'

'But if you can hear now, why worry?'

'*But what did it mean?*'

Jeanie frowned. She was losing interest in Ahlia's story, her thoughts turning back to her own experience. *What* had she seen? *You have one week to live.* That was it. *You have one week to live.* Now what the hell was that supposed to mean?

'... do you think it's an omen?'

'Oh, be quiet!' Jeanie snapped, suddenly exasperated and wanting to think. What *did* the words mean? And after a week what would happen?

'Are you angry with me?' Ahlia pleaded, suddenly vulnerable.

Jeanie sighed. 'No. I was just thinking about what you said.'

She was tempted momentarily to confide in her employer, but resisted. Perhaps she *had* only imagined the message and was merely unsettled by what Ahlia had said. Her head thumped. No, it *had* happened. She had received a message and now she was suddenly and unexpectedly afraid. *You have one week to live.*

One week, how long was that? Seven days, a handful of time. And what was she supposed to do with such a warning? Her practicality vanished; all the years of common sense bolted, and in their place was only a sense of impending doom. Uncomfortable memories returned too; memories which had been suppressed, forgotten; old guilts which for decades had been squashed under the weight of pragmatism. But no longer – a message had come; it had come unnaturally and it brought unnatural remembrances; and it promised unnatural ends.

Rachel Crossley's meeting with the deaf man had gone surprisingly well. All the dull unease of the past weeks had lifted, the weight of anxiety gone. The deaf man had helped her. He had taken the misery away, just as he had promised. Rachel's relief had been so intense that she had been almost euphoric. The dreams would stop now, she thought, the shadow which had hung over her life would disappear. The deaf man had helped her, saved her.

Rachel returned to her flat and made herself something to

eat, then curled up in a chair. She fought sleep but soon her eyelids closed and after another moment she dozed off. And she fell. Fell immediately into the old dream, tumbling into the foul little pit which was waiting for her.

Leon was unravelling a ball of wool, laying it along the street in a long red thread.

'Go on,' he said. 'Walk on it.'

She hesitated – as she always did. She was very young again, frightened again. The road was empty, without houses or people; just a narrow road, along which the long red thread of wool extended out into the distance.

'Walk on it, or I'll tell! I will, I'll tell everyone!' he said, stretching up and putting his head on one side. She saw the mole under his right eye and saw the vein pulse at the side of his neck.

A high sun burned.

'Walk on it!'

She began to walk, obediently, not wanting to and yet knowing with certainty that if she didn't, he'd tell – and then everything would be over. No one would believe her, not her mother, no one. If she told they would take Leon away; he was handicapped, after all. They would put him in a home and then her mother would have no one to dote on, to pet, to remember her husband by. Without Leon – the eternal dependent – she would have no duty, and no reason to live.

So Rachel walked along the red line. She walked and the thread began to shift under her feet and suddenly, as it always did, the road disappeared and she was walking on a tightrope, the earth hundreds of feet below her. The sun clouded over and a wind blew up, threatening her balance and as she looked ahead, panicking, she saw that there was no end in sight, just the red wire extending onwards and onwards.

Every night she had the dream, and every night she woke sobbing, never reaching the end of the wire or safety, but never falling either. Every time it had been the same – except for this time. The dream had begun as usual, but now, when she was left on the tightrope the deaf man had appeared, facing her on the wire.

She expected help, but he ignored her and simply reached down and tugged hard at the rope.

Terrified, Rachel called out to him.

'Stop it, or I'll fall!'

He tugged at the wire again. Jerked it, juddered it.

'You said you'd help me! Stop it!'

Trust me, Rachel, I can take the misery away. I can eat it up. Suck it up. I can take it all away.

'Stop it!'

He jerked on the wire again viciously, he jerked on it and it slackened suddenly, it looped in the wind, it lost its tautness – and Rachel lost her footing.

Trust me.

She fell on to the back of a bird; then fell *through* its skin and *entered* it, and was carried with it as it wheeled above the red wire and left the round earth. Time ceased; breathing ceased; thought ceased. And as the land fell away, Rachel could feel the bird's body closing around her, hear the thump of its heart, and smell the hot scent of its blood as it flew upwards and onwards until the sky ended and she felt only a deep rocking motion and the warmth of skin closing over her.

And then she woke. She woke quickly, white with distress, dizzy with unease. The deaf man had promised to take away the misery, promised to make the dreams stop – but they hadn't. Now *he* was in her dreams too. Frantically, Rachel struggled to her feet. She must find him again. *She must.*

CHAPTER FOUR

The priest was sleeping badly. His bedroom, at the top of the house, was depressingly low-ceilinged so that it had taken him several months when he first moved there to get used to the idea of ducking when he approached the window, where he now stood, round shouldered, gazing out at the mean little garden. Two filled dustbins waited for collection, the lid of one slanted at an angle, a plastic bag peeking out at the top, the word Tesco eerily clear. Father Michael opened the window, letting the cold in quickly. It pulled at the poor curtains and snatched at the dressing gown he had slung over his shoulders.

He looked up longingly at the sky; but there was no full moon and only a few indifferent stars. It was a maudlin little night, without inspiration or intrigue. It made no hostile shadows and transformed nothing. Under its listless gaze the yard remained as bleak as it always was, the walls in need of pointing, the windows unwashed on the second floor. The priest leaned out, braving the cold and glancing towards the church on his left. It rose out of the dark ground like a man who had fallen over and was hurrying back to his feet. Not for the first time, he acknowledged that there was little dignity to his place of worship. It was not a highly spired church; there was only one stained glass window and that had been broken years earlier, only to be replaced in parts by plain glass. The once noble story of the stations of the cross was now condensed, the journey abridged, the poignancy interrupted by sheets of unblinkingly clear glass. In this version, Christ hop-scotched to His Calvary.

The priest sighed and turned his head towards the right, where the graveyard was. It had fascinated him when he first came to live there; it had seemed to remind him of his calling – living between the church which offered redemption and the graveyard where that redemption was to be found, or denied. Live a good life, he had told his parishioners, and here you will find everlasting peace. *Rest in peace*, he said repeatedly at funerals, scattering clods of earth over fresh coffins. *Rest in peace*, he had promised and predicted, although he saw the dead space behind the eyes which watched him and also knew that resting and peace were two words which lay uneasily together. He was neither at peace, or able to rest. His faith was at odds with his sexuality and his vanity. *Rest in peace*, he insisted, demanding from his congregation the very state of mind he longed and prayed for.

At first he had presumed that all young men felt the same anxieties about sex. He was disturbed by it, and found that he could only avoid the complications of women by insisting that he had a higher calling. The perfect solution – for a time. The perfect solution in the day. But at night such logic was misplaced. The priest who had such control over his thoughts and actions awake had no such discipline asleep. He might ignore a woman on the street; might deny the length of leg or the outline of breast, but in the sneaking hours of the early morning he had visitors to his sleep. And then these women mocked him. They took the communion wafer from his hands and allowed their tongue to run along his palm; they drank from the communion wine and slid their hands around the cup, their fingers moist against his. In his dreams they confessed to him all the sexual fantasies he had ever suppressed; they sighed through the confessional grille; they whispered throatily, describing their sins; their sins committed in parked cars, in bedrooms, in a thousand men's arms. And all the time he listened, until he awoke, wet with disgust, and waited longingly for the day to come.

For years he lived between two worlds. Between the purity of his religion and the nightly succubus who tugged at his longings. His looks, already outstanding, took on another emphasis. As he converted himself internally into an emotional martyr, he began to transform externally too. His eyes were heavy with uneasy sleep; his movements slow, languid with tiredness. He glanced at women and looked away, giving an impression not of rejection, but longing. Even his voice deepened, turned down into his spirit, losing its footing so that words shuddered in sentences uneasily – especially during the Mass.

Take, eat, this is my body.

He said to the women in the congregation: Take, eat, this is my body ... The words he had loved as a boy, the commitment of Christ to His disciples, became instead a supplication of another kind – and the realization disfigured him. The women were destroying him, the priest realized. They were taking away everything he valued. His faith was being tainted by them, his equilibrium destroyed. For years he had been at ease with himself and now, because of them, he burned.

And the church offered no comfort. It was too cold, too small and too wearily pedestrian to inspire him. If he had been attached to a cathedral; if he could have knelt under a Gothic arch, in front of a marble altarpiece flanked by pillars and peopled with stone effigies of saints. If he could have wept and begged for forgiveness under a painted cupola resplendent with angels. If he could have kissed the bronzed feet of St Peter and scourged himself, if he could have tormented his flesh until he was too tired to think *then* he would have found peace. But not here, not in some poor, downtrodden, despised little church.

A cathedral might have saved him; might have elevated his suffering to sainthood. He would have struggled against himself and in the end found peace in the devotion of others. It was not his fault that he had come to such a pitiful state, the fault was God's. So the priest decided to *punish* God, to strike back, to injure Him as he had been injured. Sick from lack of sleep and driven by frustration and longing, the priest set out to take revenge, and on a sultry evening in May eight years previously, had allowed himself to be seduced.

The woman had been all but forgotten. The colour of her hair and the sound of her voice were long gone. Her memory was no longer the memory of a person, but of a sensation. The feelings she had inspired in him were stronger than anything he had ever experienced before. She moved with him and her heart seemed to pass from her body into his, to occupy some space against his own heart; she consumed him almost to his blood, and under a summer sun she melted through his skin and sank into the very organs of his body. They made love without sound; not even summer sounds from outside interrupted them. They made love without exchanging names or promises. They made love – and the final outcome of the priest's revenge was simply a deep and unyielding vibration in the chest: the opening of the world's heart, and the closing of God's. He had lost himself in the woman, but when he had climaxed felt only the breaking loneliness of abandonment. The priest had found his revenge, but God had found His also.

The days which followed left him limp with anguish. The woman tormented him. She was always waiting at the gate or seated at the front of the congregation. Her eyes fixed on his. She dragged her own guilt along with her and gradually tied it to his so that the priest's whole body was joined and tormented with hers. He could no longer pray because all prayer was now hypocrisy; he could no longer ask for forgiveness because he had realized that no one on earth, or beyond, could forgive him. He had challenged God, and was now beyond God.

The woman was also beyond God. She begged the priest with her eyes, and wrote indiscreet letters. Her passion for him was so intensified by guilt that he became not only her lover, but her Saviour. In the end, horribly and damnably, Father Michael had finally achieved the devotion he had longed for – but the price was the shutting out of his soul. Helplessly he tried to free himself from the woman, but she clung on, and in the weeks which followed she began to sicken, and her sickness passed on to him. As her body had consumed him, so did her malaise. He felt pity for her, but more pity and fear for himself, and as she changed from seductress to hysteric he felt only revulsion.

But he did nothing. He merely avoided her, and when he was in her company he reverted to the role of priest and insisted that she forget what had happened and beg God for forgiveness. He crossed her and himself. He made the motion with his hand – and the sign of the cross seemed to hover luminously in the air for a long instant afterwards. His eyes fixed on the apparition, but the woman saw nothing; her head remained bent, her eyes on the floor.

She told him in June. Confessed it through the grille of the confessional. *I'm pregnant* . . . He heard the words and turned his head, trying to make out the contours of her face, but it was blurred. She had no reality. The only reality was the priest's child inside her. What had he done? the priest asked himself helplessly. All the longing, all the torment, what was it all for? To make love to a woman and then feel only a dull and unending sensation of guilt? To shut off the peace of mind without which there *was* no peace? Sex had been the reason he had lost God and himself, and now this woman, this wan, asexual, exhausted and exhausting woman was telling him that she was carrying his child.

'You have to do something.'

Her head moved behind the grille, but he could not read her expression.

'Do what?' she asked, bewilderment obvious. Her voice had a dead ring, not a voice at all, more like the echo of a voice.

'Get rid of the child,' Father Michael said, then closed his eyes.

The confessional booth was cramped, the curtain musty, the dim light hardly able to illuminate the top of his bent head. I am asking her to kill the child, he thought disbelievingly, waiting for the enormity of the decision to engulf him; waiting for the guilt which would follow – but nothing happened. He had gone too far to be able to *feel* any more. He would, he realized, have seen the woman dead without remorse.

'I can't do that!' she said finally. 'I can't, it's against God'.

'I am the father, and I am a priest—'

'A *priest*?' she replied, her tone rising. 'Since when did that matter to you?'

He ignored her.

'You have to get rid of the child,' the priest repeated, relieved that the words had been articulated. There was almost a sense of peace starting up within him. Perhaps if he got rid of the child and the woman, perhaps then he would be able to begin again . . .

'I can't!' the woman said again defiantly. 'I want to have this child, and you have to help me – or I'll go to your superiors.'

He flinched in the confessional booth. She was so close; he could – had he chosen to – have pushed his hand through the grille and clutched her. The musty smell of the curtain nauseated him as he breathed in, controlling himself.

'There's no point threatening me, I can't marry you, and even if I was free, I wouldn't.' He paused, but there was no sound from the other side of the grille. 'You have to abort the child for your sake as well as mine—'

'It's murder.'

Murder. He hadn't thought of it like that, not as murder. For all his years of sermonizing to women, of forbidding birth control, he had now no hesitation in ending his own child's life.

'It's murder,' she repeated, certain that his hesitation implied a change of heart. '*Abortion is murder.*'

'God will forgive you,' the priest said quietly, knowing even as he spoke that God would forgive neither of them. 'This child must not be born.'

'It's murder,' she said hopelessly again, her voice sinking, her face turned away from the grille. 'I love you.'

The priest's eyes opened suddenly and he leaned towards the grille, his fingers clutching at the wire. 'Listen to me!' he hissed, watching her back away in the confines of the booth. '*There is no future*; we are damned together unless we do something. Apart we have a chance. You must get rid of the child and go away. *There is no future for us.*'

'God is good,' she said almost hysterically. 'God will understand.'

The metal of the grille bit into his fingers.

'No, God will punish us. He will *punish* us – but we might be able to save the child.' He went on coldly, knowing how much he was frightening her. 'Abort it. Terminate it. Take it out of this life. *Save the child!*'

She breathed heavily, not knowing whether to believe what he said or not. Was he really trying to save the baby, or wanting to avoid punishment?

Her words came with difficulty: 'It's against God—'

'Making love was against God!' the priest retorted vehemently, his hand dropping from the wire grille. 'Do as I say. *For the love of God*, do as I say. This decision is not yours, it's mine. I'll take the responsibility for it.' His voice softened with momentary pity.

Tentatively, the woman rested her hand against the grille, waiting. He hesitated, then laid his palm against hers. The metal gridding chilled both of them.

'Kill the child.'

She flinched.

'Kill it.'

Then she nodded once.

He never saw her again. He heard that she had left the district and waited, tensed, for the scandal which was sure to follow. He would be disciplined, thrown out of the church, and all his ephemeral glimpses of glory would be shattered. Out in the world he would be no one, an ex-priest, a man who would be viewed as an oddity without status – without even the pitiful kudos of a cleric in a neglected parish.

The days continued to pass, but when there was no exposure the priest underwent a change. As his secret remained hidden he rediscovered his faith and unconsciously made a bargain with God – *I will serve you and love you if you will let me escape punishment*. He did not realize what he was doing, he just clung to the intermittent snatches of peace which began creeping back into his life.

He never thought of the woman; never thought of her naked; never dreamed hot dreams or woke sticky with lust. He had been through the flames and absolved himself, and God had begun to forgive him ... So the priest believed, and so he dismissed the woman and the child, and turned back to God. He prayed extra prayers and attended Mass with added fervour. He assumed the role of saintly priest and found that others wanted him to take on that persona as much as he wanted to. God had finally found a place for him, and before long Father Michael believed that he would finally be at peace.

Then three months after the woman left the neighbourhood, he woke in the middle of the night in agonizing pain. Clutching his stomach, he struggled to rise, his hand groping for the light switch. His steps towards the door were laboured, staggering, and as he snapped on the light his remaining strength failed him and he fell heavily to the floor. His legs curled towards his body, his hands pressed deep into his stomach, his hands coated with sweat as he groaned on the floor, his eyes burning, his lids pressed tightly shut, until, with one final hoarse scream of agony, he glanced down at his stomach.

The blood seeped through his pyjamas. It pooled on the bare floorboards. It spread greedily and clung wetly to his skin. Screaming, the priest tried to staunch the flow and then began praying. But the words came out as gibberish, the pains contorting his body and his mouth while the blood kept coming, swimming out of him, greasing over the floor, the walls splashed along the skirting board. Madly, the priest kept praying. Screaming and praying. Begging for forgiveness, seeing in his own blood his own death, and after death, judgement.

Then, as his hands continued to press into his stomach and his lips kept up their gibberish, the priest began to slide into unconsciousness. His mind misted over, his fingers coated with blood, and in that instant he had a vision of something close to God. Blindly the priest grovelled on the mean little floor, crawling over to the bed and clinging to the bloodied sheets. He prayed. Repeated God's name over and over; thanked Him for His goodness and for His compassion ... The priest had been absolved. He had been *chosen*.

He was bleeding from his side, as His Lord had done ... A sense of euphoria welled up in the priest. It mingled in his madness with the shock of the pain and all the old guilts. It swam in his head. It turned circles with the name of Christ, and only when he believed implicitly that he had finally found his salvation, only *then* did the priest stop praying.

The room with its faded paper and thin curtains seemed colder than before; the rug by the bed having been kicked away, the iron bedhead, its bars reflected against the wall behind. The priest glanced around him, then realizing that the pain had lifted, looked cautiously down at his stomach. His pyjamas were thick with blood. He felt it, smelt it and touched it; he revelled in it, seeing it as his death into glory – *then he saw the floor in front of him.* Where he had lain bleeding, screaming in agony, on the boards where he had howled, was a congealing patch of his blood.

It darkened as he looked at it; it darkened and thickened and assumed a shape; it became a body. Small and clotted. The blood body of a child.

Eight years passed. Father Michael lived – although for a number of years he had *longed* to die – but his vanity saved him; his looks developing even more the haunted romanticism of his own inner life. But he never touched another woman. The priest may well have lived on indefinitely in this way – always one step ahead of his guilt – had it not been for the message which had appeared on the communion wafer. *You have one week to live.* 'You have one week to live,' he repeated to himself, feeling an echo of the despair he had suppressed for so long.

One week, the priest thought, gazing out of the bedroom window into the grubby backyard. One week to live. And then what? He never thought to question the validity of the warning. He would not have dared. He assumed that it was a spiritual sentence passed on him, and was surprised to find that he was, in a way, relieved. At last he had something to fight for. He wasn't going to die. Not in a week, not in seven days . . . He smiled, amused to discover how much he wanted to live and then realized that there was no choice – to die was to be punished. One week, he repeated again, such a little pocket of time. He leaned heavily against the window ledge. Who could he turn to? Who could advise him? he wondered, glancing towards the church. The building was dark, the graveyard blacked out.

His thoughts wandered to the conversation he had had that afternoon with Harry Binky. The MP had been frightened, asking for forgiveness. Afraid.

'Something very terrible is coming, Father. Something very much beyond what I believe I can stand.'

Hurriedly the priest moved away from the window and pulled his coat on over his pyjamas, making his way downstairs and passing the mirror in the hallway without glancing at his reflection. The night was ugly and peevish, the wind quick with spite. Urgently he moved into the graveyard, pausing in front of the first row of headstones and looking at them dispassionately. *You have one week to live.*

And if I don't live, he wondered, what will happen then? Will I take my place here? The priest shivered. The ground was wet, heavy with earth, the odour disturbing him. But he didn't move. He tried to steel himself for the horrors to come, to face death in preparation for it. But he couldn't even find the emotion to be *afraid* and, after several long moments, moved on.

The keys were clumsy in his hands as he opened the church door and hurried in. For some reason, the same dark smell of earth seemed to follow him there, and he frowned, wondering if there was something wrong with the damp course. Automatically he flicked the switch and two lights came on over the altar. Dim lights, poor lights, cheap low wattage lights which gave a cold, hostile illumination. Impatiently he tried the third switch and then mumbled under his breath, angered to find the bulb had gone again. The church, apart from the area around the altar, was in darkness.

In the aisle, Father Michael genuflected. The cold was numbing, his feet, still in his slippers, chilling rapidly. He would pray, he had decided, he would pray for guidance. The thought did nothing to comfort him; he was acting on instinct rather than belief. Stiffly the priest knelt in the pew three back from the altar. The hymn books made dark shapes on the ledge in front of him, the hassock on which he knelt casting a hard shadow. Without looking up he mumbled his prayers, completing them and then beginning again, trying to keep his thoughts on the words.

But they gave no consolation and, after another moment, Father Michael straightened up and leaned back in the pew. Around him, the smell of earth seemed to be increasing. It was a dark smell, a deep smell, a scent of something primeval, a scent from *under* the world. Suddenly and unexpectedly frightened, the priest turned round. But there was no one there and he turned back to face the altar. It stood straight ahead of him, coldly white, the window behind it black to the night outside, beside it a metal tray full of burnt-out candles.

The smell of earth intensified. The dead smell, the deep smell, creeping noiselessly around the church and under the pews, coming finally to rest on the pew next to him. Alarmed, the priest glanced around again, and as he did so two candles in the tray suddenly spluttered into life. They flickered. They flashed. They burned with a horrible brilliance. Tall new candles, standing high in the tray. And, as they burned, others appeared beside them, filling the rows with ranks of fire.

The priest leapt to his feet, watching disbelievingly as the rows kept filling with candles, white rank after white rank of them taking the place of the sad little burnt-out stubs. But even as the candles burned, the earth smell increased, and the priest, suddenly terrified, backed away from the lighted rows, his hands gripping the top of the pew as he edged away from the candlelight.

His eyes fixed on the living flames, his nostrils filling with the scent of earth, the candles flickering and making vast shadows on the barrel-shaped roof above him. Then suddenly he saw a movement from the furthest corner of the church and flinched.

'Who's there?'

His voice echoed in the empty church.

The candles kept on lighting, filling up the rows.

'*Who's there!*' he repeated, his voice loud with fear.

There was no reply, only the quick movement of a figure behind an arch.

'Who is it?' the priest repeated again, running down the aisle, and wrenching at the door. It was locked. '*For God's sake, who's there?*' he shouted, his voice shrill with terror.

The figure moved out from the archway in that instant. In the dim light it moved, passed across the church, then paused momentarily before walking on. The priest narrowed his eyes, straining to see more clearly, but the light was too dim, and only when the figure stepped in front of the tray of candles did he make out the outline of a man.

His face could not be seen, only the outline of his head and body silhouetted against the candlelight.

'Who is it?' the priest asked again, hardly able to breathe for the smell of earth in his nostrils. The heat from the candles was so fierce that, even from the doorway, he could feel it burning his skin. 'Tell me who you are ... For God's sake, tell me who you are!'

But the figure remained motionless, the earth smell still emanating from him, his body black against the white light of the burning candles. And then, as the priest stood transfixed and struggling for breath, gasping in the overpowering stench of earth, the man finally moved. But he moved *back*, not forwards, *back* into the candlelight, into the heat and the blaze from the myriad ranks of flames.

And there he stood, his arms against his sides, his head thrown back; and from his mouth came not sound, but smoke, the black form of his body being consumed from inside.

Chapter Five

The deaf man was writing, the book open in front of him.

24 February

So it continues, drawing them in, one by one. I saw Rachel this morning, following me from Smithfield. Does she think I don't see her? Does she wonder about me? Oh, I hope so, I do hope so. I know she talks to Titus Brand, asks questions about me, maybe even scribbles notes on her pad. Reference notes.

I told her I can take her misery away. I want it. She doesn't know that, none of them do. I need it, I can use it. What does he do? she asked Titus Brand. Well, I live, Rachel, and I live on you – and on others like you. Misery sustains me; hopelessness, despair. What you experience, feeds me. Just as the others will feed me. Your helplessness keeps me alive. Keeps us alive. The deaf man and the deaf house.

I give the house presents, Rachel. I love her. I love her as I would have loved a woman once. As I might have loved you. I give her what she needs to live. I bury in her garden books and food; I walk on her earth and push cubes of bread into the soil. I talk to her as I feed her. I sleep under her, rub myself against her, feel her as keenly as any woman. The house is alive; a partner to me. We feed and live off the same energy. The misery which hobbles you and the others, keeps me on the earth — and a part of the earth.

The house loves, Rachel, she loves.

You won't like that.

The heat was unexpected; too hot for the time of year. Harry Binky walked out of the House of Commons and stood for a while on the street, hesitating, not knowing what to do next. The incident had been embarrassing, horribly so. One minute he had been rising to his feet to ask a question of the Prime Minister, fully aware that Question Time was being filmed, and the next minute he had found himself suddenly *unable to hear*. The question he had asked had come out easily enough, the Prime Minister rising to his feet to answer; Harry confident, balanced on the balls of his feet, looking good, and then suddenly — silence.

The cut-off had been complete. Not a fading in sound, a slow dying of volume. No — from all the clamour of the House to complete noiselessness. He had reacted badly. Sweated, feeling the familiar nervous ticking begin over his left eye. And he knew that his face would look shiny on the screen, just as he knew that he would look guilty. Uncertain. Shifty. All the adjectives congregated in his head; all the suspect parts of his nature which he had hidden so successfully were now exposed; glaringly obvious for anyone with a television to see.

And as Harry floundered, his fellow MPs watched him with interest. Greedy, hungry interest. He saw the looks on their faces, and knew that they were interpreting his discomfort as uncertainty — and that meant weakness. But what could he say? *I can't hear you, I can't hear a damn thing!* Harry closed his eyes, suddenly reminded of an unwelcome memory of his youth, the muscle in his cheek twitching as he thought of it — 'Winky Binky, Winky Binky!' they used to call him at school.

'Winky Binky' – picking on him, chanting the taunt, repeating it over and over again.

Mortified, Harry had fought to regain his composure and stood his ground, watching the Prime Minister's mouth move silently, expecting at any moment for his ears to pop as they did on a plane flight. *They'll clear in a moment*, he told himself, skirting panic, *hang on*. But they didn't. They stayed deaf, just as they had done the previous day in the restaurant. But that hadn't been public, televised. That hadn't been a grand, cringing humiliation in front of his peers.

Harry's palms began to sweat as he kept looking at the Prime Minister and the hundreds of mute faces in front of him, all turned in his direction. In an instant he would pause and Harry would have to respond; would have to reply to the unheard answer. His eyes burned with panic, his mouth dry; he thought he might pass out – and then calmed himself. No, no one was going to have the satisfaction of seeing him defeated. No one. Not the bloody House or the bloody Prime Minister. He would bluff his way out of it, just like he bluffed his way out of everything.

His hands shook violently as he looked down for an instant, then he gasped hoarsely. On his papers, in heavy black type were the words:

You have one week to live.

They rose off the paper; they skimmed the air; they floated in front of his eyes and then passed *into* his eyes, so that for one hideous second his whole mind was flooded and wrapped and suffocated by the image. The words drummed against the soft tissue of his brain, they bit into his cells, they pinched at his nerve ends and ate deep into him until the pain blacked out all thoughts and Harry Binky pitched headlong over the bench in front of him.

The House was sympathetic. Confused; but sympathetic. When Harry finally came round he was in a side room, having been carried out of the chamber, and as he opened his eyes he immediately covered his ears against the sudden impact of noise. His deafness had gone.

'You should see a doctor.'

Harry struggled to sit up. 'No . . . I'm fine. I'll just go home for a while.' He sounded uneasy and was violently embarrassed. The whole bloody country would have seen him pass out; the whole bloody country would have laughed at him. Jesus, what a mess.

'Harry,' a voice said quietly, 'listen, we all know you're under a lot of strain, anybody would be after Chris's accident.'

After Chris's accident, Harry thought wonderingly. So they thought his collapse was paternal anxiety. Of course, he realized, almost smiling to himself, after all, who knew the truth? Who knew that he was going deaf and receiving messages on parliamentary papers? *You have one week to live.* Harry shuddered, caught between relief and anxiety.

'I'm sorry, I suppose I made a fool of myself in there,' he said, his old cunning reasserting itself. There *was* a way, he realized suddenly; a way to preserve his integrity and even make himself seem a sympathetic figure. 'You're right, Chris's accident has been a big strain.' His voice was low, his head turned away from his companion. 'I hadn't realized how much it had taken out of me.'

The ploy worked, just as he had hoped.

'Everyone's behind you a hundred per cent, Harry,' the man replied. 'We're all rooting for you, remember that.'

But outside the House, Harry's confidence faded again. It seemed, in the unexpected sunlight, as though his shabbiness of spirit was exposed for everyone to see, his hypocrisy as obvious as a birthmark. Head down, he walked along, keeping his eyes averted. Yet when he took out a cigar he felt suddenly foolish with so obvious a prop and tucked it back into his pocket, buying a copy of the *Evening Standard* instead.

And he waited; waited for the silence to come again; for the sudden and terrifying descent into deafness, and the message which always came with it. *If it was true.* Harry shook his head suddenly, impatiently. *How* could it be true? It was just his imagination, that was all. People imagined things all the time, but they weren't real. Just fantasies.

Harry paused, conspicuously breathless. Having never thought of death until that minute he was suddenly confronted with a fear which immobilized him, together with a guilt which had been suppressed for decades. He didn't want to die, not now, not for a long time. He wasn't ready, he had too much to do. His breathing laboured, Harry leaned against the stone wall of an office building, sweat making his clothes cling to him, his expensively cut hair sticking to his forehead.

And he remembered. He remembered the time after he had left Gateshead, taking his nickname with him, only by now the sobriquet was embellished, not 'Winky Binky' any more, but 'Witty Winky Binky'. His tongue had saved him; his humour forcing grudging respect. Oh yes, he might still have remnants of a facial tic but unless he was under pressure he could control it, and most of the time it went unnoticed. But by this time the nickname was a part of him, and Harry Binky got the most out of it.

His ambition and wits finally brought him to London, and luck brought him an introduction into a jewellery business. He had been newly married then, Chris just a little boy, and he had been urgent with ambition. Too urgent. He had been greedy too, not wanting to be poor any longer, wanting to escape the unremarkable flat in Battersea, to be a part of the life he glimpsed through Kensington curtains. So eager to be a success that he had put his morals on hold. Always a glib and ready talker he listened to anyone who could tell him about the trade and soon became invaluable to Gregor Fylding, an old man who had been in the gem business for generations. A lonely man, Fylding had been only too willing to adopt Harry Binky and his family as his own, and eagerly passed on his knowledge.

Harry knew that Gregor was fond of him and he, to his credit, returned some of the affection. No Christmas went by without an invitation to the Binky home and in return Gregor looked on Harry as his natural successor, the inheritor of his business. Having no other relatives, Gregor taught Harry everything he knew, willingly, lovingly, without any hesitation or suspicion. And under Gregor's sophisticated European instruction, Witty Winky Binky soon moderated his garish taste, learned about wines, cigars, and culture. From being an ignorant provincial, he was smoothed and moulded into a cultivated man, a man capable of achieving much.

And he did achieve, using his basic business acumen to open out Gregor's business and expand more into Europe and the USA, harnessing contacts that proved invaluable. With the backing of the established Fylding name, Harry became a force within the field in which fate had so luckily placed him, and for a while, he was happy with his lot. But only for a while. As his clothes improved and his salary increased; as his flat in Battersea gave way to one in Holland Park; as his son attended the finest preparatory school on London and his wife shopped on the Brompton Road; as he worked and climbed – he also plotted.

Because greed had come out to play with him. It sneaked into his life, blind, unthinking, immoral avarice tainting his success – and his perception. By this time Gregor was retired and had left Harry to run the business, taking a percentage of the sales as a salary. It wasn't a huge amount of money, and yet every time Harry made out the cheque for his mentor, it rankled. He forgot what Gregor had done for him, preferred to think that he had been the one who had made the business what it was – Gregor had needed *him*. Or so he convinced himself. Before long, Gregor was no longer the wise old sage, but a nuisance, an old, unwelcome fool.

The more Harry had, the more he wanted; the more money he made, the more he resented the percentage he gave to Gregor. Gradually the relationship between them began to sour, although Gayle, Harry's wife, tried repeatedly to reason with her husband.

'He gave you your start. You owe him.'

Harry bridled. 'Listen, I pay him a good salary—'

'Without him you wouldn't have a business, Harry! He's old now, you owe him gratitude at least.'

'He has everything he needs.'

She shook her head disbelievingly. 'No, he doesn't! He lived for the business before we came along, and then he lived for us,' she said quietly. 'Don't break his heart, Harry. He's an old man, don't fail him.'

It was a pointless discussion and it had no effect. Harry wanted more money and more kudos, and gradually his infrequent trips to see Gregor ceased, the invitations at Christmas no longer extended.

Harry didn't see the effect of his actions, neither did he want to. He had what he had longed for – prestige – and he believed he had earned it. Luck was no part of it. The good fortune of meeting and being tutored by Gregor Fylding was forgotten. Harry had made his mark on the world and from then onwards, anything was possible – with money and status, he could do anything.

So when Gregor Fylding was too frail to look after himself, Harry had him put into a nursing home and when the old man was taken ill he had him declared incompetent and, taking full advantage of the situation, had him sign over the company to him. Lock, stock, and barrel.

'Sign here,' he said, passing the papers to the old man.

Gregor looked straight ahead. Coughing; small in a narrow

bed. 'It's my business. My father started it . . .' he trailed off, trying to dig for the words. 'You're like a son to me . . .'

Harry didn't want to hear it. The papers lay impatiently on the bed, under the old man's hand.

'Gregor, sign. I'll look after everything,' he said in a singsong voice. 'You don't have to worry about a thing.'

The old man looked at him despairingly, remembering the impatient out-of-towner who had come down from Gateshead with all the ambition of the world. Witty Winky Binky, what happened to you? Gregor wondered, with a breaking sense of loss as he remembered teaching Harry how to cut gems. Long into the night, at the back of the shop, the worktop covered with baize cloth, the tools clumsy in the young man's hands.

'You have to *love* the gem,' Gregor had said, holding an emerald between his thumb and forefinger, a magnifying glass expanding the size of the jewel, swelling it. It had glinted seductively in the lamplight. Green to the core, green as envy. 'Imagine it worn against the skin of a beautiful woman; imagine it warming against her.'

Harry imagined.

'Each gem is like a soul,' Gregor had continued, intoxicated by his own love for the objects. His voice, quiet with wonder, he spoke as a lover might. 'A perfect stone is God's way of making us remember our shortcomings.'

'Sign,' Harry said, his tone impatient.

The old man's thoughts came back sharply to the present, his fingers lying heavy on the papers. He had believed he had found his moral son; not a son born of his body, but of his heart and his beliefs. He had been happy to see what he loved pass on to the man he loved – and now the betrayal was too terrible to bear.

'Harry, I . . .'

'Sign,' the younger man repeated, wanting to be gone.

Gregor tried to reason with him, but there were no words

left. He was a nuisance, a bore, a drag on the ambitious grasping stranger in front of him. In the end, his mind had been sucked as dry as his heart. To be cheated of his business was intolerable; to be cheated of love was unbearable.

So he signed.

And Harry sold the business three weeks later, using the funds from the shop and the jewels to dabble on the stock exchange. But the money which had been so lucky before had lost its lustre, and the investments failed, Harry pouring more and more of Gregor's finances into schemes which he believed would eventually recover. They had to, he assured himself, he had been lucky before, he would be again. But he wasn't, and when he finally realized how much he had lost, he banked what was left abroad. For safety. His safety.

Rapidly Gregor's condition worsened and when he was finally bedridden after a stroke, Harry, with impeccable logic, had him transferred to a geriatric ward in an NHS hospital. After all, the old man didn't know where he was, so it wouldn't hurt him – and it did save money on private nursing fees. Such was his logic. As he ran through Gregor's money he allowed his provider and one-time protector to die by ounces, alone.

By this time Gayle was too preoccupied with money worries herself to think of the old man, and was working frantically – never realizing that there was a sizeable sum put away abroad as she tried desperately to find a way to meet Chris's school fees. Whilst Harry plotted to retrieve his previous glory, his wife worked and worried, and his old friend waited to die. Ruthlessly unfeeling, Harry never worried about Gregor's condition, or phoned the hospital for news, and as the months passed he knew nothing of the old man's mental or physical state – and worse, he didn't care.

The memory had been suppressed for so long that when Harry remembered it he was rocked by the sheer brutality of the recall. When he was told that Gregor Fylding had died he denied it at first, insisting that it was a lie; his mentor was not dead – he couldn't be – because with Gregor Fylding all his hopes and peace of mind were dead also.

I broke his spirit and he died alone, Harry thought, leaning against the wall, unable to move. *I broke his spirit. I stole from him, I killed him.* The guilt returned with staggering force. An old guilt rising triumphantly on the London street. Gregor Fylding, the man who had taught him and loved him, the one he had betrayed. Harry felt nauseous suddenly and found himself dizzy, turning away in horror, his head cold with sweat.

I killed him as surely as if I had strangled him, he thought, maddened by the violence of regret, his cheek beginning to twitch, the old familiar tic starting up. His memory jumped back instantly; he had wanted to make amends for Gregor's death, but had been unable to, and when he had confessed the full extent of his betrayal to his wife she had hit him. She didn't slap him across the face as expected, she struck him with a clenched fist deep in his stomach, winding him. He remembered the sensation and felt the same humiliation at her loathing.

She was a Catholic, Gayle explained, and she didn't believe in divorce. But there was more to it than that, Harry knew. She might not believe in divorce, but by God she believed in guilt. Each day she reminded her husband of what he had done to Gregor Fylding, dragging the corpse through their life like the rotten carcass it had become.

And Harry stayed with her because he couldn't leave and gradually Gregor Fylding stepped between the two of them. He sat at their table and lay between them in bed. His ghost was everywhere – in the money in Harry's wallet, in the conversation, in the food. Before long Harry was driven by guilt; his wife would never forgive him and his son was distant.

His confidence dipped and all his wit and charm mouldered under the ghost of Gregor Fylding. He was ended, his spirit imploding within him, his facial tic constant. Witty Winky Binky, no. Just Winky Binky, the sparse kid on the playground who twitched with insecurity.

But the crisis, when it came, was unexpected. Gayle going out to work one day and not returning. He had waited for her, dreading her, but needing her, and yet she didn't come. The four o'clock afternoon shifted on an hour, and she still didn't come; another hour turned over and only when evening began did Harry suddenly remember that Chris was still at school.

He rose with the heavy effort of a sick man and made his way ponderously across town, arriving to find his son standing in the entrance hall talking to a teacher. Chris seemed composed – although by this time he would usually have been met by his mother on her way back from work – and turned as Harry made his way towards him. Unshaven, stooped, angry with discomfort.

'Where's your mother?'

Chris could smell the staleness of his father's skin. 'She didn't come. I've been waiting for her.'

His voice was steady. He was neither judgemental or patronizing, although the teacher was staring hard at Harry and making his disapproval obvious.

'Well . . . come on then,' Harry said, suddenly aware of the impression he was creating, his hands vainly trying to straighten his hair. 'We'll go home together.'

'She might still come,' Chris said quietly. 'Maybe I'll wait a bit longer.'

The tic in Harry's cheek intensified. It fluttered under his skin like a caught insect.

'Oh, do what you like!' he snapped. 'You're old enough to find your own way home anyway, you don't need a bloody wet nurse.'

The teacher took in his breath, but Chris stood his ground impassively. 'We walk home together because she comes this way after work, not because I need an escort.'

Harry smiled weakly, cowed with embarrassment and aware of the teacher's obvious disgust.

'Sorry, Chris, sorry . . .' he mumbled, suddenly aware of his son and the damning difference between them. As Chris faced him, Harry felt ashamed, his own sour image mirrored in the unbending dignity of his child.

'Will you come with me, Chris? Please.'

The boy hesitated, stared at his father and then nodded.

Gayle never came back. In fact for years she disappeared and never contacted either her husband or her son. To all intents and purposes she could have died. But Harry knew she was alive, knew that the slivers of her disappointment would keep the blood running in her veins. He thought then that he had escaped; that his future was wiped free of any reminder of Gregor Fylding, and in the two years which followed Harry thrived. He won a parliamentary seat and became Harry Binky MP, and he ran his surgery and attended to his constituents faithfully, smugly grateful for their attention. The television was kind to him, he looked good, and his quotes were often employed as sound bites, his face cropping up with increasing frequency on the news.

Restored to good health and fortune, Harry had become complacent with his success – until the message had appeared on the menu the previous day: *You have one week to live.* The words had terrified him, as had the accompanying deafness. His security was now teetering, his stability slipping away from him. He did not know where the message had come from, or what it meant, he only knew that he could not escape its consequences. Oh yes, he had thought for a while that he might cheat his fate as he had cheated so many times before, but that was before the paralysing embarrassment of his collapse in the House.

The street glared with cold February light, Harry still leaning heavily against the wall, unable to move, his eyes fixed on the pavement in front of him. It glowed wickedly under the hard sun, clear except for the dark outline of Harry's shadow, falling in front of him. His eyes fixed upon it, he stared at it, and then blinked, uncertain of what he saw.

Beside his shadow was another. The shadow of a man standing beside him. Startled, Harry glanced round – but there was no one there and the street was merely terrible, and empty.

Chapter Six

Kaine Lukes stared at the open page in front of him and then slowly began to read what he had written. Behind him the clock ticked rhythmically – although without his implants he couldn't hear it – the pendulum swinging endlessly in the dim light, the noise echoing within the wooden confines of the case.

This has been a busy day, and the weather has been beating in time to our moods. Unnatural weather, rapidly changing. Brilliant and then overcast, the sun giving way to the bolting rain. There's such a lot to do, but one by one they are drawn in. First Chris, then the priest, then the MP – such a cunning man, full of spite and greed; chock-full of arrogance – and now Rachel. They all hurry about, running here and there, wondering what the message means. Frightened.

It's good to be afraid. When I fought I was always afraid, and when I lost my hearing I was mad with fear. Desperate – for a while. Only a while. I learnt how to control, how to gobble up the terrors. In fact, I developed an appetite for them, so that after a while nothing satisfied me as much. I have grown muscle and fat off misery.

Tonight I won't go out. Tonight I'll wait, and continue tomorrow. There are two women left to visit, only partially disturbed, only wondering. Not yet really afraid. Jeanie

Maas and Ahlia Bell. One getting older, one getting madness. Both looking to escape. Tonight I'll lie down by the fire and sleep until the heat dies out. Cold ashes feel like the brush of feathers on the hands, and they smell of dry earth.

Rachel's afraid. Fascinated. Waiting and watching. She could lie here with me, under me, with the deaf house around her. We could watch over her... When I was young no one watched over me. I came and went without comment. Later, in the fight game, I made an impact and won respect – only to lose it. The earth carries us on its back, and in the the end covers us for the final sleep. I believe that the soul can breathe underground and hear the world's heart beat; that when I am dead I can turn in my body and touch visions as they brush against my limbs.

I believe that we only lie easy when unseen, unheard and unmarked, and that we are all promised one shroud of earth to call our own.

Kaine Lukes stopped reading and closed the book, dipping into his inner pocket and drawing out the plastic bag filled with the diced bread. Absent-mindedly he crumbled one cube in his left hand, then slowly smelled the crumbs before his tongue flicked into the food and he began to eat.

And so ended the second day.

The Third Day

Chapter Seven

Jeanie Maas was taking the rubbish out to the priest's bin. Although Father Michael had a housekeeper, Jeanie came in once a week to do the menial tasks. She never told Ahlia exactly where she went on her day off, she liked to think she had some secrets. She just said she did some cleaning for a priest. An *old* priest; old and infirm, she implied.

'Father Michael's acting odd again. Pacing about,' the housekeeper said, walking into the kitchen and looking at Jeanie. 'He asked if you'd vaccuum the front room.'

Jeanie nodded and pushed the hoover along the corridor, passing the priest as she went. He *was* a handsome man, she thought, imagining how Ahlia would react if she saw him. Have a hard time trying not to drool! Jeanie thought, laughing to herself, her mind wandering as she began to hoover.

'Damn and blast it!' she snapped suddenly, as the machine made a harsh grinding noise. 'What now?' Flicking off the power, Jeanie banged it up and down on the carpet several times, a bent hairpin finally flirting out from between the rollers and bouncing with a metallic ping against the skirting board.

An old memory shifted inside Jeanie's brain. Her father had always complained about the hairpins she had left lying about. He had muttered about them, picking them and putting them into an old tobacco tin. Dozens of little pins of all shapes and sizes rattling in the little rusty tin with a picture of a ship on it. He had been a priggish man, narrow shouldered, stooped, with a bald head and round glasses; a man who had a tailor's shop at the top of the town, inherited from his uncle.

George Maas had been an indifferent tailor and when the Co-op came to town with its ready-to-wear suits, his business suffered badly. Grandly arrogant, he chose to believe that the falling off of his clientele was due to his customers' ignorance rather than his own mediocrity, and determined to keep the shop afloat, whatever it cost him or his family. And it cost a great deal, all their meagre savings swallowed up in the purchase of unsold cravats and out-of-date Homburgs. It had never been an impressive place, but as time went by the shop disintegrated, the three changing booths, lit by low wattage lights, growing grimier by the month, the privacy curtains faded and the mirrors fly-blown. At nine he arrived every morning, except Sundays, turning around the CLOSED sign to read OPEN and lifting up the yellow blind on the window. As they had done for years, two weathered dummies peered dolefully out into the changing streets in an eternal double act, the sign above them – GEORGE MAAS—GENTLEMEN'S OUTFITTERS – altered now by time to read G ORGE AA—ENTLEM N'S OUTFI ERS.

Without the money to employ a professional, George had set about restoring the sign himself, but his efforts were clumsy and his crudely added letters swayed drunkenly amongst the originals. He didn't notice, or care; the shop was his kingdom and as such he ruled it, as he did his surly staff, in his own fashion, and brooked no criticism. In fact, when he ran out of money to pay the staff, he was secretly pleased – now he could escape his home and spend all his time in the shop doing exactly what he wanted.

So for a number of years George eked out a mean living for his family. Pretentious, he was also narrow spirited, and although he adopted a ludicrously grand manner he was quite prepared to see his daughter go into service in her teens. Her wages would be useful, he reasoned, and besides, when she was out of sight he could fantasize about her, making fairytales out of the dross of reality.

Then when his wife died a year later, George's last grasp on reality slipped and he withdrew into his little kingdom, the dull wooden shelves and musty changing booths becoming the focus of his prissy attention. In his pressed grey suit, with its greasy cuffs and shiny knees, he hovered outside the drawn curtains, holding conversations with imaginary clients.

'I think we might have it in another colour, Lord Birkenhead . . . another tie might be more appropriate, sir, if you don't mind my suggesting it . . .'

Then he would move away, bustling around the half empty shelves and pulling out a variety of articles. Bearing them like jewels laid out on a cushion, he would pause outside the drawn curtain:

'When you're ready, sir . . . but only when you're ready . . .'

In this gently potty way, George Maas drifted into his late sixties, the shop becoming a curiosity in the town as his previous fastidious arrogance gave way to genuine instability. The fact that he developed Parkinson's disease exacerbated the deterioration; he now stood with his arms trembling under the weight of suiting, his voice at times pitched eerily high as he served his phantom customers. Boys from the town came to watch him through the window, laughing at the hunched little man scurrying clumsily about.

'Oi, Mr Maas,' said one cockily, 'I need some help.'

'I'm busy,' George said firmly, cocking his bald head towards the cubicles. 'The Mayor's having a fitting.'

'The Mayor! Like hell!' the boy scoffed, a gaggle of his friends laughing in the doorway.

Unbalanced George Maas might have been, but his dignity was intact and he fixed the youth with a basilisk gaze.

'Get out of my shop! I won't have language like that in here – especially in front of His Worship.'

Egged on by a growing audience, the youth dived towards the cubicle and pulled back the curtain. He hadn't used much force, but the material was threadbare and parted from the iron rings almost as he touched it, falling with a puff of dust on to the bare floor.

'There's no one in there, you old fool!' he sneered victoriously.

George Maas paused for an instant, glanced into the cubicle, then at the ruined curtain, then finally looked back to the boy. His face was unreadable. Without a word he picked up the curtain and folded it, pressing it against his chest, his hands shaking fiercely as he did so.

'Did you want the grey serge, sir? I'm so sorry, I don't think I quite heard you,' he said, his eyes blinking vaguely behind glasses.

The boy was suddenly alarmed and backed away.

'You're mad, you are! Bloody mad.'

George continued to move towards him, his gait unsteady as he laid the curtain down on the counter. A smudging of dust marked the front of his worn suit where he had pressed the material against him.

'Whatever you say, sir,' he said deferentially. 'But if I could just suggest that you tried the—'

'Bugger off!' the boy shouted, running out of the door and calling to his friends to follow him. Only at the end of the street did he stop, turning round to see George Maas standing on the pavement outside the shop.

'Crazy old man!' he shouted. 'You're bleeding crazy.'

The words shifted in the air, trembling uneasily, just as George Maas's hand trembled, as he waved the boy goodbye.

From then onwards only old customers visited George Maas; the young were too afraid of madness to penetrate the dank shop. But the older men were George's age and felt sorry for him; so sorry that they were prepared to play along with the charade in order to purchase a pair of socks. Daily more afflicted with Parkinson's disease, George shuddered amongst his old stock, the bald crown of his head mirrored in the two round circles of his glasses, his voice either an ingratiating whine or a shrill protest.

'Oh, no, sir!' he howled, the top half of his body poked into an empty cubicle as he talked to another ghost customer; 'Please allow me to suggest something more *suitable*.'

He teetered out, raising his eyebrows to one of his few real customers, an old man like himself, who was waiting by the counter. 'No taste!' whispered George. 'And a Count! Would you believe it?'

The man hesitated then nodded sympathetically as he glanced at the cubicle. 'George, I just wanted to get some socks—'

'In a minute! In a minute!' he replied pettishly. 'Can't you see I'm busy?' He scuttled across the shop jerkily, then stopped, stock still, his eyes fixed on the floor. 'A hairpin! How many times have I told the girl not to come into the shop when I'm busy?' He winked conspiratorially. 'It's Jeanie, she wants the Count. You mark my words, there'll be a marriage here before long.'

The story had been passed on amidst much laughter, as Jeanie Maas was at that time working as a maid for a doctor in Shropshire and had as much chance of marrying a Count as she had of being made Prime Minister. Inheriting her father's weak eyes, Jeanie had the parboiled look of all women who expect little love from men, and was violently embarrassed by her father's behaviour. In her halting, ill-educated letters she reprimanded him, but in his bewildered mental state he took her rebukes as female coyness and replied skittishly.

Dear Jeanie,

What a silly girl you are! You almost make me angry, but I forgive you. I saw your Count today and he spoke of you at great length – perhaps you should see him more often? Not that it's for me to say, but I do feel that he needs a little more encouragement.

Business is good. Word travels and I have many new customers.

Fondest love,
Your father

Working from six in the morning until ten at night for an unappreciative family, Jeanie was initially impatient, but her temper faded quickly, the mischievous streak in her nature reasserting itself – together with a real pity for her father. He was ill, sick in the head. Poor fool, she thought. Poor silly fool. She jerked her head up defiantly. What the hell did it matter what people thought, or how they laughed at her? If it made him happy to live in a fantasy world, why should she care?

Eagerly Jeanie picked up a piece of lined paper and in her best handwriting penned back a note to her father:

Dear father,

Thank you for your letter. I should have known I couldn't hide anything from you, but you see I don't love the Count...

She laughed softly and pushed her glasses further up the bridge of her fleshy nose.

... I have met someone else instead.

Frowning, she wondered what was better than a Count, and then wrote on:

. . . a Prince. He's from Spain and loves me terribly. We adore each other. Please tell the Count that it's over between us.

With love,
Jeanie

For a year the two of them kept up this bizarre correspondence. George, severely disabled both mentally and physically by his Parkinson's disease, shuddered around his shop and his phantoms, and longed for his daughter's letters, believing every word implicitly. Jeanie's fantasy romance grew mistily in his brain, her words passed on to the ghost customers, her virtues extolled constantly. She was transformed by his mental instability and by distance into a luminous beauty, much desired, much loved – and she was *his* creation.

Jeanie Maas's thoughts stopped short. The hairpin still lay against the skirting board and for an instant she could again see her father's worn tobacco tin with the ship on it. It had been that summer, that last summer in Shropshire . . . Jeanie's eyes closed against the remembrance, but it played on in her brain relentlessly. A warm English summer of smudgy afternoons and quick evening rains; of birds singing into twilight; of boys calling out from street corners, whistling at the girls. Even whistling at Jeanie that summer. Oh yes, when she had taken off her glasses and fluffed out her hair she was passable; no beauty, no one's first choice, but she had a kind of spirit which passed for attraction – when it was a warm evening and the air smelt of mown grass, the last bus droning by idly, the conductor leaning against the boarding rail.

Summer sounds, summer senses. Summer came in and picked up Jeanie like that last bus home; it carried her over the dry lanes and away from the drudgery; its engine humming in time to the humming of her own hopes. Short-sighted without glasses, her hair loose, she laughed with the fierceness of someone at last accepted, but expecting at any moment to be rejected again. Living in that one balmy instant of security Jeanie went willingly with the boys up the hill, with them, and with her girlfriend, Mary Keller. Up the sloping hill, steamy with late sun, towards the barn still warm from the day's dry heat.

Don't go with boys, her mother used to say. *Don't go with boys* . . . Her employer and his wife had warned her too, hinting at instant dismissal. Hinting even at pregnancy – the end of her chances.

'You're not a pretty girl,' the doctor's wife had said bluntly, 'but you could make someone a sound wife – if you keep your reputation.'

It had been effortless to be good. So easy to keep a reputation that no one wanted. So simple to retain something undesired. Jeanie Mass's virtue had never been threatened; instead it dragged behind her like an unwanted mongrel. They were forced companions – she and her virtue – no one wanted either of them.

Until that evening in Shropshire. The hill was not steep, only undulating, rising towards the barn on the bank, growing darker by the instant as the sun set. Early pipistrelles flirted in the steaming air, the boys murmuring, calling to Jeanie and her friend. Then one extended his hand to Jeanie and she took it. The skin was heated, the fingers greedily catching hold of hers. Without her glasses the boy was unclear, hazy as the falling evening, a shimmering and enticing form.

And she went up the hill, holding hands with a boy she couldn't see and didn't want to see. She followed him into the barn, Mary and Jim running in front of them. The air was full of the smell of dust and the warmth of the ended day, bales of hay piled up against the walls, a worn ladder leaning against the upper portion of the barn. Gingerly, unable to see clearly, Jeanie climbed upwards, following the boy who was still holding her hand. The straw scraped against the bare skin of her legs and prickled against her arms as she sat down, the boy beside her. Alan's face, now only a foot away from hers, came into sudden focus, and she closed her eyes to distance herself. Hurriedly the other couple pushed past them, nestling and giggling behind a bank of hay bales, their voices thick with excitement. Jeanie kept her eyes closed, sensing the boy beside her, allowing him to touch her, allowing clumsy kisses and fumbling, the scent of the straw and the summer dust filling her nostrils as she leaned against him.

His skin was heated, his voice low, his words inane, the soft murmur of laughter from the other couple drifting, disembodied, from the far corner.

Still with her eyes closed Jeanie clung to the boy and then felt a wrench of anguish as he pulled away from her.

'Here, try this,' Alan said.

Her eyes opened. In the dim light his face was indistinct, only the burning tip of a forbidden cigarette glowing brightly.

'I . . . I don't smoke,' she said, hesitating. If she refused maybe he would be angry and leave her. 'I don't know how to.'

Alan moved, leaned towards her, placing the cigarette between her lips.

'Do it like they do in the films . . . go on.'

She breathed in and coughed, passing the cigarette back to him, scarlet with humiliation. From behind the far bales, someone laughed.

'I don't like it!' she said sharply, then softened her tone. Don't anger him. Don't, or he'll go . . . Eagerly she leaned against him, wanting to regain the closeness and wanting him to kiss her again.

'How old are you?' Alan asked, drawing on the cigarette in the half dark. The question spiralled uneasily with the smoke.

'Seventeen.'

'Never!' he said, trying to see her face in the dimness. 'You look younger. I *know* you're younger.' His voice dropped, his lips against her ear. 'Is this your first time?'

She nodded. 'I told you, I've never smoked before.'

His laugh was unexpected and for an instant she bristled, only relaxing again when he caught hold of her. The intimacy of his body made her drowsy with longing.

'I meant – was this your first time with a boy?'

The full implication of the question shocked her and Jeanie bit her lip. If she moved away now he would be annoyed with her, there would be no more kisses, no closeness. She would have to walk home alone across the dark field, back to the doctor's house. And worse – Alan would laugh at her and tell his friends how useless she was. No one had wanted her before, maybe no one would again. She moved her position slightly, feeling the steel wire of the glasses in her pocket dig momentarily into her hip.

'I . . .'

'It is, isn't it?' he said, his tone a mixture of amusement and excitement. 'Well, you just relax and I'll show you how it's done.'

He said nothing else, just pushed her back against the hay bales and moved on top of her. All the world's sounds melted in the barn's closed air, together with the scents and the feeling of heat and warmth. Under her limbs the straw moved like scented water, the dark vault of the roof above her an unfocused and protecting shell. Their limbs in the darkness lost form and indentity, their mutual desire masking any awkwardness, and then suddenly, Jeanie sat up.

'What's that?'

'What?' Alan asked irritably.

'I can smell burning!' Jeanie said, jumping to her feet and refastening her blouse. 'Look, over there!' she shouted, pointing to a small patch of flames from the far corner of the hay barn. 'Oh God!' Her voice rose unsteadily as she called to her friend. 'Mary, are you there? Come out! Something's burning. *Come out of there!*'

Beside her, the boy peered into the darkness, coughing as the smoke wafted over to them. 'Come on!' Alan said urgently, panicking and dragging Jeanie towards the ladder. 'Let's get out.'

Impatiently, she shook off his arm. 'Not until I know where Mary is. And what about your friend, what about Jim? They were over there—'

'So if they're not answering they must have got out!' the boy snapped, dragging her to the ladder. 'For Christ's sake, let's move!'

Jeanie stood her ground, the flames blurring in front of her eyes, only yards away.

'*Mary!*'

He pushed her then, so savagely that she nearly fell down the ladder and only saved herself when she grabbed the wooden rungs, her feet scrambling for purchase as she slid awkwardly to the floor. Above them the smoke was so intense that her voice choked in her throat, her eyes streaming as she looked up.

'*Come on!*' a voice called out suddenly.

They turned to see Jim silhouetted in the doorway of the barn, beckoning to them. In blind relief, they ran towards him.

'*Come on!*' he shouted again. '*The place is going to fall in! Run!*'

They ran out without looking back; ran out of the burning barn, away from the smoke and flames now rising frantically up to the dark summer night. Gasping for breath, Jeanie followed the others into the darkness, her chest filling with smoke. Still without her glasses, she ran down the hill, running for her life, unable to see them clearly, only grateful that they had escaped. Her limbs, before so light and loving, pounded heavily on the dry grass, her breaths rasping, her lips dry. The night was darkening as she ran, and only when she reached the bottom of the hill and stopped beside them did the others come into focus.

'Mary?'

Silence.

Her hands shaking, Jeanie scrabbled in her pocket and pulled out her glasses. All the night's horror came into sudden clarity.

The boys stood transfixed in front of her.

'You can't tell anyone, Jeanie . . .' Jim said coldly. 'Promise.'

The night collapsed around them. The three of them. *Only three.*

'But . . . I thought Mary was with you . . .' Jeanie stammered. 'You called us out, you called us out!' Her voice was pierced with hysteria. 'You knew she was still in there and you called us out!' She turned clumsily, her eyes on the blazing barn on the bank of the hill. 'Oh God, she's in there . . .'

'She could have got out—'

Jeanie swung round: 'But you don't *know* that, Jim. *You don't know!* You didn't care, did you? You just wanted to save your own neck!' Her hands moved up to her mouth, panic rising. 'We have to get help, get someone. We have—'

Roughly, Jim caught hold of her arms and shook her.

'We can't do anything now. It's over. Besides', he said evenly, 'how would you explain why she was there? Are you going to let everyone know what you were doing?' His voice was hard with fear: 'You'll lose your job, Jeanie, and people will talk—'

'She was my friend!'

'She's gone,' he said flatly.

'*No!*' Jeanie screamed, pulling away and looking up at the hill. The flames were massing in the sky, the smoke rising black against the indigo night. 'She can't have gone ... she *can't* have.'

'We can't say anything. We can't tell anyone,' Jim went on. 'We have to stick together. If we go into town now we can say we went to the pictures.'

Jeanie began to sob but he continued.

'Then we can say that Mary was supposed to come with us, but she never showed up. Jeanie? Are you listening to me?'

'We killed her.'

He struck her then, once, hard, a blow to the shoulder, knocking her off balance. 'Listen, *we have no choice*. There's nothing we can do now. If we told everyone the truth, what good would it do any of us? It can't bring her back. We'd all have to go to trial. They might even say it was murder—'

'*No!*' Jeanie wailed. 'They can't, we didn't know she was in there.'

'*Didn't we?*' Jim asked.

The night chilled suddenly. Against the skyline the two boys were silhouetted, facing her. Jeanie's seventeen-year-old brain raced on frantically. *Murder*, that would mean prison, disgrace. Her father would be humiliated and she would be sent away for years. The cold weight of fear, compounded with guilt, swamped her.

'So what do we do?'

'We stick to the story I told you,' Jim said, breathing more easily now that he knew she was an accomplice, not an adversary. 'No one will ever know.'

From the first, their story had been believed. When Mary Keller's body was found it was presumed that she had been with some stranger who had deserted her when a cigarette end had started the fire. Some out of town man who had abandoned her.

Don't go with the boys up the hill, Jeanie. Don't go.

'It's such a terrible business, but she did have a bad reputation,' the doctor's wife said. 'You see how important it is to be careful?'

Don't go with the boys up the hill...

'It's a horrible way to die, but there you are. I suppose it will act as a warning to all young girls.'

It acted as a warning to Jeanie. It warned her about life. For the next three months she lost weight steadily and in the end could hardly work. Her doctor employer put it down to grief. After all, she had been Mary's best friend. He even tried to console her.

'Be thankful it wasn't you.'

Oh, but she *wanted* it to be her. *How* she wanted it to be her. She wanted Mary to be alive and herself to be dead, because nothing could suppress the memory of that night. The sound of a boy whistling, the smell of hay, the crackle of a fire, all brought back the nightmare. And one particular question always came with the memory – why didn't she call out? Why did Mary Keller stay silent?

But there was never an answer. Had she been overcome by the smoke? But *how*? If Jim got out first, why didn't she go with him? Why didn't he lead her out? *Why*? What were they doing? What was *he* doing? The questions were unending, just as the last question was unanswerable. If she had gone for help when they reached the bottom of the hill, could Mary have been saved? Logic told Jeanie that it was unlikely. She knew that by the time they left the barn it was almost impossible to breath in the smoke, so Mary must have been dead or unconscious by then. There was nothing she could have done, nothing. Or was there? *Was* there?

But horrible as it was, the tragedy was soon overshadowed by the war, and when Jim Curtiss and Alan Grant were called up, Jeanie anticipated some kind of relief. Having avoided them for months she seriously thought that their absence might lead to forgetfulness. And in a way, it did. Unable to work properly at the doctor's house, Jeanie was sent home; back to the Northern town and back to her father. But by this time George Maas was seriously ill with Parkinson's disease. He didn't recognize his daughter. He thought she was a servant.

It was a role Jeanie believed that she deserved; a punishment fit for her crime. Others might marvel at her stoicism, but Jeanie was merely serving her time. Her sentence had been passed, and her prison was exquisitely apt. As her father moved further and further from reality and more into the grandiose world of his imagination, Jeanie retained her sanity by necessity. He needed her, so she became capable. There was room for only one lunatic.

The punishment was perfect – she had wanted to be dead and now, to all intents and purposes, she was. She no longer ached for male companionship and was relieved to be thought plain. There were no ambitions for her to chase, or realize. Her invisibility was her best defence; from now on she was to serve her parent's whims – and serve them as a stranger. Her father had mentally disowned her. Jeanie Maas was no more.

He died in his eighty-seventh year, and only then did Jeanie believe that her sentence had been finally served. She sold the shop and with the little capital she had saved advertised for a position and went to work as a lady's maid in London. Serving and service were the principles of Jeanie's existence. To give pleasure, to look after, to make amends in many lives for the one life lost. That was her aim and the whole tenet by which she lived. So when fate threw Ahlia Bell into her path, Jeanie took up that challenge as well. Hysterical, unbalanced, beautiful Ahlia came like a saviour to Jeanie and together they lived, needing each other for their own salvation.

Apparently the past had been absolved. Or so she thought – until she received the message yesterday:

You have one week to live.

It was not ended after all. There was still some other recompense to be made. The message was chilling; Jeanie even wondered if the messenger had been the long dead Mary Keller, but dismissed the idea immediately. No, this was more than any ghost could contrive. Her eyes were still fixed on the hairpin, the dull cream skirting board sour in the noon light. *I could give up*, she thought, *I could just let go* . . . But the notion was unpalatable to her. She had struggled to hold on to her life, and no one, not God or man, would take it from her now.

Her life might be nothing. Small, narrow, apparently without hope, Jeanie realized; but her will to live was implacable. *This is my life, this is* all *I have, and I'll keep it.*

You have one week to live.

The words danced in her head, whistled to her. Blinking, Jeanie took out her hearing aid and tapped it against her hand, impatient that it was malfunctioning again. But when she put it back in her ear it still whistled – just like the boys in Shropshire had done one summer night, long ago. The memories struggled with each other. *Don't go with the boys up the hill, Jeanie . . . don't go . . .* They skimmed in her consciousness, picked at her memory . . . Fire, whistles, hairpins . . . They spun in her mind; they teased her while her hearing aid hummed and hissed, the words etching themselves like wood smoke in the still air.

'Morning.'

Chris Binky heard the voice, but didn't move. *Couldn't* move. The ventilator breathed for him, lifting his lungs in and out, living for him. Under his taped eyelids he could just make out the faintest dark blur, but he knew who it was. The doctor.

'How are we today?'

I'm great, you bloody idiot, how are you? Chris thought impatiently. *How about getting me off this machine and letting me go home? Call my father, he'll see to it. Call him.*

'No change, I see.'

No change! Chris thought incredulously. *Well, I'm changing in here. Inside, I'm changing, doctor – and I've got company too . . .* He tried to smile grimly, to move, but his limbs were immobilized. Transfixed. Dead body, breathing brain. *Get my father, he'll sort it out. He's an odd man, but he'll do something . . . Get him, please.*

'I think we should let his father visit for a while. Can't do any harm.'

Thank God, someone's actually listening at last! Chris thought jubilantly, his inertia lifting. The previous night he had lain awake, under the taped eyelids, next to the breathing machine. Awake and paralysed. He had gone through many crises that night. Whilst the staff thought that he was insensible, unfeeling, he had been lying screaming in his head. Paralysed. Unheard.

He had wanted to die; then wanted to live. He had made bargains with God, deciding that he could live in a wheelchair but not fully paralysed. His sexuality had been considered carefully – could he live without sex? Could he? To live without wanting sex would be possible, but to *want* sex and be unable to perform, could he live with that? His thoughts had turned automatically to Rachel. He loved her – in bed and out – loved her when she was moody, funny, sexy. Loved her completely . . . well, had done – until now.

Please God, don't let me live if I'm paralysed for life. And don't leave me on this bloody machine while I can think and no one can hear me . . . Panic descended horribly, without warning. His limbs were useless, there was no way to indicate distress, even his tears had dried up. *I want my father*, Chris had pleaded silently. *Get my father.* And now they were letting Harry in; now he was coming to see him again.

Patiently, Chris waited. But before his father arrived, another man came in. Not through the doors of the intensive care unit but straight into Chris's head. The deaf man came in alone – stood for an instant watching him – and then touched Chris's forehead with his thumb. Startled, Chris could actually *feel* the touch as though it had come from outside, and winced.

The deaf man touched him again, pressing his thumb into the flesh and then speaking in his eerily rhythmic voice.

'YOU HAVE
ONE WEEK
TO LIVE.'

Chris felt the pressure of the man's thumb against his forehead and heard the words. Fear trickled from his pores like sweat.

One week?

Kaine Lukes nodded.

But I can't move. I can't help myself.

'I WILL
HELP YOU.'

Chris hesitated; he didn't trust the man, felt only a dead weight of terror. *If you don't help me, will I die?*

'LET ME
HELP YOU.'

Why, who are you?

Silence.

Are you alive? Chris persisted, scrutinizing the deaf man's face. He was motionless, watching. Dangerous. *Am I imagining you? Or are you real?* Chris faltered, terror making him childlike. *My father's coming*, he said firmly. *He'll help me.*

'HE CAN'T
HELP YOU.'

He can! Chris answered desperately, his unresponding body leaden on the narrow hospital bed. *Go away! Leave me alone. GET OUT!*

Unmoved, Kaine Lukes paused, his thumb still against Chris's forehead. Slowly and firmly he pressed into the flesh, the thumb going through the skin and into the muscle beneath, then between his forefinger and thumb he pulled a thread – *and Chris's right hand moved*.

He felt the movement and his heart lurched. This man *could* cure him, could save him!

Once more, the deaf man pulled on the thread. Again, Chris's right hand fluttered.

Help me, please! Chris begged. *I'll do whatever you say. Just help me.*

'WAIT HERE
FOR A
LITTLE WHILE.'

All right. Chris agreed, feeling another flicker of movement in his arm. *All right, whatever you say.*

He thought he was going to be helped, to be cured – but instead he saw the deaf man hold up the thread and bite through it with his teeth. It snapped into two immediately, Kaine Lukes swallowing the piece left in his mouth, the other end sliding back slowly, sinuously, into the bloody indentation in Chris's forehead.

Jesus, no! NO!!!! Chris pleaded. *Don't do that. Let me move, please. Please, let me move again . . . please.*

But Kaine Lukes said nothing, merely leaned forwards and placed his lips over the bloodied hole on the young man's forehead and closed the wound with his teeth.

'I saw him move!' Harry Binky said excitedly, leaning over Chris's bed.

'Mr Binky, your son is paralysed.'

'Why don't you bloody look before you speak!' Harry said hotly. 'I tell you, I saw his right arm move.'

'Wishful thinking, I'm afraid.'

Impatiently Harry pushed past the doctor and stood looking down at his son, searching his body and face for any sign of life. Half mad with his own problems, he still was aware enough to know that Chris was trying to communicate with him. *His son had moved*. He *had*.

But as he stared Harry saw no other flicker of activity. The dead still limbs lay unmoving, the face blank without feeling. He stayed for over an hour and then rose to leave, defeated and more debilitated than he had ever felt before. The machines hummed behind him, the nurses whispering at their station, Chris immobile on the bed.

Live, Harry willed him. *Live*. His anguish was genuine, his grief crushing. Then he bent to kiss his son, his lips brushing the skin where the deaf man's thumb had lain.

Chapter Eight

Slowly, Ahlia got out of bed and walked into the bathroom, her bare feet noiseless on the carpeted floor. She ran the bath quickly, taking off her negligée and standing in front of the full-length mirror which ran the length of the wall. Age had not touched her. A beauty at nineteen, she had realized the power of her attraction and had committed her life to its preservation. No treatment, cosmetic, or exercise routine was neglected; the skin which had been firm at twenty was still taut at thirty-eight; and the face which had enticed two decades before still held its potent sensuality.

As ever fascinated by her own reflection, Ahlia stared at the face she owned. The wide visage, with its dark, heavy lidded eyes, regarded her thoughtfully, her lips rising with the familiar undulating smile. Her head tilted to one side, her hair brushing against her shoulder and exposing the line of her neck. She moved, as she always did, slowly, certain of her ground, without hurrying, her actions languorous and hypnotic. She made love in the same way, smoothly, expertly, with ultimate confidence.

Her body, her face and her whole concentration was centred on her sexuality. Nothing in her life was as important to her. Her eroticism had bought her status, wealth, enjoyment and a powerful husband. Ahlia sighed, the noise coming unexpectedly from her lips. She didn't like to be reminded of unpleasantness – it was ageing. She turned away from her reflection and slid her hand into the water, checking the temperature before lowering her body into the bath.

You have one week to live.

The words came back without warning, Valium failing to obliterate the warning of the previous night. Ahlia moaned brokenly. It had been a dream, that was all, just a nightmare. After all, her hearing was fully restored and when she had gone back to bed there was no trace of the writing on the pillow. *But it had seemed so real*, she thought, fighting panic. So horribly real. Her wet hands moved up to her ears and she touched them gingerly. To lose her hearing, never again to enjoy the flattery, the adoration of men, to be pitied, not admired . . .

Unexpectedly she thought of her late husband. Ahlia had made a career of her widowhood, the enforced celibacy soon abandoned as she found innumerable men to appease her sexually; she had even incorporated her widow status into her lovemaking, telling each man that he was the first lover she had taken since her husband died. Timidly, hesitantly, she had pretended to be afraid, her own sensuality increased by the charade, the black clothes and underwear enhancing the effect.

It had served her well for a while, until the sheer number of her lovers made such pretence impossible. But Ahlia still clung to the illusion and the men went along with it. They wanted her and if she wanted to pretend, then so be it, it was only a delusion and one well worth pursuing in order to possess her. They laughed about her behind her back, naturally; they compared notes too; but they still came to the house in Cleveland Square. They used her rooms and ate her food and slept in her bed; they fingered her possessions and showered in her bathroom and thought they were using her. But when they had gone they would have been unnerved to know how little they had left behind.

Because as the door closed behind them, Ahlia called for

Jeanie and together they underwent the ritual they always employed – methodically and grimly cleaning the bedroom and the bathroom. They stripped the bed and wiped down every surface the lover had touched; they washed the bath and the bathroom walls; they disinfected the toilet; they boiled the china and the glasses he had touched. In short, they obliterated him.

At first the rite had seemed bizarre to Jeanie and she had reacted with amused disbelief, only to be silenced by the expression on her employer's face. The thunderous sensuality was gone, in its place was an unexpected glimpse of a fierce and feral nature. And at such times Ahlia resembled a fox; wide-faced, huge-eyed, remote. Jeanie never laughed at her employer again, and from then onwards joined forces with Ahlia until every scent, impression and fingerprint of the lover had been removed. Only then did Ahlia dismiss Jeanie and draw a bath. It was always hot, as hot as her skin could stand it, and in the water she poured a solution of Dettol before getting in and scrubbing herself clean.

The ritual cleansing always followed lovemaking. It soothed Ahlia, it absolved her, and for the next week or month she regained her equilibrium, until the next time she made love. The alternate desire and self-loathing she did not understand; another woman would have realized that such behaviour was abnormal, but Ahlia neither admitted her phobia nor sought its cure. It was something she did to calm herself. That was all she knew, and all she would admit. Besides, to tell anyone about her foible would expose her to ridicule, and might even imply that she was frigid, or guilty about sex – and that was unthinkable. It was a secret between her and Jeanie, and Jeanie would never tell.

A plane flew over the house and made Ahlia flinch. Planes flying overhead, flying, crashing . . . She moved her legs under the water, admiring them, but the memory was resistant and persisted. A plane, a plane flying away ten years ago . . . She scowled, unnerved, trying to avoid her thoughts. But she couldn't. She had always suffered from premonitions; predicting the death of her grandfather, and the sudden, crippling illness of her aunt. She didn't like to think of such things, but she couldn't stop them wading into her mind. They crawled in relentlessly; unbidden, unwelcome omens trailing disasters and losses. At first, Ahlia tried to dismiss the precognitive glimpses and warnings, but as she grew up she realized she was never wrong. The future of which she caught snippets was the future which could not be avoided. So she learned to listen to the warnings and act on them.

But not always. A decade ago she had watched a plane leave Heathrow, watched it lift up to the skies, watched it without blinking as it levelled and then watched it as it crashed. The news report had confirmed that there were no survivors. Of course not, she had known that already. It was a disaster, unexpected to everyone – except her.

Because she had already seen the plane fall. In a dream she had seen the DC10 plummet to earth, and had known then that no one would survive. No one – not even her husband. But then that had been the point, he was *supposed* to die, because he wasn't going to be allowed to live after what he had done to her. Ahlia opened her eyes and stared fixedly at the curtained ceiling above her. Her husband could have been saved; she could have told him about the dream; begged him to stay home. But he had betrayed her – and so she let him go to his flight and his death. He had rejected her, *her* for a mutual friend, a woman without her beauty. He had taken this other woman to bed, made love to her; he had wanted her more than he had wanted his wife. And his longing had killed him.

You have one week to live.

The warning sounded evilly in Ahlia's mind as the plane

moved overhead and she winced, turning on the hot water tap and heating up the water hurriedly. Years had past, it was over, finished surely? She wasn't prepared to feel guilt; *she* hadn't sabotaged the plane; *she* hadn't killed her husband. She simply hadn't warned him. But the logic was inadequate and she knew it. Filled with intense foreboding, Ahlia felt the water burn her and turned off the tap, her eyes fixed ahead sightlessly, her lips opening as she sank further into the bath and dipped her head under the water. Her hair floated eerily around her face and then, just as she was about to rise up again, she felt the base of the bath fall away.

She plunged immediately into darkness, the water pushing her down, folding over her head, drumming in her ears as she gasped in panic, a trail of bubbles punctuating the surface. Hysteria gripped her, her falling body turning over in the depth of water, the bath suddenly an unending well without a base. The temperature dropped, not bath water any more, but cold well water, sea water, without end. Frantically she tried to fight her way back to the surface, but was pushed downwards instead, her lungs bursting.

Then, with disbelieving terror, she felt someone grasp her foot.

The hand jerked at her leg, pulling her further under. Down, down, under the weight of the drowning mass, her lungs burning with pressure, her arms reaching upwards desperately as the hand continued to cling to her foot. Mad with terror, Ahlia kicked out blindly, straining to see who was holding on to her. But the water was black, cloudy, and she could see nothing, only feel herself finally losing consciousness. Her eyes opened blindly like a doll's, her mouth slackening – and then, in that instant, she came face to face with the person who was dragging her down.

The deaf man's face came suddenly through the dark water towards her, Ahlia screaming in terror, the last bubbles of air leaving her lungs as she did so. Her head jerked upwards, her limbs flailing uselessly, but as she fought to free herself from his grip, he pulled her towards him and moved his mouth over hers. Repelled, she felt the force of his lips and the teeth underneath, as she struggled frantically in the last moments before drowning.

Then, dying, she finally relaxed, and in that moment realized that the deaf man was pushing air *into* her body, using his own breath to thrust life and oxygen back into her. She clung to him fiercely then, her nails ripping deep into the flesh of his back, her eyes rolling upwards. And he kept breathing into her while their bodies moved together under the water; kept holding her and passing his life and breath into her mouth, allowing her to take comfort and air from him.

Then, just as suddenly, he released her. Suddenly he let go and swam away from her, his body disappearing into the blackness of the water. Deprived of air, Ahlia panicked, groping around in the dark water for him, her mind clouding with terror.

Look up.

Ahlia heard the command and obeyed, her eyes fixing on a light burning high above her. Then, agonizingly slowly, she began to swim towards it, fighting against the weight of water, struggling upwards by inches, making for the surface with what little air she had left. She could see the bath above her, the open rectangle above the water, and swam desperately towards it, dragging herself through the suffocating water, her eyes fixed on the daylight above.

She came up suddenly, thrusting herself out into the air, gasping for breath, her hands grabbing the side of the bath as she heaved herself out of the tub and fell heavily on to the bathroom floor. For nearly a minute she gulped for breath, gradually refilling her lungs, and then, only then, did she glance back into the bath.

It was shallow, the water only inches deep, and warm to the touch.

Kaine Lukes crossed London at five o'clock in the morning, walking up the dark streets towards the market, his eyes fixed ahead. He paused outside Smithfield, then moved on to the Cock Tavern, walking in and gesturing to the landlord. His usual beer was brought to him in his usual seat, a small group of porters – bummerees – sharing a joke on the next table. They saw him and nodded, but did not invite him to join them, knowing that he would refuse the invitation as he always did.

Realizing that he could lip read, a few had taken the trouble to talk to him slowly, and once he had responded by feinting a few blows at a hanging side of beef. The roars of approval had rung down the aisleway, several of the porters whistling and banging their feet on the stone floor. But they soon realized that such communication was rare, as the deaf man apparently neither wanted nor needed companionship. He just wanted to walk around the aisles, criss-crossing the market hall, stopping occasionally to watch as a carcass was cut up and then weighed, the old metal weighing machine reminding him of the days when he had been weighed before a fight.

No one bothered him – they knew that he didn't like to be pestered – and, well aware of the fact that he was an ex-boxer, they kept their distance.

But occasionally some wanted to talk.

'I saw you fight Terry Norman – you were good,' one of the men said, a puller-back who worked on the vans outside, literally pulling back the meat towards the front of the lorry as it was loaded. 'You go deaf because of a fight?'

The questioner was standing on the landing board of a van, his hands livid with cold as Kaine Lukes stood looking up at him.

Slowly Kaine nodded.

'I bet that was a bit of a kicker,' the man went on. 'Wrecked your career, good an' proper. Can't you fight if you can't hear?'

The deaf man frowned, not understanding, and then waited for the man to repeat the question. Carefully he lip read the words, watching the man's mouth, and then he hesitated, his gaze moving upwards to the man's eyes where it locked into the porter, hooking him as effectively as a side of meat on a skewer.

'Jesus Christ, you should have seen him,' the man said afterwards to Titus Brand. 'I thought he was going to flip.'

'It was a bloody stupid question,' Titus replied laughing. 'You're lucky he didn't plant one on you.'

'He just looked so bleeding odd, that's all.'

No one started a conversation with Kaine Lukes after that. They treated him with respect instead and kept their distance, and although some thought that he was brain damaged from his years of fighting no one had the courage to challenge him and all gave him a wide berth. Apart from Titus Brand. He was just as afraid of him as the others, but he was curious about the deaf man and after a while he and Kaine Lukes developed a curious rapport.

But when Rachel started coming to the market and asking about the deaf man Titus was uneasy. He had seen the young woman come and go for weeks and had been willing to answer her questions, but over the last couple of days her interest in the deaf man had increased unhealthily and Titus was disturbed by it. He had tried to warn her off, but she kept coming, drawn to Kaine Lukes by some misplaced and unlucky compulsion.

Titus had a daughter of his own, about Rachel's age, and felt the same unease he would have felt for his own child. So he watched Rachel, and he watched the deaf man – and in his turn, the deaf man watched him. Sometimes Titus would be at the weighing machine at the back of his stall and would see the deaf man pass, studying him as he paused by the white railings and looked into the vast walk-in freezer.

Kaine Lukes knew of the old man's interest. He hadn't made it obvious that he had noticed it, but he been aware of the scrutiny and the previous day had spent longer around Titus's stall than anywhere else. The two men, so dissimilar, watched each other, the deaf man outside the bars, the old man inside, cutting meat, the front of his apron liberally splattered with blood.

Later, Titus was standing in an aisle eating a bar of chocolate as Kaine Lukes passed. When he saw him he offered him a piece as he usually did.

'Want some?'

The deaf man paused. He could smell the blood on the old man's hand mixing with the sweet scent of the chocolate and nodded.

'Good,' Titus said simply, chewing the chocolate and measuring up his companion.

The deaf man was many inches taller than him and at least six stones heavier, but had lessened his physical impact by leaning against the stall. His head was turned away from the old man, his eyes averted as he ate the chocolate, so that Titus had to nudge him to get his attention.

'More?'

The deaf man nodded, smiling briefly. The smile was unexpected and did nothing to lighten his features.

'You want a beer?'

Kaine Lukes touched his ears.

'Yeah, I know you're deaf. We go through this performance every time,' Titus said easily. 'I just asked if you wanted a beer. Sure as hell you don't need ears to drink.'

Kaine Lukes thought for a moment and then shook his

head, his gaze moving towards the door, his mechanical voice suddenly materializing in the frozen air.

'WALK WITH
ME PLEASE.'

The sound was no more a voice than the scrape of metal hooks on the butcher's pole. Titus accepted the invitation and fell into step with him. They walked for a long time across the early streets, day breaking, then the deaf man's steps turned back towards St Bartholmew's church across the road from Smithfield. He walked around the outside of the church hurriedly, turning to beckon to the old man who followed. The dark stone brickwork was gloomy in the half light, the gravestones blackened as Kaine Lukes suddenly knelt and leaned his head against the stone flags upon which they had been walking. His right ear was pressed to the ground, his eyes closed, and for an instant Titus stepped back, aware suddenly that he was watching something primeval.

The deaf man crouched over the earth, his head bent to the ground, his back, in its heavy overcoat, humped in the semi-darkness. He was no longer human, no longer a man, simply a form, and when he moved it seemed as though the flagstones opened for an instant, his head moving downwards, *into* the earth, the white flesh drawn into the black ground.

Startled, Titus caught his breath as the deaf man rose, getting to his feet so quickly that the disturbing image disappeared almost as suddenly as it had occurred.

Together they walked back in silence – and when they reached the entrance to the market, Rachel was standing there.

'Morning,' Titus said, frowning and glancing over to the deaf man. 'What brings you here again so soon?'

Her eyes were dark, shadowed, tired. She's worried about something, Titus realized, something that matters a great deal to her.

'I just wanted to have one last look,' Rachel said quietly.

Titus could *feel* the deaf man watching her.

'Well, that's OK. I'll go with you, luv,' the old man said hurriedly.

But as the words left his lips, Kaine Lukes moved over to Rachel and took her arm.

'Come on.'

She blinked slowly, like someone half asleep, then walked away with him.

Anxious, Titus fell into step behind them, his voice edgy: 'Hey, come and have a cup of tea. Both of you. It's cold and I could do with the company.'

Rachel glanced over her shoulder. She seemed resigned, oddly calm.

'I'm OK, Titus. Honestly.'

'But, we could—'

Slowly the deaf man turned, stopping Titus in his tracks. Kaine Lukes's face was impassive, the full impact of his fury coming like an odour from him. *Go away*, he willed the old man, *go away* . . .

Immediately Titus stepped back, and stood, inwardly cursing his cowardice, as he watched the couple move towards the exit.

'So?' Rachel asked as they stood on the pavement outside.

The deaf man was surprised at her lack of fear. Her eyes were shaded, her skin smelling faintly of perfume. Worn scent, dying in the cool air. Fascinated, he studied her for a long instant, noting the faint indentations by the sides of her mouth, and the fine down of hair at her temples. Then he touched her.

She jumped. Opened her eyes slightly, glanced away.

Look at me.

She did so obediently, feeling him take her hand, his fingers separating her forefinger from the others. Then he unfastened the collar of his coat and shirt. Under the lamplight Rachel

could see the white ridge of the scar running across his throat.
I'm not saying he did it, or they did, but someone *did* ...

He was studying her, watching her face carefully as he lifted her hand and stroked her forefinger slowly across the scar.

Aaah ...

The skin felt hard, rigid under her touch. Startled, Rachel tried to pull her hand away.

He held on.

Frightened, she tried to tug her hand out of his grip, her fear mushrooming. His eyes were dilated, his breathing rhythmic.

'Stop it,' she said, her voice hard with panic. 'Stop it!'

But he wouldn't stop, he merely pulled her hand upward again and then held her palm flat against his throat.

Listen.

And then he talked through her hand.

I can take the misery away, Rachel. I can take it all away ... Let me have it. Give it to me ...

The words whispered against her skin, soaked into her blood, forced themselves into every pore and frightened Rachel so much that she stepped back, taking in her breath and wrenching her hand out of his grasp. Enraged, the deaf man moved closer towards her, but she ducked out of his reach and ran, his feet echoing behind her as he followed.

She ran blindly, weaving her way between the porters who were unloading the vans outside. And she could hear the deaf man behind her, gaining on her. *Jesus, God*, she thought, *help me* ... The cold tore into her, her eyes running, the savage wind snatching at her as she paused, suddenly disorientated and rocking uneasily on the spot. *Run, Rachel, run*, she willed herself. But another voice came into her head more loudly.

Stop. Wait for me. Wait for me ...

Her mind blurred and in that instant Rachel lost all sense of reality, lurching forwards blindly into the loading bay. Startled, several porters called out to her but she didn't hear them and continued weaving an erratic course – straight into the path of an oncoming truck.

The headlights picked her out. Spotlighted her, suspended her in a pool of illumination as she stopped, rigidly immobile, the blast of a horn sounding in her head many many miles off. She knew then that she would die, and anticipated the pain, but in the moment she faced death Rachel felt herself being lifted upwards and felt the impact as her chest thudded against someone's shoulder. The movement was so fast that it seemed fluid. To be pinned in the headlights, then lifted, then carried out from the path of the truck – to be within death, and to live.

Her consciousness folded inwards like a falling tent as she was carried into the market hall and heard, like a burst of water overhead, the noise and chaos. Then just before she passed out she smelt the rough wool against her face and the shaded scent of earth on the deaf man's coat.

Harry Binky hesitated by the phone and then lifted it on the fourth ring. The young woman's voice was calm, almost detatched.

'Mr Binky?'

'Speaking.'

'It's Rachel.'

He paused for only an instant: 'Rachel. How are you?'

'Fine,' she replied without conviction. 'I just rang about Chris. I've just phoned the hospital again—'

Harry felt a slap of guilt. 'I was going to call you—'

'I want to see him, and I wondered if I could visit . . . I mean, would you mind?'

He was bemused: 'Rachel, Chris loves you—'

'Yes, I know, but the hospital said that he couldn't have visitors, except for relatives.'

'You can come with me, if you like,' he volunteered quickly. 'I could pick you up.'

She hesitated at the other end of the line. 'Would you mind if I met you there? I'd prefer to do that.'

If another person had said it, it would have sounded like a rejection, but this was Rachel.

Harry agreed reluctantly. 'OK, I just thought it would be easier for you, that was all.'

She nodded at the other end. The gesture was silent and unseen. 'So I'll see you at eight,' she said simply, ringing off.

Harry arrived to find Rachel sitting outside the intensive care unit, with her coat on her lap. She was still, her dark hair tied back at the nape of her neck. When she glanced up she smiled politely although the gesture was automatic, without feeling.

'I'm sorry I'm late,' Harry began. 'The traffic was impossible.'

Her eyes were steady; the words seemed to have no importance for her. 'Can we go in?' she asked simply.

Harry extended his hand to her, but she ignored it and stood up, keeping a yard of space between them.

'They wouldn't tell me how he was,' she offered, shrugging. 'I'm not a relative.'

Harry nodded and together they moved towards the doors of the ward, Rachel entering first. She stood unmoving in the dimmed ward for a long moment, Harry at first thinking that she was nervous before realizing that she was, in fact, merely adjusting to the difference in light. Her composure was awesome, and when she finally moved she walked straight over to Chris's bed without waiting for Harry to follow. Silently, she studied him. Then she glanced at the ventilator, then the tubes, and finally the ECG machine, her hand resting against the steel side of the cot.

'Can I talk to him?' she asked, without looking at Harry.

'He can't hear you.'

Rachel glanced at him with placid surprise. 'Oh, he can . . . I know he can.'

Her hand slid from the rail and rested lightly on the upper part of Chris's left arm. He didn't move. She leaned towards him and murmured.

'Chris? It's Rachel.' Her voice was even, without any perceptible emotion, but her hands spoke for her as her touch moved from his arm to his face. For an instant her fingers rested against his cheek and then, with infinite tenderness, she touched the taped eyelids.

The action was peculiarly moving and Harry felt oddly embarrassed by it.

'Careful.'

Rachel didn't even look at him. 'I wouldn't hurt Chris,' she replied, almost reprovingly. 'You're going to get well,' she said, ignoring Harry and talking to the still form on the bed. 'Believe me, you'll recover.'

Oh Rachel, I didn't want you to see me like this, Chris thought despairingly. *Not like this.*

'He's unconscious,' Harry said stubbornly, with a guilty nudge of envy as he watched her. 'You can't get through to him.'

Rachel closed her eyes. The gesture effectively distanced her and silenced him. Externally removed, she appeared simply to be thinking, but was actually feeling around, judging the atmosphere, sensing Chris; gently trying to find a way to reach him. He's forced into silence, she thought, so I'll talk to him in silence. I'll talk inside my head.

Chris, listen to me.

No response. No movement.

Harry watched, uncertain of what was going on, only aware that there was some connection between the two that he couldn't fully comprehend.

Chris, something odd is happening. I need your help, your advice.

Nothing.

I've seen a man, I think he wants to help me, but I'm not sure. I had a message, Chris, and it frightened me...

Rachel paused, waiting for a response. The message hadn't really frightened her, neither did the deaf man, but she believed that by making herself appear vulnerable she could reach Chris. By asking for help, she hoped that she could call him back to life. But her understanding was limited, and without realizing it she was terrifying the unconscious man. She was telling him her experience without knowing that the two of them had received the same message, and that Kaine Lukes had entered both their lives.

Rachel! Chris called suddenly, with alarm.

He knew she was there, he had known as soon as she walked into the hospital, but had been unable to communicate with her. He had listened to her instead, marvelling at her intelligence, hearing her as she talked telepathically to him. For an instant he had almost believed he could actually break through and communicate with her – until she mentioned the message and the deaf man. His wits had failed him then, panic clouding his concentration. *The deaf man had reached Rachel.* He knew without her telling him who it was – and that it was the same man who had come to him.

The knowledge shuddered through him. *Why me?* he asked himself, panicking. *Jesus, why did he want me? What have I done? Why should he come for me?* Chris's heart rate accelerated and he forced himself to calm down, thinking longingly of Rachel. But why had *she* been given only a week to live? Rachel, of all people? Rachel who had been damaged, who had suffered at the hands of others in ways he could only guess at. Why her? His thoughts shuddered. In a way it made sense that he'd received the warning. After all, he'd wanted to die; longed to escape paralysis. In fact, in the quiet of the small hours, he *still* wanted to die, wanted to give up, to let go. But not *her* surely. Not Rachel. Unless... Chris's mind scuttled clumsily under the sedation of the drugs. Perhaps she wanted to die too; perhaps she had some misery from which she wanted to escape. Something he could only guess at.

No, not Rachel. Surely she wasn't that unhappy? He thought of her; saw her face, the way she turned her head to one side when she was listening; the deep unreached calm which he had taken for strength. Damaged she might be, haunted yes, but defeated? No, not Rachel. He sifted through the little she had told him about her family. Her mother had lost her second husband and was left to look after her handicapped step-son, Leon. Chris tried to concentrate although the effort exhausted him, his thoughts jumbling under the drugs.

He had seen her step-brother only once; waiting outside Rachel's office. He had been unremarkable, dressed in jeans and listening to a Sony Walkman, his foot tapping. A little idiotic, but not conspicuously so. Unremarkable, except for the fact that on seeing him Rachel had stiffened, her conversation ceasing. They had measured each other up and their eyes had challenged each other – meeting without greeting.

Rachel had excused herself suddenly. 'I have to go, Chris.'

'I'll walk you home.'

Her gaze had been implacable. 'No, I'll go home alone.'

He had thought she wanted to go with Leon but she had walked off, away from him and passed her step-brother without even glancing in his direction. Leon seemed surprised by her action and was obviously uncertain how to react, waiting for an uncomfortably long moment before following her.

Why had she behaved that way? Chris wondered. Why? Was she afraid of him? No, it wasn't fear. Rachel's action had been one of dismissal, not intimidation. Her gesture, her almighty coolness had implied disgust . . . Disgust. The word yawned into Chris's head, together with a thundering sense of unease. Oh God, he thought, I know. *I know*:

Chris, listen to me. It's Rachel. I need you, you have to get well.

He felt her hand against his arm and ached to reach out to her, but his muscles refused to move, his eyes blind under the tape. His heart seemed to fill with a rushing of blood, his skin fired with heat. *Rachel*, he pleaded inside his head, *Rachel* . . .

'I think you should go now,' the doctor said suddenly, glancing at the ECG machine. The monitor was showing excessive activity, Chris's heart rate accelerating, the green line bleeping erratically. 'He needs rest.'

Harry looked at the machine. He too could see the sudden reaction and touched Rachel's shoulder.

'We have to go.'

She jumped, turning away from him, her eyes fixed on the monitor. 'He can hear, I told you!' she said excitedly, for once expressing emotion. 'Chris *can* hear us.'

'You have to go,' the doctor repeated, ushering them away from the bed.

Rachel moved reluctantly away, her head still turned towards the bed where Chris lay. She felt oddly removed from the scene; she never even noticed Harry's hand on her arm, or the fluster of movement from nurses as they gathered around the bed. All her thoughts, all her strength, centred on the still figure of Chris Binky. Her energy bolted from her to him; it galvanized him, and for an instant she heard his voice calling her.

Rachel!

She felt the increasing pressure of Harry's hand on her arm and impatiently shrugged it off, turning back, trying to return to the bed, but he barred her way.

'We have to go!'

Chris's body was hidden, surrounded by medical staff, but she could still hear him calling to her.

Rachel, be careful. Rachel...

Her mouth opened, helplessness making her desperate. If she could just be with him, talk to him, comfort him. If only she could be with him on her own, then she could help him. No one understood, no one. They just didn't understand how it was between them. Her eyes fought to catch sight of Chris, but there were too many people around him and she could only catch glimpses of him – an arm, the shape of his feet under the sheet, the top of his head. Fragments of him, little particles. He *understands*, she wanted to scream, he can hear and feel... Oh God, she thought hopelessly, he's alive in there, and they're going to kill him.

'Chris!' Rachel shouted suddenly, her voice gigantic in the cocooned ward.

Startled, the medical staff turned towards her impatiently, the doctor gesturing to Harry as he struggled to get Rachel out.

But Chris had heard her call out his name and answered her. From somewhere in his own panic and desperation he conjured up the strength to throw his thoughts into her mind, and she heard him. She heard the words and winced at the impact, his voice coming loudly and clearly into her head.

Rachel, get help!

Chapter Nine

Kaine Lukes made no reference to the incident at Smithfield in his journal. He had other concerns on his mind.

All of them know now. All six of them have been told that they have one week to live. And how frightened they all are. Now that they see the one thing they didn't value threatened, how they all panic. We come into life without asking permission; we are born without earning our existence, and so we never appreciate it. If we had to fight for it, to struggle for it, to earn it, we would never give in so easily. No one would wish to be dead if they had fought to be born. No one would wallow in misery if they knew that at any time, their lives would end.

They don't know what I want. They don't know what the message really means. All they want now is to live. After they had all wished to die at some point, now how they want to live . . . One week left. No, actually less than a week. Four days, to be exact. Four days to find a way to stay alive; four days to find a way to value what they never earned and what they once found so easy to give up. They don't understand any of it. Yet.

So it goes on. Six people, six hearing people looking to live. Looking to survive. And how? How will they do it? Some will try to cheat, some to bargain, some to plead, and they will all turn to others to try and find help. Just as, in the end, they will all turn to me.

I see six people coming; six hearing people coming. Coming to the deaf man, in the deaf house.

Jeanie Maas walked into the hospital waiting room at nine a.m., glancing round and taking a seat by the door. She thought it was the best thing to do. That way the nurse would see her first and maybe, just maybe, it would mean that she could be seen first. She doubted it though. Due to a myriad cuts the hospital was under pressure, the different waiting rooms all amalgamated into one so that there were nearly thirty people all crowded together, waiting for their turn to be called.

She needed her hearing aid repairing, that was all. But not all to her. It might not be a matter of life or death but it was of great import to Jeanie. After all, it was difficult enough to answer the phone normally, now it was downright impossible, and Ahlia had been less than patient.

'Go to the hospital and get it fixed!' she had said that morning, more than usually jumpy. 'I need you, Jeanie. You know that.'

'I'll go as soon as I can—'

'No,' Ahlia had replied shortly. 'Go now.'

So she had, arriving soon afterwards to take her place in the queue. Mournfully, Jeanie glanced around. A pregnant woman looked back at her dispassionately, a man with his arm in a plaster cast trying to turn over the pages of his magazine. The room sizzled with resentment, and after another moment Jeanie made her way to the hospital canteen. A cup of tea would help to pass the time. She glanced round, looking for somewhere to sit and then sat down opposite a young dark woman.

Curiously, Jeanie studied her. About twenty-four, twenty-five, she reckoned, with that straight dark hair which went grey early.

Apparently unaware of the scrutiny, Rachel continued to stare at the table in front of her, her ears straining for the sound of Harry's voice. But she knew it wouldn't come; knew she had ruined her chance of visiting Chris again. She shouldn't have called out like that, it wasn't like her. She should have been calm, just as she usually was, but when she heard him call to her . . .

'Pardon?' Rachel said, suddenly aware that someone was talking to her. 'I'm sorry, what did you say?'

'I asked who you'd come to see, luv.'

'A . . . friend,' Rachel replied, studying the old woman in front of her. Jeanie was wearing glasses, her hands toying idly with her hearing aid, a misshapen felt hat pulled low over her forehead.

'Been waiting long?'

Rachel shrugged. 'Over an hour.'

'Over an hour!' Jeanie said, snorting with disgust. 'I can't afford to wait that long.' Her curiosity was tickled. 'Do they know you're here?'

'Oh yes, they know,' Rachel said with resignation.

Jeanie misread the tone in her voice. 'I'm sorry, luv, I didn't mean to pry.'

'Oh, you weren't,' Rachel responded kindly. 'I'm waiting to see my boyfriend.'

Jeanie smiled. Kids.

'What's up with him?'

'He was knocked off his motorbike,' Rachel said calmly. Too calmly. 'He's on a life support machine.'

Jeanie leaned towards her, trying to catch every word.

'I'm sorry . . . really sorry,' she said, touching the back of the young woman's hand. Rachel was surprised to find that she didn't move away. 'It must be hard for you.'

Unexpectedly, Rachel's eyes filled and she stared down at the floor.

'How long's he been here?'

Her voice was remote when she answered. 'Only two days.'

'Bet it feels like weeks, hey, luv?'

Rachel swallowed, fighting an overwhelming impulse to cry. The moments yawned out as she struggled to control herself, the man across the waiting room dropping his magazine and swearing softly.

Disgusted, Jeanie raised her eyebrows.

'Typical,' she whispered, eyeing the man's torn jeans and leather jacket. 'Still, what d'you expect from a pig, but a grunt?'

Laughing, Rachel glanced round. 'Would you like a drink? I mean, I was just about to go for another coffee – d'you want one?'

Jeanie nodded, smiling, her false teeth impressively even and large. 'Oooh, that would be nice, luv. Milk and two sugars, please.' Hurriedly she rummaged in her purse. 'Here's the money, have yours on me.'

Rachel hesitated. 'No, I couldn't—'

Jeanie would brook no argument. 'Yes, you can. Never look a gift horse in the mouth, that's what I always say.'

Rachel returned only moments later, offering a polystyrene cup to Jeanie. 'I warn you, it's vile.'

'Oh well, it'll do to pass the time,' she replied easily, putting her handbag by her feet and turning to the girl. The steam from the cup rose up and momentarily misted her glasses as she sipped at the coffee.

'I'm Rachel,' said the girl suddenly, introducing herself. 'Rachel Crossley.'

Her companion smiled. 'And I'm Jeanie, Jeanie Maas.'

'As in the bar?' Rachel queried.

Jeanie chuckled. 'I wish a had a fiver for every time someone asked me that,' she said. 'No, it's spelt M – A – A – S. It's Dutch.'

Rachel opened her eyes wide. 'You don't look Dutch.'

'Oh, and how is someone Dutch supposed to look?' Jeanie asked quizzically. 'Should I be wearing a white cap and carrying a milk pail?' She paused, her thoughts wandering. 'There used to be some cheese with the picture of a Dutch girl on it; some silly bitch with a cow standing behind her and a row of mountains.' Again, Rachel laughed. 'I never could stand her, simpering away like that.' She pulled a gormless face. 'Put me off cheese for life, she did.'

Cautiously Rachel sipped her coffee, longing for the woman to carry on talking. She was light-hearted, amusing – and she kept other thoughts at bay.

'So what do you do?'

'Me?' Jeanie queried. 'I'm a cleaner. I work one day a week for a priest in Peckham, Father Michael,' she grinned rakishly. 'Now, *he*'s a incredible-looking man. Wicked-looking, if you know what I mean. Not like a priest at all. When I was young there was a movie star called Tyrone Power – well, Father Michael looks like that.'

Rachel smiled.

'You think I'm joking!' Jeanie admonished her. 'I'm not. I work for two of the best-looking people in London. No kidding.'

'So who's the other one?' Rachel asked.

'Ahlia Bell. I'm her housekeeper in Cleveland Square – she doesn't know about Father Michael. I let her think he's some old duffer, due to peg out at any time.'

Rachel leaned forward in her seat, fascinated. 'What's Mrs Bell like?'

Jeanie thought for a long moment before replying. 'Very beautiful. I mean that, too. Not just attractive, but beautiful. Men love her. It's like Beauty and the Beast in our place. No prizes for guessing who's the Beast,' Jeanie said, grinning good-naturedly. 'Is your young man handsome?'

Rachel sat unmoving in her seat. She didn't think of Chris, instead she saw the spool of wool in her dream, watching it unravel almost as though it was on the floor in front of her. And then she saw Leon. And finally she saw the deaf man.

'Well, *is* your young man handsome?'

Rachel turned back to Jeanie and the image vanished. She was just an old woman, asking about Chris. Nothing else. She was being kind, that was all.

'He's very attractive.'

'Oooh. Blond or dark?'

'Sort of mid colours. But tall.'

'And how old is he?'

'Twenty-five.'

'Is he smart?'

Rachel paused. 'Special.'

'Like how?'

Oh, like *how*? Rachel wondered. 'He's very careful. You know, he never says anything to hurt anyone. He's trying to be a writer. His father's Harry Binky, the MP.'

'Harry Binky!' Jeanie repeated, stunned. Harry Binky, one of Ahlia's ex-lovers. Harry pompous Binky, who always left the toilet seat up.

Rachel looked at her in surprise: 'Do you know him?'

'My employer does – or rather, she *did*,' Jeanie replied, looking around her. 'But I don't understand, Harry Binky's an important man, so why isn't his son in a private clinic somewhere?'

'They can't move Chris at the moment – he's too sick.'

Jeanie considered the information carefully. What a coincidence. Who would have believed it? Harry Binky.

'So, why are you here?' Rachel asked, suddenly changing the subject.

'My hearing,' Jeanie said, sighing. 'I've been having trouble with this thing.' She waved the hearing aid in front of Rachel. 'Bloody thing's more trouble than it's worth.'

A slow memory trickled inside Rachel's head. *Deafness.* Loss of sound.

'I couldn't hear a damn thing the other night,' Jeanie went on, trying to explain what had happened, trying to make it light-hearted, unimportant. 'It just packed up on me and I was left high and dry. It's a curse, not being able to hear properly.'

You have one week to live.

The thought entered both their heads at the same instant, and left them both silent. Without understanding the sudden unease between them, Jeanie struggled to sound cheerful.

'But then, what can you expect? These things happen as you get older.'

Rachel could hardly hear her any more; she was thinking of the board room and the sudden turning off of sound. The deafness swallowing her whole. And she was thinking of the deaf man... She stared at Jeanie and wanted suddenly to confide, to cling on to the woman, to beg comfort.

But she didn't, and instead Jeanie sat looking at her hearing aid, her head bowed, apparently unconcerned. But she too wanted to reach out. As scared as Rachel, she too wanted to seek comfort, but she couldn't... Both of them twitched with uncertainty; both longing to take from the other. Yet neither moved and, only inches apart, remained petrified in their own anxiety.

'I don't have many friends,' Rachel said, surprising herself.

Jeanie nodded. 'Same here.'

'Why is that?'

'Some people are just born that way, luv,' Jeanie explained, putting the empty polystyrene cup on to the windowsill behind her.

'I can talk to you easily enough,' Rachel went on, praying

that the woman would understand what she was saying *under* the words.

Jeanie did. 'Where did you say you lived?'

'Maida Vale.'

'Which isn't a long way from Cleveland Square, is it?' Jeanie said, tentatively risking rejection. 'You could come and say hello sometime. If you wanted, that is. I'm usually banging around.'

Rachel hesitated: 'Well . . . I . . .'

'Just a thought—'

'No,' Rachel said hurriedly. 'I *want* to come and see you. Really,' her voice was eager. 'I don't have anyone to talk to, you see, and since Chris's accident . . .'

'You need to talk,' Jeanie said quietly, dipping into her pocket and bringing out a paper bag. 'Liquorice?' she offered.

Rachel shook her head and watched as Jeanie began to chew. The sweet darkened her lips, her false teeth clicking intermittently.

'I'm at number 54, Cleveland Square,' she said matter-of-factly. 'In the basement. You just drop in any time and we'll have a cuppa.' Her head jerked towards the machine in the corridor. 'It'll be better than that muck, I promise.'

'And you won't mind?'

Jeanie stared hard at Rachel's face. The smell of hay and the dark sound of a boy whistling spun in her head. *I was your age once; I was young, once. But now I'm old and frightened and I need you, Rachel Crossley. I need you.*

'No, luv,' Jeanie said quietly. 'I won't mind.'

'Well, I bloody do!'

'What!'

'I need you!' Ahlia wailed, her nerves shuddering. 'You said you were coming round tonight—'

'I have to work.'

'Since when was work important to you?' she snapped.

'Ahlia, listen to me—'

'Why? You never say anything worth listening to,' she retorted, violently slamming down the phone and leaning breathlessly against the table in the kitchen. Bloody fool, who the hell did he think he was, messing her around like that? She wouldn't have it. She bloody wouldn't. *No* man messed her around without regretting it.

A plane passed overhead.

Or did it?

Startled, Ahlia glanced up, but the sound had gone, and only the expensive white ceiling looked back at her. Picking up her handbag she turned slowly, her reflection mirrored in the surface of the fridge, the cooker, the microwave and the back door. Lots of Ahlias, looking back at her. Hurriedly she moved out of the kitchen – and then in the hall, she hesitated.

Why in God's name had she had mirrors put everywhere? she wondered suddenly, knowing full well that her vanity demanded a constant reiteration of her beauty. Jeanie might walk past with her eyes fixed straight ahead, but Ahlia needed to see everywhere that her magic was intact. But now the mirrors annoyed her and she turned away, irritated, letting out a hiss of real anger as she came face to face with herself again.

In the end her temper forced her out of the house and into the street, where she stood for a moment trying to collect her thoughts. The sensation of dread had been increasing steadily, an omen of foreboding gaining on her. Fiercely Ahlia strode along, tugging on her coat and pulling her handbag on to her shoulder. Maybe she could walk off her temper, dodge the inevitable... The day was unremarkable, Cleveland Square quiet apart from a removal van parked outside the corner house. Absent-mindedly, Ahlia walked on, an hour passing. She wasn't thinking of where she was going, she was just walking, passing all the familiar expensive streets and then stopping when she came into unfamiliar territory. Surprised, she glanced at her watch and realized with amazement that she had been walking for nearly two hours.

What the hell was she doing? she wondered disbelievingly. A dull wash of unease crept up her spine. Something was coming, something bad... *Stop it!* she warned herself, fighting panic. *Stop it! It's nothing. Just your imagination.* But it was never *just* her imagination... She glanced round the street, looking for a taxi. The area was unknown to her, the area code on the street name telling her that she was in Peckham. Peckham! she thought disbelievingly. How in God's name did she get to Peckham?

Ahlia paused uncertainly on the street, a billboard towering behind her, a pub on the opposite corner. Anxiously she glanced round for a cab, but there wasn't one in sight, only a bus stop already sporting a growing queue. Suddenly aware of her expensive clothes and jewellery, Ahlia nervously began to walk on, passing the curious gaze of the bus queue, her eyes raking the street ahead for a signpost. Peckham! she thought again, wasn't this where Jeanie's priest was? She frowned, trying to remember the name. The church of *what*? What *was* its name?

Hurrying on, Ahlia ignored a man who called out to her from a shop doorway and kept looking for a cab. The man called out to her again, fascinated by the fabulous creature who had suddenly materialized. Ahlia automatically quickened her step, realizing as she did so that he was following her. Tightening her grip on her handbag, she fixed her eyes straight ahead, her footsteps sounding loudly on the pavement. Surely a taxi would come? Swing round the corner at any moment? The winter street ended suddenly, forking into two other identical streets, leading into others, all similiar... And as she stopped, wondering which way to go, the man paused several steps behind her, calling out again, making Ahlia chose, *forcing* her to move on.

She took the right fork. The street was indistinguishable from the last, the sky sullen with approaching rain. *I could go into a pub*, Ahlia thought, *and phone for a taxi from there* . . . The man was still following her. Logic told her to slow down, to appear nonchalant. Didn't they say that a woman should never act like a victim? But she *felt* like a victim, Ahlia thought despairingly. She didn't feel strong, she felt threatened.

So when she saw the church she stopped, light-headed with relief, and hurried up to the wrought-iron gate, pushing at it fiercely. St Barnabas. *St Barnabas!* Ahlia thought incredulously. That was the name of the church she had been trying to remember all along. This was where Jeanie worked for the priest. Ahlia's spirits rose. Maybe she had been wrong for once; maybe her unease was misplaced. Maybe she had been guided here; maybe a priest was exactly what she needed to help her; to explain what was happening to her. The gate swung back moodily, the short gravel path to the church mottled with weeds and a couple of empty crisp packets. Her feet scuffing on the chippings, Ahlia rushed on, finally grasping the black iron handle of the door, turning it hurriedly, and walking in. Only then did Ahlia glance back. The man who had followed her was gone.

A resonant voice sounding out from the belly of the church made her jump.

'Can I help you?'

Ahlia turned, a smile of apology already on her lips.

'No, I—' She stopped short, watching as the priest walked towards her.

'Surely I can do something to help you?' he asked, his voice implying a need to help. A plea to be useful.

Her expression was incredulous. Sly old woman, Ahlia thought. Sly, wicked Jeanie, letting her think that the priest was old, infirm . . . just wait until she got home. Wouldn't she have a thing or two to say! Jeanie had been lying to her! Keeping the truth from her – when they usually shared everything. It was too bad of her. Almost cruel . . .

Father Michael walked down the aisle slowly, Ahlia feeling, rather than noticing, the impact of his appearance. Knowing herself remarkable, she had seldom found others as stunning, and was, in one shimmering instant, as impressed by his beauty as much as by her own. This man, this pungent reminder of all she valued in herself, mesmerized her. He was her bodily equal, and more – he was a priest and, as such, could offer a sexual conquest beyond anything she had achieved before. The bad dreams, the events of the past two days had unbalanced her – so she responded in the way she always did, not by seeking a solution, but by swamping her anxiety with sex. Besides, it would be a way of paying Jeanie back. Of teaching her a lesson, of making sure that she never kept any secrets from her again . . .

And while Ahlia thought all this Father Michael paused in front of her and felt within himself the drumming of resurrected desire. He had not slept the previous night after seeing the man consumed by fire in his church; he had not even been able to turn off his light, afraid that once he did so he would see the figure with its head thrown back and feel himself suffocating slowly under the pressing stench of earth. He had whimpered softly through the dawn hours and scourged himself, and fingered his crucifix – but without comfort. God and the church offered no peace. He was damned and took his damnation with him everywhere.

Everywhere . . . He had finally realized the full horror of that truth when he rose at six. But even as he realized it, the priest knew that he would not give up. He wanted, fiercely, blindly and illogically, to live. He *had* to live . . . But he had been given only a week and the days were already passing.

There had to be an answer! he thought wildly, *there had to be!* He knew he couldn't find it in himself, or in his faith; so as dawn began to soak into the ending night he decided that he would find the solution *in someone else.*

The solution. Or the absence of fear. And whichever it turned out to be, it was his escape. So he looked at Ahlia and wanted her, knowing, then, how to achieve forgetfulness.

Although she had waited patiently for hours, the doctors refused to let Rachel see Chris again. Disconsolately, she left the hospital, her mind turning suddenly to the memory of the accident at Smithfield that morning. Terror immobilized her again; the screech of the brakes, the blaze of the oncoming headlamps. She saw the truck coming for her, the wheels on the black road... *But the deaf man had saved her. Why? Why?...* Rachel stared ahead blindly. *Who in God's name was he?*

The question shimmered in front of her and before she realized it, she had driven to Smithfield. But this time she did not approach him. Instead she waited until he left, then followed him on foot. Keeping her distance as he walked ahead, she crossed the streets he crossed, paused when he paused, and when he finally reached the house, she watched him enter.

The front garden was empty; a dry lawn only, without flower beds, and the path which led to the house was gravelled, without weeds. Shuttered windows added to the atmosphere of neglect, although a single light over the front door and smoke rising from a high chimney gave the place an unexpectedly domestic air. Frowning, Rachel pulled her coat around her, the February cold of the morning striking the exposed skin at her throat.

It was only then that her courage faltered. The house was forbidding, bleak, and her determination was suddenly replaced by a crucifying anxiety. If she continued now, what would happen? *How close have you got to him? How close?*... What would happen if she went into that house? If she went into *his* house? ... Rachel hesitated. The glare of the late morning light invaded the dark garden, shadows sliding back. Then suddenly – out of the corner of her eye – she saw a movement and gazed down disbelievingly at the pathway.

Against the dull grey of the gravel a ball of wool was unwinding; a red thread extending from her feet to the closed front door.

Transfixed, Rachel stared at the cord, her breathing short, panicked, her lips parted. She felt the deaf man watching her, willing her onwards. But when she finally glanced up there was no figure standing at a window and the door was closed. But the porch light still burned. The house, she realized, was holding its breath. It was waiting.

Repelled, Rachel backed away from the red thread and moved towards an area of wasted hedge. Cautiously, she peered through a gap in the vegetation directly in front of her. The back garden was as untended as the front, but lacked the overgrown lushness of neglect. Instead it was sick with emptiness. The earth which had once supported flowers was now bare, *although the beds were scored with markers*. Curious, Rachel stared at them. The slats of wood had been set out in meticulous lines, arranged carefully in rows, and although some were worn and splitting, others seemed new and freshly painted. But for *what*? she wondered. There were no bushes, no shrubs, no greenery at all.

So what *had* the deaf man been marking out? Seeds? Little grains of vegetation under the earth which would break through in spring? Or perhaps vegetables, lettuces creeping up through the shifting earth? But she thought not, and suddenly tensed. In the dull winter light the markers glowed luminously like headstones, graded in colour from dull ochre to a blinding and unearthly bone white, the black printing indecipherable.

And it was then that Rachel recoiled, suddenly violently afraid, her hands releasing their grip on the gap in the hedge. The privet snapped savagely back into place, the branches welding toether, the hedge turning her away and guarding the house behind. And she knew then that the deaf man was watching her; and that he was waiting.

Finally Jeanie was ushered in to see the doctor. She didn't like the surgery. It was cramped, dusty, and without windows, the walls sporting a few plastic-coated medical charts of the inner ear. Thoughtfully, Jeanie sucked a piece of liquorice from under her false teeth, her hands crossing and re-crossing themselves on her bag. It was a bloody disgrace letting the room get in a state like this. All it needed was a dust. Unhygienic, she called it. Her thoughts hummed in time to the hum of the fluorescent lighting above. She was a nice young woman, that Rachel Crossley, all her life ahead of her . . .

Drowsily, Jeanie closed her eyes. The room was stuffy without a window to open and the air seemed muzzy with chemical smells. Why did they have to keep anyone waiting this long? she thought, yawning noisily. Why not just say come at twelve instead of ten?

The room's cream-coloured walls blurred before her eyes as she fought sleep, the charts childishly garish, their drawings leaping out from the wall like holograms. Slowly, Jeanie felt herself doze, her left hand sliding from her bag on to her lap, her breathing deep and rhythmic.

The doctor was harassed and discourteous, his sudden entry startling her. He came in without uttering a word, read Jeanie's notes, picked up her hearing aid, and then began to tinker with the mechanism. Over his shoulder loomed the chart of the inner ear bones, the painted ear around it gigantically large. If I had ears that size I wouldn't need a bloody hearing aid, Jeanie thought to herself, struggling not to laugh. Flaming doctors. Who did they think they were? Moody, every one of them. Treated you like cattle.

The doctor continued to fiddle with the hearing aid, his head bent down over the desk where he worked, his white coat in need of an iron. Jeanie thought of her father, wondered what George Maas would have said about that. Unprofessional and ungentlemanly, no doubt. A man should take care of his appearance – especially a medical man. The warmth of the room was increasing, the radiator beside Jeanie throwing out waves of stifling heat. They talk about having no money in hospitals, but if they turned down the heating they'd save a bloody fortune, she thought, suppressing a yawn.

Oh, why didn't he get on with it? The other doctors never took this long, Jeanie thought impatiently. It was only a sodding hearing aid, not a hip replacement. The heat was still rising, Jeanie unfastening her coat and pushing back her hat although the doctor seemed immune to the temperature and simply continued to work, occasionally glancing over to her medical notes. Finally, after another five minutes, he turned and leaned forwards, inserting the hearing aid into Jeanie's ear with practised ease.

Then he turned it on.

Don't go with the boys up the hill, Jeanie.

YOU HAVE ONE WEEK TO LIVE.

And then a whistle, a boy's whistle, and the sound of a nightjar in an evening field.

Rigid, Jeanie sat in her seat as her head filled with the babble of noise. Her first instinct was to call out – but she couldn't, neither could she wrench the device from her ear. Her hands tried to move, but they seemed paralysed, and just lay uselessly on her lap while the sounds poured maliciously, and piercingly loud, into her head.

Don't go with the boys up the hill, Jeanie.
Just be grateful it wasn't you . . . it wasn't you . . .
You can't tell, Jeanie. You can't. What would people say if they knew? . . .

Gasping, Jeanie looked pleadingly towards the doctor, but he had moved away, apparently oblivious to her distress, his back still turned to her while she sat transfixed in the treatment chair and the sounds bored into her head through the hearing aid.

A nightjar sang again, and then came the noise of fire, flames crackling. Boys calling, the wood splitting and dry after a choking summer. Crackling hay splitting in the heat.

Don't go with the boys up the hill, Jeanie . . .

She could feel her eyes fill and useless tears well up behind her glasses as she continued to listen, unable to turn off the hearing aid or even gesture to the doctor. The noises were so loud that Jeanie could no longer hear or see anything else, no hospital noises, nothing, only the scream of memory and the burning heat of the radiator filling the tiny room and suffocating her.

Then finally the doctor turned. He frowned, seeing the distress on Jeanie's face and rushed over to her, snapping off the hearing aid and taking it out of her ear as Jeanie's head slumped forward on to her chest. The noises ceased then. Nothing, only stillness, and silence. The blessed noiselessness and end of sound. For an instant, too much in shock to move, Jeanie could only gaze at the doctor and wince as he bent down and laid his hands over her ears.

She expected further pain, excruciating distress, but his flesh seemed to alter as he touched her and became water. It was liquid and soothed; it lapped at her brain; it curled into the tortured corners of her ears and licked them; it bathed and cooled her; Jeanie's tears drying on her face, her flushed skin chilling under the touch – and in that instant she fell asleep again.

The door opened suddenly, the blast of a voice startling Jeanie and forcing her eyes open.

'Well now, Miss Maas. How are you today?' a large, red-headed doctor boomed.

Jeanie shuddered at the onslaught, trying vainly to marshal her thoughts. The room was unusually cold; the radiator turned off.

'I'll just have a little look at that hearing aid of yours.'

Jeanie found it difficult to talk. 'But the doctor's already seen to it—'

He frowned impatiently.

'I'm your doctor, Miss Maas. No one's been in to see you yet,' he said, and then smiled, exquisitely patronizing. 'I think we might have kept you waiting a little too long today. You've been day dreaming, I'm afraid.'

Chapter Ten

Rachel had never thought of losing Chris. He was too young, *they* were too young. People their age didn't die. Or did they? *You have one week to live.* Rachel frowned, a hollow emptiness opening inside her. Would she die in a week? No, now it was less than a week, only four days. Or was it Chris who would die? Or was it both of them?

She couldn't live without him, she knew that now. She had no other love, no other security except for Chris. Her mother and she were not close, and at home there was Leon, still grinning madly, turning over sick memories in his sick little brain. I won't tell because of what it would do to my mother, Rachel swore, but I'll never forget what you did to me. Never.

It had taken some time for her to trust a man, the hideous luck of her childhood finally changing when she met Chris. Their lovemaking had been tentative, careful, Chris quick to realize how fragile she was. He was curious too, but never asked her outright why she was so nervous. I'll tell him in my own time, Rachel reassured herself, when the moment's right, I'll tell him.

Oh, but the moment came and the moment went. And now Rachel knew that when Chris recovered – because he would, *she* would see to that – then she would tell him. Chris, of all people, would understand. He wouldn't be disgusted, he would know that what had happened had nothing to do with her. Others wouldn't have believed it, but Chris would know the truth.

Just as he had known that she was there in the hospital, calling him. The nexus binding them had gone beyond normal life. Now she could hear him calling in her head. *Get help* ... Get help I will, Chris, she promised, I will. But where? The deaf man, where else?

You have one week to live.

Rachel paused. Was it him? Was it Kaine Lukes who'd sent the message? But *why*? Why would he do it? And if it *was* him, why would he have saved her? No one saved someone they wanted to destroy. *Unless there was goodness in him somewhere.* Yes, Rachel thought, there *was* some goodness in him – and that meant she had a chance. She would go to him, appeal to that tiny speck of kindness in him. Beg him for help ... Hurriedly she made her way back to the deaf house, standing on the pavement and staring up at the blank windows. *I came back*, she said to herself, suspecting that he could pick up her thoughts. *I came back to ask for help.*

I know you're in there, I know you're waiting for me ... she paused, her heart sounding in her ears. *Go on*, she willed herself, *he's the only one who can help you now. Don't show him you're afraid. Go on* ...

I knew Rachel would be the first. She had to be the first to come to me ... Come on! Keep on walking, it's only a few yards more, up the pathway, up to the door. There, you've nearly made it even though you don't really want to come. You don't like the house, do you? That's understandable, I know how forbidding she can be. But she LOVES, Rachel, she loves. And she has *loved me; behind her windows and doors; under her ceilings and against her walls; she* has *loved me. Could you love me as well? I think maybe you could, you could feed me anyway, keep me alive, give me all your despair, let me suck the misery out of you.*

You think I have goodness in me. But you're wrong. How wrong you'll have to discover yourself... See how the wind moves the tree branches by the gate? See how it skims the crown of the hedge and buffets the wooden markers in the garden behind? Hear it rattle the slats? Hear it? How does it sound to you? Tell me... You can hear it, Rachel, I can't... I have something for you. For your bravery. A little reward for courage. I admire that, Rachel. I've always had courage myself. In this world it's courage that pumps the heart and rules the brain. Not talent, not instinct, but courage. Go on, knock; call to me. Knock and I'll open the door to you. Knock... I'll feel it. The sound will reach me, be certain of that.

Aaah... there it is. The knock at the door. And so it begins for you, Rachel, so it begins.

'You need a sabbatical.'

'I need a fucking psychiatrist,' Harry Binky thought wildly, staring out through the taxi window as it approached Westminster Bridge.

'You've had a bad shock, Harry,' the man went on. 'It's terrible, what happened to Chris. How is he?'

'No change, Gordon. No change.' Harry replied, glancing at his agent and noticing a minor rash around his collar. Hardly due to his age, he thought grimly. Not exactly a rush of teenage acne; more likely junk food.

'He'll recover, you'll see,' Gordon went on, violently embarrassed, his words inadequate, forced. 'Chris is young. The young can get over anything.'

He droned on uselessly, the taxi stopping at some lights, Harry's mind wandering back to the time he had first been elected as an MP. Chris had been away on holiday that week with friends and Harry had, in his triumph, bought a new flat in Westminster, hurrying to get it ready for his son's return. It was on the fifth floor of a modern block, with a drawing room whose walls were composed mainly of windows, the furniture modernistic, hasty. It was a bachelor's home, but not entirely. Segregated off was a bedroom with its own bathroom and study – for Chris.

Harry had had the common sense to leave the decoration in there alone. If it was to be Chris's area, then it had to be in Chris's taste. Childishly he had waited for his son to come back, picking him up from the airport and driving him to their new home. Chris walked in slowly, absorbing the new furniture, the views over London, the bridges lighted against the night sky. He saw the moulded library shelves and the Etruscan busts, the floral arrangements, the latest video and compact disc technology, and he remembered the flat where they had lived after his mother left. The flat with the kitchen which smelt of old cooking fat and the bathroom with the water heater and the sloping roof. And he wondered if his father would be any happier here.

'Is it yours?'

Harry hesitated, remembering the old joke about the Irish girl who told her father she was pregnant. *Are you sure it's yours?* he'd asked her.

'Of course it's mine,' he said, a little churlishly. 'I mean, it's *ours*.' He hurried his son along the corridor and opened the door which lead to his apartment. 'I didn't decorate it, I wanted you to chose the things you wanted . . .' he trailed off, embarrassed, afraid that his gift might seem banal. Maybe his son didn't want to be with him any more. But if Chris left, what was there? *Who* was there? Without Chris there was only him, alone with his own thoughts.

'So, what do you think?' Harry had asked his son anxiously.

Chris walked around his rooms and then turned back to his father. He said nothing, merely walked over to Harry and put his arms around him. It was the first time his son had touched him for years.

'I think a holiday would do you good,' Gordon went on. 'Just for a weekend somewhere.'

Harry sighed, his thoughts pulled back to the present. The platitudes! Christ, nothing changed, did it? People mouthing off without thinking.

'Use your head, Gordon. I have to be here. I have to be in London so I can see Chris—'

'So take a few days off from work and stay at home.'

Harry's temper flared: 'I don't want to stay home! What would I do? Rattle round the bloody place all day? Work's the only way to take my mind off the situation. Besides, I have to think of something to do. I don't have time to waste—' he stopped, suddenly aware that he was about to give himself away.

The message, at first so casually dismissed, had left its indelible mark on his subconscious and was now playing frantically on his nerves. *You have one week to live.* One week, Harry thought despairingly. No, less now. Four days – and this idiot was telling him to take time off.

'I'm sure Chris will recover,' Gordon said fatuously. 'I don't think you should worry about . . . well, you know . . . I mean, no one said anything about time, did they? I mean, about the time he had left?' he blustered, the skin of his neck reddening. 'After all, he's expected to recover . . . isn't he, Harry?'

We are talking at cross purposes, Harry thought idly. As ever. My agent is babbling whilst my son is dangerously ill and I have four days left on this earth. He groaned inwardly, his gaze turning away from Gordon and out into the street outside. There were a group of tourists standing outside Simpsons, looking into the window where some dummies nodded their heads inanely. Dummies of famous people, all nodding like morons... Suddenly Harry wanted to escape and on a whim, jumped out of the taxi at the lights, Gordon's startled face staring out of the back window as he ran across Piccadilly and paused outside Boots.

Four days left, Harry thought again. What could he do in four days? Who could he turn to? If Chris had been well – *if* – he would have asked his son for advice. Chris would have known what to do. Chris was special like that. Intuitive. All the things Harry used to sneer at. Until now. Now he needed his son's sensitivity; needed him to keep the demons away.

Harry thought suddenly of the priest. He could go to see him, ask for comfort. He had been arrogant before, unyielding. But not now, not after his collapse in the House. Now he felt anything but arrogant. Perhaps the message was a warning, that was all. No one would send a message like that unless there was a way to avoid the outcome. It made no sense otherwise. Unless the message came from someone wanting revenge.

Could it be Gregor Fylding? Harry wondered, cold with unease. Could it be the old man coming back? Harry walked along aimlessly. If it *was* Fylding, what could he do to appease him? Give him back his money? Harry snorted, surprised by his own stupidity. You can't repay the dead; they don't have bank accounts... So if it wasn't Fylding, who was it? A relative of his? Someone who had discovered what he had done? Or was it Gayle?

The thought nearly comforted him. If it was Gayle; if it *was* his ex-wife, he could deal with that. Pay her off. Set her up somewhere comfortably. Buy her a house, a car. Open a bank account.

'Look where you're going!'

Harry jumped back, startled by a young woman with a

Fortnum and Mason carrier bag. He stared at her. Was it her? Was she about to say something to him?

But the girl simply stared at him, then walked off with a snort of irritation.

God, get a grip! Harry admonished himself. She was a shopper, that was all, not some kind of supernatural visitor. He stopped, glancing into a nearby window where a gilded angel stretched its arms protectively over a selection of confectionery. No, it wasn't Gayle, it couldn't be. She had remarried. And Gregor Fylding was dead. The spire of St James's church looked black against the daylight, the roof ebony. I have to find help, Harry thought helplessly, I have to. But not here. Not in some expensive church in W1. His thoughts winged back to Peckham, to the mottled little chapel where he had first gone to talk to Father Michael after Chris had been hospitalized. He would go back there, he had to go back. There he would find the answer.

'I have no stomach for this,' he said aloud, then turned away, mortified by his outburst.

Embarrassed, he hurried towards the underground, fighting his way on to the platform. He had forgotten how busy it was, the lines of people ranked up to the edge of the platform, the signal board above his head indicating the oncoming trains. Harry had little idea of where he was going; he would simply catch a train to the end of the line and then continue by bus to Peckham. A woman next to him coughed, reading a paperback, the boy beside her tapping his foot in time to the music coming through his headphones. The platform swung with noise and the smell of bodies; its walls reverberated with the sound of passing trains entering other platforms; the wind sucked through the gaping tunnels; and on the line an old wallet lay hoplessly beside the steel track.

The heat was making people listless, a portable phone bleeping from the inside of someone's briefcase as they waited, all eyes turning towards the tunnel at the sound of a train approaching. Carried forward by the crush of bodies, Harry found himself hustled on to the train and automatically reached upwards for the rail, his hand fastening on to the warm metal. The doors closed as they moved off rapidly, an Indian girl pushed up against Harry's side, her body swaying to the rhythm of the train.

The first stations came and went, travellers getting off only to make way for a further crush, an old man dropping his stick on the platform as the doors closed at the Elephant and Castle. Harry hung on grimly, the Indian girl finding a seat at the next stop, a whole group of people getting off and leaving some welcome standing space. Taking in a deep breath Harry willed the train to move on – and it did – only to pause in the next tunnel. The moments passed, the travellers all conspicuously avoiding each other's eyes.

Harry glanced around him impatiently. Every head was turned down, or away – except one. One man caught Harry's gaze and held it rigorously. Surprised, Harry looked away, then looked back. The man was still staring at him; watching him. A faint unease crept over Harry, and then he controlled himself. He was an MP, not unknown; he had been recognized, that was all. But he knew that wasn't it. Just as he knew that the man was making no effort to hide his curiosity. He *wanted* Harry to know that he was watched.

Discomfited, Harry turned away. But the man's eyes crept over him, down his arms and legs, along his shoulders, over the back of his head. They consumed him, feasted on him, and Harry found himself turning, unable to resist. The man was still there. A heavy man in a heavy overcoat, watching.

Further stations came and went, and each time the train stopped Harry willed the man to get off, knowing as he did so that he would only leave the train when he did. Unsettled and hot with anxiety, Harry stared out of the window, only to find himself looking straight at the man's reflection. But it was impossible! he thought disbelievingly. He couldn't be reflected *opposite* him when he had been behind him before. But he was. In some way the man was moving himself around the carriage, finding seats where there had been none before, making sure that wherever Harry looked, he was looking straight at him.

The train juddered along the track, stopping and starting, a woman with a crying child climbing on at the next station. The child howled with an indignant and fractious whine, the sound filling the carriage and irritating all the remaining passengers. Except one. The man in the overcoat seemed immune, unnoticing, his eyes anchored on Harry. The end of the line was coming, Harry realized, and then what? His cowardice infuriated him. He would get off, that was all, and catch a bus. The man would get off too, he had to, there were no further stops, and then he would go his own way. Wouldn't he?

No, Harry realized. He wouldn't. He would stay with him, and follow him, and then, what? *What?*... The train stopped, the passengers alighting, Harry panicking suddenly and moving up the EXIT stairs as fast as he could go, knowing as he did so that the man was behind him. He ran up the first escalator, then took the second more slowly, out of breath. He turned round twice, but there was no sign of the man in the overcoat. As Harry approached the exit he was almost smiling with relief. He had been imagining things again, that was all – just his imagination. The man was even now crossing to another platform somewhere under his feet, or making his way up the first escalator. He wasn't following him. Or if he had been, Harry had left him behind. Oh yes, he'd outsmarted him all right.

The man in the overcoat was standing at the exit.

Harry stopped dead in his tracks, only yards away, facing

the man disbelievingly. It wasn't possible, he couldn't be standing there. He had been *behind* him! It was impossible, there was no way he could have passed him without being seen. Harry had watched the people coming up the escalator and he hadn't been among them. He couldn't be there! Spooked, Harry turned, about to return to the platform, and then paused. What the hell was he running away from? What could the man do to him? This was a public place; an underground station full of people; he wasn't going to run away. No bloody chance! With his eyes fixed defiantly on the man, Harry moved towards the figure standing waiting in the exit.

He expected him to step back, to move, but the man in the overcoat held his ground, almost willing Harry on. Then, as Harry tried to walk forward, he found himself unable to progress. His feet moved, but he made no advance, only marked time, stepping uselessly on the same spot over and over again, his shoes tapping on the tiled floor. Knock, knock, knock, echoing in the now empty exit hall. Transfixed, Harry looked down at his feet and then glanced over to the man. The exit was empty.

A movement behind him made him turn. The man in the overcoat was now *behind* him, moving towards the escalator. Maddened, Harry called after him, still unable to move, as the man's body disappeared down the escalator until all Harry could see was the top of his head. And then, suddenly, Harry could move again. His feet lifted, jerked up and, half falling, Harry hurtled forward and ran towards the escalator, almost tumbling down the steps, the man in the overcoat well ahead of him.

He reached the bottom just as the man turned into the tunnel which led back to the platform. Furiously Harry called out to him, still running, his voice hoarse. His heart pounded from the unexpected exertion, and his temper was rising. He wasn't going to be made a fool of, he was going to tackle this bastard, have it out with him. He called out again more loudly – but the man ignored him and merely moved on, on to the platform, walking towards the end where the tunnel was. Only there did he finally pause. Harry halted too, three yards away from him.

The platform was empty, deserted, as they faced each other, Harry breathing heavily, the other man expressionless. Maddened by the previous day's events, Harry recklessly moved towards him, his skin coated with sweat, his suit creased; and as he walked he could hear the sound of a train passing in a nearby tunnel. The man in the overcoat watched Harry's approach without reacting, merely waited until he was within a few feet of him and then, suddenly, he lifted his hand.

Harry knew it hadn't been close enough to reach him; knew it couldn't have done; and yet he felt the blow resound against his chest, knocking him off balance. He fell back, spiralling in the thin air, and landed on the track, automatically scrambling away from the live rail. All too aware of the danger he was in, Harry crouched against the side of the platform, his back flat against the wall. His breaths came in grunts, fear mixed with pain, his impact of the fall making his thoughts blur momentarily.

Then he heard the footsteps coming towards him. Panicked, he scrambled to his feet, scurrying along the track – away from the man watching from the platform overhead. He began to run, his eyes fixed on the edge of the platform as he stumbled along, striving to put some distance between himself and the man above him. If he could just get a little way ahead he could stop and haul himself off the track, then make for the exit . . . Panting, Harry ran on wildly – and then realized that he was making no progress, his feet slipping uselessly away from him, his legs unfeeling. Incredulous, Harry looked down.

His legs were crumbling under him, giving way, his limbs

turning to dust as he ran, his feet, ankles and thighs powdering. Screaming, Harry threw himself against the side of the platform, his arms groping at the floor, his legless trunk swinging helplessly.

He heard the train coming then. Fast, along the track, through the tunnel towards him. He heard it and pressed himself further against the wall of the track, his hands groping along the cement floor of the platform as he tried to lift himself – the man in the overcoat moving closer and closer to him. As did the train. Gibbering with fear, Harry tried to pull himself upwards, but his hands suddenly lost all feeling and when he looked at them they too began to disintegrate, trails of powdered dust left where the fingers had been. He howled, screaming hysterically, wriggling his trunk against the wall, trying somehow to clamber upwards, the wind from the tunnel making his empty trouser legs flap uselessly, his arms crumbling further and further until Harry finally lost his grip and felt himself falling back on to the track.

And the man kept coming, walking to the rhythm of the oncoming train. The engine lights flared on the track as it cleared the bend in the tunnel; they came on full, illuminating the track and the screaming, limbless man, his head thrown back, his mouth black as the tunnel entrance, as he writhed on the track. On, on, on came the train. On, on, on came the man on the platform. The windows of the train were full of faces, the lights flickering over the posters on the station walls. On, on, came the train, on, on went the man's feet overhead, until finally Harry stopped screaming and stared straight ahead of him.

The train driver's face was rigid. He stared at Harry and at that moment Harry looked up to see the man in the overcoat standing on the platform directly above him. He closed his eyes then, waiting for the impact which would slam into his crippled body; waiting for the machine to smash the blood and bone out of him. The noise of the train filled his ears, it screamed at him, the ground vibrating underneath, the piercing shriek of the machine bearing down on him. The sound tore into Harry; it flayed him; it burned him . . .

. . . And then it stopped. There was suddenly nothing. No impact, no noise. Only a terrible stillness. Silence.

Slowly Harry opened his eyes. He opened his eyes and found himself moving up the escalator and out to the world outside. Trembling with shock, Harry felt his legs buckle under him, and leaned against the moving rail, looking down. His legs might be ready to give way under him, but they were *there*. Real legs. Blood and bone legs. Frantically, Harry felt his arms, but they were whole too. His body complete again.

The up escalator continued to move upwards, up to the cooling streets; up to reality; up to safety. Almost incoherent with shock, Harry slumped further against the escalator rail, glancing listlessly across to the down escalator opposite him.

The deaf man passed him in that instant. As Harry moved up, he moved down: his eyes fixed ahead, his ears deaf to the repeated cries which echoed after him.

CHAPTER ELEVEN

When Jeanie came back from the hospital she let herself into the basement at Cleveland Square and turned the cold water tap full on. The water splashed against the steel sink and sprayed down the front of her coat until she turned down the pressure and filled a glass of water. Slowly she sipped it. Swallowing hurt her.

Jeanie sighed. Her ear burned fiercely and she wrenched out the hearing aid, pushing it into a kitchen drawer and slamming it shut. The memory of the pain, of the patronizing doctor, drummed into her head. All the resentment of the years clawed at her. Her wasted youth after the death of Mary Keller, the time spent caring for her father – a man too sick even to recognize her. I've been buried alive for decades, she thought, suddenly panicking, adrift in her own inescapable despair. For year after year I have hidden away, for year after year consoling others ... her temper rose with shuddering force, the control of a lifetime slipping from her grasp as she suddenly threw the glass on to the kitchen floor.

The hard smash of its impact startled her and she glanced down incredulously. The slivers were mismatched; some almost powdered, others mean and triangular. She continued to stare, a loathing for herself growing instant by instant. *I have four days left*, she thought helplessly, four days ... But I've wasted *years*! she howled impotently, tears filling her eyes. All those years gone, for nothing, and now only four days left... Someone had to help her, someone young, someone with no guilt, no past... Her own past smacked into her. Her wasted life. It was closing in on her, creeping over her... She *had* to find help.

But not from upstairs. There was no help there, only a woman who drained what little resources she had left. The answer had to be elsewhere. She just had to find it. Surely someone, somewhere, would comfort her as she had done so often for others. Surely she had earned that right? Maybe Rachel would help her. She *had* to! Jeanie thought, panic rising. Rachel Crossley would come to see her and make everything all right. *If* she came. If she came...

'Jeanie!'

She looked up suddenly. Without her hearing aid she hadn't heard her employer calling her, and was startled to find Ahlia in the room.

'This really is too bad...' Ahlia began, Jeanie straining to catch her words. She seemed sparky with the usual afterbloom of sex smoothing her features. But for all Ahlia's thunderous beauty, her eyes were altered; they were quick with satisfaction, but something else, something bothersome.

'I've been calling you for ages, why didn't you come?'

The basement kitchen seemed dowdy, ill-suited to the breadth of this woman's sexual aureole. Ahlia was growing somehow, filling out the room's atmosphere.

'You'll never guess what happened this morning,' she said, suddenly confiding and leaning towards Jeanie. 'I met someone. Someone *very* different.'

Jeanie remained transfixed, leaning back against the sink. The metal felt cold through her skirt.

'Someone *different*,' Ahlia continued, her eyes flirting from Jeanie to the street outside. Footsteps paused, then passed. 'I've been very naughty. Tell me it doesn't matter, Jeanie. Tell me.'

The older woman hesitated, words balling up in her throat. *She's been with a man.*

Don't go with the boys up the hill, Jeanie.

She's been with a man, slept with a man. Whilst I've grown ugly and old down here, in this dank little hole, she's been glutting herself, and she's done it again this morning...

'Tell me it doesn't matter, Jeanie. Tell me,' Ahlia pleaded, suddenly aware that her employee was looking at her in a disturbing way. Jeanie wasn't listening! After all these years, she wasn't listening to her. She *had* to listen, had to tell her everything would be all right. She *had* to. Ahlia's tentative grip on reality faltered.

'Jeanie, talk to me! It's your fault anyway. You were so sly; you never told me about Father Michael. You let me think you were going to clean for an old man. You never told me what he was like, and that's not fair, we never have secrets from each other... Jeanie, listen to me!' she howled, grabbing the older woman's shoulders. '*Talk to me!*'

But Jeanie remained immobile, watching her employer, her whole being consumed with the bitterness of decades. *So she found out about Father Michael, did she? And she slept with him...* Jeanie felt a sudden inescapable loathing – not for Ahlia, but for herself – the fierce resentment climbing moment by moment, and as Ahlia shook her, Jeanie remained silent, merely slipping off her shoes and stepping forward, the soles of her feet pressing down on the shards of broken glass.

'Talk to me, Jeanie! Talk to me!' Ahlia insisted, her eyes freed of the triumph of lovemaking, her voice pitched high like a dog whistle.

A whistle. A boy's whistle. A whistle. A hearing aid whistle forced into Jeanie's ear by a doctor who never existed.

'JEANIE, FOR THE LOVE OF GOD, TALK TO ME!'

But Jeanie didn't talk, she simply moved her feet around, only centimetres, but enough to force the glass further into the flesh of her feet. She felt the blood come, and sighed indolently, her gaze blurring before she finally slumped against Ahlia's shoulder. *I'm in the presence of madness*, she thought without fear, *this woman is mad*.

'*Jeanie!*' Ahlia continued, trying to pull away from her; embarrassed by the reversal of roles. She was the one to be comforted. She needed Jeanie, she needed her. '*You have to listen to me.*'

And then she glanced down. As Jeanie leaned against her, Ahlia looked at the floor and saw the snail trails of blood and the torn stockings on her employee's ill-formed feet. She saw them and blinked, fighting an impulse to run — but if she ran, who could she run *to*? She needed Jeanie; Jeanie knew all her secrets; Jeanie kept her sane. Without her there was nothing; only the dreams and the four days left. Without Jeanie, there was death . . .

'Oh God, what *have* you done?' she said quietly, lowering her employee into a chair and glancing round wildly. 'I'll get a cloth, Jeanie. That's right, isn't it? A cloth.' Uneasily Ahlia got to her feet and, avoiding the bloodied glass on the floor, wrung out a cloth in the sink. Then she knelt down and began to pick the glass out of Jeanie's feet, wiping the blood away as she did so.

Her voice took on a crooning quality:

'Now that was a silly thing to do, wasn't it?' she asked the unmoving woman. 'What a silly thing to do.' Her gestures were uncertain, awkward, her long nails plucking at the embedded glass. 'I can't have you doing crazy things, Jeanie, you know that. After all, I rely on you . . . I need you. What would I do without you?'

Jeanie looked down at the immaculate head bent over her bunioned, ungainly feet. She watched her employer and felt embarrassed — but the feeling was only fleeting, replaced immediately by a riveting sense of purpose.

You're almost mad, Jeanie thought. *I've seen madness and it's in you. But not in me. Not in me.*

Gingerly Ahlia continued to tend Jeanie's feet, chattering on inanely as the older woman's brain clarified and reason returned with knifing clarity. *You need me so you'll help me, just to make sure I'll always be here for you. You need me...* Jeanie sighed, revelling in the comfort offered, in the rare expression of another's concern. If only you knew that I had four days left; if only you knew, she thought. How would you help me then, Ahlia? What would you do to make sure nothing happened to me?

And as Jeanie thought all of this, Ahlia continued to wash her feet, her own mind humming incessantly with the one idea. *I need her, I need her, I need her...*

Rachel flinched. The deaf man was standing at the gate. Motionless, watching her. She smiled nervously, without expecting the gesture to be returned. But it was. A slow smile, slow and slight. Wordlessly he passed her and walked to the door, unlocking it and standing back for Rachel to enter – which she did without hesitating, the door closing behind both of them.

She was then in another world – his world – for the house was as silent as he was. It was stilled, without carrying the noise of their footsteps or the echo of the road outside. Mesmerized, Rachel glanced round. The hall was shady and very cold, the deaf man crossing it and guiding Rachel towards a room on the first floor. The stairs were without carpet, the walls bare, the windows curtainless. It had the atmosphere of a house left empty for too long.

Yet the room into which he showed her was occupied, and it smelt of him. The earth smell was strong here, two leather chairs flanking the fire, the wood panelling of the walls, the shuttered windows and the low ceiling, making it shadowed. In the wide grate a meagre fire still burned, and against the left wall a clock ticked sombrely in a massive maghogany case. Rachel walked over to it, and in the face of the brass pendulum she saw the reflection of the deaf man behind her and watched as he bent down and threw a log on to the struggling fire.

The pendulum swung soothingly, languidly, the sound filling the room. *The only noise*. There had been no sound as the logs hit the fire grate; no sound as the deaf man moved; and no sound as Rachel dropped her bag on to the floor. She saw it land – expected to hear a noise to confirm it – but there was none. The house was silent. A deaf house for a deaf man.

Oh, but she loves, Rachel, she loves.

She turned, startled, but the deaf man had not spoken aloud and was now sitting, staring into the fire.

She has loved me, Rachel, behind her windows and doors; under her ceilings and against her walls. She has loved me.

'I love Chris.' The words seemed to make the room wince. They landed heavily on the walls, the light coming in through the gaps in the shutters, trembling. Cautiously Rachel moved over to the deaf man, kneeling beside his chair, the firelight highlighting the right side of her face and body.

'Talk to me.'

He glanced up at her slowly, regarding her for a long instant.

'You've helped me,' Rachel said simply. 'I want to thank you for that.'

The deaf man raised his hand, gesturing for her to lower her voice, then his eyes fixed on her mouth.

'Why are you helping me?' she asked. He read her lips and then glanced into her eyes. 'Did you send the message? *Was* it you?' she asked, her voice cushioned by the room's dead weight. 'Is it true? Do I only have a week to live?'

Four days.

The thought came into her head, an unspoken reply, the deaf man watching her.

'Yes . . . four days,' she agreed. 'So it's true?'

Noiselessly he moved, reaching into his coat pocket and taking out two hearing aids. They seemed fragile in his unwieldy hands, the knuckles swollen from the years of fighting. But his movements were deft as he fixed first one aid into his left ear and then the other into his right. He then took in one deep breath, exhaling slowly through his nostrils. Then he spoke:

'CHRIS HAS
HAD THE
SAME MESSAGE.'

The words rocked to the rhythm of the clock; swinging with the pendulum, the surreal, metallic voice in harmony with it. He was talking in time to the clock.

'Chris had the same message?' Rachel repeated, chilled with fear: '*Chris* is going to die?'

'YOU MAY
ALL DIE.'

'*All?*' Rachel reiterated. 'How many are there of us?'

He sighed, but the sound was noiseless.

'All right, don't tell me about them . . . But what about Chris? Can I help him? Tell me, what can I do to help him?'

'THIS HOUSE
LOVES ME.'

Rachel frowned. Was he likening his love to the love she shared with Chris? *Could* a house love? Her gaze wandered; in the corner there was a table on which was an unlit lamp, and a book, open, the pages glowing in the semi-darkness. The book seemed to draw her, to call her over, to compel her. If she could just read what was written there, maybe it would help. If she could just read it . . .

Cautiously Rachel rose to her feet, skirting the deaf man's

chair and moving towards the clock. The pendulum swung easily, the reflection of the room reproduced perfectly in the brass disc. Back, forward; back, forward. Left, right; left, right. The clock ticked on, moments measured, the reflection perfect in every detail; so perfect that Rachel had an impression that the *image* of the room was the reality, not the room itself. She stared, transfixed, the pendulum swinging, her image swinging with it; *her* image – and the image of the deaf man standing behind her.

Frightened, she tried to move away, but instead she found herself forced *towards the clock* and felt a sudden unwelcome sensation of pressure on her back. The smell of earth was increasing. Rachel saw the reflection of the deaf man stand up and walk towards her. Her eyes were fixed on his image, unable to turn away from the clock, the pressure on her back increasing by the second as the deaf man approached. Panic winded her, her mouth drying, her body suddenly bending under the weight of the deaf man leaning over her.

The pendulum swung on, swinging, swinging, reflecting her agonized face, the deaf man behind her, consuming her, his body on hers. Rachel tried to move, but couldn't; tried to scream, but couldn't; and when she looked at her face in the pendulum she saw her features suddenly and hideously distorted. Pain exploded inside her head; the skin of her face splitting, ripping; the pressure from behind forcing itself through her. *The deaf man pressing his own face through hers.*

And the pendulum swung on. It swung and reflected the room, the table, the firelight, and then it reflected Rachel – wearing the deaf man's face.

'*Stop it!*' she shouted suddenly, turning away from the clock. 'It's a trick.'

The deaf man raised his hands.

'I THOUGHT
YOU MIGHT

KNOW THAT.'

'You're not going to hurt me,' she said firmly, fighting panic. 'That's not what this is all about.'

'MAYBE SO.
MAYBE NO.'

'I need help,' she said flatly. 'And Chris needs help. Has he seen you? Has he? Please, don't frighten him, he's helpless . . .' Her voice softened, took on the aura of a plea. 'Listen, punish me, I don't care – but not him. Not Chris.' Rachel's eyes moved over to the table and the book. If only she could read what was written there. 'Chris doesn't deserve to die—'

'HE WANTS
TO BE
DEAD NOW.'

'He's sick. Paralysed!' Rachel snapped. 'He can't think clearly. He doesn't *really* want to be dead – not Chris. I know him. He wants to live.'

Tick, tock, went the clock.

Tick, tock, went the rhythm of the deaf man's speech.

'HE HAS
FOUR DAYS.'

'Take me instead!' Rachel shouted, then stopped short. 'No! I don't mean that. I want to live.' She moved towards him slowly, keeping a yard between them: 'What do *you* want? Tell me, I'll help you if I can.'

'STEP BACK.'

She heard the command and hesitated – then stepped forward again, her voice gentle:

'You're not evil. You don't really want to hurt us. There's good in you, I know there is. You've been kind to me . . . Tell me what you want. Tell me how I can help you. I know some things about you, Titus told me about your boxing, your accident—'

'STOP NOW.'

But she wouldn't. Couldn't. 'Why do you want to hurt us? *Why?*' her tone steadied, forcing down the panic. 'What have we done to you? Why would you need to punish us?'

'I NEED

YOUR PAIN.'

She frowned, bewildered. 'Why?'

'IT LETS

ME LIVE.'

The clock ticked behind them. Back and forth, moment by moment, the room darkening. *Get out, Rachel, get out!* her hands were suddenly moist, the smell of earth overpowering. The deaf man didn't move, but the air around him seemed to pulsate with menace.

'You can't frighten me,' Rachel said quietly, trying to keep her voice steady. 'I'm not going to die – and neither is Chris. Please, can't you help him?'

The deaf man said nothing. He simply watched Rachel's lips and imagined her voice in his head.

'Please, help him,' she begged. 'Have you seen him? I know you can go anywhere. You came to me in a dream. Did you go to Chris the same way?'

Her voice rose again; it lapped against the dim walls and reverberated in the shadowed corners.

'What do you want?'

Nothing, again nothing.

'Just tell me what you want, please,' Rachel said. 'I want to understand. Please, tell me.'

'I CAN'T

(tick, tock)

TELL YOU'

(tick, tock)

THAT MUCH.'

(tick, tock)

'But I have to know!' Rachel pleaded, watching the deaf

man. 'You're good, I know you are.' She reached out to him, offering kindness. 'Tell me,' she said, dropping to her knees in front of him. The firelight made a copper goddess out of her, her hand golden as she extended it to him. 'I won't hurt you. I promise . . . Talk to me, help me.'

Then she took hold of his hand.

He howled once.

She rocked with fright, but held on.

The room winced at the sound, the walls shuffling around them, the fire dimming, the book on the table slamming closed behind her. But still she held on, Kaine Lukes throwing his head back against the chair, his eyes closed, his mouth working, howling. The noise expanded, it scraped at the walls, it tore into Rachel. And then, just as suddenly, it stopped.

And then he moved. He jerked, moved forwards towards her, his face only inches from hers, his eyes fixed. The look of pain had gone, in its place was a sensation of unexpressed longing. Startled, she tried to pull back, and felt his hand drawn away from hers. Painfully, his skin peeled from hers; torn away from hers; taking with it some of her skin. And then he held his right hand in front of her eyes.

The palm altered, the skin becoming a moving membrane, and on the deaf man's hand an image appeared, a image of two people – her and Leon – *and the image moved*. The abuse played itself out on his palm, the bedroom, the smell of cold coffee from a half emptied cup, the muffled noises. *Don't tell, don't tell . . . keep quiet, Rachel, keep quiet . . .* The scene was re-enacted in every sordid detail, Rachel transfixed on the image before her.

And when it finally ended she saw herself crying, curled in a foetal position on her bed.

'Oh God, let me die . . . let me die . . .'

Then, nothing . . .

The deaf man's hand returned to normal, the palm only

flesh again. Immobilized by shock, Rachel sat unmoving at the deaf man's feet and then watched, mesmerized, as he felt at the scar on his neck. He fingered it urgently, tearing at it, the healed wound opening, blood trickling slowly down his throat. Then he stood up and slowly, tenderly, wiped his bloodied hand down the wall. The blood seeped into the wood greedily, making a sinister mark.

'Jesus . . .' Rachel whispered, getting to her feet and backing away. 'Dear Jesus . . .'

The deaf man hadn't heard, but he paused, his palm flat against the wall, his back turned to her.

'GO NOW.'

And she left.

One, two, three, turn. That's the way, the nurse will read the chart now and then put it back on the end of the bed. It will scrape on the metal . . . yes, that's it. Go on, cough now. A nervous habit, you don't need to cough, you don't have a cold. But you'll cough anyway. There! I knew it.

Chris would have smiled, if he could have. But he couldn't, he was paralysed. Unmoving. He heard the nurse and measured her movements. He had learned to do such things to keep his mind off the horror of his situation, to keep himself sane. He imagined the intensive care unit too. Although he hadn't seen it, he had watched enough television to have a clear idea of what went on, and the rest he imagined. Or heard. The swoosh of the plastic doors flapping closed, the clink of the glass waste bottles taken away and replaced. *Funny to think that even paralysed you continue to pee and crap yourself. Apparently your bladder and bowels keep working – what a judgement on the human race. To all intents and purposes, you're dead to the world, but you still function in the gut. Maybe the soul of man is in his bowels*, Chris thought bitterly, *maybe that's the only part that exists after death. The bowel.*

He would have laughed, but couldn't.

I beseech you in the bowels of Christ, think it possible you may be mistaken.

Maybe Cromwell had it right after all, Chris thought madly. *Maybe he wasn't such a nutter ... I should be writing now, working on that piece about conservation. Not here, listening to the time passing ... He'll come again. The deaf man. If I wait long enough, he'll come. At least he knows where to find me. I'm not going anywhere. But what about Rachel?*

Then panic took a swing at him. He felt it come and ducked mentally. That was the way to do it, he knew that. Dodge it, or it consumes you, and he couldn't let that happen. He had to stay sane because he was going to get out of this. Somehow he was going to get out of it. With the deaf man's help.

But he didn't like the idea. Didn't like the thought of turning to him for help. *But who else was there?* Chris thought hopelessly. He was the only one able to help. After all, hadn't he let him move for the first time since his accident? There was no one else ... But the deaf man was terrifying, unnatural, evil. *Evil ... Oh God*, Chris thought, what was it all about? If the deaf man did help him, what would be the price for his help? It wouldn't, couldn't, be free. He had to want something in return. Chris shifted in his bed. Or tried to. Instead he felt the weight of his body press into the sheets. *I'll have bed sores on my rear end, like a nappy rash, and my teeth, who's cleaned my teeth? No one, not in all the time I've been here and how long is that now? How long?*

He tried to measure the time, but failed. The panic which had descended on him at first left him stupid and disorientated, and it had taken him a while to control his hysteria. But he had. Just as he had managed, through force of will, to limit his reactions. The heart monitor had been the giveaway, he knew that on the second day. If he was alarmed it gave off a different sound and then they pumped him with sedatives, and whilst they depressed his anguish they also suppressed his thoughts. And that was dangerous. So now Chris mastered his reactions, and as a result they didn't dope him so much.

They thought they were monitoring him! What a laugh, *he* was monitoring them. Chris paced his thoughts. The deaf man was like the drugs, only dangerous if you didn't control him. If you *couldn't* control him. Chris had to control him and get help from him – there was no one else. Besides, he thought, trying to calm himself, he was helpless. If the deaf man had wanted to injure him he would have done so already. Unless he was going to injure him through Rachel . . .

A touch on the arm made Chris jump, his thoughts shattering. So it was that time already. Time for tea. He felt the gastro-nasal tube adjusted in his nostril, the liquid filling his throat. *Swallow, Chris. Be calm, take the food, you'll need it. You have to be strong.* He swallowed again. *Make it steak and chips next time, hey? And a coffee.* Again he swallowed, then felt someone wipe a cloth at the side of his mouth where he had dribbled.

A wash of self-pity welled up in him.

No, not now! I can't give in now. I have to concentrate, work it out. Work it all out. Think. *And I have to call him. The deaf man. I have to call him back.*

Chris shivered, fear creeping over the bedclothes and nestling round him. *Come on*, he concentrated, *come on, there's no choice*. A nurse laughing broke into his thoughts and he flinched, then settled again, trying to conjure up the deaf man.

Where are you? Come on, come back. I'm calling you. Come on . . .

Down down down. Down into darkness, under consciousness, swimming under reason. Down down down. Down to the earth's womb which carries the deaf man. *Go on*, Chris willed himself, *go on* . . . Down down down. Down under feelings, under sound, under daylight, under wood and under earth. Under bodies past and under bodies to come; under death. *Go on, Chris, go on, find him. Find him* . . .

'COME IN.'

'I am in,' Chris said evenly, facing the deaf man.

'I SAW

YOUR FRIEND.'

'Rachel?' Chris asked, startled. 'Are you going to help her?'

'WHAT ELSE?'

What else indeed? Chris wondered. They were not in the room where they usually met, but in the kitchen instead, a pair of torn leather gloves on the windowsill and an old kettle whistling on a gas cooker. The noise shrilled in Chris's ears and he turned it off quickly, knowing the deaf man would never hear it.

'YOU HAVE

FOUR DAYS

LEFT NOW.'

'And Rachel, how long has she got?' Christ asked.

'THE SAME.'

'What's the price?' Chris asked, the deaf man turning and looking at him. He seemed not to understand what he said. 'I asked the price – how do I pay for your help? How do I get you to help Rachel and me?'

Without answering, Kaine Lukes sat down at the kitchen table and dug into his pockets, pulling out a poster from one of his fights. It was folded many times, and when the picture was spread out, it was crazed with dark lines. Frowning, Chris sat down opposite him and looked at it, seeing the deaf man's photograph and his name printed underneath.

'You're called Kaine Lukes?'

He nodded.

'Strange name. Is it your real name?'

He nodded again.

Chris studied the poster, sensing some of the deaf man's pride. An ex-boxer, a fighter, of all things. He had never thought of him as being a real man, not a living being, not a man with a name. Yet here it was – Kaine Lukes – a man with a place in the world. He was real, after all, Chris thought incredulously. *But if he's real, how did he get* inside *my head*?

'Four days isn't enough time,' Chris said, jumping as Kaine Lukes lunged out and grabbed his hands across the table.

'WATCH THIS.'

Kaine Lukes released the young man's hands and turned his own over, the palms exposed. The skin altered, undulating, the scene of Chris's accident played out on the flesh. The weaving of the bike between the cars, the snort of the air brakes from the lorry, the one elongated moment in which Chris passed from life in unconsciousness, his body landing lifeless on the road. Then there was more – a young man in a hospital bed unable to move, willing himself to die. Willing his life over . . . swamped, shrouded in misery.

Watching, Chris felt the overwhelming agony of helplessness and sucked in his breath. Kaine Lukes suddenly closed his fingers over his palms, and the image disappeared. Then he rose noiselessly to his feet and prepared two cups of tea in thick white mugs, walking back to the table and placing one in front of Chris. The young man's head was still down, his desolation palpable as the deaf man walked behind him and laid his hands over his face. Chris had no chance to struggle before the odours entered his nostrils, climbing avidly into his brain and triggering his recall.

Petrol. The hot smell of burning tyres, then the dark, lonely perfume of the hospital ward . . . Fiercely the deaf man pulled back Chris's head, pressing it against his stomach and breathing in. Chris could feel his diaphragm expand, then contract, the pressure of his hands increasing against his face.

Help me, Chris willed him, *help me*. The hands still clung to him frantically. *For the love of God, help me* ...

'NOT YET.'

The priest had woken to find Ahlia lying in the crook of his arm. She had been sleeping, breathing greedily, her face vulgarly sensual, her head weighty against his chest. Moving carefully, Father Michael had slid out of bed, taking in a sharp breath as his feet hit the cold, uncarpeted floor. A wan sun had glowed grimly through the over-washed curtains, making patterns, the shadow of the iron bedhead criss-crossing the wall behind.

Ahlia's clothes lay half over the chair and half across the chest of drawers, her shoes by the door. Even her clothes took up space, he had thought meanly, she couldn't leave them in a little pile, but had to scatter them over every inch he owned. Not that he hadn't understood what she was doing. He had known that she was marking out her territory, leaving her scent and touch on every trivial thing he possessed. Making sure that nothing he had was free of her.

He had wanted that. At first. Wanted to forget the imminent threat. His fear had made him want her; made him make love to her; he had despaired of salvation so he had turned to obliteration instead. Sex offered, sex taken. Vows broken, trust betrayed. He had done it before and was willing to risk the wretchedness of guilt which would follow the euphoria – but he hadn't realized how swift the fall from grace would be.

That had surprised him, and emptied out the remainder of his hope. Now there was only the punishment left – in four days. Four days. The priest looked at his watch and then at the sleeping woman. She had been his final grasp at forgetfulness, a ludicrous and, in a way, brave act of defiance. But God, as ever, was not impressed. And Father Michael hadn't even the satisfaction of saying that he had enjoyed his lapse.

The dial of the watch had glinted in the afternoon light, the priest sitting down on the side of the bed. He had wanted to lose himself in a sexual fervour and, after the first act of intercourse, had been mortified to find himself suddenly impotent. It was almost amusing, he had thought, to risk everything for an act, not of consummate eroticism, but of humiliation and failure. What better way to punish a sensualist, than to take away his desire?

And who was this woman, he had wondered. Who was she? And who had sent her? He gazed at the figure in the bed and felt a quick revulsion for her. It had been her fault, not his. Many women had wanted him and he had resisted, except for that one lapse ten years before. Self-pity tugged at him. He had suppressed his sexual needs, stored them away, controlled them, and then when he wanted a woman, *needed* a woman, Ahlia had materialized. This undulating, fabulous creature had suddenly come into his life – what was left of it. But why? She should have been able to help him. He had only four days left! Only four days.

She was evil, he had realized. She was poisonous – someone had sent her to test him, and he had failed. He had fallen into the trap, and now there would be no escape. Infuriated, the priest had rubbed his forehead, willing Ahlia to wake, wanting to argue with her, to punish her for his own agony. But she hadn't, instead she had slept on, long limbed and violently lovely in the shaded night.

His mind had woven unsteadily. Someone had to help him, there had to be someone, if not her, someone else . . . He thought of the night he had woken bleeding, and of the blood child on the bedroom floor; then he remembered the man in the church, the man he had seen the previous night, the man burning inside . . . He wasn't mad, no, not mad. Sick maybe, but not mad. Overwrought, but not mad. People saw things when they were under pressure, all kinds of things. It was commonplace, imaging things.

The priest had glanced over his shoulder, half expecting the bed to be empty; half wanting to believe that he had tried to make love to a ghost. But Ahlia had still been there, alive and breathing. It was her breathing which had disturbed him the most; her rhythmic, measured, greedy breathing . . .

Restlessly, he had risen to his feet.

'What is it?' Ahlia murmured, sitting up in bed.

'Go back to sleep.'

'Don't worry,' she said yawning. 'I've told you, it happens to every man now and again.'

The words, said half heartedly, had prickled at his skin. She irritated him so much, he thought furiously, why didn't she go? Get out?

'You worry too much.'

'Shut up!' he had snapped, flinging himself on the bed beside her, his arms folded behind his head.

Ahlia had frowned, unsettled. Her confidence plummeting, her hand reaching for the sheet, the edge tucked into her mouth automatically.

'This has to stop,' Father Michael had begun, then paused. There were only four days left, it seemed hardly worth ending anything, time would end it for him.

'Are you angry with me?' Ahlia whispered.

He had sat up suddenly. All his movements had been staccato; like his thoughts.

'I shall die twitching.'

'What?' Ahlia asked, her voice childish, uneasy with the threat of her own imminent death. 'Who's going to die?'

'Nothing.'

Slowly she had risen up in the bed, kneeling and laying her naked chest against the priest's back, her mouth against his ear.

'Tell me . . . let me help.'

He had closed his eyes longingly, more seduced by those few words than by any of her sexual tricks.

'Tell me . . .' Ahlia had crooned. 'Are you ill?'

'In the head,' he said listlessly. 'Sick with guilt.'

Guilt. Like the guilt over her husband's death. Guilt she understood.

'Tell me about it,' Ahlia coaxed him. 'Tell Mama . . . Tell Mama.'

Her mouth had been so close to his ear that the priest had imagined he could almost hear her heart beating. Her voice had been misted, muted; it had stirred inside him; drawing him in.

'You can trust me. Nothing is going to happen to you. Nothing, you're safe, safe. Mama's here . . . Mama's here . . .'

He had sighed then, the sound mixing with Ahlia's own intake of breath, the two in sexual union. Freed momentarily from the madness of his own fear, the priest had felt the woman's warm breasts move against his back and moaned. And in response her hands had moulded him, flicked at his skin, combing him with the old lusts.

'Tell me . . . tell Mama . . .'

He had felt himself change then, had felt the urgency of wanting her, and turned, grasping Ahlia and forcing her back against the pillows. The sheets had tugged at his ankles, the blanket hot against his legs as he'd moved on top of her, and then, in the moment of ultimate sensation, the priest had felt himself lifted away from her.

The room had lost him . . . He could still see her on the bed, still feel her under him and yet the room was no longer his, it had become a dark room with shuttered windows and a closed door, a room with only a bed in it. Her face had been only inches from his, and yet *between* them there had been something else. Or someone else . . . Sickened, the priest had tried to pull back, but Ahlia had clung to him, crooned to him, clawed at him. Her actions fierce, desperate, violently needy – but silent.

Because something else had changed. *There was no noise, no sound. Only silence* . . . Suddenly terrified, the priest had fought to escape, but had remained fixed, locked, held on top of Ahlia, his body changing, his shape and hands altering, turning into another man. And then he had lost himself; his face and body turning into another person's, his blood absorbed by someone else's, his thoughts in another's head, his actions performed by another's hands.

And he had been forced to watch. Trapped inside a stranger, he had been forced to watch himself make love, becoming a voyeur of his own shadow. He had been compelled to spy on his own lusts, to watch Ahlia respond to his needs expressed by another. And all the time he lay with her, on top of her, within her, he had felt the other body between them. Felt the other hands like gloves upon his own, and the other face like a death mask on his own features. Caught in the mire of his own desire, he had finally felt him climax and had known, with bitter frustration, that the release was not his own.

They had lain silent afterwards, the priest too afraid to move – knowing that the other was still in the bed with them. Waiting. Ahlia had not noticed the change of room, merely stirred languidly as the priest had groaned and watched helplessly as his hands moved up to his face . . . The gesture had not been his; it had been enacted for him; and as his hands came closer and closer, he had been forced to watch, his eyes staring, as the whole horror of his past was played out on the palms. The horrors had uncurled image by image in the dark room, the scenes glowing luminously before finally concluding with the image of the priest begging God for release. For death.

And then it had ended. Tormented beyond endurance, the

priest had closed his eyes and slumped on to the sheets, his head falling heavily against Ahlia's shoulder. She had stirred, languid from lovemaking, and laid her hands against his face. But the touch had been different; the man between them taking possession, for an instant, of her compliant skin.

Paralysed with fear, the priest had then felt the hands move over his face, Kaine Lukes's palms pressing down against the handsome head, crushing into the fine bones, blood exploding from the priest's ears and nose, his eyes collapsing under their lids.

Then the pressure had suddenly evaporated – and the priest left the deaf house screaming.

White-faced with shock, Harry had plunged back into the underground after his tormentor, and followed Kaine Lukes back to the deaf house. As he approached the shuttered building, a figure emerged. It was Rachel. She walked quickly, without looking back, her head bowed. Now, what the hell was that all about? Harry wondered as he stared at her receding image. He was acting like an idiot – he knew that – but he didn't care any more. He might be doomed, but he'd be buggered if he'd go down without a fight.

So Rachel must know something, he thought. A hunch. Whatever. The way she had got through to Chris the previous night at the hospital; the way his son had *known* she was there – that had been uncanny, creepy. It might have been telepathy, but Harry wasn't convinced. He wasn't impressed by what Rachel said either. It was more how she *looked*. She had the aura of someone ready to fight – and that was what alerted him.

But *what* was she fighting? Chris's illness, or something else? Harry frowned. There was something unearthly going on . . . He was surprised to find that he could accept the idea easily. After his terrifying experience in the underground he had admitted to himself that some things were beyond reason. Like fear. And death.

The man had tried to kill him. But why? Was it another warning? Like the warning of the week to live? Harry shook his head impatiently. Logic was no use any longer, it offered no answers. His eyes moved back to the house. Why had Rachel visited Kaine Lukes, he wondered. What did she know? Or maybe she was the one with the answers; maybe she knew how to save him and his son. After all, she loves Chris. *Rachel loves Chris*, Harry repeated to himself. It was the only nuance of hope left. A love between two young people. *Was* there a kind of magic in that? he wondered. Love was supposed to be stronger than anything, wasn't it? Hadn't he read that somewhere?

Rachel had come out of the house hurriedly, almost afraid . . . or was it *his* fear he was feeling? Oh God, grow up! Harry thought furiously, what the hell can Rachel Crossley do? *She might be able to help Chris*, came back the answer. Well, help was exactly what he needed. Help was what they *all* needed.

But still Harry paused, sweating slightly even though it was cold. The house was unwelcoming. Hostile. There had to be an answer there, or why would Rachel have come? He hovered nervously outside the gate. What would happen in the house? What? he wondered, an image of the deaf man flashing into his head.

Harry stepped back, a quick wind blowing the gate closed.

'Jesus!' he snapped, startled by the sound, his heart pumping. *Calm down. It's only a gate, Harry, calm down.*

Slowly, he moved forwards again. The windows were lidded with shutters, but he knew that someone was watching him, willing him in . . . He turned, glancing round. Maybe he should take something with him, something heavy. A log of wood or something... Harry paused, imagining the headline – MP MUGS LOCAL RESIDENT IN MIX-UP. Oh God, he thought incredulously, what the hell is going on?

I'll just go and knock. After all, what's the harm in it? I can always say I've made a mistake, got the wrong address. Rachel's been there, for God's sake, so what can happen to me? The reasoning was sound, but Harry still couldn't move. The day skimmed over with cloud, rain mottling his suit as he waited.

And then, as he watched, from the chimney of the deaf house came a little spiral of smoke. Benign. Safe. Welcoming.

Ahlia was watching Jeanie, staring at her bandaged feet and wondering what had happened to turn her safe, practical ally into this withdrawn and distant stranger. The snow had begun early that morning, London snow, she thought, the type that would melt almost as it landed. Yet this time it didn't, it lodged against the windows instead, taking hold of the house in Cleveland Square, the basement steps coated with a frosting of white.

The lovemaking had not soothed Ahlia for long. Almost as soon as she left, she had felt the dwindling satisfaction evaporate. Worse, Jeanie hadn't reacted as she had expected.

Beside her in the dim basement bedroom, Jeanie stirred in her chair.

'Are you all right?' Ahlia asked, hurrying over to the older woman and pulling up a chair next to hers. The cover was worn, rough to the touch.

Jeanie turned, glancing at Ahlia without recognition.

'*Jeanie!* Don't look at me like that.'

'Fine...' she said listlessly. 'Fine.'

Ahlia frowned, straining to understand. 'Are you hungry?'

'I'll make us something,' Jeanie said, moving forward in her chair.

'*No!*' Ahlia replied, laying her hand on the woman's shoulder. 'I'll do it.'

'Don't be daft, you can't cook, you know you can't.'

But Ahlia wanted to be busy, wanted to be occupied – and she wanted to make Jeanie better. Normal. So she ignored her employee's pleas and slipped into the kitchen, flicking on the light switch and wrenching open the fridge door. The shelves were crammed with food, an uncooked chicken on the second shelf. Thoughtfully, Ahlia chewed her lower lip. Having never had to cook for herself she was uncertain where to start, and timidly eyed up the trussed chicken.

Finally she took out three eggs and searched for a mixing bowl. The snow crusted the window ledge outside, the temperature dropping. Uncertainly Ahlia cracked the eggs, whisking them sloppily, the eggs yolks pooling together into a frothy yellow. If she stayed busy, she would be all right. She would have lunch with Jeanie and a chat, and things would be back to normal. She turned on the gas, the jet popping loudly in the still air as Ahlia jumped back, startled. Slowly, she lit one gas ring, and the grill, putting two slices of bread on to toast. Keep calm, she willed herself, there was a way out of this mess. When she felt better, Jeanie would know what to do; Jeanie knew everything.

Gingerly Ahlia dropped some butter into the pan. It hissed on the hot metal, bubbling suddenly as she dropped in the eggs, her gaze moving to the grill where the toast was browning. She had to stay fit, well; and she had to keep Jeanie well too. She couldn't get sick on her now, not when she needed her . . .

From the sitting room came the sound of a radio and Ahlia smiled nervously. That was better, Jeanie always liked to have the radio on. Besides it was too quiet down here and the basement smelt of damp. She frowned, stirring the eggs. It had never smelt damp before. Or been this cold. But was it damp she could smell? That deep, earthy smell . . . Ahlia inhaled, drawing the odour into her nostrils. Maybe there was something wrong with the plumbing, she thought idly, still, nothing a plumber couldn't fix. She would get Jeanie to call one in.

The toast browned on one side and she turned it. The other side of the bread was white as the snow falling outside. She didn't want to see the priest again; she had thought it would be fun, a diversion, but he was sick. Ill in the head. Odd. And she didn't like that. She had enough problems of her own and besides, she couldn't cope with other people's anxieties. Except Jeanie's. Jeanie's she *had* to cope with, unless she wanted to lose her.

The thought spat at her and Ahlia dropped the spoon, a yellow trickle of half-cooked egg landing on the faded lino.

'Jeanie,' she called, forcing a light-hearted tone into her voice. 'Come on, it's nearly ready.'

The old woman walked in slowly, tucking the hearing aid into her ear, her skin pale.

'Sit over there.'

'You haven't set the table,' Jeanie said, immediately laying out the mats and cutlery. 'You should have done that first.'

'Sorry . . . I forgot the table,' Ahlia replied sheepishly, their roles suddenly reversed. 'I just wanted to make something for you. You look cold.' She laid down the bowl of unappetizing eggs and cut the toast into halves, passing some to Jeanie. 'Eat up, you know that's what you always tell me.'

'I'm not hungry.'

'Eat it, Jeanie!' Ahlia said firmly, her tone pitched high. *Eat, Jeanie. Keep well.* 'You look very pale, are you OK? I could get a doctor—'

'*I don't want a doctor!*' Jeanie snapped suddenly, putting on her glasses and looking apologetically at her employer. 'I'm sorry, I just feel a little down, that's all. Probably flu.'

'Eat, Jeanie . . .' Ahlia repeated, her voice taking on a lost air.

In silence, they both began to eat.

The clock ticked behind them.

The snow fell outside the window.

Between them lay the same knowledge, yet neither referred to it. They both thought of their pasts and of the sentence passed on them – four days. The fear of the impending threat made eating difficult and speech impossible. They did not confide each other, they *could* not confide, and each said nothing.

'I haven't even looked at the second post yet,' Jeanie said at last, reaching out for the batch of letters on the table. There were six; five passed to Ahlia, the other tucked into Jeanie's pocket.

'Bills.'

'What?'

Ahlia glanced at the envelopes. 'I said that they were only bills.' She expected Jeanie to return the compliment and tell her what her letter had been. But she didn't. She merely sat down and began to play with her food again.

The sudden distance between them intimidated Ahlia and she felt herself begin to panic, her tone forced, over-eager to please.

'I was thinking that we could go on a holiday. Would you like that, Jeanie?'

No response.

'We could go to the Lake District, or somewhere hot. France, Italy . . .'

Silence.

'It would be a change. You need a change. You do so much for me.'

Her panic increased in the face of her employee's unfamiliar reserve. *You know my secrets, Jeanie, you keep me sane. Come back, please, come back.*

'We could go next week.'

Next week. The words jingled like loose change. Next week neither of them was going anywhere. Fear lodged in them both like ice, Ahlia babbling on incoherently, filling the mordant pause.

'Or if you'd rather, I could have this place redecorated. It smells of damp.' The thought pleased her, it seemed the right thing to say. It was comforting just talking about banalities.

'I could get a decorator in to re-do the kitchen, Jeanie, make it all modern and warm for you. And the sitting room, even the bedroom. That old flowered wallpaper could go, and the tiled fireplace. You never liked that, did you?' she asked, desperate to elicit some response. 'Not that you complained – you never complain about anything, do you, Jeanie?' her voice was nearly a whimper. 'You're not going to leave me, are you?'

Four days left, Jeanie thought, *there are only four days left and she knows it, but how?*

I have only four days left unless she does something, Ahlia thought in the very same instant. *If she goes there's no hope, no chance . . .*

Their eyes looked – then slowly Jeanie pushed away her plate.

'I have to lie down, Mrs Bell—'

'Ahlia!' she replied, startled by the sudden formality of her employee's tone. 'Since when have I been Mrs Bell to you?'

Unmoved, Jeanie walked out.

She knew that Ahlia would remain in the kitchen for a while and then retreat upstairs, probably to pace around, or cry. The thought would normally have upset her but she was long past feeling and wanted only to be quiet. So Jeanie took out her hearing aid again and, with the sounds around her muffled, began to read the letter.

The handwriting was unfamiliar, her name dark on the cream envelope, the paper stiff in her hands as she prepared to read what was written there. But here was nothing. The letter was blank. The page bare. Mystified, Jeanie turned it over, but there was nothing on the reverse side either and she was just about to throw it away when it moved.

It moved in her hands. Almost jumped out of her hands. Then it shifted and threw up an image – the picture of a room, a room with a low wood ceiling and a table and two chairs. A room which was occupied . . . Alarmed, Jeanie tried to drop the paper but it clung to her fingers and in one shuddering instant she found her whole body drawn towards it. The paper expanded, the room increasing, and she felt herself incredibly and disbelievingly lifted from her chair *into* the paper.

And then she passed through the sheet; passed into the room waiting in the deaf house, landing on the wooden floor in her bandaged feet, her slippers left behind. The paper slid away, and she was marooned . . . Her hands moved to her ears automatically, Jeanie realizing at once that she had left her hearing aid behind. Fear welled up in her as she strained to listen . . . The silence was immense. Complete. Not the silence of someone hard of hearing; no muffled noises indistinctly heard. Just total silence. I can get out, she thought practically, logically; there *has* to be a door . . . But there wasn't, only a shuttered window and a fire. And a man.

It *was* the doctor, Jeanie thought incredulously. It was the doctor from the hospital! Timidly, she skirted the perimeters of the room, avoiding his chair, her eyes fixed on him. But he didn't turn, just kept staring into the fire, a dark overcoat in place of the hospital white. Without hearing the ticking, Jeanie saw the clock and glanced hurriedly away, her eyes fixing on the open book on the table instead. Uneasily she edged towards it.

'GET AWAY
FROM THERE.'

She jumped at the sound of his voice. The noise was strained, a voice without emotion or the usual rhythm of speech. Fear made her whimper.

'COME TO
THE FIRE.'

No, not fire! No, not to the fire, Jeanie thought wildly. Anywhere else, but not the fire.

'COME TO
THE FIRE.'

The deaf man repeated, and as he said the words again, Jeanie began to move, inexplicably drawn towards him and towards the flames. The heat crept out to meet her, tickling her face with its warmth ... She expected at any moment to be thrown into the flames; to be roasted in the agony of the fire ... but she wasn't, and as she reached the deaf man's side, it was he who moved first.

He moved quickly, leaning forwards, his hands outstretched; reaching *into the grate*, digging his fingers in amongst the burning flames, his hands gobbled up in the yellow heat. Hysterically Jeanie screamed, her head jerking back, her mouth filling with spittle. But he remained there unmoving for what seemed to be minutes, then finally, almost reluctantly, he withdrew his hands and extended them to her.

The fingers were dancing with fire, the palms curling with smoke and blistering even as she watched. The stench of burning flesh came from them, the oozing of blood and fat spitting from the end of his fingers ... But in amongst the blackened and dying flesh there was one cool patch of skin, and on that skin Jeanie saw the death of Mary Keller replayed; saw the hay loft and the nightjar; saw herself and the two boys running down the hill, away from the burning barn; saw herself calling out desperately for a lost friend; saw the fire against the night sky; and then saw herself later, thin with misery, crying out repeatedly in her guilt: I want to die, I want to die . . .

The flames continued to consume the deaf man's hands, they burned with the bitter memories and the guilt, and when the flesh was nearly all consumed, Jeanie smelt the keen dark scent of deadness and the sourness of earth.

Jesus, dear God, I shall die here, she thought suddenly, *I shall die here* . . .

Then the deaf man moved again. She flinched, then watched as he held out his burning hands, his eyes fixed on her face. He appealed silently to her, as her father had done, as Ahlia had done, as everyone had done . . . and then he moved closer towards her.

The room stepped forwards too, enclosing the two people, the deaf man and the old woman facing him, small in her bandaged feet.

Pathetically, Jeanie began to beg: 'Let me go, I can't help you . . . I can't . . .' Her words were pitched high with hysteria, her mouth widening into a long scream of terror as he caught hold of her hands.

He grasped them firmly, pulling her towards him, the pain of the fire passing from his hands to hers, agony driving the breath from her lungs. The skin melted between them, the old woman gibbering, dropping to her knees. But still he held on, the fire passing from his hands into her body, burning through her flesh and muscle and into her lungs until, finally, she could no longer breathe and her head fell back, a black trickle of smoke coming from her open mouth.

Then suddenly he let go of her . . . and the fire snuffed out like a candle. The flames had gone, the flesh magically restored to both of them. On her knees, Jeanie gulped in air and then stared at her hands. They were fully restored – as were the deaf man's. His palms were blank; without a mark. No images, no burns. Nothing.

And then she began falling, the deaf man moving away from her as Jeanie was drawn back, away from the room in the deaf house, and away from the fire ... She fell back through the letter, back into Cleveland Square, landing in her sitting room, the paper floating to rest by her feet. Her legs gave way under her then, her body falling, her head landing on the floor, her eyes open and staring at the blank sheet of paper in front of her.

Ahlia's hand was pressed against her mouth, her eyes open with shock. The priest had been in her bedroom! She knew that; she could sense it. But how? She wondered. He didn't know where she lived, she had been careful not to give anything away. And Jeanie wouldn't have told ... So how had he found out where she lived?

Angrily, Ahlia strode into the bathroom. Her towels had been used too! Her toilet, her shower – all used. The priest had been here touching her clothes, her bed linen, her underwear. Fingering her possessions. Damn him! she thought furiously, he had no right, none at all. Now she would have to call Jeanie and clean everything.

But what if Jeanie wouldn't come? She was behaving so oddly. What if she wouldn't help? What if she stayed downstairs instead, cold and defiant? ... Ahlia exhaled sharply with irritation. Jeanie *had* to help her, she always did. They had to clean up, to get every trace of the priest removed from her house ... A sudden noise behind her made Ahlia spin round. But there was no one there; no priest in black standing at the door; no shadow of a man moving up the stairs.

She shuddered with unease. Something was wrong, horribly

wrong... She thought of the deafness which had descended so unexpectedly; of the incident in the bath; of the man who had suddenly emerged in the water... Her mouth dried, the old sensation of dread creeping over her. Something bad was coming; something terrible... Reluctantly Ahlia turned, her eyes moving over the room, the bed rumpled, the painted coverlet pulled back, the white linen sheets obscenely creased.

There was a sudden noise on the stair.

'Jeanie?'

Silence.

It's just the cold, Ahlia reassured herself, it's just the sound of the floorboards shifting... She turned round again, listening; rigid with anticipation.

Silence.

Her limbs were heavy, exhaustion dragging on her. She would go and see the priest... she would talk to him... But later, not now. Now she had to lie down and rest for a little while... Heavily she sat on the edge of the bed, moving her fingers idly over the sheets...

The bed was still warm. Startled, Ahlia leaned over quickly, her hands running frantically over the creased bedding. She was right, there *was* a warm area, about the size of a body. Dear God, she thought furiously, the priest had been in her bed and slept there. But how? He *couldn't* have got in without her knowing it... Ahlia shook her head disbelievingly. She was going mad, that was obvious, she was going crazy. Her panic was childlike, fretful. She had to find someone to help her. None of it was real, she was just imagining things...

But the bed was still warm when she touched it again. That was real; she could feel the heat. Even though the sheets were exposed to the cool air, they were warm – as though someone was still lying on them.

Her hearing faded in that instant. Closed off. The room was getting colder by the instant, Ahlia's expression blank as she slowly and dispassionately began to undress. Her clothes fell from her, the snow banking the windows with the white cold, pressing against the glass, then slowly sliding through the panes and over the floor. It came silently, over the used bed, over the spreadeagled woman. It folded over her; touched her; soaked into every crevice, and entered her. The snow mingled with the white bed sheets and took shape in the dying air.

In silence, in coldness, a white body bled the warmth from the living woman, it coiled around her, smelling of dead ice, twisted and mated with her in stillness. Ahlia no longer responded, she lay unfeeling, the final quiet death of her senses transfixed under the white stillness. Her mouth opened, her limbs moved in a ghastly parody of orgasm; but she felt nothing, and when she opened her eyes and saw the deaf man, there was no response.

He took her away then; to his patch of earth. To the deaf house. And there, in his bed, he used his hands to tell her. He used his palms to recreate her past, her guilt and her misery. He used his white snow palms to show her what she had done and what she had become. On the deaf man's skin she saw her own cruelty; saw re-enacted her husband's departure; and saw herself later waiting for the confirmation of what she already knew – that he was dead.

And when he had finished showing her the past, Ahlia didn't move. Never tried to escape, or repel him. She clung to him instead; to the white chill of the killing cold, filling herself with the deaf man's deadness and sucking from him a comfort which could only lead to madness. And he let her; he let her use herself, and abuse herself, and watched her in the dark room of the deaf house as she whined, and crawled, and begged to please him.

And then he repulsed her; sending her, soiled and naked, away from the deaf house and back to her own room.

The snow stopped. It fluttered against the window and then began, finally, to thaw. The afternoon darkened, day going, twilight standing waiting. Ahlia moaned, turned against the bed, her hearing returning, her hands moving frantically over the cold sheets which now smelt, darkly and unmistakably, of earth.

Harry saw the snow land on the roof of the deaf house and shivered. The chimney kept smoking; the day fading; coming down to evening. The end of the third day, Harry thought. Only four days left. And what was he going to do with those last four days? Chris was in hospital, and he should be on his way to vote at the House of Commons – but he didn't care any more. Nothing mattered now. Not his career or his ambition. Instead he had followed a man across London, followed him to a deserted house... Harry smiled ruefully. The world was all madness and God had left his Heaven for a while.

The chimney smoked on. Then a light came on over the front door... So someone was in there, Harry thought, someone was moving around... He sighed, hoping that Rachel had got home before the snow started. But then of course she had, she had been gone for a while now; a lot of time had passed whilst he had stood there, waiting.

His courage had failed him at the end. He had only made it to the pathway and then backed off, watching the house from the safety of an overgrown wall opposite. Absentmindedly, Harry touched his cheek. Above his left eye, a tic fluttered. *Winky Binky, welcome back, I've missed you*, he thought grimly.

Suddenly angry, he stepped out from the shelter of the wall. The snow landed on his suit and on his hair, his hands damp. *I'm scared*, Harry thought with wonderment, *it's been a long time since I've felt so uneasy.* The pathway to the house was short, only thirteen steps, and Harry's hand was already poised to knock when he reached the front door and rapped at the wood impatiently. *Come on, you bastard, whoever you are. I'm ready ...*

The knocking seemed hollow, as though the house was empty, and there was no sound of footsteps – so when the door opened suddenly, Harry jumped.

'What the hell!' he snapped, then stared at the deaf man. The man in the underground; the man who had tried to kill him. 'Who *are* you?' he asked, his temper rising furiously as the deaf man turned away and walked back into the house. 'Now listen to me!' Harry blundered, following him, crossing the threshold of the deaf house, the front door banging closed behind him.

The house ushered him in, the silence closing over him. Harry paused, suddenly scared again. The shuttered darkness was relieved by only a single paraffin lamp, glowing eerily in the corner of the hall, the staircase a black shape against the wall. The smell of earth was strong, the same smell he had noticed in the underground. As he followed the deaf man, Harry could hear no trace of footsteps – not from the man, nor from himself.

'You owe me an explanation!' he snapped, stopping as the deaf man turned.

The man was standing in a doorway, his shadow looming huge against the wall, magnifying his size.

'I want this thing sorting out once and and for all, do you understand?'

Harry knew he was talking, but the words made no impact either on the house or on the deaf man.

'Who the hell are you?' Harry asked irritably.

Who the hell are you?

He knew he hadn't repeated the words, just as he knew

they hadn't been articulated out loud. Apparently they were being echoed off the deaf man, and resounding inside Harry's head. The realization jolted him and he wanted suddenly to run. *Calm down, Harry... he's just some nut, some loony. Talk to him, find out what he wants...*

The deaf man had already turned away and was moving into the room beyond.

'I think we have a mutual friend,' Harry said, wincing at the banality of the remark. '*A mutual friend*' – *God almighty, this wasn't a cocktail party.* 'Do you know Rachel? Rachel Crossley?'

The deaf man continued to walk, crossing the room and standing beside the table, Harry following him. Another paraffin lamp illuminated the area, the blue-white light casting wicked shadows. The fire had gone out.

'Talk to me,' Harry said impatiently, his tone cold.

The clock swung into motion in the instant he said the words. Back and forth the pendulum went, ticking, ticking, marking time. Unsettled, Harry could feel the flutter of a muscle twitching in his cheek. *Witty Winky Binky, it's not so funny now, is it?*

'Oh, come on, talk!'

The deaf man turned, touching his ears, carefully setting in place the hearing aids – and then he paused, measuring his speech to the clock's metre.

'DO NOT
TRY TO
BULLY ME.'

Jesus, Harry thought, the unnatural voice echoing in his head. *He's talking in time to the clock... Dear God...*

'YOU ARE
THE LAST.'

Harry frowned. 'The last? What does that mean? The last of what?' Realization dawned on him. 'There are *others*? You gave the message to others?' he asked incredulously, thinking back to the young woman he had watched. 'To Rachel?'

Another, more powerful thought struck him. 'To *Chris*?'

'YOU WILL
FIND OUT
IN TIME.'

'In *time*? We've only got four fucking days left, or did you forget that?' Harry shouted. 'You can't do this, you know, it's not possible. All this is just a con, isn't it?' he rushed on, trying to make sense of what had happened to him. 'The message was clever – *You have one week to live* – I don't know how you did it, getting it on the menu like that, but it was bloody clever. And the shadow – that was clever too.' Harry slowed down, to show fear was to lose. 'It was a trick, I know that, but a good one. Even the underground – I've thought about it, but there's an explanation. There always is. It was a drug, or a hallucination, something like that, wasn't it? But *why* did you do it?' Bravely, Harry walked towards the deaf man, their shadows vast against the panelled walls. 'What do you want? What could you want from someone like Rachel? Or my son? Me, I understand. I'm a successful man and I have money—'

The deaf man howled once.

The room shuddered with the noise, swinging as though on rockers, like a child's crib. Almost losing his footing, Harry grabbed the chair next to him, landing heavily on one knee. The deaf man exhaled quickly, the clock's pendulum swinging crazily.

'YOU ARE
A FOOL.'

The words came out fast, hurried, staccato, spat out to the rhythm of the clock whose pendulum was swinging too fast now, violently rocking in its mahogany case.

'I COULD

HAVE KILLED
YOU ALREADY.'

Get out, Harry thought, *get out now. This is no trick. This is real. This is madness*... He rose to his feet cautiously, the deaf man standing facing him, taller, heavier, his eyes highlighted with the glow from the paraffin lamp. The tic in Harry's face intensified, flickered under the skin, giving his fear away. He was suddenly a child again, bullied in the playground by the bigger boys. *Get out, Harry, get out*...

He lurched towards the door in one quick movement, his hand fastening on the handle only to find the knob melting, absorbed back into the wood. He scrabbled at the closed door frantically, sensing the deaf man coming closer, his shadow looming over him. Harry's mouth worked uselessly, his tongue dry with fright, his eyes blurring, altering, filling with a sudden and grotesque pain.

Screaming, Harry put his hands over his face, trying to close his eyelids to shut out the pain; but he couldn't; his eyes were locked open, staring out at the deaf man. *Who was now dark green*, evilly, foully, green; and the room was green; the light green. Harry continued staring, his eyes wedged open, tears pouring from the corners, his vision tinting everything an unearthly, terrible emerald.

'Do something!' he begged. 'Do something!'

The agony screamed inside his head, his eyes forced open, bulging out, too big for their sockets.

'Do something!' Harry howled again, feeling a tearing from behind his eyes, and his vision altering. The green had suddenly gone, in its place was blueness – cold blue, hard blue, infecting everything. The room was a blue tomb, the deaf man an indigo waxwork.

'Help me...' Harry pleaded, his eyes straining from their sockets.

'LOOK INTO

THE CLOCK.'

Harry heard the words and staggered forwards, staring at his reflection in the swinging pendulum. His face was blue, his eyes massive and glassy, splitting the sockets, blood oozing down his cheeks. Indigo blood. He stared, his heart pumping with terror. His eyes were not real eyes any more. They had no pupils, no whites, there were only two ovals of jewel, sapphire blue . . .

And then he knew . . . He had betrayed Gregor Fylding, cheated the old man out of his jewellery business. He had wanted the gems so much that his greed had made him desert the one person who had befriended him. He had longed for the jewels, dreamed of them, been seduced by them, and in his greed he had finally stolen them . . . And now *they were embedded in him*; he was seeing the world *through* them. Now he was locked into them, for ever staring out in agony through the very objects he had wanted most to possess.

And it *would* be for ever, Harry knew that. His lids would never close. The daylight, the sun itself would pass into his brain and burn him, as he stumbled through an evil, bejewelled world of his own making . . . Hysterical with pain, Harry saw the deaf man approach and backed against the wall, trying to turn away from the upturned hands which were held out to him. But couldn't. His eyes couldn't, *wouldn't*, close; and so he was forced to watch his past played out on Kaine Lukes's palms; forced to see what he had done, and what he regretted, and the guilt he had wanted to escape.

He stared at the deaf man helplessly. 'Stop it, please, stop it . . .' His face twitched, his lids burning with the pressure of the unearthly eyes scratching the soft flesh inside. 'Dear God, help me . . . help me . . .'

And so ended the third day.

The Fourth Day

Chapter Twelve

'You did say I could come and see you, didn't you?' Rachel asked uncertainly. 'When we met in the hospital, you said I could pop round.'

Jeanie smiled with relief and then stood back for the young woman to enter. 'I meant it too. Come in, flower, I've just been baking.'

The basement kitchen was warm, the homely smell of hot pastry tickling the senses. A row of pies covered the worktop, three cakes and a pile of biscuits laid out on the table, a stew bubbling on the hob.

'Are you expecting company?' Rachel asked, surprised at the amount of food prepared. 'I could come back later.'

'No need, luv,' Jeanie replied, offering the girl a seat and making tea for them.

The cooking had taken her most of the morning, the preparation meticulous, the labels written clearly and concisely. In three days she would be gone and she wanted to leave something for Ahlia. She had worked it all out very practically; she had made enough food to last a week, some to be put into the fridge, the rest in the freezer, a list of instructions left to make sure that her employer would understand what to cook, and how to cook it. She was making things simple, leaving her own kind of culinary last will and testament. A week's supplies would last until Ahlia hired someone else, Jeanie reasoned, until another woman took over her job.

The thought was oddly comforting, the only way she had found of fighting despair, and of coping, albeit fleetingly, with the threat hanging over her head.

'Help yourself,' Jeanie said, passing a scone to the young woman opposite her. 'They're fresh.'

Gratefully Rachel took one and split it, spreading a liberal amount of butter on the two halves. The kitchen was comforting, soothing her.

'Have you been to see your young man again?' Jeanie asked, settling herself in the seat next to her visitor, and pulling open the door of the Aga. A hum of warm air settled on both of them. It was pleasant talking like this, she thought, achingly lost; it was as though everything was normal again.

'They wouldn't let me in at the hospital,' Rachel replied softly. 'But I'll keep going. They can't stop me trying.'

'He'll be all right,' Jeanie replied automatically, then flinched as she heard the front door open.

The deaf man would come for her again, she knew it, he would come and then what? Her stomach lurched, her throat drying. Maybe if she tried to reason with him. After all, he had to have a purpose for doing what he did, there had to be a point in frightening her, in reminding her of Mary Keller. Maybe if she just tried to talk to him...

Again, the door banged overhead... *Get on with it!* Jeanie thought suddenly, *don't bait me. If you want to come and get me, then make a move, don't leave me hanging here*...

The kitchen was suddenly heavy with unspoken thoughts, Jeanie's anxiety spilling over on to Rachel. Neither of them realized that they were thinking of the same things; the same ominous winding down of their lives.

But if Jeanie was afraid, Rachel wasn't. She knew that Kaine Lukes could have killed her in the deaf house. If that had been his intention he would have gone through with it already. He knew everything about her, and could do anything to her. *If he chose.*

I can take the misery away, Rachel. I can take the misery away.

She thought of the slats of wood in the garden of the deaf house and shuddered. All those rows of markers, all laid out so precisely. Not for bodies, nothing so melodramatic. But *something* lurked under the earth in the garden of the deaf house, something left a memento of its passing there. Another image conjured itself into her mind. Kaine Lukes smearing his blood on the wall of the deaf house . . .

'Have another.'

Rachel jumped, then accepted a second scone.

'Is there any change in his condition?' Jeanie asked gently. 'I mean, is your young man any better?'

'No, there's no change.'

None that the doctors would admit to anyway. But Rachel knew better. Knew it as certainly as if she had been told. The deaf man had visited Chris. Why else would he have told her to get help?

'Do you believe in telepathy?' she asked suddenly. 'You know, people reading other peoples's thoughts?'

Jeanie was baffled by the question. 'In what way, luv?'

'I think I know what Chris is thinking,' Rachel went on evenly, 'I think he's afraid.'

'But he can't feel anything—'

Rachel shook her head. 'Oh, but he can! He can feel *everything* and knows exactly what's going on.' She longed for the woman to understand, to make sense of what she was feeling. *Kind Jeanie Maas, practical Jeanie Maas, help me to get through the next few days.*

'You have to put it out of your mind,' Jeanie said firmly, using the old tactics she employed with Ahlia. 'Stop dwelling on things.' But her voice faltered, her own strength of will suddenly deserting her. 'What's written, is written.'

'I don't believe that,' Rachel said with disappointment. 'I'm sure we can change things, alter the future.' Her tone was urgent, desperate. 'We must be able to alter fate. We *must*.'

'Why?' Jeanie asked, suddenly hopeful. Perhaps this girl did have some of the answers, after all.

'Because we're human. Because we think.' Rachel's certainty merged with the kitchen warmth, making them both believe, for an instant, that their futures were controllable. 'If we don't fight, we die.'

And there it was – the word. Die.

Such a little word; only one syllable. Hardly a word at all, yet meaning more than all the words in the language. Their conversation faltered, locked between gears, caught between truth and myth. And neither of them could comfort the other.

'I'll keep visiting Chris whatever they say. I'll keep going until he wakes up . . .' Rachel hurried on. 'I'll get through to him in the end. I know I will . . . I love him, you see . . .'

Jeanie watched her without taking in a word. She had heard enough and couldn't listen any longer. She didn't want to talk about dying, because dying meant the deaf man and Mary Keller. The old ghosts took a swing at her . . . *No*, Jeanie told herself, *just think about the things you understand*. Her body stiffened suddenly – she'd forgotten the washing! There was a whole pile of laundry to do, *and* the ironing. If she hurried she could get on with it, and clean the paintwork too; then there was the front door brass to polish, and the downstairs cloakroom. If she started this afternoon she could finish it in plenty of time before . . .

'Chris will live, won't he?' Rachel pleaded.

Jeanie glanced at the girl, surprised to find her still there. Really, what was the good of talking in riddles? She couldn't help her, she didn't have time. Besides, she had other commitments already, pressing commitments, she couldn't take on any more . . . Impatiently, Jeanie marshalled her thoughts. There was no point trying to understand what was going on, she just had to carry on as normal, and then maybe, just maybe, things would settle down again.

She had been wrong about Rachel Crossley. She couldn't help her, no one could. Quickly Jeanie got to her feet, folding a tea towel and glancing at her visitor. Time was passing and there was so much to do; no time to spend gossiping.

'Well, luv, I must get on.'

Embarrassed by her sudden dismissal, Rachel rose to her feet. 'I'm sorry ... I didn't mean to keep you.'

'You didn't,' Jeanie said distantly. 'I just have to get on with the work now.' She opened the door and then smiled. 'Drop in anytime, luv. You will, won't you?'

Automatically, Rachel nodded. 'Yes, I'll come back.'

But they both knew she wouldn't.

The River Thames was unlovely that morning as Harry stood on the balcony of the House and tried to remember the argument with his agent. Poor Gordon, only trying to do his best, and he had shouted at him. It wasn't fair. But then, what else could he do? How could he possibly explain his sudden lack of interest? After so many years of grubbing for power, how could he explain the violent loss of ambition?

The water moved coldly under the blank sky. For years Harry had dreamed of entering Parliament; grafted for it, longed for it, and now it meant less than nothing. He touched his eyelids tentatively, the pain had gone, the blue orbs disappearing, Harry own's eyes returning, soft and living – and with those eyes he raked the horizon, but the city looked back at him, unwanted and undesired.

The deaf man terrified him. He admitted it. Never in his whole life had he been so afraid. The house, the smell of earth, the ghastly nightmare of everything that had occurred there ... He buttoned his coat against the wind, frowning.

He couldn't remember how he had got out of the deaf house; only remembered waking up in his flat and crying out, then touching his eyes repeatedly, reassuring himself over and over again.

The Thames slid past, the air filled with the cry of seagulls. It was the fourth day, Harry realized, there were only a few days left now. Such a little time. He bowed his head, leaning over the parapet, the Palace of Westminster behind him, the seat of democracy. What he had experienced was the most perfect example of democracy he could ever have imagined – the spirit of social equality come to life. Or if not social – moral equality at least.

We all die. And we all are revenged or punished . . . How simple the moral truth was, so simple and yet so denied. Harry nodded, as though agreeing with his own thoughts, and felt the first glimmer of humility. How *could* he have imagined that he would escape judgement? How could he have been so bloody stupid? So arrogant? His greed and cunning had blinded him, just as they had brought him here, to this pinnacle of power; just as they had bought him a Mercedes and two homes; just as they had paid for Chris's schooling and the exotic and erotic holidays. He had grown slick and greasy in his own mire, and now he was forced to pay for what he had done.

But not Chris, Harry thought, *not* Chris. Not his son, who had done nothing. He wasn't to be punished . . . But how could he protect him? How could he make sure that the deaf man didn't reach Chris? Harry stared ahead blankly. *Oh God, don't let him get to my son – or to me. Save us, keep us, watch over us. Don't let him come back*, he begged, *please, don't let him come back* . . . A movement beside him made him jump. But it was only a tourist, taking a photograph of a London scene. Deep inside Harry's chest an emptiness opened, a hollowness which he could not shake off, and with it came a hopelessness, dull with loss.

I can beg all I like, but he'll come for me, I know it, Harry thought blindly. *Some day, somehow, the deaf man will come for me.*

He was in agony, boiling alive. There had been no pity in the night, no peace, only the replay of his past and of his betrayal. The deaf man was going to destroy him, the priest told himself, he had come from God to destroy him. There was no escape, no way of avoiding the horror to come, not with a woman, not with forgetfulness. He was damned and a man had been sent to kill him.

There were only three days left. Then what? Death? But how would the deaf man kill him? The priest wondered. *How?* He knew everything, everything he had ever done, every foul and blasphemous act. There was no escape. Unless it was true that God forgave all sinners. The priest struggled to find comfort. Maybe it was God's will. Another thought struck him harder than the first. If it was God's will, was the deaf man sent from God?

That was the real problem, the real uncertainty. God might have sent the deaf man, but then again, he might have come as someone else's messenger... The thought scalded the priest, panicked him. Made him remember what he had done, and how he had challenged God. *No*, he pleaded, *punish me, punish me all you like, but don't desert me. Don't leave me...* The fear of abandonment sucked him down, threatened to draw him into a chasm from which he could never be lifted. To die and be damned... *No!* the priest howled; *no!* there had to be a way to be forgiven.

But no solution came to him. Nothing, only the teachings from his childhood, the Catholic damnation beckoning him, the Devil against God. He struggled with the thought, and with the fear; struggled against the black night. But when four o'clock came round, the priest knew who had won.

He lay unmoving in bed, without thought, wiped of logic. He lay in the nest of his own fear, and continued to lie there until nine, ignoring his housekeeper's knock on the door, ignoring everything, plotting instead.

The church was empty, the early Mass having been undertaken by some other priest. He didn't care, what did responsibility matter any more? His movements were alert, watchful, as he inspected the church, pacing the length of the aisle and the nave, counting the windows, measuring the limits of his domain. The depressive meanness of the place seemed like a criticism; but it wasn't the church which was flawed, it was him. He knew that now. Knew that his hypocrisy had negated the goodness which had once been here. He had corrupted himself and, through his actions, his church. The thought rocked him, too huge to deny, too vast to repair. His chest tightened, his mind racing. His foulness had contaminated the very air, the priest realized, and he was cursed . . .

'*Damn you! Damn you!*' he screamed wildly, suddenly lifting the cross on the altar and hurling it down the aisle with all the force of his body. It landed heavily, skidding towards the door, Father Michael following it, walking in its path, step by step, half crouched. His face was distorted, his body naked except for his trousers, his feet bare on the tiled floor.

'*Damn you!*' he roared again, saliva gathering at the side of his mouth, his hair falling over his forehead, his back crisscrossed with the marks of flagellation.

His voice reverberated against the arched walls of the church, it shook the windows, sounded in the vault below as he continued to shout, hurling abuse and profanities at the air itself. Then he stopped, finally turning away from the cross. For several moments he hesitated, his eyes widening, and then he began to run. He ran back the full length of the aisle with his arms outstretched, rigidly extended away from his body.

He ran with frightening speed, taking the distance almost

in one jump, then slamming his body into the stone altar with all the force he could muster. The impact jerked his head back, the pain in his chest forcing the breath out of his lungs as he half stood, half slumped, against the altar. Then slowly, the priest began to slide downwards, his blood marking the stone and the white altar cloth, his head striking the floor first.

And still he screamed.

'*Damn you! Damn me! Damn me to Hell!!!*'

The roof took the sound and magnified it. The words gunned into every corner, ricocheted around the nave, into the Lady Chapel – and then returned to him, the volume swelling, the curses drumming into his ears and brain. The magnificent head convulsed on the floor, juddered in the shadow of the altar, the freezing temperature mottling the priests's flesh. And still he screamed.

'*Damn me to Hell!!!*'

The echo fell on to him heavily as, clumsily, he began to move, to crawl towards the pile of clothes he had torn off earlier. Frantically he scrambled amongst them, tearing at them, looking for the inhuman thing he had made that morning. And then he found it, picking it up, studying it.

The makeshift crown of thorns was crude, the barbed wire scraping at his fingers as he lifted it, holding it high above his head, his naked chest already darkening with bruising, the skin split around his left nipple. He lifted the crown and the light from the window fell on to it, throwing a malevolent shadow in front of the priest, distorting it and extending the sharpened metal points.

Taut, his body strained upwards, his knees pressing into the freezing stone floor, his arms and hands extended upwards, holding the cross.

'*In the name of God, forgive me . . .*' he howled once, then jerked his arms downwards.

The steel ripped through the flesh on his scalp and

forehead, the crown jamming above his eyes, a fierce and unstoppable flow of blood spurting from the ring of wounds.

His eyes opened.

Transfixed.

A figure shimmered at the end of the aisle.

He blinked, the pain distorting his vision.

The figure moved towards him, towards the kneeling, bleeding priest.

It moved slowly, without speech, without sound. Closer and closer it came.

The priest tried to focus, blood pouring down his face.

'No . . .' he whimpered. 'No . . .'

The figure continued to move. Something dark and forbidding in the shabby little church. Something all powerful and damning; something not sent from God.

'No . . .' the priest whispered, staring at the nearing image, the figure caught for an instant in a bolt of sunlight. 'No. Oh, Christ, no! . . .'

Morning, Chris thought. *Morning already . . . Aaaah . . . and now what? What? What was the next move, and who would make it? Not me*, Chris thought. *I can't move; can't do anthing but think. But think, that I can do. There's no problem in that, no problem at all; the trick is to stop thinking.*

Rachel . . . The name whistled in his head like a night train passing. *Rachel . . .* He had tried to warn her; tried to tell her to get help – but had she understood? Had she known what he was trying to say? And did she know who to turn to?

And who was that? Chris asked himself. *Who exactly was that? His father?* He moved inside himself, trying to alter his position, but failing. The hospital bed was unmoving, unyielding, the rubber undersheet pulling the sweat out of him. The monitor bleeped on, the sound ominously cheerful.

The deaf man is coming for me, and for Rachel. I know it, I can sense it. He wants to punish us – but why? He thought of Rachel again, an image of her step-brother, Leon, jumping into his head. *I'll kill him for what he's done to her*, Chris swore violently. *I'll kill him ... If only I could bloody move, if only I could get out of here ...*

The monitor altered its tone, the inane bleep speeding up to something altogether more urgent, the green line juddering on the screen. For once Chris had forgotten how his emotions changed the read-out; in his fury and frustration he had lost his control and now the monitor was calling the doctor over; alerting him, and betraying Chris.

Alarmed, the medic noticed the increased heart rhythm and signalled to the nurse, calling for an injection. Chris heard the words and realized what he had done ... Helplessly, he moaned to himself, tried to calm himself, tried to steady the monitor's rhythm – but it was too late, it had given him away, and the last thing he remembered before the drugs took effect was the sight of Rachel calling for him.

Ahlia sat in front of the desk, a piece of paper lying next to her right hand. She had attempted to write down her thoughts, but had failed, realizing that she had no one to write to; no one who would care. Not even Jeanie. Even *she* had betrayed her in the end. Oh, she seemed more composed than she had the previous day, but she was still distant, and had spent all morning cooking. Now there were piles of food down there, Ahlia thought incredulously, what for? Who for?

Not that she had had the courage to ask. She didn't want to risk any further estrangement, so she had kept out of Jeanie's way instead and let her carry on. The baking smells had curled out of the basement and up the stairs to Ahlia; deceitful smells, promising comfort but offering none. Ahlia raised her hand to her mouth, rubbing her forefinger against the bottom of her upper teeth. It was a gesture she had used as a child and seemed to soothe her; and she had needed soothing then, just as she did now.

Ahlia suddenly realized how tired she was, how completely, hopelessly tired. Her limbs dragged on her torso, pulled on her trunk, her skull heavy, too cumbersome to hold upright. Wearily she laid her head down on the writing desk, her eyes looking straight ahead. A piece of pink blotting paper lay ahead of her in a cubby hole and it stirred a memory, taking her back, right back to her childhood. It was mottled with ink, just like her mother's had been, pink, marbled with navy. Her mother had had a pen stand too, a heavy Victorian object, old fashioned and grim, the front heavily encrusted with the initials L and B.

Laura Bell . . . She had been a big-voiced woman and a clever lawyer, respected in her field, holding centre stage everywhere – even at home. Especially at home. There had been no attempt at femininity; no grace; no soft notes; only a masculine fierceness which took her to the pinnacle of her profession. Alone. Oh, yes, Laura was married and had a child, but she was emotionally as alone as any spinster. Her husband was tolerated, her child dismissed, disliked. And why? Ahlia wondered, why did you hate me so much? The thought which had hung over her childhood hung over her now. Various reasons had been offered up by therapists – envy, irritation, lack of maternal feeling – but it was deeper than that, and Ahlia knew it. Her mother hated her for her face. Had she been born plain, Laura would have accepted her, helped her, encouraged her. Pitied her.

But she couldn't pity a child whose whole image reminded her daily of what she lacked. Brilliance was never enough for Laura, she had wanted to be lovely too. But, over-tall and heavily boned, she had been cheated of such bounty and instead had capitalized on her abilities. Which had taken her far, even ensuring her a husband another, prettier woman, might have been expected to marry. Then Ahlia was born – late in life, late in spirit – a changeling child with all the magnificence Laura had been denied.

The gods adored Ahlia. And fatally, so did her father... the pink blotting paper danced in front of Ahlia's eyes, its colour kind. She had loved her father, and taken from him everything her mother withheld. Admiration, adoration, kindness. The care Laura denied, he offered two-fold, three-fold, giving easily to his child, and receiving Ahlia's devotion in return. And he listened to her too. Never laughed when she sensed things, even encouraged her to talk about her 'feelings' and comforted her after she prophesied her aunt's unexpected and hideous death. He was her confidant, her ally, her friend.

So when he left his wife, on that terrible white summer day, his daughter couldn't accept the fact that he would never return; couldn't believe that love so easily and consistently given could be so suddenly and brutally cut off.

With bitterness and some little warped triumph, her mother told her what had happened; how her father had met some younger woman and had left her.

'He left you too. He didn't think much of you in the end did he, Ahlia?' she said, the powerful voice carrrying the words as though she was addressing a jury, not a child of twelve. 'After all you thought about him, he's turned out like all the rest, no good, no good at all.' She leaned towards her child. 'Don't fall in love, Ahlia, don't love. There's no point, they'll damage you.' She grasped her daughter's hand. 'You have to learn not to feel, not to care. You have to learn how to use men.' She ushered Ahlia towards the stairs, pushing her upwards into the master bedroom and pulling open the wardrobe doors. 'We have a job to do, child. Something very important – you will help your mother, won't you?'

Ahlia stared at her mother, terrified, and nodded.

'We have to clean up,' she went on. 'Clean up the dirt that he left behind. Clean up after the dirty man has gone . . . they're all dirty, Ahlia, all men . . . remember that.'

The memory had been suppressed for so long that Ahlia first thought she had imagined it, but slowly other remembrances followed – her father's death abroad, her mother's humiliating professional decline, and later, her slow descent into mental illness. She died in Leamington Spa, only hours before her daughter was due to visit her. Died alone.

As I shall. Ahlia thought dully. As I shall . . . Her eyes closed against the memory of the previous day, against the thought of the man who had made love to her, the same man who had tried to drown her . . . What was it supposed to mean she wondered blindly, fighting panic and trying to think of someone to whom she could turn for help. But there was no place of safety. Every man wanted her and every man left her – every man followed her father's example.

And what of the priest? she wondered. What of him? He was the same as the others, taking from her, wanting the kind of erotic oblivion she offered. Taking all the small power she possessed, the power of herself; her body, her sex. And now he had left her, just as they all did, and she was alone – with three days left.

You have one week to live.

Ahlia closed her eyes. What she had done she regretted. She could have saved her husband, but she had murdered him . . . the thought made her cold with shock. *I'm sorry*, she thought helplessly. *I'm sorry* . . . But the words meant nothing. Her husband was still dead; she had killed him and regret wouldn't bring him back.

Somewhere, down below, there was a sound of someone talking. Ahlia frowned. Was it Jeanie? But who was she talking to? She listened. Maybe it wasn't Jeanie, after all. Maybe it was someone altogether different. A deaf man, unlike any other man. Or was he? Ahlia sat up, thinking, a timid hope flickering inside. She didn't want to die; she was afraid of death and punishment. Besides, she had killed already and had no morals to lose.

'This is my life and I chose when it ends – and who ends it,' she said quietly, turning round, almost expecting to see the deaf man standing behind her. *You think you can kill me?* she thought to herself. *Well, we'll see. You're only a man, whoever you think you are. You're a man, and I know men.*

Unsteadily she rose to her feet and looked round. She waited, half expecting him to materialize – but the house was silent; without any unfamiliar sound or movement. Except one. As Ahlia waited and watched, the clock in the hallway began ticking more loudly than usual; the sound reverberating up the stairwell and ticking in time to the beating of her heart.

Chapter Thirteen

The market hall was crowded, the scuttle of bummerees hurrying in at the entrance doors, the sides of beef hooked rapidly on to the metal rails, the scrape of steel piercingly loud as the carcasses were pushed back, the cadavers swinging grotesquely in the bitter air. A strong February wind had blown up soon after midnight; it rattled the iron gates and made the overhead lights rock in the vaulted ceiling, each sound sharpened, intensified, in the echoing vault. The cold was terrible. Even the men, used to the chilling conditions, found their grip loosening on the meat, the steel weighing trays drawing any warmth from their fingers as they worked, their white coats stiff with the hellish damp.

Kaine Lukes watched them. Leaning against the side of Thomas Fortune's stall he studied the men, and clenched the steel bars in front of him, his hands fixed with cold. Beside him a fridge door was opened suddenly, the chill roaring out, a mist following, a line of frozen sheep's carcasses ethereally pale against the metal sides of the freezer. The smell was stilled, hardly a smell at all. Finally Kaine Lukes moved. He stood, feet astride, with his body blocking the doorway.

'What the shit is he doing now?' one of the porters asked, jerking his head over to where the deaf man stood. 'Is he crazy, or what?'

'He likes the atmosphere here,' the other man responded, blowing on his hands. 'After all, who wouldn't want to be here at one in the morning freezing their nuts off?'

'Maybe he doesn't have any.'

The man grinned. 'Tell you what – why don't you go and ask him?'

The deaf man didn't hear the exchange, merely remained where he was, staring at the hanging rows of meat, his face expressionless.

Fascinated, the men continued to watch him.

'Maybe he's doing research for a book, like that bloody female who came in the other day.'

'Come off it, he doesn't look like he could read a book, let alone write one.'

'Then maybe he's a cannibal and he's trying to work out how to keep his victims fresh.'

The first man folded his arms. 'Of course, he could be a Health Inspector.'

'A deaf Health Inspector? Do me a favour!'

He shrugged. 'Maybe he isn't deaf. He might be pretending.'

'Nah, he's deaf all right. You know the story – he got deafened in a fight.'

'Do you think . . .' the first man began tentatively, touching his forehead, 'd'you think he's gone a bit funny?'

'Well, he doesn't make me laugh,' the other replied, turning quickly when he felt a tap on his shoulder.

'So what's going on?' Titus Brand asked, thin and wheezy in the morning chill.

'You tell us,' the man replied, pointing to the deaf man. 'Your mate's been stood there for ages.'

Titus frowned, and glanced over to the freezer. He expected to see Rachel there as well, and was relieved to see the deaf man on his own.

'Jesus, he'll freeze there,' he said, hurrying over to Kaine Lukes and touching his arm.

The deaf man turned slowly, ponderously, recognizing Titus and nodding.

'So how's things?' Titus asked slowly, mouthing the words so that the man could read his lips.

Kaine Lukes moved his hands quickly, the old man watching, trying to follow the hand signals.

'You've been busy?'

Kaine Lukes nodded, then signalled again, jerking his head towards the exit.

'Walk?' he signed. He seemed subdued, almost sad.

'Just give me a minute and I'll be with you,' Titus replied, hurrying over to his stall for his overcoat.

Together they walked out of the market hall and over to the old execution site opposite Smithfield, now a circle of rough garden overlooked by a solitary statue. The cold dragged at the winter trees, the earth hard underfoot, a van blasting its horn as it turned into Cheapside. Titus wheezed noisily, pulling his coat collar up and breaking a bar of chocolate in half.

'Christ, it's cold enough for the Thames to freeze over.'

The deaf man accepted the chocolate, then exhaled, watching the vapour of his breath as it misted in the light from the street lamp.

'So, what you been doing then?' Titus asked, his eyes running with cold.

'Busy,' the deaf man signed again.

'Yeah, I got that. Busy with what?'

Kaine Lukes shrugged and turned away.

Aware that he had somehow overstepped the mark, Titus sat down on a nearby bench, the deaf man following suit. Their shadows were ill-matched, one vast and bulky, the other spare. *I should get back to work*, Titus thought, *I should be weighing that last batch of deliveries* ... But he didn't move, he sat waiting instead. And then suddenly Kaine Lukes turned to look at him.

His expression was hard to decipher; the light was bad, and the cold had paled his skin to an unnatural white. Against the dark collar of his overcoat, Kaine Lukes's face was stone coloured, the deep-set eyes shadowed, the short hair almost bristling with cold. Titus felt suddenly threatened . . . *Get back to the market*, he willed himself. *What the hell are you doing? This man's not right in the head; leave him alone today.*

But it was Kaine Lukes who looked away first, drawing in a breath and turning.

'Can I help?' Titus asked anxiously.

The words were unheard. Cursing his own stupidity, Titus touched the deaf man's arm and when he turned, repeated the question.

Kaine Lukes watched his lips and then stared into the old man's eyes. His gaze was steady, and then slowly he shook his head. The gesture seemed to tire him, his shoulders slumping under the dark coat as he lifted his hands and looked at them for a long instant.

Titus looked at them too. They were square, powerful, the fingers short. Years of boxing had swollen the knuckles, the little finger of the left hand crooked over, the thumbnail split. Under the dark sky, under the white street lighting, the hands told the deaf man's history. The fights, the power of temporary strength, the descent from status. Titus blinked, shifting with the cold, and yet he still looked at the hands, seeing, or imagining – he never knew which – the noise of a crowd before a match, the pummelling noise of the sound system, the names of the boxers called out. It was all so real – the applause of the supporters, the cat calls of the rival punters, the ringing of the bell, the first sounding of the gloves on flesh, the rhythm of the punches.

The hands told the deaf man's history that early morning before dawn broke. In the circle of the old garden Kaine Lukes laid out his glory past for Titus Brand, and then, when he had finished, he paused and said, painfully slowly:

'THIS IS
WHO I
ONCE WAS.'

Titus frowned, unsure how to respond and surprised at the deaf man's admission of vulnerability. Kaine Lukes, to all intents and purposes, was cut off, his place in the world taken from him. The ex-boxer was never again to feel a pride in his skill; never to experience the euphoria of fighting and winning; never to feel the bruised and bloody satisfaction of hard won victory; never again to walk the slow walk to the ring. And never to hear again. To be for ever silent, remembering noise, remembering applause, remembering praise, remembering where he had been, and who he had been – but only remembering, not hearing. He was deaf, beaten. He was over.

'I'm sorry,' Titus said simply.

The deaf man didn't respond, he merely fingered the scar at his throat, his eyes fixed ahead.

'Can I do anything to help you?'

The deaf man turned, frowned, read the lips of the old man and then, unexpectedly, he smiled.

Titus flinched, his eyes fixed on the deaf man's face. *He's laughing at me*, Titus thought incredulously. *The bastard's laughing! He made me feel sorry for him, and now's he laughing at me* ... Embarrassed and afraid, Titus made a move to go, wincing when Kaine Lukes took hold of his arm.

'Hey!'

Hey!

Titus heard the echo of his voice and flinched, badly frightened.

'Let go of me!'

Let go of me!

'Let go!' he repeated, struggling to his feet, the deaf man still holding on to his arm. 'What the hell do you want from me?'

With his free hand Kaine Lukes was still fingering the scar on his neck, Titus watching in disbelief as the wound suddenly opened, weeping blood.

'Jesus!'

'*Stay out of my way.*'

The voice was hard, unfamiliar – *and it was coming from the deaf man's throat.*

Panicked, Titus tried to pull away, his eyes fixed on the open wound. *Dear God, he was talking through it!* The deaf man was talking *through* it . . .

'What do you want?'

'*To live,*' Kaine Lukes replied.

'You *are* alive,' Titus stammered.

'*Don't you want to know who I am?*' the deaf man asked.

Titus hesitated. 'All right, who are you?'

'*Don't you want to know how I live?*'

The old man could feel the pressure on his arm increase. 'All right! all right! So how do you live?'

The deaf man's eyes were steady, unblinking – then they closed for an instant; and in that moment the wound in his neck healed over and he released his grip on Titus's arm.

'I HAVE

TO GO.'

Kaine Lukes spoke simply, his voice returning to the flat, distorted voice Titus recognized. Quickly he rose to his feet. His figure was bulky, heavy in the dark overcoat, his shadow thrown out in front of him.

Breathing rapidly, Titus watched him go with relief – and then he leaned forward, alerted, his eyes straining to see more clearly.

On and on Kaine Lukes walked, but now, beside his own shadow were the shadows of six others.

I see six people coming; six hearing people coming. Coming to the deaf man, in the deaf house.

*

Work was impossible, Harry realized. He might go through the motions, but he was only fooling himself, there was no possibility of his functioning normally. The gaps in hearing were increasing in frequency; he had been talking to one of his constituents on the phone and had been suddenly plunged into silence.

At first he thought that the line had gone dead, but then realized that he couldn't hear anything else; not just the conversation, *anything*. The room was noiseless. Frantically he tapped his pen on his desk. Silence. Then he kicked out at the wall. Silence. Sweat pooled over him, the world suddenly altered. He couldn't speak; couldn't respond to the unheard words; could only wait, heart pounding, for his hearing to return. *If* it did.

The minutes shivered in the office air, they yawned maliciously, the soundlessness complete – except for the drumming in Harry's ears, the rushing of his own blood, magnified in his head.

'Hello? Hello?'

The sound came back, the woman's voice irritable.

'Hello? Hello?'

'Sorry,' Harry said automatically. 'There must be a fault on the line.'

A fault on the line. Which bloody line, he thought, hysterically, my life line?

'Well, I was just saying...' she went on factually, impatiently, angry with British Telecom.

And Harry sat there, not taking in a word. How many times was this going to happen? he wondered helplessly. How many times, and where? In the House of Commons again? While he was giving a speech?... He thought of the dinner he was supposed to attend the next night, and of the after dinner talk he was excepted to deliver. But how can I, Harry wondered, how the hell can I?

His world ran on speech. Talk, conversation, persuasion, bullying. And in order to function he had to hear. To hear what people said, to respond to their words. Without hearing there was no career, no future. But then, maybe that was the point, maybe there *was* no future. He thought of the three days left, panic rising. *No. Hold on, Harry*, he willed himself, *hold on. There has to be an answer; there always is.*

The deaf man has the answer, he thought suddenly, stiffening in his seat. No, not him. There was no way Harry was going to ask help from him . . . But maybe he wouldn't have to. Maybe the deaf man would come back of his own accord . . . Harry struggled to his feet, knocking the telephone on to the floor. His thoughts were hazy, panicked. The fourth day was drawing to its close. It was now seven o'clock in the evening. He couldn't just sit around. Couldn't wait for something to happen. Couldn't let the days simply pass. There had to be an answer, there had to be!

But there was no solution offered, no comfort, only the intermittent loss of hearing which effectively crippled Harry.

'What the hell is the matter with you?' Gordon asked him impatiently, walking in to find Harry slumped, with his head in his hands. 'You can't just cancel—'

'Tell them I've got flu, tell them anything, for Christ's sake!'

'I think,' his agent said carefully, 'that you need to see a doctor.'

No time, Harry thought, remembering the conversation from that morning. No time for medics, and besides, what could they do? Refer him to a psychiatrist?

Tell me about your dreams, Mr Binky, and your childhood . . . no, this shouldn't take long, about six months perhaps, if you come every week . . .

There wasn't time. Time and reality were no more. There was only the threat of death.

Clumsily Harry rose to his feet, grabbing his coat and walking out. The House of Commons had no magic for him any longer, it meant nothing, he was facing death and all the tinny traumas of ambition seemed pointless. He held his career, his loved, adored, magnificent career, at less than nothing. All that mattered was salvation: to find a way of saving his life and his son's life.

Someone *had* to help him? But who . . . *Hold on*, Harry willed himself again, *hold on*. He flagged down a cab and arrived at the hospital minutes later, walking down the familiar stretch of corridor to the intensive care unit. As he turned the last bend he saw Rachel in the waiting room and felt a sudden pang of guilt, but moved on.

The ward was unchanged, as was Chris. Wearily Harry sat down beside his son, and watched him. The doctor came over and exchanged a few words, but the prognosis was the same. Unchanged. Harry studied his son's face. *Are you in there, Chris? Are you?* he wondered, leaning forwards. Chris's skin was bland, smoothed out, unfeeling, empty. Harry winced, having a sudden creeping sensation of unease. Perhaps Chris had already gone, out of the body, out of the mind. The machine bleeped steadily beside him, but his mind ran on, his thoughts disjointed. Chris had changed; this wasn't Chris. So where was he? Where was his son?

Timidly Harry touched his son's arm, willing Chris to move, to turn to him. But he didn't, he remained undisturbed, removed. Above everything; beyond the world. *Don't go, Chris*, his father willed him desperately. *Without you there is nothing. Nothing* . . . his fingers locked over his son's hand, his warmth bleeding into the coolness underneath. *Chris, come on, come on, fight. We've always fought, you and I, always. We've come through everything, haven't we? And we can do again. We can, Chris, we can. Rachel's outside, she's waiting to see you. Let me give her some good news, let me tell her you're*

OK. Talk to me, talk to me . . . Jesus, talk to me . . .

Dad? Dad? Chris woke in his head, drawing on his concentration. *It's you, isn't it? And you're panicking. Stop it! It doesn't help anyone, you know that. That's what you always told me. 'Panic is piss-all good', you used to say.* He smiled in his head, feeling his father's hand on his. *Well, this is a hell of a way to hold a conversation, Dad. I can't talk and you can't hear me . . .* Chris's thoughts nose-dived. *Deafness.* He had been deafened suddenly that afternoon, his hearing cutting off, the noise of the monitor ending, the sounds he relied on, ceasing.

His aloneness in that instant had been complete. Blind, paralysed and deaf, he had felt then something beyond death, the collapse of the soul. Perhaps I'm dying, Chris had thought, perhaps this is end . . . but the thought had been no comfort, in fact the reverse. In the instant of utter hopelessess he had wanted to live, and had been desperate to save himself.

If he had been able to, he would have explained. But now his father was sitting there, listening, and he couldn't say a word. His frustration nearly maddened him.

'Listen, Chris,' Harry went on, 'I've been thinking, when you're better we can go on holiday – with Rachel, if you like.'

Aaaahh . . . Rachel, did I ever tell you that I loved you? Of course I did. Well, I'll say it again – I love you, Rachel Crossley. Love you . . .

'Greece maybe, or Egypt,' Harry continued. 'You always said you wanted to go to Egypt.'

I always said I wanted to be an actor, but I was lying, Chris thought. *I've had enough unreality for one lifetime. When I move again I'll play squash and go to the cinema, and I'll sell the bike and buy Rachel something. And you, Dad, I'll buy you a box of cigars . . .* he frowned to himself. *But I haven't smelt smoke on your hands lately, maybe you've given up. Good, it's bad for you . . . Bad for you, like dying's bad for you.* Chris was suddenly fiercely alert. *Have you seen the deaf man, Dad? Have you? I think maybe you have. You see, I've had a lot of time to try and work this out and now it's beginning to make sense. I think you saw Kaine Lukes, just like Rachel did. All three of us have met him; 'a mutual acquaintance,' as you would put it.*

'Chris?' Harry said softly, touching his son's hair and staring at the taped eyelids. 'There's a way out, I know it, there's a way.'

You've seen him! Chris thought wildly. *You have, or you wouldn't be talking like this. You're afraid of him too. I know that feeling. I know it well. Did he tell you that you had only three days left? Oh Dad, I bet that came as a shock. All you've worked for, all that marvellous career ending in three days. Do you lie awake at night, Dad, thinking? Wondering, worrying? Did he show you what you had done, did he? God, I wish you'd talk to me. Talk to me, damn you! Talk to me, tell me what he said . . .*

'There's a way out, Chris, believe me.'

Oh, I believe you, but who's going to show me *the way out? You? No, otherwise you'd already be doing something. You've never been short on courage, Dad. If you knew how, you'd help me. So now someone else has to. Someone has to show us* all *how to get back . . .* Chris's courage dipped suddenly, helplessness overwhelming him. *He'll come back, Dad, he'll come back . . .*

'You have to hang on for a little while longer . . .'

There are only three days left! How much longer can *I hold on?* Chris concentrated his thoughts, willing his mind to reach out to his father's. *You have to get help. You have to get help, get someone, but get help – before the deaf man gets us. Find help, Dad. Find help . . .*

Harry shivered involuntarily, and then stared at his son. Chris was trying to say something, trying to communicate, he realized. Desperately, his mind focused on his son, his whole being reaching out towards the unconscious figure on the bed. Then he heard something faintly, hardly discernible, a thought more than a voice.

Get help. Get someone to stop the deaf man ... Stop him, Dad, stop him ...

Harry gripped his son's limp hand, clung to it, willing him to continue.

And Chris responded.

That's it, Dad! That's it, you can hear me now. So listen. Get help, for all of us. You, me and Rachel. Get help – you have to stop the deaf man.

'Yes, yes, Chris,' Harry cried, 'Yes ...'

Stop him ...

'Yes, Chris, yes!'

Get someone to help us ... Find someone ...

'Time's up,' the doctor said suddenly.

'What!' Harry snapped, frantically turning back to his son. 'Go on, Chris, go on!'

But he was struggling, fading.

Get help ... get help ...

'I have to ask you to leave, Mr Binky. You see, we have to give your son his medication,' the doctor persisted, surprised by the look on Harry's face as he spun round.

'Get out! Get away from me. I have to hear what he says – *I have to listen to my son*. You've no idea what you're doing – leave us alone.'

The doctor was startled, staring disbelievingly as Harry pressed his ear against his son's mouth, his eyes wide with panic.

'Tell me again, Chris, tell me again—'

'Mr Binky, your son is unable to talk—'

Fiercely, Harry flung out his arm, striking the doctor on the shoulder. His panic terrorized him, screamed at him, as he turned back to Chris and flung his body over his son's protectively.

'Get away from us! Leave us alone! I have to hear what he says . . . I HAVE to listen.'

'Mr Binky,' the doctor said cautiously, keeping his distance and signalling to the nurse. 'It's time to go now. You can come back later.'

Harry was almost sobbing. He could no longer hear Chris, the moment had gone. His son had faded, the tentative communication between them lost.

'You're going to kill him!'

'I'm his doctor,' the man said patiently, calm in the face of the deranged father. 'I'm trying to save your son.'

'You're trying to save him?' Harry said, straightening up and looking at the doctor with desperation. 'You know nothing, nothing . . . You're losing my son, Dr Mitchell. He was here, he was coming back to me, and you lost him, you bloody bastard, you *lost my son*!!!'

The priest was sitting in the front pew, staring at the altar. He was silent. Unmoving. *Deaf.* He knew it would pass, if he waited. It had done earlier and it would again. He just had to wait and be still. *Be still, and know that I am God.*

His housekeeper had phoned his superiors as soon as she found Father Michael, and an older priest had arrived within half an hour, responding to the panic in the woman's voice. He had found Father Michael in the church, still kneeling, still with the barbed wire crown on his head, his whole body bloodied. The sight had rendered him speechless and as he moved towards the priest his foot had stumbled against the altar cross on the floor, still lying where Father Michael had thrown it. Shocked, the priest had lifted it, kissed it, and returned it to its rightful place.

Then he had gone over to Father Michael. His eyes were closed, fiercely closed, as though to block out light and vision, and the blood on his face had dried. Gingerly, the priest had tried to lift the crown of wire, but in that instant Father Michael had moved, scurrying away from him and crouching against the wall.

'No!'

'Sssshhh, it's all right, it's all right.' He knelt down in front of Father Michael whose face was turned upwards, his head cocked to one side as if listening.

'Be quiet!' snapped Father Michael. Then he asked, more gently: 'Can you hear it?'

The priest paused, listening. He was not afraid of the man in front of him, he seemed harmless. Deranged, a disgusting parody of the crucified Christ, but not dangerous.

'I can't hear anything.'

'I can – I can hear the traffic.'

The thought seemed to please him, to soothe him.

'Come back to the house,' the priest said gently. 'It's cold here. Too cold to sit around.' He wanted to add 'half naked' but stopped himself. All Father Michael wore was his black trousers, his clerical robes torn off and discarded. 'You should rest, a week's holiday will do you good.'

'I don't have a week,' mumbled Father Michael.

'What?'

'I don't have a week left,' he repeated evenly, touching his ears. 'I can hear though . . .'

'Yes, you can hear,' the priest agreed, wanting help, wishing he had brought someone else with him. Father Michael was ill, seriously ill, he had seen breakdowns like this before – crises of faith, the Church called it. 'Come with me.' He extended his hand tentatively, but the crouched man refused it.

'Don't touch me!' he shouted.

The sound echoed in the church.

'You have to come with me,' the priest insisted. 'What if someone came in—'

'Did you see him?'

'Who?'

'*The man* – did you see him?' Father Michael repeated. 'He came to me. He's going to try and kill me. But I won't die, I won't.'

'Michael,' the priest said gently. 'No one is going to kill you. You're not going to die, you're a young man.'

Father Michael bowed his head, his expression searching. 'I can't die, can I?'

'No,' the priest assured him. 'We'll help you—'

'You can't! No one can,' Father Michael shouted. 'He'll come back, you see. I know he will.'

The priest sighed. He was hallucinating. Obviously something had affected him and he was disturbed, paranoid. 'Come with me, Michael.'

'No! This is only place I might have a chance. In church . . .' Father Michael looked bewildered, but determined.

There was no way the older priest could move him physically – and there was obviously nothing he could say to persuade him to leave – so he sat down in front of him and took off his jacket, passing it to Father Michael.

'Put this on.'

He hesitated, then obeyed.

'Now let me move this . . .' the priest continued, leaning forward to lift the crown from the confused man's head. It came away with difficulty, reopening the dried wounds and drawing fresh blood. 'That's better,' he said, grimacing and then laying the crown on the floor between them. 'Now tell me what's troubling you.'

'Confess?'

The priest nodded.

Father Michael hesitated. He couldn't confess, couldn't

admit what he'd done; there was no absolution for the breaking of vows, not once, but twice. No, he would be punished by his superiors, thrown out from the church, abandoned in the outside world. And then what? There were only three days left. If he was to die he wanted to die here, where he was known. In his church, with his people. Here he would be mourned, even God would allow that. This was his home, the only home he had – and he couldn't risk losing it.

'I'm not well . . .' he stammered.

'So we'll get you a doctor.'

He nodded, the betrayal was only a small one. Hardly anything, after all the colossal betrayals which had gone before. He would say he was sick, would gather people round him, good people, priests. If he couldn't find his peace with God, maybe they could find peace for him.

'We'll take care of you, Michael,' the priest said kindly. 'You're amongst friends.'

Yes, he was. But even as the thought comforted him another took its place. There might be safety here, but no answer, the solution was elsewhere, not with a priest but with someone entirely different. Bewildered, Father Michael tried to decide what to do; he was afraid to leave the church and the sanctuary it offered, and yet the help he needed could only come from the outside. Dear God, how could he get help while keeping himself protected?

Hurriedly, he grasped the priest's hand.

'Pray with me.'

The man sighed with relief. This was the first sign of recovery, a normal response for a priest. Thankfully, he helped Father Michael to his feet and then guided him over to the altar rail, kneeling beside him. He heard the younger man's breathing and closed his eyes, concentrating his thoughts and praying for guidance, while Father Michael clenched his hands together and repeated silently, over and over.

'Keep the deaf man away.'

There are only three days left.
'Keep him away...'
Three days.
'Keep him away...'

And so ended the fourth day.

The Fifth Day

CHAPTER FOURTEEN

The deafness increased. All five of them found that instead of suffering seconds of hearing loss, they were deaf for minutes at a time, and then, by the morning of the fifth day, a whole hour passed by without sound. Still cleaning the house at Cleveland Square, Jeanie dismissed her hearing aid. She no longer believed that the device was responsible for her lapses in sound. She knew the truth, and, as her memories came back to her, each was accompanied by silence. And noiselessly, each was played out.

She stumbled around the kitchen in her enforced silence, her whole being concentrated on the routine of housework, her thoughts with her employer. For a time she had believed she could cope, but as the fourth day ended and the fifth began, her hopes faded. She was going to die. Horribly. The deaf man would come back, and then – what?

Every sound threatened his appearance; the night lengthening, each step outside, each banged car door, each sudden voice making her flinch. Even the most benign objects startled her; a movement of the shower curtains, a coat hanging behind a door. Every time she opened the curtains she expected his face; every time she answered the door she expected him. He would come for her, and he would kill her . . .

But he didn't. He had tormented her instead, tortured her, and left her with only two days to live – and no hope of redemption. There was no one she could turn to; confess her past to; no one from whom she could beg help. Death was coming. It was unavoidable. All Jeanie could do was to wait – but as the time passed and the week drew to a close, she began to panic. Someone had to be able to help; someone had to . . .

A loud thud above made her look up. Ahlia was moving around, waking early after a weary night. Jeanie wanted to give some kind of explanation to her employer, but couldn't; could only make things easier and hope beyond hope that Ahlia could cope when she had gone. But she doubted it. Even consumed by her own fears she had seen a quick deterioration in her employer, a jerkiness of voice, a hopelessness she carried around with her like a scent. Ahlia had never been balanced, never been stable, but in the last few days there had been a nervousness about her which bordered on frenzy.

She was waiting for something, Jeanie realized, immediately presuming that it was a man. She was waiting for a lover, a new adventure, a fresh conquest. The thought almost cheered Jeanie – if Ahlia's unease was only due to that, she could relax.

It never occurred to her that it was due to something else entirely, and that as the time pressed upon Jeanie in the basement, it also pressed upon Ahlia upstairs, both women accompanied by the same dread. Having distanced themselves from each other, neither noticed the periods of deafness in the other, Ahlia locking her bedroom door and waiting for the sensation to pass, Jeanie sitting patiently, rigidly, in the kitchen downstairs.

All their old sins swung about the house; singing in corners. All the old guilts, injuries, and fears clung to them. Nothing existed outside 54 Cleveland Square and neither of them went out any more – neither daring to risk the loss of hearing while away from home. Food was delivered instead, the telephone put on the answering machine, the door unanswered. The world was on hold – and there were only two days left.

Ahlia's response to the threat of death was typical of her. She looked back, not forward. The future was too terrifying, so it was to the past she turned for comfort. She remembered the men, all the men. She remembered their words, the mumbled endearments, and the vulgarity of their sex talk. Compliments on her beauty were mulled over, treasured; as another woman would have looked at her children's photographs to give her a sense of accomplishment, Ahlia remembered her lovers' words.

Never to hear those words again would be agony. To be deaf and dismissed, to be pitied. There was no ending more cruel for a beautiful woman than to be handicapped. So as the incidents of deafness increased, Ahlia retreated into her memory bank of words. She shifted them, weighed them, rolled them on her tongue. Sometimes – when she couldn't hear – she sat on the bed holding a mirror, her mouth moving silently, repeating over and over the compliments she would soon cease to hear.

And she wondered about the deaf man. She wondered as she wondered about all men. But this time she wanted revenge. Whilst he terrified her, he angered too, and her rage burned as she rocked on the edge of her bed, her hands over her deafened ears. Terror made her sly; she had been weak all her life, dismissive of her advantages, spoilt by her father, cosseted, protected by money and then later, when all the men had deserted her, there was Jeanie. Always there, always listening, always practical. But this time even Jeanie couldn't help her, Ahlia realized. All her brisk common sense would be useless in the face of such a threat.

Slowly Ahlia slid her tongue along her bottom lip, animal with cunning. He was a man, and she knew everything about men. The memory of the water and the snow swamped her, entered her, folded over her – and then the memory of her husband's death came back to her too. But she hardly responded any more. The event had been replayed unceasingly during the last two days; over and over, until it became a part of her, until it wedged inside her, a canker as real as a piece of bone. It had been unbearable at first, but as the time passed Ahlia learned to sit out the images, to ride them, to pace herself, waiting for them to fade and for her hearing to return to normal.

Her ears popped suddenly, sound coming back so loudly that she winced. Slowly Ahlia glanced back into the mirror; her face was heady with sensuality, drowsy with lust. If the deaf man came back she would know how to protect herself. She would seduce him, bargain for her life. The thought comforted her. She wasn't beaten yet. She had searched for and found a solution. If he came back, she had a chance.

And meanwhile Jeanie continued to iron in the basement downstairs, her head intermittently silent, then full of noise. The hot iron moved over the clothes, back and forwards to the rhythm of the footsteps overhead. Her eyes focused on the creases, but she saw only Mary Keller's face rising from the bed sheets, and the hill with the burning barn. The kettle whistled and became the sound of the last bus home, the nightjar, the bell in her father's shop, and every scrap of metal, every railing outside the window, every wire rack became a hairpin . . . She worked blindly, thoughtlessly, mindlessly.

She dragged herself around the basement and walked into and out of her own hearing. Back and forth she went, without knowing how or why, just working, working . . . Only a floor apart, the two women paced out their destinies alone. Had they chosen to confide, they could have become allies. But each had remained silent; in the one most important event of their lives they had estranged themselves, and waited in a ghastly disharmony for the re-emergence of the deaf man.

*

Gingerly Rachel leaned down in the garden of the deaf house and touched the nearest slat of wood. It felt chilled, winter cold, but then it was February and the frosts were not over. Her fingers lingered on the piece of wood, her thoughts wandering.

The previous day she had waited to see the deaf man again. Had expected to see him outside Smithfield, or in her dream. But he was nowhere. Gone. Even his presence had vanished, the atmosphere he carried with him, the scent which preceded him, all gone. The day had lingered, intolerable with memories of the past, and the night had been even longer. In between she had suffered, like the others, from the terrifying patches of deafness, making work impossible. So she had called into the office sick, walking around the London streets, hiding in toilets when the deafness came on, sitting with her arms around her knees, waiting for it to pass.

She knew it would. The end was not yet. It was too soon ... Finally, reluctantly, she had gone home to her flat, and then to bed, jamming a chair behind the door of her room and imagining the soft footfall in the early hours when Leon used to come for her. Half asleep, she thought she saw the doorknob turn, pictured his face, heard his threats.

And don't think of locking the door or I'll tell ... I'll tell ...

Go on then, Leon, she willed him. Tell on me. Tell on us. Tell. *Tell.* TE-E-E-E-LL ...

Rachel looked down at her hand, surprised that she had gripped the wooden slat so tightly that the edge had pierced her skin and bloodied it. It was all coming to the end. There were only two days left to wait. And only two days left to reach Chris and save them both.

When she had heard nothing from the deaf man the previous day, Rachel had still hoped. But by the time the afternoon of the fifth day came she was sufficiently disturbed to go in search of him. So she returned to his home. To the deaf house. And as she had done before, she knocked and waited for him to emerge. But there was no answer at the door, and no smoke came from the chimney. Slowly, disbelievingly, Rachel walked around the house, but all the windows were shuttered and the doors barred. Her only ally had gone – deserted her – just as he had deserted the house.

Oh, but she loves, Rachel, she loves. And she has loved me.

Startled, the girl looked over her shoulder, but the deaf man wasn't there. He was talking to her, but not from anywhere she could see or reach. He loves the house, she said to herself, struggling to understand; he loves this place so he would not leave it for long. Cautiously Rachel turned to gaze up at the windows of the first floor. Blankness. Then the second floor. Nothing, no sign of Kaine Lukes anywhere ... Oh, but I feel you, Rachel thought, I feel you ... or if not you, *who?*

Her skin prickled suddenly, fear aroused. The long afternoon was fading, the shadow of the house stretching towards the flower bed where she knelt down again, the slats of wood each casting their own shadows around her.

She loves, Rachel, she loves.

And she *lives*, Rachel thought suddenly. Dear God, the house *lives!* ... The shadow crept over towards her, the smell of earth coming strongly into her nostrils as she tried to rise – but couldn't. The ground held her feet and, as she struggled, the slats around her began to move violently. All the wooden markers began to vibrate, to shudder in the dark earth, to rock, and then to strike against each other. The noise was faint at first, then grew, the sound becoming ominously loud; the wooden clicking of the sticks increasing every instant; the steady, deadening drumming of the posts echoing in the freezing air.

'No!' Rachel screamed out. 'It's a trick! I know you're in there. Come out.'

Her voice carried over to the house, to the shuttered windows and the empty rooms. He *had* to be in there somewhere, hiding, watching.

'You helped me. You're not evil, I know that. I need you . . .'

Her voice rose fiercely, but it was drowned out. Gasping, she clapped her hands over her ears to shut out the noise of the wooden slats banging together, her eyes widening as the sound suddenly changed to the beat of a thousand footsteps, marching in time. Startled, Rachel stared ahead. *The sound was coming from the house*, she realized suddenly. It was coming from the house! Her eyes fixed on the deaf house, and in that instant she felt the ground move, the shadow of the house moving closer towards her.

No, Rachel thought, her mouth dry, it couldn't be *moving*, it couldn't be . . .

But it was. The house was creeping over the ground, moving to the applause of the clapping wooden markers. Terrified, Rachel glanced at the earth, then violently she wrenched the nearest marker from the ground.

The noise stopped immediately.

Silence.

Silence in the garden.

Silence in her head.

The house stopped moving. The air froze. It shuddered with tension, it held its breath. Then from the hole in the earth where the marker had been, there came a sound.

A faint sound, a familiar sound, from deep in the womb of the world. The sound of a clock ticking.

And then she knew.

CHAPTER FIFTEEN

'Harry? It's Rachel, I have to see you.'

He sighed inwardly. 'Hello, Rachel, what is it?'

Hurriedly she pushed some more money into the phone and leaned back against the glass door of the booth. 'I have to see you – it's important. It's about Chris.'

He was alert immediately: 'What about my son?'

'Can't we talk face to face?' she asked anxiously. 'Please . . .'

'Yes, yes, of course,' he agreed. 'Where?'

'At the hospital, in an hour's time? In the waiting room.'

He was surprised by her assertiveness.

'All right, in an hour then.'

Relieved, Rachel put down the phone and then walked back on to the street, deserted apart from a tall, elegant woman who was hurrying past. She noticed her because she was beautiful, terribly lovely on the dark winter day, but she seemed troubled, anxious to be somewhere else, nervously crossing the street and looking round repeatedly.

Ahlia didn't notice Rachel, her thoughts were elsewhere, her quick voyage to the shops rationed in time. *Hurry*, she willed herself, *hurry.* There was so little time to waste. She had gone out to buy some new cosmetics, a whole batch of lipsticks, make-up and perfume swinging from a collection of initialled bags. She was preparing herself, setting the scene for the deaf man's re-emergence, calling into power her incredible beauty. *If he comes back I'll be ready*, she told herself. *If he comes he'll find me at my best.*

She moved hurriedly back towards Cleveland Square, crossing a set of lights and pausing momentarily outside the window of a television showroom, the bank of screens throwing up myriad images of Harry Binky, MP. Startled, Ahlia recognized her old lover, but could hear nothing of what he said. The sound was turned down, no voice materializing from the working mouth, and after a moment she walked on.

At precisely four-thirty she opened the door of her house and walked in, and at the same moment, across London, Rachel saw Harry Binky's Mercedes pull into the hospital car park. Her relief was followed quickly by anxiety. He looked older, uncertain, his movements uneasy as he locked the car door. Slowly he moved away and then turned back, checking the door again, his actions disorientated, his hands fumbling with the keys. He's slipping, Rachel thought with alarm, he's losing control.

He walked over to her and smiled woodenly, the tic above his left eye jerking under the skin.

'Rachel,' he said simply.

She smiled and touched his arm briefly.

The action seemed to affect him and he glanced away to compose himself.

'What can I do for you?'

The air was moist, promising rain now that the snow had gone.

'I want to ask you something,' Rachel began hesitantly. 'I had a warning... a premonition... and I think Chris had one too.'

Harry stared at her. His mind shifted, fixed on the young woman in front of him. He had suspected something, but hadn't been prepared for her to admit that what had happened to him had happened to her also.

'Did you . . . have *you* had a similiar experience?' she asked, hurrying on. 'I don't want to pry, I've no right to ask you to confide in me, but I think that Chris is in danger – I have to help him and I think I might know a way. If you'll help me.'

Harry continued to stare at her, transfixed.

'I know a deaf man called Kaine Lukes.'

Harry flinched.

'He came to me, he . . . knew all about me . . . and he went to Chris too.' She paused. 'Your son didn't tell me that, I just *know*.' Her voice rose, high-pitched with anxiety. 'Harry, I think the deaf man will help us—'

'Jesus.'

Rachel frowned. 'What, what is it?'

'Leave him alone,' Harry said fiercely. 'He's crazy. He won't help anyone.'

'I think he will.'

He grabbed her arm. 'No!' he said bluntly, letting go of her and glancing blindly around the car park. So Rachel *had* received the warning and now she had only forty-eight hours left to live. Just like him – and just like Chris. The weather sank gloomily into him as they stood, motionless in the car park, and he shivered, bleak with cold.

'I was told I had a week to live.'

Rachel nodded. 'But you weren't told why?'

'No . . .' Harry trailed off. 'I've done some shitty things in my time. I suppose it's a punishment.' He glanced at her and then glanced away, embarrassed. 'I don't know what to do.'

'Neither did I. I thought I could find a way out. In a week I thought I'd find an answer – or find someone who would give me that answer.' She thought of Jeanie Maas and then continued. 'But I didn't, and finally I realized that *he* was the only one who could help.'

Harry's face was white with terror.

'You're mad.'

'No, believe me,' Rachel insisted. 'It *is* him. He's the *only* one who can help.' She paused. 'He helped me—'

'He's evil.'

'I don't think so. There *is* some goodness in him.' She caught hold of Harry's arm. 'Trust me. I know him and I think that we're meant to turn to him. When I realized that, I waited for him to come back, to help. I waited for two days, but I was wrong. He never came back . . .'

Thoughtfully, Harry looked at the girl. 'Why did he come to you in the first place? Why you, Rachel?' he asked. 'I know what I've done. I know why I should be punished – but *you*? What did you do?'

'I wanted to die.'

'Some sin,' he said quietly. 'I suppose we've all wanted to die at some time or other.' The wind pulled at his hair. 'Why's he doing it?'

'Who?'

'The deaf man!' he snapped impatiently. 'I want to know why the bastard's doing this. *How* he's doing it, and what he's getting out of it.'

Let me take the misery away, Rachel. Let me have it.

'Why should there be anything in it for him?' she asked, touching his arm.

Harry raised his eyes. 'Jesus, grow up! No one does anything for nothing, Rachel. This sod's getting his kicks out of jerking us around.'

'Maybe,' she said coldly. 'Or maybe not. I don't know why he's doing it, but I know one thing – I don't want to die, Harry.' She spoke softly, so softly that he had to strain to hear her. 'I want to live. And I want Chris to live. And you.'

'I don't care any more—'

'You do!' she snapped.

'No,' Harry insisted. 'I want to save Chris, and I don't

want anything to happen to you, Rachel. But for myself, I no longer care.'

'But Chris would,' she said gently. 'He loves you. You must know that.'

Moved, Harry glanced away. Regret, loss, fear all welled up in him. I'm tired, he thought, so tired, and so empty. Rachel's young, she'll survive, but what hope is there for me? The two days yawned out in front of him. Two days, and after that, what? Oblivion? The end of life? He felt the muscle twitch in his face and, embarrassed, covered it with his hand.

'I think I know what to do,' Rachel said at last.

Harry felt nothing. There was nothing left to feel.

'Listen to me,' she pleaded, '*I think I know what to do*. We have to get the deaf man to help us.'

The words burned in his head and he looked at her disbelievingly.

'No! No way—'

'Hear me out,' Rachel insisted. 'We need him. He's the only one who can do anything now ... I can get him back, Harry. I know a way ... but I need help. Will you help me?'

The question hung between them. It shuddered in the listening air; it begged him; pleaded with him. The deaf man, Harry thought. No, not him. It *couldn't* be him. He wasn't going to help them ... and yet Rachel had said he'd helped her. She believed in him. But I don't, Harry thought. If we go to the deaf man, what the hell do we disturb? If we go to him, plead with him, what will he do?

His mouth thick, dry with fear, Harry glanced away. He thought of the pain in his eyes, of the horror of the previous days, and automatically touched his eyelids, frightened beyond measure. To face the deaf man again, to take him on, to turn to *him* ... Dear God, how could they risk it? And what if they were wrong?

'No, I can't face it.'

Something very terrible is coming, Father. Something very much beyond what I believe I can stand.

'I can't. I'm sorry, but I can't . . .'

Rachel stared at him coldly. 'You have no choice.'

'It might be just a threat!' Harry blustered. 'In two days nothing might happen. We might simply have imagined it all.'

She looked at him incredulously. 'But you don't believe that, do you?'

'No!' Harry said sharply, angrily. 'No, I don't bloody believe it.' He thought of the way his son had tried to reach him the previous day. *Find help, find help . . .*

Rachel could see his indecision and pushed him. 'He would have done it for you so willingly.'

'What?'

'Chris – he'd have helped you without giving it a second's thought.'

Shamed, Harry looked away. 'Are you sure there's no other way?'

'No,' Rachel replied softly. 'No other way.'

'We might be wrong—'

'For God's sake!' The words tore out of her. 'Just help me!'

A moment passed between them, and then finally Harry nodded.

In silence they climbed into the car, Rachel sitting in the passenger seat next to him and giving Harry directions. They cleared central London as the light faded and early evening set in. Preoccupied, Harry remained silent, and when the car phone rang he ignored it. *Time was when I loved to answer it,* he thought, *when I drove along making plans, arranging social events, talking to constituents.* He remembered suddenly that he was due on television that night; the phone call must have been from Gordon; panicking, wondering where he was.

On they drove, over the Thames, towards the deaf man. The phone rang again, Rachel glancing at Harry questioningly. But he simply turned on the radio to drown out the noise. His recklessness was phenomenal; it had taken him decades to build a career and only days to destroy it.

'Sometimes I go deaf,' Rachel said suddenly. 'I have gaps in my hearing.'

'Me too,' Harry agreed.

'Often?'

'More and more so lately.'

She stared at his profile: 'But you're OK now?'

'Pardon?'

She began to repeat the question, but Harry laughed.

'I was only joking – yes, I'm OK now,' he said, surprised at his own levity. *I feel light-hearted*, he thought, *as though everything was perfect; as though I had everything I wanted in the world.* He shook his head incredulously.

'Turn here,' Rachel said.

Harry turned, and suddenly he realized where she was taking him and shuddered. The deaf house . . . *How long ago was it that I first came here? A day, two days? . . .* He couldn't remember, time had no limit or meaning any longer. We are going to the deaf house, he thought simply, turning at the next bend. We are going to walk into Hell.

Rachel looked at him curiously. 'Have you been here before?'

'Yes.'

'Ah . . .' she said simply, lapsing into silence.

She expected him then to ask her what she intended to do. After all, he had agreed to help her, it would be a reasonable response. But Harry remained silent, driving carefully, the radio turned full on.

Then suddenly the house was before them. It rose up, lonely, from the bleak ground, illuminated for an instant in the headlights before Harry parked the car, turned off the engine and then the music. The silence was oppressive. Tomb silence... Together they sat in the car and waited. The house was dark, no lights, only its bulk black against the failing sky. Soon it would be dark.

'Is he in there?'

Rachel glanced over to him. Her bravery had a grim urgency. All she felt now was coldness and complete, blind determination.

'Well, is he?' Harry asked.

'He must be,' she replied finally. 'You see, he loves the house, and the house loves him... If he's not there now, he'll return. He has to. He'll come back because of her.'

Jesus, Harry thought to himself. *We're all going mad.*

'Are you ready?'

'What for?' he asked, watching as Rachel took a torch out of her bag and opened the car door.

'Come on, you have to help me.'

He sighed and slid out of the car, following her to where she stood on the pavement. The house was still, the temperature dropping as the night came on.

'Rachel, look, I don't think—'

'No!' she snapped, her expression fierce. 'No excuses, we have to get him to help us. Chris asked me to get help.'

He asked me too, Harry thought, shamefaced.

Cautiously, Rachel opened the gate and moved into the front garden of the deaf house. The light from the far-off street lamp no longer made an impression on the darkness so she switched on the torch, training it on the ground in front of them. Reluctantly, Harry followed, tugging his coat around him, his skin prickling with tension. The house was blank, without lights, and no sign of smoke was coming from the chimney.

Slowly, Rachel traced the building's outline with the torch beam, the light picking out the crumbling stucco and the damp green moss around the edges of the door.

She loves, Rachel. And she has loved me.

'He can't be in. There are no lights on,' Harry whispered.

Rachel didn't reply, she simply turned the beam of light back on to the ground as she moved round the house and into the garden beyond. The earth was hard underfoot, even though rain had recently fallen.

Harry stopped dead. 'What the hell is that?'

Rachel swung round, the torchlight picking out the rows of wooden markers.

'God Almighty, it looks like a cemetery,' Harry said hoarsely, kneeling down and reading the nearest label. '*Thérèse Raquin* by Émile Zola.' He shook his head incredulously. 'He buries his books here ... he *buries* his bloody books.'

A sudden sound behind them made them jump, Harry snatching the torch from Rachel's hand and fixing its beam on the house.

'Who's there?'

Nothing.

'Who is it? I know someone's there.'

Silence.

He turned back to Rachel; in the half light, her face was pinched, terrified.

'Let's get out—'

'No!'

'Listen, Rachel, this is madness,' Harry said, his breathing erratic. 'The man's not here.'

'Then we call him back,' she replied simply.

He was sweating: 'How?'

'We hurt him.'

Harry frowned, bewildered. '*Hurt him?* How?'

Rachel's voice dipped. She seemed to be trying to avoid being overheard.

'We hurt the thing he loves,' Rachel went on, surprised

that Harry didn't already understand. 'We hurt *her*.'

She pointed towards the house, Harry staring at her in disbelief.

'It's a bloody house!' he said incredulously. 'It's just a house, Rachel, a *house*—'

'It's *his* house!' she said savagely, 'and he'll come if we hurt her. I swear, he'll come.'

Harry shook his head, backing away. 'No,' he said firmly. 'This has gone far enough. We're going home now. Come on, Rachel, come on. Time to go.'

She stood defiantly on the dark earth, the shadow of the house gathering over her. The air froze into stillness, the cold sucking the warmth from them.

'You want him to help us, don't you?'

Harry hesitated, then nodded.

'And you know he won't come back unless we call him?'

'He might—'

'*HE WON'T!*' she shouted.

The sound echoed in the empty trees, scuffed against the white plasterwork of the house, shuddered in the basement, under the earth. 'He'll only come to save the house. I know it's true, believe me. We have no choice.'

'It's madness—'

'Do you have a better idea?' she countered, turning back to the house and then bending down to the earth. Carefully she picked up a stone and weighed it in her hand, then slowly and deliberately, she paced towards the house, pausing by the shuttered back window.

'No!' Harry warned her. 'NO!!!'

In one quick movement, Rachel drew back her arm and then flung the stone forwards. It rode the chilled air, it swung on it, skidded on it, moved on towards the house and then, with a huge, resounding blow, struck the wall above the window.

*

The deaf man stirred, clutched at his arm, staggered to his feet. Then paused.

Clever Rachel, how clever you are. The youngest and smartest of all of them.

He moved out from the cellar, lurching against the dark wall and groping towards the stairs. A deep patch of bruising showed on his upper arm, the skin mottled, the deaf man climbing, naked, up the steps.

You couldn't wait, could you? Couldn't wait until I came for you. You came for me instead. You came to hurt me. It was a good blow, Rachel, unexpected. Always catch your opponent off guard, that way you win. But not always...

At the top of the stairs, Kaine Lukes paused. His skin was covered in earth, his eyes steady, his deaf ears useless, his instinct hearing for him. The house was dark above him, but he needed no light. He knew her, knew every inch of her walls, and when he reached the hall, the deaf man paused again. In the fraction of light which remained, his white body showed in relief against the wooden panels, the deep and savage bruising on his arm darkening rapidly.

Go on, he willed her. *Go on, Rachel, strike out again. Hurt me.*

For a moment, time hung motionless. The house was deaf, without noise, as Kaine Lukes leaned against the wall and then slowly and luxuriously rubbed his head against the wood, a deep guttural sound resonating in his throat. Unable to hear, he could decipher nothing of the noise, but the hall caught at it and magnified it in the stillness – the sound of the deaf man purring.

You don't like the house, do you, Rachel? Oh, but she loves, she loves. She loves me ... and she'll save me.

Frantically, Harry traced Rachel's outline with the torchlight.

She was crouched among the wooden slats, listening, her face intense, frenzied.

'He's here!' she shouted. 'He's here. The deaf man's here!'

Quickly Harry caught hold of her arm. 'For Christ's sake, come on. Come on!'

'No!' she shouted. 'We have to get to the deaf man. We have to!'

Her voice was vicious with determination, her hands reaching out towards the first wooden markers, her eyes fixed on the slats in front of her, her breathing rapid. And then, before Harry could stop her, she began furiously to wrench them out of the ground.

Inside the dark hall of the house, the deaf man jerked, his body arching upwards, his hands flat against the wall behind. Then suddenly on his chest bruises began to appear, some small, some larger, welling under his skin, and darkening, swelling in patches.

He breathed heavily, his head still rubbing against the wall behind, his feet planted wide on the floor.

Oh, but she loves, Rachel, and she loves me . . .

The marks widened, swelled, the dark bruises covering his torso, appearing one after the other, increasing instant by instant, until the deaf man's body was disfigured and discoloured, his skin twitching wildly with the repeated onslaught of pain.

She loves me . . .

'Dear God,' Harry said, kneeling down beside Rachel.

She had pulled all the wooden markers from the ground and was shaking, looking down at what she had done, the vacated gaps in the soil giving off the dark and familiar scent of earth.

'*He's here*,' she said blindly. 'I sense him – and I smell him.'

Harry tried to grasp her arm, but she pulled away.

'He's here!' she repeated, beginning to dig at the disturbed earth, her fingers clawing at the soil.

'Enough!' Harry said sharply. 'Stop it! It's wrong, it's all wrong . . .' He glanced round nervously, checking the outline of the house with the torch, its light sliding across the deaf windows and the closed doors. 'For God's sake, Rachel, come away.'

But she continued to dig, to grope at the earth, her hair falling forward over her face, her eyes shadowed.

'Help me!' she pleaded. 'Help me – we have to reach him, you know that. You promised to help me find him, you have to help. Please . . . please . . .'

Harry shone the torch on to the black earth. 'Rachel, he isn't there, he *couldn't* be there.'

She paused momentarily and then began to dig again. Her hands worked at the earth in a frenzy, her fingers finally closing on the books, the volumes plucked out and discarded, thrown to one side, as she continued to dig.

Horrified, Harry watched her.

'A man can't live underground,' he said firmly. 'Be reasonable, Rachel. A man couldn't bloody *breathe* underground.'

She stopped suddenly, listening.

'*He's coming*,' she said. '*He's coming* . . .'

Harry shuddered, his skin crawling, his body rigid with terror. He too could sense a movement, could smell the dead scent of earth and hear a deep guttural sound coming from below. His hand shook holding the torch, the white beam of light shivering in the darkness.

'He's here.'

'Jesus,' Harry whimpered, dropping the light and scrambling to his feet. Rachel turning, reaching out for him.

'Harry, wait . . .'

But he was too terrified to listen and backed away, his eyes fixed on the earth before them.

Oh God, he thought desperately, what have we done? What have we done?

THE SIXTH DAY

Chapter Sixteen

'You came back,' said Jeanie timidly. 'I thought you might.'

She was in the basement on the morning of the sixth day, waking intermittently, weary from a disturbed night. Tiredness had made her disorientated, muzzy in the head, a slight ache starting over her eyes. She had sat up until past two, waiting for some kind of signal, for someone to help her. But the night hours dragged by slowly, taking away the fifth day and hurrying in the sixth – and still no one came.

Someone *had* to help her, someone had to show her how she could avoid death ... The word made her lip tremble and Jeanie moved, turning on the lamp by her bed and picking up the letter lying there. Her last will and testament. There was little to leave. A small amount of money in a post office savings account, the few indifferent pieces of furniture she had brought with her to Cleveland Square, and her father's old velvet smoking cap. Delicately, Jeanie fingered the cap. The old gold tassle had lost its colour long ago and was now tarnished, the velvet a dull mole brown. She remembered her father wearing it, ludicrously proud, his body jerking with Parkinson's disease; and she remembered the shop and the deep wooden drawers lined with brown paper.

The recall tugged at her in the quiet hours; its poignancy almost too much to bear. And yet tired as she was, Jeanie couldn't sleep. The night wound on, her eyes often closing, then opening again, startled by a sound. Then by silence ...

Her mood swung between despair and blank, uncomprehending terror, and when at last the morning broke, Jeanie dressed and began, blindly, to work.

And then he came. He came down the steps noiselessly, or so Jeanie presumed. How else could he have entered the basement? He hadn't been there when she bent down to empty the washer, it was only when she turned.

'Oh, God . . .' she said simply, dropping the sheet she was holding.

He was dressed as she remembered him last. Not as the doctor, but as the deaf man in the deaf house. The same dark overcoat covered his bulk, the same closely cropped hair surrounded the wide features. Slowly, the deaf man nodded and beckoned for her to approach.

Timidly, Jeanie walked over to him.

'COME WITH
ME NOW.'

'But I have to finish here,' she blustered. 'Make Mrs Bell's breakfast . . .'

He silenced her with a look, and then beckoned to her again. Jeanie moved forward, glancing over her shoulder towards the kitchen. She should have washed up, and the bin needed emptying . . .

'COME ON.'

She jumped. Hesitated. Where was he going to take her? she wondered. Where was there left to go?

He paused, turning to climb the basement steps.

'COME ON.'

Breathing heavily, Jeanie followed him, falling into step with the deaf man as she pulled on her coat. Then she noticed that she was still wearing her apron and slippers. *Dear Lord*, she thought to herself, *why wasn't I more prepared? Why wasn't I ready?*

Through the London streets they passed in the seven o'clock quiet. The morning was cold, snow threatening again, the wet moisture of rain giving way to a deep chill, only a few people passing them as they moved quickly on. Jeanie could feel the uncomfortable cold creeping through the thin soles of her slippers and slapping her cheeks. God, she thought, shivering, it was going to be a bitter day. She should have worn something warmer. Something suitable – but for what?

The bus came as they reached the stop, the conductor extending his hand towards Jeanie for money. Automatically she showed him her bus pass and then paused, glancing over to Kaine Lukes – but he took a seat without paying, and the conductor said nothing, merely stared ahead, apparently not even seeing him.

Frowning, Jeanie sat down next to the deaf man, leaving a gap between them, and then she looked at the passengers sitting opposite. A teenager was slumped in his seat, his mouth hanging open as he slept, and besides him a man in glasses read the morning's copy of the *Telegraph*. Curiously he glanced up, raised his eyebrows on seeing Jeanie's slippers, and then quickly looked away.

She could make a run for it. Jump off at the next stop ... but where would she run *to*? she wondered helplessly. There was nowhere left. The deaf man had come for her.

She turned, nervously eyeing her companion: 'Where are we going?'

He said nothing. But the man with the paper looked at her strangely.

'Please tell me where we're going,' she begged the deaf man, then paused, embarrassed by the pointed stare from the man opposite.

'What the hell are you looking at?' she asked fiercely.

Blushing, he turned back to his paper. But when Jeanie looked over to the conductor she saw, to her amazement, the man smile at the passenger, jerk his head in her direction, and then touch his forehead.

Bloody cheek! she thought furiously, folding her arms and

leaning back in her seat. *There's nothing wrong with me, nothing at all. I mean, if you can't ask someone a question, what the hell is the world coming to? You'd think I was talking to myself...*

Jeanie shivered, tentatively glancing at the seat next to her. The deaf man was still there. *She* could see him – even if the others couldn't... The thought skimmed on her nerve ends, her spine tingling with unease. Frantically she tried to calm herself, the roads passing outside the window, Cleveland Square falling behind them.

They travelled for nearly three-quarters of an hour, some passengers getting off, others taking their place. In one hysterical moment Jeanie wondered what would happen if there was a sudden rush for seats. If no one could see Kaine Lukes, would someone sit on him?

She giggled to herself, suddenly childish, but stopped laughing when the conductor looked at her again. *He thinks I'm knocked!* she thought madly, then decided that she didn't care and put her tongue out at him. *Now, what d'you make of that?* she wondered as he scowled disgustedly and turned away.

Her spirits plummeted suddenly, unexpectedly, despair setting in as her body slumped against the seat, the deaf man beside her. Maybe there was *still* a chance, she thought. Maybe if she told the conductor what was happening. Or the man opposite... Jeanie sighed brokenly. No, they would just think she was a mad old woman, rambling. Senile... the bus moved on. Maybe if she rang the bell, begged for help... But it was too late, she knew that. It was virtually over. No one had come to save her and now the deaf man was taking her away. But *where?* Jeanie wondered, staring blindly out of the window. Oh God. Where?

They arrived at the gate of the deaf house minutes later, Kaine Lukes walking to the front door and standing back to let her in. The wide wood hall looked out at her sullenly.

'I never meant Mary Keller to die,' she said frantically as she hesitated on the step. 'It was an accident, I never meant—'

He took her arm and guided her into the house.

'It was an accident,' Jeanie babbled. 'You believe me, don't you? Don't you? . . . I never meant it to happen.' Her body tensed, strained to escape. 'I didn't kill her – it was an accident.'

Soundlessly, the door closed behind them.

Father Michael turned in his bed, moaning slowly. Beside him, the older priest sat deeply asleep, his head lolling forwards, the housekeeper slumbering in another chair by the window. The three of them crowded the narrow room, the sound of the woman's slow breaths moving in time to the priest's heartbeat. Waking momentarily, Father Michael was surprised to see her there, and then remembered having asked her to stay, begging Father Shelan to remain with him as well, wanting people around him – even a woman had had never truly liked.

He had been terrified, out of his wits quite literally, gibbering with fear as Father Shelan had helped him back to the house, and up to his room. At first horrified by the wounds, the housekeeper had tended Father Michael with the kind of pinched charity which offered aid, but no comfort. She bathed his wounds, never asking what had caused them, and then fed him, and then later that night, she and the priest stayed with him. Sleep had come quickly to her then, but the rug over her knees had slid off around three in the morning, and the chill had wakened her. Stiffly she rose, turned on the electric fire by Father Michael's bed, and then leaned towards Father Shelan.

'He's sleeping. Do you want a cup of tea, Father?'

He nodded, putting his forefinger to his lips in a gesture to be quiet.

Stiffly the woman left the room, stretching in the corridor, her arms reaching up as she yawned. What in God's name had Father Michael been doing? she wondered, thinking back over all the hints of scandal and remembering their numerous domestic frissons. Her feet moved wearily down the stairs, the dark green walls shadowed, the hall only half-lit as she switched on the lamp by the telephone.

He had looked petrified when Father Shelan brought him in, she thought. His eyes had been fixed, his mouth hanging open, and all that blood . . . She had seen some things, but that was the limit. A priest shouldn't act that way, it wasn't godly. The kettle began to whistle as the woman set out two cups and saucers and reached for the biscuit box. But when she realized there were only her favourites left, she ate two quickly and then put away the plate. What the eye doesn't see, the heart doesn't grieve about, she thought meanly, as she moved back up the stairs.

Father Shelan took his tea and then glanced at her questioningly: 'No biscuits?'

She smiled stiffly. 'Surely, Father, I'll just get them,' she said, walking back out on to the stairs and cursing softly under her breath.

The steps were shaded, shadowed; the front door, with its painted glass panel, standing wide open. The housekeeper frowned with disbelief. *But I locked it*, she thought, *I know I did*. Quickly she glanced out into the street and then closed the door again, firmly clicking the locks. The hall was cold, the night air doing its damage, and she was tired, snatching a plate and bad-temperedly slamming a few biscuits on it, one breaking in two halves as she did so. Then wearily she made her way back upstairs.

There was no light coming from under Father Michael's

door, and she hesitated, seeing only the faint red glow from the electric fire as she walked in, its colour bleeding over the priest's sheets and over his sleeping companion. Father Shelan's empty tea cup laid by his feet, and as she bent to pick it up, the woman felt a sudden chill move over her. Alarmed, she turned hurriedly – but there was no one behind her and after a moment she settled herself back in her chair and tucked the rug round her legs.

Father Michael slept; Father Shelan slept; the housekeeper drank her tea, ate all the biscuits, and slept. The two bars of the electric fire glowed into the room, sending long shadows across the bare floorboards and the priest's black shoes, the iron bedstead distorted in the half light and looming massively over the sleeping priest.

He stirred. The fire glowed. The door opened and then closed.

Ahlia had left the basement door open, but had not glanced out. The sixth day had come. Only one day left; tomorrow he would kill her. But only if she let him; only if she *let* him kill her. The music was turned down low, sultry music, music to which she had made love many times. The notes from the stringed instruments swirled in her head, the crescendo building as she bathed and then slowly, and deliberately, dressed.

She wore no underwear, her body cool to the touch, her bare feet padding on the carpeted floor. In time to the music, she walked to the mirror; in time to the music, she pulled out a pair of high black mules and slid them on to her feet. The music soared inside her, the beat drumming in her ears as she poured some perfume on her hands, rubbed her palms together, and then spread the scent under her breasts and along her thighs.

He will come soon, she told herself. Soon, very soon he will arrive... The long line of her eyes, accentuated by black liner, closed and then re-opened. There was no time for sleep, she had done all the sleeping she would do. It was time. Carefully Ahlia packed her case, and then turned to her handbag, pushing her make-up and a hair brush into it before zipping it closed.

The daylight was white, snow-promised white, as she turned off the light and leaned against the window, looking out. A car stopped in the street outside and she tensed, but it wasn't him. A moment later the postman came to the door and dropped in the mail, pausing to sort his remaining letters on the step before moving on. All the trivia of city life passed by the window, the morning waking the capital gently. Then suddenly a girl ran out on to the street, the remnants of the previous evening's make-up on her face. *She stayed with her lover last night*, Ahlia thought, with a rush of envy; *she made love last night*.

As I shall do soon, Ahlia reminded herself. Just as I shall do... She thought of the priest then, and of her father, and lastly of her mother. How you'd hate me now, she thought, how you'd hate what I've become. Her reflection in the window was faint, insubstantial, only a half image, her beauty ghostly. Disembodied. Dead. Startled, Ahalia stared at it, at the impression of herself, the flesh transparent, without body. Without life.

Her fear, vast and unexpected, winded her, and she turned, suddenly knowing that she was wrong. Terribly, terribly wrong... Her hands ran over her face frantically as she rushed into the bathroom and began to wash. Her hands rubbed against her eyes, scouring away the make-up, then while the water dripped from her, Ahlia hysterically pulled off her clothes, snatching up the loofa and working at her skin. I have to destroy myself, she thought, I have to make myself ugly...

Her skin was soon raw from the onslaught, her body roughened when she finally stopped and turned to the mirror.

Scrubbed and unkempt; reddened and naked, her beauty remained. The thing she valued above everything, remained. Impatiently Ahlia turned away, pulling on a pair of trousers and an old jumper, hiding herself. He'll expect to see me beautiful; he'll expect me willing and waiting... She was suddenly frantic with hope, suddenly certain that she could save herself. I can cheat him, I can beat him. If I take away the thing he wants, he'll leave me alone. He'll go away, tomorrow will come and I'll escape...

Clumsily, she tied a headscarf over her hair and took the stairs two at a time, opening the front door and looking out hurriedly. The street was empty; only a few birds sang in the garden square. Clasping her handbag and suitcase, Ahlia moved out of the house and towards the main road, keeping her head down. He'll never recognize me like this, she thought, no one would... Her feet, in the flat shoes, moved noiselessly, timidly, as she walked, her mind working quickly. I'll go to the airport and take a plane. I've got my passport. I can be gone in a couple of hours.

I can run away, she thought disbelievingly, almost dizzy with relief. *I can run away*... A taxi came round the bend at that instant, the driver nodding when she asked to be taken straight to Heathrow airport.

'Which terminal?'

Which terminal? Ahlia wondered, then said quickly: 'Terminal Four. And hurry, I've a plane to catch.'

He pulled out into the traffic, passing the first knots of pedestrians, Ahlia scrutinizing each face, looking for the deaf man. At the lights she drummed her fingers on the window, her impatience building. Hurry up, hurry up... The driver was humming to himself, the tuneless noise irritating her as they drove along. The roads were reasonably quiet, only becoming more crowded as they neared the airport. Repeatedly Ahlia willed herself to be calm, willed herself to relax . . . Only a few miles more, she thought, and then I'll be on my way. I'll go anywhere, take whatever flight is available. I'll just leave, get away . . .

When the taxi finally stopped, Ahlia leapt out, paying off the driver and turning to cross to the terminal. Her heart beat faster with every step, her spirits soaring. I can do it, I can get away, she thought, hurrying on. He's not going to stop me. No one's going to stop me or kill me . . . Swiftly she moved across the concourse; past couples embracing; past businessmen; past staff; her eyes fixed on the ticket desk, her whole being concentrated on the girl behind the counter.

There were only four people queueing in front of her. Four people, Ahlia thought, only four people between her and safety . . . the first one moved forwards slowly, spoke to the girl, and then moved way. Go on, Ahlia thought, willing the next couple to hurry; go on, buy your tickets and go. They paused, arguing with the girl about something, pointing to the arrivals board. Oh God, Ahlia moaned inwardly, move, move!

Her eyes raked the concourse urgently, a sigh of relief escaping her lips as they finally moved away. Now there's only one left, Ahlia thought, her breathing shallow as she waited behind the businessman, tapping her foot, urging him to hurry. The moments expanded, elongated, became hours and days, ate into the little time she had left as Ahlia's chest constricted, her eyes fixed on the man's back.

Move, move, she screamed inwardly. *Move!!!* Painfully slowly the man bought his ticket, and then at last, walked away. It was her turn! she thought frantically, stepping up to the ticket girl, her hands shaking, her eyes momentarily glancing down into her bag to get her passport.

But when she looked up, he was there. The girl had gone and in her place stood the deaf man.

THE DEAF HOUSE

'IT'S TIME.'
He said.
'IT'S TIME.'

CHAPTER SEVENTEEN

Kaine Lukes stood in the deaf house and looked at the clock. Slowly he took off his hearing aids and then, for an instant, relished the silence as he exhaled. He knew it would only last momentarily, that after the first burst of soundlessness, the tinnitus would follow, the buzzing, moving noises in his head. The brain mewls. And he waited for them, like another would wait for the sound of a friend calling over a gate.

Ssshhhhh, what noise! What noises in the head! Sounds, like the earth shifting, like the passing of a train. When I could hear there was never enough silence, now there's too much. Rachel Crossley... how clever she is, how cunning. As I was. She understands, some of it, at least. Years ago, I would have talked to her. Years ago, I would have loved her. But not now, now there is no speech, no love. Only silence, and in that silence I walk, I feel and I live.

They are all here now. Six hearing people; all come to the deaf man in the deaf house. All frightened. All guilty, miserable, hopeless. All of them have wanted to die once, to give up. Cowards – every one of them. Except Rachel. She thinks I'm going to help her. She's waiting for me... When I was a child I waited once, waited for four days and four nights, locked in a cellar, under earth, under street level, under foot. I waited in the earth and smelt it, and lay in it, and it held me. I was a child then. I was a child once. And the earth mothered me for four days and four nights, shielded me, loved me.

When I was found, when they rescued me, I never forgot. I never forgave and I never forgot. Time passed and I never forgot. I fought and won, and I fought and lost, but I never forgave and never forgot. And I never loved – as I should, as I should . . . Later, when I was deafened, I was lost, defeated. They turned on me then. Crept up on me. Beat me. I didn't hear them, and so they cut me. They made a red gash in my throat so my blood poured from me.

I wanted to die then. There was nothing left. I was over. Beaten. I had lost my place in the world and lost any hope of love. For days I turned on myself. Bit myself, cut myself, hated myself. Wanted to die and then finally learned that I could live another way. On hopelessness. On loss. On misery. I grew strong on my own despair; I dipped my food into my own anguish; sucked it from my memories; gorged myself on my own hatred – and then I came here, to the deaf house.

The world turned on me, but not the earth itself; she held me and she held the deaf house. And she loved me. She has loved me. So I learned how to preserve her and thank her; to feed her; shore her up. I gave her my anger and she loved me in return . . . But time passed and I realized I had used up all the misery. There was nothing left in me. Ssssh. Think, think . . . I did. For a long time, I thought and tried to plot. To protect myself. But slowly, irrevocably, I sickened, and the house sickened with me. My security, the walls which held me and shielded me, began falling. We were dying. We were hungry unto death.

Then, one freezing winter dawn, I went to Smithfield. I stood at the entrance and looked at the carcasses and at the men. I read their lips, and others's lips – and I knew then what I had to do . . . The world is thick with misery, coated in despair. So I chose six people more guilty or more hopeless than the rest; six people who wanted to give up. I chose them . . . to feed on.

Ssssh . . . listen, listen to me. The house is sleeping, quiet, satisfied. Inside her the six of them wait . . . It's not my fault, I didn't commit their crimes, I didn't make them hopeless. They all wanted to die, so I'm merely granting their wish. And in feeding from them, killing them, I continue.

I would have loved, if I could. Rachel, dark-eyed, white-souled. I would have loved her, if I could. I would have helped her once, because she touched me. But not now.

I believe that the world bears us and buries us; and that the soil takes us all in the end. No more than this; no more than this.

'What is it?'

The deaf man turned. He hadn't heard Rachel, only sensed her.

'What are you writing?' she asked, trying to keep her voice steady as she stood behind him. 'Please, let me look.'

In answer, he spread his hands over the open pages.

Rachel swallowed, fighting panic. She was in the deaf house, in the room with the fire and the clock. Harry had been with her, but had suddenly gone. She'd heard him screaming – and then silence. Minutes had passed while she waited, and then finally, the deaf man had come into the room. He had ignored her and sat down, writing urgently, his head bowed over the book as she stood silently and listened, straining for any sound.

But the house was noiseless . . . She had expected it, Harry's screams fading into silence. *Oh God, I'm sorry*, she thought helplessly, *I'm so sorry, Harry . . .*

'Please, let me look,' she said again.

He glanced up. His expression was unreadable, but something moved behind his eyes, some fleeting impression of what? Rachel asked herself. Pity? Desire?

'Let me look,' she repeated, stretching out her hand and taking the book away from the deaf man.

She read what he had written with disbelief, her hands turning the pages hurriedly, the solution – presented in black and white script – horrifying and inescapable. When she had finished reading, Rachel heard him move and turned, glancing up at him.

How close have you got to him? Titus had asked her once. *How close?*

'You don't have to do this,' Rachel said softly. 'You could let us all go.'

Expressionless, the deaf man leaned down, staring into her eyes, studying her face. His breath felt warm against her skin, his right hand taking the book away from her.

She clung on to it fiercely: '*No!*'

He pulled, tugging it away from her and then bending down again. He seemed to be scrutinizing her, looking for something.

'You don't have to live like this . . .' Rachel said gently, trying to keep her voice steady, the deaf man's face only inches from her own. 'I could help you.'

He sighed, then slowly reached out and touched her breast.

She flinched, moving his hand away and taking it in hers. 'Don't kill us. No one deserves to die.'

I could have loved you once.

She heard him in her head.

'You could still love.'

Don't lie to me. You read the book. It's over. I need you, need all of you. I can take your misery away, Rachel. I can help you. I can make it all stop. That's what you wanted – that's what you all wanted. Once.

Her grip tightened on his hand. *Make him understand*, she

thought, *whatever it takes, make him understand. Oh Chris*, Rachel thought poignantly, *I love you. Forgive me.*

'Help me,' she said softly, mouthing the words.

The deaf man watched her lips, then slowly leaned towards her, his mouth moving above hers, over hers – but not touching hers. She could feel his breath, the warmth of his skin, and looked up into his eyes. His gaze was fixed on hers.

'Help—' she tried to repeat the words but he suddenly breathed in, taking the syllables into his own lungs, drawing the words into his body, the echo sounding between them.

Help.

Around them, the house jumped like a snake struck by lightning.

The room in which Harry woke was vast, the walls hung with paintings, or draped with the heaviest velvets. Antique French furniture and damask-covered chairs stood impressively on the marbled floor, Aubusson rugs placed under pietra dura tables, plinths supporting busts flanking an Adam fireplace, where, on either side of the grate, caryatids stood peering into the lighted room. In the centre stood a table, the top a splendid marquetry display although little could be seen because much of the polished wood was covered with boxes. And the boxes were open.

Harry walked over, his curiosity drawing him to the three opened chests. They were varying in size, one tiny, one about a foot square, the last a larger oval, and each was full. The first was overflowing with gems; the second with silver and coins; the third with money. Paper money. Bank money. More money than Harry had ever seen. His fingers trailed over the contents of the boxes, lingered over them, luxuriated in the warmth they seemed to give out and then he turned.

He was deaf. Totally deaf. No sound at all moved in his

head. Nothing. Only stillness, and he knew then that he was inside the deaf house. But *where* inside, he wondered, touching his ears and sweating with dread. Where? In which room? Silently he moved around; the other tables also sported ornaments, silver bowls, priceless *objets d'art*, possessions so valuable that a man would have spent a fortune on them, and a lifetime collecting them. But which man? Kaine Lukes? Harry's eyes moved back to the table, compelled to return, to touch.

There was more money here than he had ever seen or hoped to earn; objects which only the greatest collectors could have amassed. The silence bore down on him, absolute, final. And then he realized something else. That amongst the comfortable splendour there were no windows and no door. Alarmed, he sucked in his breath, his heart rate increasing even as his eyes moved back to the table. There was so much, no one could have so much; no one *should* have so much. He had worked all his life and had never come close to such bounty.

The thought dug into him, rankled in him. That the deaf man, that weighty, uncouth man could own so much... Harry struggled with his envy, tried to suppress it, but his eyes kept moving over the objects and, try as he might, he couldn't resist picking up some of the jewellery and weighing it in his hands. The room seemed to smile at him, encourage him.

Look at me, touch me. Love me...

It seemed to welcome him like some friend once loved, then lost and then re-met. Harry hesitated, swinging between fear and longing, waiting for the deaf man to arrive. Waiting, with the heavy weight of gems and silver in his greedy hands.

It was the sixth day; tomorrow was the last day. The only day left to live. How could he stop his death? Harry thought for the thousandth time. And why was he here? His mind blurred uncertainly with panic, his thoughts muddled by the seduction of the objects which surrounded him. I did wrong, I know, I did wrong. I'm to be punished – or am I? he wondered suddenly. Perhaps there was to be no more punishment, perhaps his guilt and the horror of what he had already experienced were punishment enough. Perhaps now the deaf man would absolve him. Forgive him, let him go ... The cornucopia of plenty shimmered in front of him, awakening all the old greeds ... Perhaps, Harry thought stupidly, he had *already* been forgiven and this was his reward.

No, it couldn't be that easy. It couldn't! there was more to come. Guilty, he wrestled with the memory of his past. He thought of Gregor Fylding; of all the mean and heinous tricks he had employed to ensure power; of his treatment of his wife; of his spite, his love of success and money. Was it forgiven? Was so much so easily forgiven? Shame struck him forcibly. Gregor Fylding had been abandoned, left to die alone and poor; his wife had been cheated; his son neglected ... but he had tried to make amends later, Harry thought with despair. He had *tried*.

But it had been too late. Gregor Fylding was in his grave. Gayle was gone. His greed had taken precedence over his morals and his responsibilities. The old man's death hung on his hands heavily, as heavily as the silver he now held. And yet he couldn't let it go, couldn't lay it down on the table. Some part of him, the innermost part of Harry Binky, forced him to hold the objects, his guilt sliding away under the seductive power of his greed. Kaine Lukes would never miss one of these jewels, never miss one, Harry thought. He had so much, how could he miss one object? His thoughts seethed; how could any man need so much?

His hands trembled with longing, the silver and money eating into his skin. And yet he hesitated, afraid. The room seemed to watch him, to wait for him, urge him on.

Take something, take something . . .

It willed him. *Go on, take something* . . . Yet Harry resisted, fighting the impulse. He had one day left; if he got through this day he would be saved; he would escape death. The thought of dying sobered him, terrified him. If he died, what would he leave? What would his epitaph be? He could imagine the footnote in the press.

Harry Binky, MP, died today. A man who

– a man who had done *what* exactly?

What would they put on his grave?

Probably a bloody car park, Harry thought grimly.

The gems seemed to nuzzle into his skin, seemed to tickle him. There was so *much*, he thought helplessly, so much. What did a deaf man need with so much? He could put it to so much better use. He could enjoy such wealth. The deaf man couldn't. He was a loner, a recluse, a man without a place in the world – not like him. Harry would *know* how to employ his wealth, where to go, what to see, who to impress with his bounty.

His mind swayed with longing. If he just took a few things, tucked them into his pocket, who would know? He glanced around timidly, the tic over his left eye beginning to flicker erratically. But if he *did* take something, how could he get out afterwards? There was no window and no door. No obvious exit. Reluctantly laying down the fabulous objects, Harry moved to the wall and began to feel his way along it.

There had to be a door; if he had been put here there had to be a way in, and therefore a way out. His hands ran over the walls, searching, pulling back the hangings, his fingers groping for a door handle and a means of escape. The room seemed to sigh behind him, the objects calling to him. If I can find the way out, I can take what I want. The deaf man wasn't here, Harry thought, he couldn't see or hear him . . . But then again, *he* couldn't hear either . . . The thought shuddered inside him for an instant and then he smiled slyly. *The deaf man couldn't hear!* Kaine Lukes couldn't hear him leave – so he couldn't stop him. All Harry had to do was to find the door . . .

The money and gems called to him from the table; they sang in his head; willed him to hurry, to find the exit, and take them away. The room was warm, luxurious, full of everything Harry had ever desired. It was pulsing with richness and promise and it drove him into a madness of greed, his hands frantically moving over the walls, searching for the exit, the siren song of the bounty urging him on.

The minutes passed, Harry's head swimming with desire; his whole body trembling. He had never felt such longing for a woman, never experienced such intensity, never wanted anything as much as he wanted those objects – and then suddenly he found the door. He found it and his hand closed over the handle and he felt a relief so intense that he was momentarily breathless.

Quickly he hurried back to the table, cramming the gems into his pockets, filling them with money and silver, his arms weighed down with the objects which clung to him and nuzzled him and leaned against him longingly. Then he moved back to the door. Weighed down with what he had stolen, he turned to the exit, his eyes burning with greed, his deaf ears filled only with the sighing of fulfilled desire.

But the door had gone – and where it had been stood Kaine Lukes.

The silver fell from Harry's arms as he stepped back, pulling the money from his pockets, throwing it on to the floor as though it was something vile and corrupting. Unmoving, the deaf man watched him – and the room became smaller, the hangings fading, the furniture melting into bare floor boards, the richness slipping into the cracks in the empty wooden walls.

Hysterically Harry glanced round, watching as everything he wanted most in the world evaporated. Before his eyes, the fantastic room ceased to exist, the richness disappearing until all that remained was a small bare cell without furniture and without any means of escape.

His mouth opened to speak but nothing came out, the tic over his eye increasing, Winky Binky standing terrified and motionless in front of the deaf man.

I'll die, he thought hopelessly. *Dear God, I'll die.*

His greed had sentenced him, his envy and avarice had given him away . . . He moved towards the deaf man; his eyes pleading with him, his deafness making him disorientated. *He has me in his world now*, Harry thought with absolute terror, *he has control here.*

'Help me . . .' he sobbed, without hearing the words. 'Help me . . .'

Kaine Lukes watched him. The room was cold now, with only a little light.

'Dear God, help me . . .' Harry repeated, knowing that he had only the one day left. 'I don't want to die. Tell me what to do,' Harry pleaded, falling to his knees and begging him. 'I want to live, I *have* to live. I'm sorry for what I did. *I'm sorry!* But I have to live, I have to . . . Tell me what to do . . . What do I do?'

'GIVE IN.'

'I won't!' he shouted.

The deaf man's face was expressionless.

'YOU WILL.'

The words carried all the weight of a threat. Harry shivered. The last of his courage had gone, in its place was merely an animal instinct to survive. This man would torment him;

would extend no forgiveness, would only demand repayment for what he had done.

The thought winded him, but there was no escape. In an instant the room closed around him and the deaf man; the day sliding suddenly into night. The hours passed by in a second as they faced each other, the temperature dropping, the whole horror of what was to come fixed in the bare room.

On his knees, Harry moaned softly in terror, seeing Gregor Fylding materialize in front of him, the old man dressed as he had always been, in his working overalls. He moved about as though he had not seen Harry, taking out his gem-cutting tools and laying them on a table which had materialized with him. He worked quickly, adeptly, setting out his bench, preparing himself.

Terrified, Harry watched him, called to him. But there was no sound as Gregor Fylding continued to work in silence. The gem-cutting tools flickered in the half light, sharp and honed, their wooden handles worn from use. They flickered, not as the gems had done, but with malice, Harry suddenly feeling himself lifted upwards and laid down upon the flat surface of the work bench. He could no longer move, he could no longer call out, Gregor Fylding looking at him without seeing him, Harry's limbs suddenly rigid, locked into immobility.

In that instant his body was paralysed, his skin chilled as he looked down at his trunk and saw his flesh encased in crystal. The gem flowed around him, then locked him into rigidity as it moved up his legs and around his chest, making his breathing shallow. Screaming noiselessly, Harry tried to struggle, but the liquid gem passed upwards, washing over his throat and over his chin, and then hardening – jewel-hard – encasing him. Unable to move, he watched helplessly as the jewel spread over his mouth, his eyes pleading silently with Gregor Fylding as he felt the coldness close over his head.

But the old man never looked at him. He simply continued to lay out his tools, as Harry, screaming soundlessly, lay buried, encased.

Transfixed like a fly in amber, he could no longer move. His blood seemed to burn inside him, his breath locked. His eyes were fixed open, looking out into the bare room, seeing the deaf man behind Gregor Fylding, and watching with horror as his old mentor turned to him and lifted his gem-cutting mallet.

Ahlia had long since given up trying to find an exit. There wasn't one. In the mirrored room to which the deaf man had brought her from Heathrow, there was no window and no door. Only the endless repeated reflections of herself played back from the walls. She was deaf. Totally deaf. She sat on the edge of the one seat looking at herself. And as she looked, her beauty seemed to increase, to pass on from its usual perfection into something supernatural, something beyond beauty.

Her skin was immaculate, her hair no longer human hair, but something ethereal, unworldly. Her eyes were fixed on her reflection, seeing in it a power of physical attraction which was ungodly. Terrified, Ahlia watched herself alter. She saw the transformation and tried to turn away, but could not escape her image; everywhere there were reminders of it and on every surface she was greeted with the enormity of her own perfection.

She knew the deaf man would come, but not *how* he would come; just as she did not remember how she had come to the deaf house. There was no memory of her arrival. Nothing. Only the realization that she was now on his territory. She could not hear, could not assess where she was, or if there was anyone else around. At first she had shouted for help, but her words were noiseless and soon she stopped, exhausted. No one would hear her, no one would know where she was – except the deaf man, and she didn't want to call him back.

So she lapsed into silence and in silence she remembered what he had shown her. The death of her husband played and replayed in her mind constantly, until she believed her guilt would drive her insane. She had not warned him, she had let him go on that plane instead, knowing he would die. And why had she done it? Because her vanity had demanded it. In Ahlia's eyes her husband had committed the worst sin in the world: he had left her, as her father had done. And worse, he had left her for another woman. A woman who lacked her beauty. He had chosen someone other than her, preferred someone other than her, made love to someone other than her – and his rejection of her had killed him.

And yet, perhaps there was some hope left, Ahlia thought. Perhaps there was some little hope left. The deaf man had made love to her; he wanted her – surely that alone would save her? But she doubted it. She had killed – not directly, but indirectly; but she had killed – and all the guilt in the world would not absolve murder. Her situation was hopeless, irredeemable.

This was the sixth day, she realized, and the day was closing fast, *too* fast, the night coming with the threat of dawn. She had only this last day to find a way to save herself. The room mirrored her image, her thoughts; it watched her silently, forbiddingly, offering no comfort and no escape... I'm locked in here, and here I'll die, Ahlia thought numbly. Here I'll die.

Unless he helps me, she thought with sudden childlike trust and hope. If he comes to me, if he sees me like this, he'll help me. Her eyes fixed on her reflection. Surely he couldn't refuse a woman so fabulous? So perfect? No man could, it wasn't possible. She had seduced and been seduced by many men, no man could resist being moved by her. No man. She would simply wait for him, that was all, she would wait and then make him want her as all the others had done. No man on seeing her, could fail to help her.

She had been staring into the mirror fixedly and yet Ahlia did not see the deaf man enter. He simply materialized, watching her, his own reflection mirrored next to hers. Desperately she turned to him, extending her hand, knowing her beauty, knowing with certainty that he could not resist.

'Help me,' she pleaded, her eyes fixed on his, waiting to see the familiar expression of longing in his face. But he was unmoved, detached. 'Help me,' she begged again. 'What do I do?'

Tentatively, her hand moved out towards him, but in that instant he pointed away from her towards the other side of the room, Ahlia turning to see her father standing there.

Frantically she moved over to him: 'Daddy . . . Daddy . . .'

It was all right! she thought hysterically. Her father had come for her, he'd come to get her out of this place. Fiercely, she held on to him as she used to as a child, kissed him, rested her head against his, her despair lifting. But there was no response and finally she pulled back, surprised by his indifference. He had loved her, been proud of her, why did he not love her now, seeing how beautiful she was?

'Be proud of me, Daddy,' she begged, 'be proud. I was always your pretty child, now look at me, look at me and help me.'

'HE CAN'T
SEE YOU.'

The deaf man's voice resounded in her head but Ahlia didn't turn, instead she stared disbelievingly into her father's eyes and saw blindness. *He could not see her*, she couldn't move him, couldn't compel him to help her; and she couldn't ask for help either; her voice had gone. To him, she was now any woman. Not his daughter, but any woman. Without his sight her father could not recognize her or be moved by her, and without her voice, she couldn't plead for help.

With a sense of utter despair, Ahlia stepped back, and as she did so, other men appeared, old lovers, all without sight, all unable to see her; all passing by her without offering affection or help. Shaking her head from side to side in total bewilderment, Ahlia backed further away, her father fading as the other men continued to approach her, their lips moving endlessly.

But she couldn't hear what they said any more. Their words were removed from her, their compliments, their husky murmurs of pleasure – all gone. The admiration Ahlia had lived for was no more. She was as beautiful as any woman who had ever lived, but her beauty was to be unseen, unappreciated, unknown. She would never see the desire in a man's eyes again, never be given that satisfaction; all that remained was sex. Not seen, not heard, not offered, but taken.

'No.' She mouthed simply, backing further away from the men who now circled her. 'No!!!'

Chris, listen to me, Rachel said, forming the words in her head, willing them over to him in the hospital. *I'm all right, I'll be all right. I'll find a way out, I promise you. Trust me. Christ, trust me . . .*

She paused, waiting to see if she could pick up a response, but there was nothing. Her head ached relentlessly from the effort of trying to reach him. Her mind concentrated on him and turned away from her own situation – because if she allowed herself to think of that she would go mad. *Stop it*, Rachel willed herself, *stop it*! Her hands were clenched, her clothes soiled, covered in earth. Bedraggled and cold, she now sat, afraid and hungry – and she waited.

THE DEAF HOUSE

Her hunger surprised her. In such circumstances Rachel was amazed to think she could actually want food. But she did; her stomach told her she was empty. Not surprising, Rachel thought, it must be late now. She breathed in deeply, trying to fight panic. *Where am I? In the deaf house*, Rachel thought, answering herself. And where was the deaf man? Somewhere in the house, or the garden. Doing what? And to whom?

Harry . . . where was he? *Stop it!* she willed herself, he'll be OK, he's too bloody-minded to be anything else . . . When the deaf man came back he'd help her, he *would*. And then she would convince him to help the others. She just had to wait for his return, that was all.

The room was empty. There were no windows, and no door, and no way to assess how much time had passed. Only her stomach told her that – and her instinct. It's coming to the end of the sixth day, Rachel told herself, tomorrow is the last. They had been given a week to live, and the time was coming to its close. Before long, it would be over. No, she told herself, not over. The deaf man would help her. She had reached him, moved him, touched him . . . he *would* help her. He would help them all. She just had to trust and wait . . .

The deafness had nearly driven her insane and had made her isolation complete in the darkness. For there had been no light to tell her where she was. Without hearing or sight, Rachel had tried to force herself to listen. But there were no sounds, no indication of people passing, or traffic moving outside the window. Nothing, only silence. In a vain attempt to calm herself, Rachel had even tried to sleep, but had finally despaired, shuffling around the room in the darkness. And so it continued for long hours, until suddenly, without warning a light came on.

Blinking, Rachel watched as the room opened before her, a room which was familiar. Her bedroom from her childhood.

Astonished, she rose to her feet and gingerly touched the furniture, thinking for an instant that it was real – until she saw that the window and the door had gone. Then she knew where she was. In the deaf house. Somehow Kaine Lukes had managed to reproduce her childhood bedroom in his house, and here she was to stay, until he came for her.

Wearily Rachel sat down on the edge of the bed. The room was familiar, but it wasn't comforting; too much had happened there for it to be a place of refuge. Leon had been there, he had abused her there ... Rachel stood up quickly, unsettled by the memory, her thoughts turning back to Chris.

Chris, it's Rachel, talk to me ... Chris ...

Nothing. Silence, as effective as the silence in her own head.

Oh, Chris, answer me ...

Again nothing. No response. Rachel sat down again, defeated. Her head fell forward on to her chest, her despair boundless. Just let the deaf man come back, she prayed silently, just let me talk to him ... She thought of the taste of his lips, of the pressure of his hand against her breast. *Oh God*, Rachel thought, *I love you Chris, just hold on. Just hang on and I'll help you. The deaf man will come back. He'll help me – he'll help all of us.*

Did I tell you that I loved you? Of course I did. Did I tell you that you were my life? That without you there's nothing? Listen to me, listen ... Rachel went on, talking in her head, sending her thoughts out to Chris ... *I love you. How simple it is. I love you. I love you.*

Stop it!

She spun round, hearing the words in her head, feeling them pushed into her thoughts, separating her from Chris. The deaf man stood in front of her, in her room, watching her.

EAT THIS.

Puzzled, Rachel glanced at Kaine Lukes's outstretched hand. A cube of bread lay on the open palm and for an instant her hunger was so strong that she nearly took it.

'No, I don't want it,' she said gently. She felt, rather than heard, him sigh.

'IT IS
NOW TIME.'

For what? Rachel asked inwardly, knowing beyond doubt that he could follow her thoughts. Time for what?

Silence.

Slowly she rose to her feet, facing him. He looked at her avidly, his expression longing, his hand extending towards her and running down the length of her throat.

'Help me,' she said, simply.

He smiled, watching her lips, running his forefinger across her mouth, letting the words slip over his skin.

'You're a good man,' Rachel said tenderly. 'I know you're good. You'll help me, won't you? You'll help all of us, won't you?'

His mouth opened slightly, his collar unfastened, the white ridge of the scar vivid in the light. Gently he cupped his hand around the back of her neck and drew her head towards him, pressing her mouth against the scar. He sighed, feeling her breath against his skin, his other hand sliding under her jacket and unfastening her skirt.

Rachel stiffened, tried to pull back.

'I can't—'

He put his hand over her mouth quickly.

Let me take the misery away, Rachel. Let me have it.

Then suddenly he was gone. The room dimmed, the furniture transformed, the bed over-large, a figure lying on it. Leon . . . Startled, Rachel turned round, glancing towards the door, knowing there wasn't one and yet hoping beyond hope that there was some escape. Idly, Leon moved on the bed, turned over to look at her and then smiled. He didn't speak; she wouldn't have heard him anyway, he merely beckoned for her to come over to him. Dumbly Rachel shook her head, watching as he frowned and then threw the red ball of wool towards her. It unwound in the dead air, falling to the floor at her feet and lying motionless on the floor. The red thread extended from him to her; it lay still; and then slowly it began to twitch.

Terrified, Rachel backed away, but the woollen thread clutched at her ankle and crawled up her leg; it tugged at her, and pulled at her, and drew her slowly and relentlessly, closer and closer towards Leon. Struggling frantically, Rachel tried to break the thread, tried to snap it with her fingers, but it still clung to her and with horror she realized her feet were losing their footing and that she was about to fall.

But she didn't fall, instead Leon gave one last violent tug on the thread – and then vanished.

The room was silent. There had been no sound during their struggle and no sound now. Breathing heavily, Rachel glanced down at her leg. The red thread was still there; still moving; climbing. Fiercely she snatched at it, her fingers clawing at it, her mouth moving noiselessly as she screamed. But the thread kept its grip on her, and then suddenly and disbelievingly, Rachel felt a movement in her stomach. Her eyes fixed on her skirt, her mouth opening in horror as she saw the material split and her own stomach, pregnantly distended. The skin was taut, the pulse throbbing, veins marbling the white flesh.

And then as she watched, the flesh became transparent, so clear that that she could look into the womb, and see the embryo there. In deep shock, Rachel could no longer move or think, she could only stare, horrified, at the child, the baby's face bearing Leon's features, the umbilical cord a thread of red wool.

I wonder if it would matter if I took my teeth out? Jeanie

mused idly. I mean, just for a minute . . . she toyed with the idea, her tongue fiddling with her dentures. He hadn't come for her yet, so she might as well be comfortable for a while. Her thoughts ran on, her eyes fixed on her slippered feet. Her teeth hurt. God, how they hurt! she grumbled to herself, looking round. The room was pleasant enough; a little front room like thousands of others up North. A three-piece suite, the covers faded, a table with some flowers on it, and a picture of Constable's *Hay Wain*. Not a bad room, except that there weren't any windows, or doors. Still, he would explain everything when he arrived.

Her stomach tightened. *When he arrived. No, calm down*, she willed herself. *Calm down. Don't let your imagination get the better of you; think of ordinary things. Normal things . . . Oh, my bloody teeth!* Jeanie thought, slipping out the bottom set of her dentures and holding them in her hand. That was better. As soon as she heard him coming, she'd just pop them back in and no one would be any the wiser . . . except that she *couldn't* hear him coming. *She couldn't hear anything at all.*

The deafness no longer surprised her. Her own hearing had been bad for years and this would be only temporary – like all the other times. No, there was nothing to worry about on that score, there were worse things coming . . . *Stop it, Jeanie*, she willed herself, *stop it!* It would have been nice to have a telly in here, or a radio. No, a telly would be better, she could watch the pictures until her hearing came back. Her hand shaking, Jeanie glanced at her watch, but it had stopped. She might be missing something good, 'Cell Block H', or something like that . . . still, if she had to wait, that was what she'd do.

But she worried about Ahlia, worried that she might not have found the note with all the instructions on it. She'd be looking for her dinner and not finding it. Her fear was fading. All right, she'd been a coward once, she'd let Mary Keller die. But not *deliberately*! It had been an accident, and now that the deaf man knew that, he'd understand. I mean, no one could be blamed for an accident, could they? It wasn't as though she had killed Mary. Not really... Jeanie ran her tongue over her bottom gums. She'd do whatever he said, and then she'd go home. Back to Cleveland Square and Ahlia. Back home...

All she had to do now was to wait for him. And when he came she would do whatever he said. That was fine, OK by her. Jeanie's eyes glanced back to her slippers. She should have taken off her apron and put on her shoes before she left. Really, what would anyone think if they saw her walking about like this? It was laughable... She thought of her father then, and of what he would have said to her:

'*If you dress like a lady, you behave like a lady.*'

Oh, and he was right, she knew that; she respected his judgement. He would have hated to see her like this, in old slippers and without her bottom set in... Jeanie thought suddenly of his smoking cap and felt an overwhelming urge to cry. It was such a silly thing to wear, ridiculous really, but he had thought it made him look like a gentleman... The memory was an uncomfortable one, so painful that Jeanie hurriedly turned her thoughts elsewhere. If she had a bit of liquorice, something to suck, she'd be happy really. Just a bit of something sweet to take her mind off things...

'GET UP!'

Startled, Jeanie flinched. She hadn't expected to see the deaf man suddenly appear in front of her and when she jumped to her feet her false teeth fell off her lap and skidded under the table. Damn it! she thought impatiently, I knew I should have left them in. I knew it!

'DO AS
I SAY.'

She nodded hurriedly. Fine, that was fine. And if I do, will

I live? Jeanie asked him, her mouth working uselessly, the words mute. Will I live?

'DO AS
I SAY.'

Jeanie nodded again, furtively looking over to where her teeth lay on the floor. When she glanced back the deaf man had gone.

The room was changing, distorting itself, altering itself into the hay loft she remembered as a girl. The air lifted her, carried her upwards in among the bales of hay, the boys laughing next to her, and Mary Keller lighting a cigarette in the dim summer night... *Oh, no,* Jeanie thought frantically, *no, Mary, don't!* Quickly she moved across the hay loft towards the girl, trying to call out to her, but she couldn't make herself heard and watched with desperate frustration as Mary lighted the cigarette and inhaled...

The air was suddenly full of sound; the boys' whistling; the call of a nightjar in the field beyond. And under the sounds came the sweet scent of summer from the long dead field. In slow motion Jeanie watched as Mary kissed the boy; watched as the cigarette fell from her hand and caught at the hay around them; watched as the smoke massed, and the first flames fluttered into life.

All the old fear and anguish welled up in Jeanie, all the old guilt re-emerged. But as she moved towards her, Mary Keller disappeared. There were no boys and no young girl left lying in the straw – only her father, crippled and helpless, his limbs jerking, his rheumy eyes fixed on the flames around him... Noiselessly, Jeanie screamed; noiselessly, she beat at the flames; noiselessly, she grabbed hold of her father and lifted him.

And then she began running down the hill, down the hill where the nightjar sang and the barn burned. Down the hill with the one person she loved above all others. And she *kept* running, carrying her father, her feet moving over the dry grass, her heart pumping, her relief too enormous to contain. She had made amends, she had saved her father – and she had saved herself.

On and on she ran, on and on away from the dead hillside, and the burning rick. But as she ran, clutching her father's body, her arms began to feel heavier, and heavier. Still she kept running, and only when she reached the bottom of the hill, did Jeanie glance down at what she carried. Her father had gone, in his place was only a bale of hay. Screaming, Jeanie dropped the bale and turned. The flames were high in the sky. Too high for anyone to survive in them, she thought wildly, her mouth drying. Too late.

Go back, she willed herself, *go back* ... But her feet wouldn't move, and her mouth remained open, screaming for her father as she saw the rick burn against the night sky.

In the name of God, help me ... In the name of God, protect me ...

The priest paced the cell relentlessly, measuring out its confines. The walls were stone, the space narrow, without a window or a door. A monk's cell, a holy man's cell, a cell in which to find peace, or forgiveness. The deaf man would only have put him there if he wanted to forgive him, the priest thought wildly. If he had wanted to punish him, he would never have left him in a religious place.

If this was a religious place ... It had to be! he thought madly. *It had to be.* It was a church, or somewhere like that. Somewhere holy, somewhere near to God. He began to pray again, although he couldn't hear his words.

Help me, help me ... Forgive me, Father, for I have sinned. Forgive me, Father, for I have killed ... I killed my child. Forgive me ...

His deafness taunted him. It threw his words back in to his

head. It caged them; held them fixed to the earth; tied them to the world – but he wanted them to reach God; they *had* to reach God, or they meant nothing. The priest paused, falling to his knees and then rising again, smoothing down his vestments. He was glad of his clerical clothes, glad of the protection they offered, glad that he had had the foresight to sleep in them, even though Father Shelan had thought he was mad. What did *he* know? He had no idea, the old fool.

Forgive me, Father, he mouthed hurriedly. *Forgive me for my pride and my arrogance and my lust. Forgive me my sins . . .*

He would come, Father Michael thought frantically, oh yes, the deaf man would come. He knew about him, he knew *all* about him, everything he had done; he had even shared some of it . . . The thought struck the priest with disgust and he crossed himself. *You drove me mad and now what?* he thought dully. Forgiveness? Yes. It had to be that. Forgiveness.

The cell was narrow, the bed hardly two feet across. A hard bed, a bed which forbade unnatural, unpriestly thoughts. *I've been arrogant, defiant. I've challenged God*, the priest thought despairingly. *But He will forgive. He will, I know it. He will forgive me; He will send this man to show me how to repair the damage I've done. One day left, and now – what time is it?* he wondered suddenly, knowing that it was late and that the end of the sixth day was coming.

The seventh day was imminent. At midnight it began. And how far away was midnight? The priest shuddered, rocked with real terror. Time was passing, soon his chance would be over. If only the deaf man would come, if only he would come and tell him what to do. It was sex that had brought him to this place; sex which had ruined him; confused him; driven him to madness. He should have controlled it, controlled himself, he was a priest . . . but he couldn't, he couldn't stop wanting the women.

Forgive me, Father, for I have sinned . . .

There had to be a way to stop it, to stop the thoughts coming into his head. But who could help him? There was no one else here, no one to hear him, and no one to come to him. If he died here, who would know? Who would care? Or maybe that was his punishment. He had broken his vows, and he had killed his own child, not directly, but indirectly, but what did that matter? The child was still dead . . . The priest stopped pacing, his big ill-formed hands pressed against his face. The deaf man was his last hope, he *had* to be his Saviour, his Redeemer: he *had* to be.

You have one week to live. The words came back, but didn't offer any solution. *How do I save myself?* he *pleaded. How? I turned from God, and turned to a woman instead. I ruined my chance of life. Dear God, I lost the one chance I had . . .* Frantically the priest paced the cell, willing the deaf man to come to him, afraid and yet prepared to face the one person he believed could save him. *Help me, show me what to do, help me. Tell me how I can save my life.*

'THIS IS
THE END.'

The priest swung round violently, the deaf man facing him in the small narrow cell. The two men stared at each other, the priest sweating with fear. But his despair had made him reckless and quickly he made the sign of the cross in front of Kaine Lukes.

There was no response from the deaf man; nothing.

Slowly, the priest's hand fell to his side.

'LET IT
NOW BEGIN.'

In that instant the side wall fell away, and two figures appeared, a couple making love only feet from where the priest stood. He flinched, as though physically struck, and would have stepped back, but there was no room. Instead he was forced to watch, the back of his knees pressed against the bed, his eyes fixed on the naked bodies in front of him. *Look away*, he willed himself, *look away* ... but the woman was beautiful and he wanted her, longed for her and, compelled by overwhelming desire, the priest wanted to pull away the man who held her and put himself in his place.

His head hummed with excitement, his body aroused, his every thought concentrated on the scene being played out in front of him. Frantically, his fingers clawed at the collar which suddenly threatened to choke him; they ripped at the long clerical garment; and then finally he stepped forwards – only to find his way barred. As the couple continued to make love, the priest found an invisible barrier blocked his way. He could see; he could long for; he could weep with the rage of desire; but he could not pass through the wall which separated them.

Wildly, the priest banged his fists against the barrier, the couple ignoring him. He howled with rage and frustration, losing his last grip on reality, and knowing then what his punishment was to be – an eternal and unending agony of the body. He was to be aroused and never to find release. To desire, without ever being allowed fulfilment, to be torn apart by his own sensuality.

Maddened, the priest continued to beat against the barrier, rubbing his body against the invisible wall, unable to find relief or to climax. Then finally he stopped and turned ... he turned slowly, his eyes wide with insanity and despair, and then he lunged forward towards Kaine Lukes. Instinctively, the deaf man stepped back, striking out as the first blow landed. But driven by a frenzy, Father Michael fought back, howling and striking out repeatedly, his big hands flailing the air, his last blow sending the deaf man backwards against the stone wall with all the force of a madman.

Kaine Lukes fell slowly, heavily, striking his head. He fell, taking with him the last of the day, and he fell on the first chiming of midnight.

Chapter Eighteen

At that moment all of the rooms opened. A door appeared in each and each person felt themselves released; and suddenly freed from their tortures, each ran to escape. Harry from his room; Rachel from hers; Jeanie stumbling out; and Ahlia wrenching open the door of her room in the same instant. They all ran out – and then all faced each other in the hall of the deaf house, staring incredulously, and recognizing each other. Yet none of them spoke. Their deafness was absolute, rendering them incapable of speech. The stillness, in that instant, was awful.

Only the priest remained in his room; even when the door opened, he stayed, standing over the body of the deaf man, and watching as the others turned and slowly moved towards him. They knew, by instinct, where he was, and after looking at him their eyes moved to the dead man at his feet. Each of them seemed long past humanity, long beyond reason, and each felt the same sensation of dread, knowing in that instant that all hope was lost. Kaine Lukes was dead; their torture might be over, but the deaf man had been their only means of escape from the house. They were trapped. The priest had killed the only person who could have saved them.

Their despair in that instant was too terrible to contain, the priest stepping back, walking back into the narrow cell, as the four people moved towards him. He moved back in complete terror, inch by inch, only stopping when he felt his body touch the wall. He offered no resistance and made no attempt to protect himself, and knew then, with absolute certainty, what his fate was to be.

The first blow struck him on the side of the head, a fist landing noiselessly against his chest. He slid down the wall, on to the floor, drowning in pain, the repeated kicks and blows thudding against his body, his murder committed in silence, in deadly, noiseless, pitiless silence. He turned over, galvanized by pain, gabbling under the onslaught, squirming as the punches and kicks pounded into him, his knees drawn up, his face tucked into his chest. And still they attacked him, their faces all pooling into one face, their noiseless grunts and howls without expression, their bodies crouching over the bleeding priest.

He felt the time pass over him and into him; days moved around him, the agony extended, elongated into a thousand deaths, into a million injuries; the blows fast, the repeated punches taking him out of life and into unconsciousness, and then, in one instant, as his mind was jolted with a blow to his cheek, the priest lifted his arms. His hands flew up to his head to protect his face, his palms exposed – and on those palms his attackers saw an image and stopped.

They stepped back in unison, watching as the scene was played out on the priest's hands. They watched transfixed, their sanity returning as they saw Kaine Lukes walking, living, and fully aware of where he was. He moved quickly, purposefully, down a white hospital corridor towards a pair of swinging doors, and there for an instant he paused, then moved on. The semi-darkness hid him for an instant, but only for an instant, before he and the ward became visible.

On the priest's palms the deaf man moved, on his palms he walked over to Chris's bed and stood by the unconscious boy – and then the image faded.

And in the instant it faded, their hearing returned. As the

picture died away, they found themselves standing in the deaf house, and listening to the final dark chime of midnight.

It was the last day.

THE SEVENTH DAY

CHAPTER NINETEEN

Who's that? Chris wondered, trying to recognize the footsteps and then frowning to himself. *I don't know those feet, they're new feet. Heavy feet. But whose feet?* He concentrated, trying to place them. Maybe a new doctor, someone coming in to cover the weekend, because it *was* the weekend, he had heard someone talking about working the late shift on Saturday night. And now it was Sunday, he had heard the twelve o'clock chimes on the nurses' radio. Sunday. A week gone. The final day was here.

He expected to die then. But nothing happened. The monitor bleeped on beside him and he continued to live. *Had they the whole day left? Or just a part?* he wondered, almost holding his breath. *No, nothing was happening yet, so there had to be a little time left.* The thought almost cheered him – but he didn't like the feet by his bed. Silent feet. Quiet feet, too quiet for a nurse or a doctor. *But not too quiet for the deaf man. Oh God, oh, dear God,* Chris thought frantically. *He's here. He's here ... Relax, don't get worked up*, he willed himself, and then changed his mind immediately. *Yes, yes, panic. Panic now!* Chris urged himself. *Get the monitor moving, get the line jerking, get the nurses over here. Panic, Chris!* he willed himself. *Panic, get help ... That's right, the monitor's moving now, bleeping out of rhythm. Get away from me, you bastard*, he said to the deaf man. *Get away from me! ... Come on, get the doctor. Get help, get someone. Get him away from me! ...*

She's here! Thank God, she's here! She's even stopped sniffing. Now look at the monitor, that's it, now lean over me and check my responses. I can feel you, that's kind, that's kind to move the pillow. No, don't dope me, I'm OK, don't dope me! Oh Jesus, here we go . . . Chris breathed in, the medication taking effect quickly, a drowsy listlessness overtaking him . . . *Is he still there? Is he? . . . Listen, Chris, listen . . . No, he's gone. He's gone . . .*

Sighing inwardly, Chris's heart rate steadied, the drug taking effect as the needle slid out of his arm, the medication bearing him out on the deaf tide of sleep.

Harry stood motionless, unable to respond for an instant, the full horror of what he had seen on the priest's hands rendering him immobile.

'That's your son, isn't it?' Ahlia asked, her voice little more than a whisper.

'Chris,' Harry said finally, brokenly. 'Kaine Lukes is going to kill my son.'

He turned round in the hall of the deaf house, his eyes raking the walls. The wooden panels were unbroken, uninterrupted by windows; the rooms leading off going further into the deaf house without offering any escape. They were entombed.

'There has to be a way out of here. There has to be!'

Alerted by the panic in his voice, Rachel also looked around, but the only door she could see led into a corridor – where the deaf man's body lay slumped against a wall. The dimness shaded his face, as it did theirs, the priest resting heavily against the staircase, his eyes unseeing.

Disbelievingly, Ahlia too studied him, noting the dead expression, the white skin and the torn clerical clothes – and the bloodied marks of their repeated blows. Sickened, she turned away, Jeanie taking her arm.

'It's all right, luv, it's all right.'

'It's not bloody all right!' Harry snapped. 'Didn't you see what was going to happen?' he asked hysterically. 'My son is going to die unless I get out of here—'

'Unless *we* get out of here,' the old woman replied calmly. 'We can stop him if we work together.'

'How?' Harry wailed helplessly, his panic obvious to everyone.

Rachel stood apart, sitting at the bottom of the flight of stairs. Exhaustion wasn't what had tired her, rage was. She had been wrong, bitterly, stupidly, wrong. She had believed that the deaf man would help her – that he would help them all. Even when she had read his journal, even then, she had believed that he had some good in him. Her bitterness was sour in her mouth. She had begged him, comforted him, coaxed him, touched him, kissed him . . . her hands clenched. And all the time he had been playing with her, laughing at her. Kaine Lukes wasn't going to help her, or any of them. He was going to kill them – and first of all, he was going to kill Chris.

Slowly Rachel glanced over to Harry. Sorry, Harry, she thought dully, I'm so sorry, I thought I could help . . . His face was bleached, hardly recognizable, the shock was so great. He's seen what the deaf man will do, Rachel thought, he's seen his son helpless; utterly, completely vulnerable. Chris wasn't able to fight; he couldn't take on the deaf man. He was handicapped, laid out, his body paralysed, exposed, awaiting injury and inviting death.

And after his death – ours, Rachel realized. After Chris, the rest of us will be picked off one by one. She glanced at the four people in front of her, knowing that each of them indentified with Harry; knowing that as they anticipated their own deaths they felt, for the first time, for another. Perhaps they even believed that in saving Chris, they could save themselves. Rachel stared ahead, trying to order her thoughts. If they had any chance of helping Chris they had to reach him – and in order to reach him they had to get out of the deaf house.

'If he's dead,' Harry said suddenly, looking down the corridor which held the body of the deaf man, 'how can he reach Chris? I mean, he's *here*, we can all see him. A dead man can't come back to life – so it's over, it *must* be. If he's dead, he's beaten.'

A quiet voice startled all of them.

'He's not dead.'

They all turned to look at Rachel. She was still sitting apart from them, her face shaded in the gloom, her eyes shadowed.

'*What* did you say?' Harry barked.

'I said he isn't dead,' she repeated. 'Kaine Lukes is still alive.'

'Then we kill him!' Harry snapped. 'We kill him.' He turned to the others, appealing to them. 'We *have* to! Surely you can see that? We *have* to stop him.'

They remained immobile, scared.

'You'll help me, won't you?' Harry pleaded, turning to the priest. 'You tried to kill him before, you *have* to help me now.'

The man's eyes registered nothing. Total blankness.

Fiercely Harry grabbed at his collar and shook him: 'Listen, you bastard, you're the one who's responsible, you're the reason we're all stuck here. You *owe* us – you have to help.'

The atmosphere was thick with panic and the smell of fear. Childishly afraid, Ahlia whimpered and turned to Jeanie, the old woman putting her arm around her employer protectively. The wood walls gave off the smell of earth, the light striking the priest and Harry, and throwing up malevolent shadows on the low ceiling.

'Leave him alone!' Rachel said firmly, walking towards the two men. 'He can't kill him. No one can.' She looked at them in disbelief. 'None of you understands, do you? Kaine Lukes *can't* be killed. None of us can kill him physically—'

'What the hell are you talking about!' Harry shouted, loosening his grip on the priest and turning back to Rachel. 'We have to kill him—'

'And then how will you get out of this house?' she asked simply.

The question silenced all of them.

'If you kill him, you damn us all to stay here for ever.' She glanced round at the walls. 'There are no doors; there are no windows. *There is no way out.*' Her voice rose, each of her words striking out at him. 'Only *he* knows the way out, and only he will tell us. If you want to save Chris, you have to find the way out through him.'

Harry breathed in deeply: 'What if you're wrong – you were wrong before. You were the one who was so sure that the deaf man would help us.'

Rachel flinched. 'Bitterness isn't going to help,' she said coldly. 'We've got to get away from here and get to Chris – and Kaine Lukes is the only one who can help us.'

'So how do we get him to help us?' Harry said meanly. 'Or perhaps you've got another good idea?'

'There *is* a way,' Rachel said softly. 'There is.'

He remembered her courage in the garden, remembered her calling Kaine Lukes back – and shook his head.

'You can't do it on your own.'

'I have to. There's no other way.' Her voice was steely. 'Stay here with the others and wait. When your chance comes, grab it. Take the others with you, and all stay together, but go when you can—'

'No,' Harry said firmly, 'I'll stay with you.'

Her voice was hard. 'Do as I say,' she said simply. 'When you *can* leave, go at once. Get out and go to Chris, protect him, keep him safe. I'll follow you. I promise, I'll follow.'

Harry stared at her and then, finally, he nodded.

She walked away from the four of them quickly, crossing

the dark hall and moving towards the body of Kaine Lukes. The corridor seemed to draw her in, and when she reached the deaf man's side, the gap in the wall closed over and they could see her no more.

She was no longer in the corridor, but in the cellar, the deaf man lying half slumped against an old leather chair. His head lolled over to one side, his eyes open, fixed ahead, his hands lying unmoving by his side. Warily, Rachel kept her distance, watching him as the sound of a clock ticked behind her.

Her revulsion was absolute. She hated the deaf man beyond reason, despised him for his cruelty; for what he had done and for what he intended to do. He had lied to her; defiled her; soiled her; tortured her; and now lay dying before her. The intensity of her hatred scorched her and for an instant Rachel was tempted to lift the iron door stop by the wall and beat the remaining life out of his body.

But she hesitated. In killing him, she would trap the others and condemn Chris. His breathing sounded shallow, tentative, his large body heavy on the bare floor, his coat falling open around him. Slowly Rachel regarded him, studied him as she would an animal. The zipped inner pockets she knew were full of his mementoes, his poster, his money, and the bread he always carried with him. I believed once that you had some goodness in you, she thought incredulously, but you're dark, dead in the soul. Inhuman.

He stirred, shifting his position suddenly and Rachel stepped back, her mouth drying. His shadow fell behind him, huge in the confined space, as the unseen clock kept ticking. The smell of earth was powerful, Rachel straining to make out the confines of the cellar, her gaze finally coming to rest on the book beside him, the pages covered with writing. Curious, Rachel's eyes moved to the volume and fixed on it.

The book's for you, Rachel. It's all for you. Love letters . . .

The clock ticked on malevolently. No, she thought, he's lying. Her bitterness rose. *Love letters!* For whom? Not for her. *Love letters . . .* Her eyes moved around the cellar slowly, over the stonework, the bare cement floor, banks of earth lying against the walls. The cellar stared back at her, its gaze steady, deadly, without compassion.

Oh, but she loves, Rachel, she loves . . .

Then suddenly the temperature cooled, and she heard a scuffing of earth shifting, falling away from the wall. It *is* the house he loves, Rachel thought incredulously . . . *It is the house*. This is all he cares for, all he wants. This is the woman he never had, the partner he protects and feeds . . . Her skin chilled, her chest tightening. This place, this building, is the heart of him – and he wants to keep her alive, because whilst she lives, he does.

The deaf man knew she was watching him and turned in her direction, his expression viciously triumphant . . . *He believes he's won*, Rachel thought enraged, *he believes he's won. He thinks that I can't stop him, and that he'll reach Chris. But he won't*, she swore to herself, *he won't.*

'YOU CAN'T
KILL ME.'

His voice was heavy, losing its footing, the mechanical rhythm for once out of step with the clock. Rachel paused, then cautiously moved a little closer. He watched her avidly. Her hand hesitated and then she reached into his outer pocket and pulled out two hearing aids, then slowly and gingerly, she fixed the instruments to the implants behind his ears. Then she turned the hearing aids on.

He heard the clock again in that instant and began to breathe to its rhythm, his chest rising and falling as the pendulum swung from side to side.

In, out
right, left
in, out
right, left.

'Where's the clock?' Rachel asked. 'I can hear it, but I can't see it.'

He stared at her, breathing evenly.

Upstairs.

'It's upstairs?' she queried. 'How can I hear it down here then?'

This is a magic house.

'This is a grave,' Rachel said calmly.

He breathed in with effort.

'IT HURTS
TO TALK.'

'Then talk to me inside your head,' Rachel said evenly, her tone emotionless. 'I'll hear you, you know I will. Just as I hear Chris sometimes . . . You're dying, I can hear everything in your head now. Everything – so you may as well talk to me.'

His eyes moved away from her, his mind shifting. The cellar was cold, damp, the smell of earth increasing, the dim light making their shadows huge on the wall behind. The place was deep in the earth, almost buried, the single lamp making little impression on the gloom. Suddenly, the deaf man shuddered, resting his head back against the seat of the chair, a dark patch of blood seeping into the torn leather.

Give up, Rachel. You're a clever girl, a very clever girl, but you can't take me on. I was always at my most dangerous when I was losing. That's what they said in the fight game. 'When he's bleeding, watch him, wait for the turn. Wait until he gets his second wind . . .'

Her hand shaking, Rachel reached into his pocket again. He winced, startled, but didn't stop her as she pulled out a folded sheet of paper and unfolded it. In the firelight his photograph stared up at him from the old poster:

KAINE LUKES
UNDEFEATED HEAVYWEIGHT CHAMPION

'You were a champion,' she said, turning his head in her direction so that he could read her lips. His skin seemed to cling to her, to mould against her fingers as she touched him.

'You were a champion,' Rachel repeated. 'A man with a place in the world.'

He nodded briefly.

I was someone once ... But it's over. It was over when I was deafened. That was the first death, to lose my hearing. That was the first of all the little deaths ...

'Go on,' she urged him, her eyes cold. *You've caused so much suffering, you've hurt so many, you should be dead, you should be dead ...*

You shouldn't wish me dead, Rachel, he said suddenly, picking into her thoughts and smiling maliciously. *To waste time wishing an opponent dead is to invite failure ... You have to outsmart them in the head. In the head, Rachel,* he said, reaching out and touching her temple. *That's where the fight's won or lost ...*

She stared at him, transfixed; his eyes were alert, cunning and dangerous. Her fear locked her into immobility: it held her rigid, unmoving – just as he knew it would. *The fear is in the head, Rachel,* she told herself, *in the head. Think, think, be smarter than he is and you'll win.*

Oh, but you can't beat me. I've had years of training, years spent in silence. The world alters when you're deaf, Rachel, it clarifies. All those sounds which distract you are gone. Promises mean nothing; actions are all; curses mean nothing; only revenge matters.

'Revenge for what?' Rachel asked simply.

For this, he said, pulling open his collar and touching the scar on his throat. *For being broken and beaten. For being thought a failure, a freak. For all the petty daily spites that dogged me for years. For the status I lost; and the money I lost; and the love I never had... I want revenge for the misery I endured – and the despair. For pain, Rachel. For indifference, for loneliness, for anguish.*

He winced, moving his position against the chair, his eyes burning.

What else is there for me?

'So murder's your revenge?'

He stared at her with malice; living, breathing spite. The clock rocked its time about the room, the fire blazing in union with his anger.

I don't murder. You murder yourselves. None of you is innocent. Ahlia Bell killed her husband; Jeanie Maas, her friend; Harry Binky, his mentor; the priest, his child.

'And Chris? And me? Who did we kill?'

Yourselves. The deaf man looked at her steadily. *Chris Binky wants to die – as you did. You've all wallowed in your own misery and guilt. I'm taking nothing from you that you didn't want to give up. And I need you... I'm greedy for you. Hungry...* he smiled, languid, feral. *I want to get fat off you; suckle your unhappiness; swallow your miseries. I – and this house – live off the world's despair. We exist because of you. Happiness would have destroyed us, Rachel. Laughter would have turned us into dust.*

She stared at him, her voice low with malice. 'What about love?'

The deaf man fingered her hair, pulled on it gently. *I am loved, Rachel. The earth loves me.* He drew her face closer towards his as he continued. *She mothered me. She took me in – and so I loved her in return. I came here when I lost my hearing, to this house which is locked in the earth and smells of her. I loved her, as she loved me ... And later I gave her things ... food ... wine ... books ... the things I treasured most, and sometimes I slept in her cellar, under her soil, and felt safe.*

His fingers moved through her hair, pressed against her scalp. *You can't kill me ... No one can physically kill me. Give up, Rachel, give up. Lean on me, tell me your troubles. I can take the misery away, I promise you. I can do it ...*

'I won't let you kill me,' she said simply. 'Or Chris. I love him and I won't let you kill him.'

You love him, do you? So you're not so hopeless any more, now that you love? he pulled her face close to his, his tongue flicking out for a moment and skimming her lips. *But how will you feel when he's dead? When he's gone, where will all that hope go? You'll come back to me then, Rachel. You won't be able to stop yourself. You'll weep and feel cheated and helpless – and you'll feed me. Just like the others. They'll die, Rachel. They'll die because of their misery. People do now. It's the way of the world ...*

'You won't kill me,' she said firmly. 'You know you won't. You can't.'

He shifted his position, his hand dropping from her hair. He seemed to be restoring himself, ready to be gone. Time was passing, he was recovering, the energy burning like a light from him. Push him, Rachel willed herself, push him. Now, *now*.

'You won't kill me.'

Why not?

'Because I mean something to you,' she said calmly, leaning towards him and putting her hands around his face, the gesture tender and unexpected. His body tensed, his expression rigid, his head rolling away from her.

Get out.

But she didn't. She leaned over him instead, her hair falling over his face, her mouth moving over his.

*

The house moved; it creaked overhead; it shuffled; the foundations rocking; the wooden panels splitting; the walls in the hallway splitting open with a defeaning crack, an exit materializing. Seeing it, Harry pushed the two women through to the garden, calling for the priest to follow him.

'Come on! Hurry!' he shouted, grabbing hold of Father Michael's sleeve as they all ran down the pathway towards the road, Harry turning once to look back at the house. He expected it to collapse, but all the violent movement had ceased. She stood upright again, and he realized with despair that it was not over yet. The deaf man still lived – and Rachel was with him.

Hailing a cab, they made their way to the hospital, Harry guiding them to the doors of the intensive care unit and then pausing:

'If he comes, he'll have to face us. Are you all ready?'

They nodded, following Harry blindly as they walked into the ward.

Chris lay silent, but alive, Harry moving to the head of the bed, the priest facing him, the two women standing by the monitor. It bleeped regularly, steadily. It charted Chris's heart rate and told them that he lived. And so they waited, in the shaded hospital. Flanking the helpless man, they waited.

She's moving, Rachel! She's moving ... Get away from me. Get away. You can't kill her, and you can't kill me. We live here ... we live ...

Hurredly tearing off her clothes, Rachel leaned over the deaf man. He was immobile under her; transfixed; threatened; his thoughts blurring.

Get her out! he willed himself. *Get her out! I can't feel anything for her. I live on misery. I can't hope and I can't love ...*

He felt her tongue working against his, his breathing accelerating, his hands moving suddenly and reaching out for her; pumelling her skin; sliding over her.

The house is mine ... the house is all I can love ...

She was above him, moving on top of him, her lips parted, her eyes closed as he watched her – and then finally he reacted, pushing her back against the earth-scuffed floor and working his body against hers. Moaning under him, Rachel continued to move, her hands cupping his face, pulling him towards her. *You'll die*, she thought violently, *you'll die. When you give yourself, you'll die ...*

He knew it too and his head suddenly rocked away from her touch – but his body kept responding, his physical resistance faltering as his mouth moved down to her breasts.

Overhead the house creaked, the floorboards shuffling.

See how she moves, Rachel, see how she lives? I can hear her in my head, turning, moving. In my head I know she's alive, I can feel her, touch her. You can't kill her ... She loves me.

The earth seemed to shift around them, the dim lamp lighting the side of the deaf man's face as his mouth suckled her breasts greedily. Closing her eyes, Rachel held him. Terrified by him, repelled by him, she held on to him and felt herself being absorbed into him and drawn into the house itself. The sensation chilled her and she breathed in deeply, but didn't release her grip, her body moving against the damp floor, the earth smell creeping over her skin.

She knew she was winning; knew she was killing him. His body was cooling, chilling against hers, his lips cold against her breasts and stomach, his breathing rapid and shallow. His excitement scoured the walls, it pulsated against the floor and crawled into the earth around them.

He felt consumed by her, obsessed by her, drowning in her – and then realized what was happening and, jerking upright, howled once, savagely and despairingly. He howled and the house juddered, the plaster falling from the ceiling, the walls creaking ominously, the whole building trembling around Rachel and falling over both of them.

NO MORE

NO MORE.

In the intensive care unit the monitor bleeped suddenly, alerting Harry. Alarmed, he glanced at the screen and saw the line flicker and then quicken, his own heart rate accelerating at the same time. Dear God, what was happening?

The deaf man's back! Chris thought frantically. *He's outside and he wants to get in. Stop him someone, stop him!* . . . Chris's mind raced, his thoughts, like his heart rate, out of control. *He's got Rachel, you left her with him. She can't be there. She can't be in the deaf house . . . She wants to help, she thinks she can stop him, but she can't . . . Get out, Rachel, get out!*

Alerted by the activity on the monitor, the nurse hurried over to the boy's bedside, felt his pulse and then signalled for a doctor to the called. The heart rate was dangerously high, too high to sustain life for long.

'Do something, he's going to die!' Harry shouted, calling to the nurse frantically. 'Do something, for the love of God, do something!'

She leaned over Chris, astounded that the injection hadn't calmed him. The monitor was going wild, the heart rhythm erratic and speeding up by the second.

He's going to get through! . . . He's going to get in . . . Stop him, someone stop him . . . And help Rachel, please, Dad, help Rachel . . . get her out of that house . . . Do something! She's with him, I can see her, she's in that room with him and she's . . . she's making love to him.

Let him go, Rachel, let him come here instead, let him do what he likes. But get out . . . Oh God, someone help her. Someone help her ... He's going to kill her ... stop him!!!

Rachel felt the house shudder and then right itself. It was not over yet. The deaf man stirred in her arms, he moaned deeply, but he didn't manage to throw her off, and instead his body pressed further into hers. Slowly and deliberately, she began to kill him. And slowly and deliberately, he realized he was dying.

The earth around them fell away from the walls; it slapped against the concrete floor and swarmed over to them. It slid against Rachel's bare legs and crawled over her arms, the sensation of cold dampness chilling her, the smell suffocating.

'No!' she said, brushing away the earth desperately. 'No!'

Watching the earth move over her, the deaf man drew back, his eyes fixed on the white flesh disappearing under the black soil ... Gasping for breath, Rachel realized suddenly what was happening. If Kaine Lukes couldn't kill her, the *house* would. The earth was pressing against her, pushing on to her breasts, creeping into the space between her body and the deaf man's.

She reached out to him, her voice urgent, pleading. 'Love me,' she urged him. 'Love me ...'

I CAN'T.

'Why?' she asked, her hands sliding down his stomach, her lips against his chest. 'Why not?'

The house creaked over her head, the sound ominous and angry. Her mouth dried with terror, but she held on to the deaf man. *I have to stay,* she told herself, *I have to stay until it's over ...* The earth moved across the floor; it slid into her hair and between her fingers, rubbing itself against her thighs.

'Love me,' she pleaded. 'Save me.'

LET ME
GO NOW.

'No!' she said vehemently, her lips moving away from his chest and covering his mouth, her skin moist with fear. He shuddered, his body growing weaker, the blood from his wound matting her hair as she held him and made love to him, and felt him, and smelt the odour of his skin . . . And while she did so the house continued, with its owner, to die. The roof slates fell down, the windows smashing, the doors swinging inwards.

'Love me . . .' Rachel pleaded again, knowing that the end was close and that the earth was beginning to cover her. Soon she would be buried, underground, lost . . . The soil crawled over her flesh and her limbs; it dragged on her, pulling her down into the earth below. Crying out, Rachel held on to the deaf man, and as she did so, the soil closed over her mouth.

Helplessly, Harry watched his son – and the medical team who fought to save him. He watched them in a daze, defeat staring him in the face. Chris was going to die, after everything they had endured, his son was going to die . . . and if he died, they all died. Each one of them would end in the moment he did. It was nearly over, Harry thought dully, it was nearly over.

The ward went quiet in an instant, Harry glancing over to the priest and seeing that he had noticed the silence too. So the deaf man was here, Harry thought, he *was* here! Frantically he glanced around – and in that instant the nurses and the doctor were suddenly stilled; locked into immobility. Only Chris's heart monitor continued to work, its bleeping noise growing louder and louder as his distress increased.

Automatically, the priest crossed himself and began to pray, the two women shrinking back as the deaf man materialized at the foot of the bed. He stood dressed in his overcoat, his eyes moving towards Chris.

'IT'S TIME.'

'No!' Harry said fiercely. 'Not my son. Take me, but not

my son!' Harry shouted. 'You can't take him. *He is my son.*'

Ignoring him, Kaine Lukes felt into his pockets and pulled out the two plastic bags of bread. Laboriously he untied them and then began to crumble the cubes and scatter the bread on the floor of the ward. Harry watched in disbelief, the priest shaking his head uselessly as birds began to appear and feed off the crumbs. Steadily they increased in number, the birds varying in sizes and pecking frantically, all winged – and all bearing human faces. They looked out from their feathered heads with human eyes and human expressions, their mouths opening and closing as they fought over the bread.

The priest moaned brokenly and stepped back, Harry watching in horror as the deaf man continued to scatter the crumbs on the floor and the birds continued to eat voraciously. The crumbs worked their way to the bed as he scattered them; the birds feeding ever more frantically; fighting savagely with each other in their greed – and then the crumbled bread fell, slowly and deliberately, on to the sheet which covered Chris.

The earth had nearly covered Rachel. It pressed against her; pushed into her ears, her eyes and her body; bruised her limbs; her torso sinking into the cold dead pit of soil. She was dying, and she knew it. Just as she knew that she could only kill Kaine Lukes if she held on to him – if the house didn't kill her first.

Overhead the framework teetered; the timbers cracked, Rachel's face almost obliterated by soil, although her mouth still moved against the deaf man's, the earth moist between their lips. He moaned, smelling the odour of the earth as it mingled with the scent of the woman under him. He saw her hair streaked with the dark soil and felt the earth rise to protect him. It was damp between them. Dark soil, smelling of secret places. Disorientated and possessed, he felt his body consumed and burning, his desire torn between the earth and the woman who was held in it.

'Love me,' Rachel begged again, her voice a whisper from the suffocating earth.

Give up

he willed her.

Give up.

But she wouldn't. She was dying; drowning under the killing pressure of the earth – and yet she held on to him. Her face was now only a white shadow under the covering of soil, her voice stilled. Under the earth he had loved – under the earth which had loved him – lay the only woman who had ever touched him.

He panicked suddenly. Frantically brushing away the earth; pushing the dark soil off Rachel's face and breasts, uncovering her beauty – and then finally, irrevocably, as he looked at her, he climaxed.

IT'S OVER,

he said simply.

IT'S OVER.

His body relaxed against hers, his hands slumping to his sides, his breathing stopped. He was dead.

Coughing and gasping for breath, Rachel dug herself out of the earth, spitting the soil out of her mouth and wiping it from her eyes. Hysterically she began to cry, clawing at the earth and then pushing the deaf man away. He rolled over, then stopped, his head turned to her.

He was watching her.

She whimpered in terror and then realized that he was, in fact, dead. His eyes were fixed open, but he was dead.

Misery keeps me alive, Rachel. Only love kills . . . happiness would turn me to dust.

Shaking, she dressed, then moved back to where he lay. His head was still on the floor, his eyes open and his mouth a bloodless hole. From him came the smell of earth and of death, the odour of lost hope and of despair. The clock ticked behind her, the lamplight flickering over Kaine Lukes's dead eyes, and then, as the house folded in around her, Rachel leaned forwards.

She hesitated, slowly moving her mouth over the dead man's – then she kissed him, drawing in his breath, her lungs expanding as his emptied. She kissed him, and in kissing him, took the last of his life away.

'Ahhhhhh . . .' Chris breathed in sharply, the sound coming huge and furious into the ward.

Harry leaned over, unable to believe his ears or his eyes as he saw his son's hand move.

'He's coming round!' he shouted. The birds had gone, the medical staff were returned to normal, and the deaf man, he realized, was finally dead.

Chris turned in his bed, coughed, the tapes removed from his eyes, and the tubes removed from his body, as he struggled to get up.

'Rachel . . .' he said hoarsely. 'Rachel?'

Harry held his son's hand and tried to speak, but Chris just kept repeating the one name, calling to Rachel, repeating her name over and over again.

And then she answered, calling to him, the words resounding loudly in his head.

I'm coming, I'm coming . . . Wait for me.

Chapter Twenty

They parted at the entrance to the hospital, Rachel remaining with Chris, whilst Harry, Father Michael, Ahlia and Jeanie stood for an instant in the morning cold. They were all drained, Ahlia white-faced, her beauty unearthly in the chill, her eyes averted from the priest. Only Jeanie seemed alert, walking to the gates and whistling for a taxi to take her and her charge back to Cleveland Square.

The priest remained with Harry at the entrance. His voice was quiet, without arrogance; without hope.

'Look after yourself,' Harry said simply, thinking of his agent, Gordon, and of all the explanations he would have to make. 'I don't suppose you understand any of it, do you?'

'No,' the priest said quietly.

Harry hesitated: 'But you think it's over?'

'I don't know—'

'You're a priest!' Harry snapped, seeking comfort and finding confusion instead. 'You *should* know, for Christ's sake!'

'Yes,' Father Michael replied. 'For Christ's sake I should know.'

Rachel walked up to Harry just as the priest moved off. They both watched him go and then she said quietly: 'I bought the book back.'

Harry frowned, then lifted the volume out of her hands. He recognized it immediately as Kaine Luke's and tried to open it. But he couldn't, the pages were all stuck together.

Confused, he gave it back to her and frowned. 'What's the matter with it?'

Rachel looked at it, and then, as she watched, the book disintegrated, turned into earth in her hands, the dark soil spilling over her fingers. Disgusted, she brushed it away.

Harry watched her, frowning. He didn't know what had happened, only that she had altered; passed into a place he couldn't even guess at.

'Did we imagine everything?' he asked her. 'Did he really exist?'

'I don't know.'

Harry pushed her: 'I saw things that no one *could* have imagined,' he said, his voice low. 'We must have experienced them. We *must*. We couldn't have done all this to ourselves. It isn't possible.'

'Oh, but it is,' Rachel said quietly. 'Because we let him into our lives. Every time we cursed our luck and wallowed in our own misery, we let him in. Every time we wanted to die, to give up, we opened the door to him. Kaine Lukes existed in each of us . . .' her voice was low, 'and we kept him alive. We fed him and made him what he was. That's why love destroyed him. It brought him into the light, it brought him hope – and it brought him death.'

Harry looked away from her. He didn't understand and his mind was already moving on.

'So what do we do now?'

'We live,' Rachel said simply, her face turning up to the cold morning light. 'We live – and we never forget.'

CHAPTER TWENTY-ONE

Ten years later.

'I can't see that it would do any harm,' Rachel said simply. 'After all, it was a long time ago.'

She glanced at Chris as he drove along and then at their child, sitting on the back seat. He smiled warmly at her, cheerfully unconcerned.

'I want to know,' Rachel went on. 'We're only a little way away . . . Oh, come on, Chris, I have to see it once more. I *need* to see it once more.'

'I just don't like the idea,' he replied coolly, although he had already turned the car in the direction of the deaf house. 'I think we should forget it.'

'We've been abroad for years,' she responded calmly. 'Having one quick look can't harm anyone.'

A few minutes later they pulled up outside the site where the deaf house had been and stared disbelievingly out of the car windows. The house had gone, in its place was a block of flats. The building was impersonal, clean, without atmosphere; nothing of the deaf house remained.

Slowly Rachel got out of the car and then, after hesitating for an instant, walked up to where the gate had once been. The open front garden was welcoming and as she paused by the door, Rachel turned and made her way round the block of flats to the back garden. Where once only a thin lawn and blank beds had been, was now a mass of colour. Flowers banked the borders, covering the earth and hiding every inch of soil, the ground alive with scent and greenery. It could have been another place; no hint of malice or of fear remained: it was an English garden, safe under an English sky.

'Can I help you?'

Rachel turned to face a middle-aged woman wearing a shell suit and glasses.

'Oh, I'm sorry, I didn't mean to pry . . .' Rachel explained. 'I just used to know this place when there was a house here. I knew someone who lived here once . . .'

'I'm afraid I wouldn't know anything about that, my dear,' the woman replied easily. 'I've only been here for about two years myself.' She paused and then gestured to the open back door. 'I think your little boy wants to have a look round too.'

Embarrassed, Rachel ran after her son, the woman following.

'I'm so sorry. It's not like him to wander off. He's usually shy,' she explained, catching up with her son in the hallway of the flats. He stood there unconcerned, apparently waiting for her. 'Come on, sweetheart, you don't want the lady to think you're rude, do you?' Rachel coaxed him, taking his hand and turning.

Then she stopped. Transfixed. Through the window she could see the garden, and at the bottom of the lawn a figure moved.

She stopped speaking. Stopped breathing. The woman was still talking but Rachel could no longer hear her. The silence came down absolute, the figure at the far end of the garden turning and looking at her impassively.

The deaf man had been digging and now stood with his foot resting on the spade. He was motionless, composed, heavy in a dark overcoat, and as Rachel watched she saw around his feet white-boned slats of wood blooming from the earth like flowers.